JUST ONE NIGHT?

BY
CAROL MARINELLI

MEANT-TO-BE FAMILY

BY
MARION LENNOX

MIDWIVES ON-CALL

Welcome to Melbourne Victoria Hospital—
and to the exceptional midwives who make up
the Melbourne Maternity Unit!

These midwives in a million work miracles
on a daily basis, delivering tiny bundles of joy
into the arms of their brand-new mums!

Amidst the drama and emotion of babies arriving at
all hours of the day and night, when the shifts are over,
somehow there's still time for some sizzling
out-of-hours romance…

Whilst these caring professionals
might come face-to-face with a whole lot of love
in their line of work, now it's their turn to find
a happy-ever-after of their own!

Midwives On-Call

Midwives, mothers and babies—
lives changing for ever…!

JUST ONE NIGHT?

BY
CAROL MARINELLI

Published in Great Britain 2015
by Mills & Boon, an imprint of Harlequin (UK) Limited,
Eton House, 18-24 Paradise Road, Richmond, Surrey, TW9 1SR

© 2015 Harlequin Books S.A.

Special thanks and acknowledgement are given to Carol Marinelli
for her contribution to the *Midwives On-Call* series

ISBN: 978-0-263-24699-5

Dear Reader,

I was thrilled to be a part of the *Midwives On-Call* series, and to work alongside some of my favourite authors.

We all have secrets, or sides to ourselves that we might not reveal, and that really is the case with my heroine, Isla—she is outwardly strong, with a demanding job and an exciting social life, but there is a side to her that she lets no one see. I knew it would take a very special hero to discover the *real* Isla, behind the rather glamorous façade. Alessi is all that and more.

I hope you enjoy Isla and Alessi's story.

Happy reading!

Carol x

Carol Marinelli recently filled in a form where she was asked for her job title and was thrilled, after all these years, to be able to put down her answer as 'writer'. Then it asked what Carol did for relaxation. After chewing her pen for a moment Carol put down the truth—'writing'. The third question asked: 'What are your hobbies?' Well, not wanting to look obsessed or, worse still, boring, she crossed the fingers on her free hand and answered 'swimming and tennis'. But, given that the chlorine in the pool does terrible things to her highlights, and the closest she's got to a tennis racket in the last couple of years is watching the Australian Open, I'm sure you can guess the real answer!

Books by Carol Marinelli

London's Most Desirable Docs

Unwrapping Her Italian Doc
Playing the Playboy's Sweetheart

Bayside Hospital Heartbreakers!

Tempted by Dr. Morales
The Accidental Romeo

Secrets on the Emergency Wing

Secrets of a Career Girl
Dr. Dark and Far Too Delicious

Baby Twins to Bind Them
200 Harley Street: Surgeon in a Tux
NYC Angels: Redeeming the Playboy

Visit the author profile page at millsandboon.co.uk for more titles

PROLOGUE

'ISLA...' THE PANIC and fear was evident in Cathy's voice. 'What are all those alarms?'

'They're truly nothing to worry about,' Isla said, glancing over to the anaesthetist and pleased to see that he was changing the alarm settings so as to cause minimal distress to Cathy.

'Was it about the baby?'

Isla shook her head. 'It was just letting the anaesthetist know that your blood pressure is a little bit low but we expect that when you've been given an epidural.'

Isla sat on a stool at the head of the theatre table and did her best to reassure a very anxious Cathy as her husband, Dan, got changed to come into Theatre and be there for his wife.

'It's not the baby that's making all the alarms go off?' Cathy checked again.

'No, everything looks fine with the baby.'

'I'm so scared, Isla.'

'I know that you are,' Isla said as she stroked Cathy's cheek. 'But everything is going perfectly.'

This Caesarean section *had* to go perfectly.

Isla, head nurse at the Melbourne Maternity Unit at the Victoria Hospital, or MMU, as it was more regularly known, had been there for Dan and Cathy during some particularly difficult times. There was little more emotional or more difficult in Isla's work than delivering a stillborn baby and she had been there twice for Cathy and Dan at such a time. As hard as it was, there was a certain privilege to being there, too—making a gut-wrenching time somehow beautiful, making the birth and the limited time with their baby poignant in a way that the family might only appreciate later.

Cathy and Dan's journey to parenthood had been hellish. They had undergone several rounds of IVF, had suffered through four miscarriages and there had been two stillbirths which Isla had delivered.

Now, late afternoon on Valentine's Day, their desperately wanted baby was about to be born.

Cathy had initially been booked in next Thursday for a planned Caesarean section at thirty-seven weeks gestation. However, she had rung the MMU two hours ago to say that she thought she was going into labour and had been told to come straight in.

Cathy had delivered her other babies naturally. Even though the labours had often been long and difficult with a stillborn, it was considered better for the mother to deliver that way.

As head of midwifery, Isla's job was supposedly nine to five, only she had long since found out that babies ran to their own schedules.

This evening she'd had a budget meeting scheduled which, on the news of Cathy's arrival, Isla had excused herself from. As well as that, she'd had drinks scheduled at the Rooftop Garden Bar to welcome Alessandro Manos, a neonatologist who was due to start at the Victoria on Monday.

For now it could all simply wait.

There was no way that Isla would miss this birth.

At twenty-eight years of age Isla was young for such a senior position and a lot of people had at first assumed that Isla had got the job simply because her father, Charles Delamere, was the CEO of the Victoria.

They'd soon found out otherwise.

Yes, outside the hospital Isla and her sister Isabel, the obstetrician who was operating on Cathy this evening, were very well known thanks to their prominent family. Glamorous, gorgeous and blonde, the press followed the sisters' busy lives with interest. There were many functions they were expected to attend and the two women shared a luxurious penthouse and dressed in the latest designer clothes and regularly stepped onto the red carpet.

That was all work to Isla.

The MMU was her passion, though—here she was herself.

She sat now dressed in scrubs, her long blonde hair tucked beneath a pink theatre cap, her full lips hidden behind a mask, and no one cared in the theatre that she was Isla Delamere, Melbourne socialite, apparently dating Rupert, whom she had gone to school with and who was now a famous Hollywood actor.

To everyone here she was simply Isla—strict, fair and loyal. She expected the same focus and attention from her staff that she gave to the patients, and she generally got it. Some thought her cool and aloof but the mothers generally seemed to appreciate her calm professionalism.

'Here's Dan.' Isla smiled as Dan nervously made his way over. He really was an amazing man and had been an incredible support to his wife through the dark times. His tears had been shed in private, he had told Isla, well away from his shocked wife. Many had said he should share the depths of his grief with Cathy but Isla understood why he chose not to.

Sometimes staying strong meant holding back.

'Dan, I'm sure that something is wrong…' Cathy said.

Dan glanced over at Isla, who gave him a small, reassuring shake of the head as her eyes told him that everything was fine.

'Everything is going well, Cathy,' Dan said. 'You're doing an amazing job, so just try and relax…'

'I can feel something,' Cathy said in a panicked voice, and Isla stepped in.

'Do you remember that I said you would feel some tugging?' Isla reminded her.

'Cathy!' Isabel's voice alerted Isla. 'Your baby is nearly out—look up at the screen…'

Isla looked up to the green sheets that had been placed so that Cathy could not see the surgery going on on the other side. 'Your baby is out,' Isabel said, 'and looks amazing…'

'There's no crying,' Cathy said.

'Just wait, Cathy,' Dan said, his voice reassuring his wife, though the poor man must be terrified.

Even Isla, who was very used to the frequent delay between birth and tears, found that she was holding her breath, though Cathy could never have guessed her midwife's nerves—Isla hid her emotions extremely well.

And not just from the staff and patients.

'Cathy!' Isla said. 'Look!'

There he was.

Isabel was holding up a beautiful baby boy with a mass of dark, spiky hair. His mouth opened wide and he let out the most ear-piercing scream, absolutely furious to be woken from a lovely sleep, to be born, of all things!

'He's beautiful,' Dan said. 'Cathy, look how beautiful he is. You did so well, I'm so proud of you.'

The baby was whisked away for a brief check and Isla made her way over as Isabel continued with the surgery.

He really was perfect.

Four weeks early, he was still a nice size and very alert. The paediatrician was happy with him and the theatre midwife wrapped him in a pale cream blanket and popped on a small hat. He would be more thoroughly checked later but that visit to the parents, if well enough, came first.

Isla took the little baby, all warm and crying, into her arms and she felt a huge gush of emotion. She had known that this birth would be emotional, but the feeling of finally being able to hand this gorgeous couple a healthy baby was a special moment indeed.

She held the baby so that Cathy could turn her head and give him a kiss and then Isla placed him on Cathy's chest as Dan put his arms around his little family.

Isla said nothing. They deserved this time to themselves and she did all she could to make this time as private as a theatre could allow it to be. She stood watching as they met their son. Dan properly broke down and cried in front of his wife for the first time.

'I can't believe I'm finally a mum…' Cathy said, and then her eyes lifted and met Isla's. 'I mean…'

When Isla spoke, she was well aware of the conflicting feelings that Cathy might have.

'You've been a mum for a very long time,' Isla said, gently referring to their difficult journey. 'Now you get the reward.'

Isla's time with Cathy and Dan didn't finish there, though. After Cathy had been sutured and Recovery was happy with her status, Isla saw them back to the ward. Cathy simply could not stop looking at her baby and Dan was immensely proud of both his wife and son.

They had made it to parenthood.

Before Cathy was discharged Isla would have a long talk with her. Often with long-awaited babies depression followed. It was a very confusing time for the new mother—often she felt guilty as everyone around her was telling her how happy she must be, how perfect things were. In fact, exhaustion, grief over previous pregnancies, failure to live up to the standards they had set themselves could cause a crushing depression in the postnatal period. Isla would speak with both Dan and Cathy about it before the family went home.

But not tonight.

For now it really was about celebrating this wonderful new life.

'I'm going to have a glass of champagne for you tonight,' Isla said as she left them to enjoy this special time.

She said goodbye to the staff on the ward then headed around to the changing room.

She'd forgotten her dress, Isla realised as soon as she opened her locker. She could picture it hanging on her bedroom door and hadn't remembered to grab it when she'd dashed for work that morning.

She glanced at the time and realised she would be horribly late if she went home to change. She knew that she really ought to go straight there as there weren't many people able to make it, given that it was Valentine's Day. Alessandro had apparently been doing a run of nights in his previous job and had booked to go away for the weekend with his girlfriend before he started his new role.

Isla rummaged through her locker to see if there was an outfit that she could somehow cobble together. She didn't have much luck! There was a pair of denim shorts that she had intended to wear with runners. Isla had actually meant to start walking during her lunch break but, of course, it had never happened. She could hardly turn up at the Rooftop Bar in shorts and the skimpy T-shirt and runners that she had in her locker, but then she saw a pair of cream wedged espadrilles that she had lent to a colleague and which had been returned.

Isla tried it all on but the sandals pushed her outfit from far too casual to far too tarty.

Oh, well, it would have to do. She was more than used to turning heads. She didn't even question if there was a dress code that needed to be adhered to. Isla didn't have to worry about such things—it was one of the perks of being a Delamere girl. You were welcome everywhere and dress codes simply didn't apply.

She ran a comb through her long blonde hair and added a quick dash of lip gloss and some blusher before racing out of the maternity unit and hailing a taxi. As she sat in the back seat she realised that she was slightly out of breath—she hadn't yet come down from the wonderful birth she had just witnessed.

Elated.

That was how she felt as she climbed the stairs and then stepped into the Rooftop Bar.

And that was how she looked when Alessi first saw her. Tall, blonde and with endless brown legs, she walked into the bar with absolute confidence. She looked vaguely familiar, he thought, though he couldn't place her. At first he didn't even know if she was a part of the small party that was gathered.

He knew, though, that, whoever she was, he would be making an effort to speak with her tonight. He watched as she gave a small wave and made her way over and he found out her name as the group greeted her.

'Isla!'

So *this* was Isla.

Alessi knew who she was then. Not just that she was head midwife at The Victoria. Not just that she must be Charles Delamere's younger daughter, which would explain why she was in such a high-up role at such a young age. No, it was more than that. Though he could not remember her from all those years ago, he knew the name—they had attended the same school.

'I'm sorry that I'm so late.' Isla smiled.

'How did it go?' Emily, one of the midwives, asked, referring to Cathy's delivery.

'It was completely amazing,' Isla said. 'I'm so lucky to have been there.'

'And I'm so jealous that you were!' Emily teased, and then made the introductions. 'Isla, this is Alessandro Manos, the new neonatologist.'

Isla only properly saw him then and as she turned her slight breathlessness increased.

He was seriously gorgeous with black, tousled curly hair and he was very unshaven. The moment she first met his black eyes all Isla could think was that she wished Rupert were here tonight.

Isla and Rupert were seemingly the golden couple. They had been together since school, where Isla had been head girl and Rupert had been head of the debating team. One night they had gone to a party and it had been there, after a very awkward kiss, that Rupert had confessed to her that he was gay.

Rupert had no idea how his parents would take the news and he was also upset at some of the rumours that were going around the school.

Isla had covered for him then and she still did to this very day.

Rupert's career had progressed over the years and his agent had strongly advised him that the roles that were being offered would be far harder to come by if the world knew the truth. He was nothing more than a wonderful friend who, in recent years, had questioned why Isla chose to keep up the ruse that they were going out.

It suited Isla, too.

Despite her apparent confidence, despite her ease in social situations, despite the questions raised by magazines about her morals, because she put up with Rupert's supposed unfaithfulness after all, no one had ever come close to the truth—Isla was a virgin.

Her entire sexual history could be written on the back of a postage stamp. She'd had one schoolgirl kiss with Rupert that hadn't gone well at all. Now she'd had several more practised kisses with Rupert but they had been for appearances' sake only.

Often Isla felt a complete fraud when she spoke with women about birth control and pelvic floor exercises, or offered advice about lovemaking during and after pregnancy, when she had never even come close to making love with anyone herself.

Yes, how she would have loved Rupert to be here tonight, to hold her friend's hand and to lean just a little on him as the introductions were made and she stared into the black eyes of a man who actually had the usually very cool Isla feeling just a little bit dizzy.

'Call me Alessi,' he said.

'Sorry, Alessi, I keep forgetting,' Emily said. 'Isla is Head of Midwifery at MMU.'

'It is very nice to meet you,' Alessi said. He held out his hand and Isla offered hers and gave him a smile. His hand was warm as it briefly closed around the ends of her fingers and so, too, were Isla's cheeks. 'Can I get you a drink?' he offered.

'No, thanks.' Isla was about to say that she would get this round but for some reason, even as she shook her head, she changed her mind. 'Actually, yes, please, I'd love a drink. I just promised Cathy, my patient, that I was going to have a glass of champagne for her tonight.'

Alessi headed off to the bar and Emily took the opportunity to have a quick word. 'Isla, thank you for getting here, I know you were held back, but I'm really going to have to get home.'

'Of course,' Isla said. 'I know how hard it is for you to get away and I really appreciate you coming out tonight. The numbers were just so low I didn't want Alessandro, I mean Alessi, to think that nobody could be bothered to greet him. Go home to your babies.'

As Emily said her goodbyes, another colleague nudged Isla. 'Gorgeous, isn't he?'

'I guess.' Isla shrugged her shoulders. She could get away with such a dismissive comment purely because she had Rupert standing in the wings of her carefully stage-managed social life. Isla glanced over to the bar and looked at Alessi, whose back was to her as he ordered her drink. He was wearing black trousers and had a white fitted shirt on that showed off his olive skin. Isla felt a flutter in her stomach as it dawned on her that she was actually checking him out. She took in the toned torso and the long length of his legs but as he turned around she flicked her gaze away and spoke with her colleagues.

'Thank you for that,' Isla said when he handed her her drink. She was a little taken aback when he came and sat on the low sofa beside her, and she took a sip.

Oh!

With all the functions that Isla attended she knew her wines and this was French champagne at its best! 'When I said champagne...' Isla winced because here in Melbourne champagne usually meant sparkling wine. 'You must think me terribly rude.'

'Far from it,' Alessi said. 'It's nice to see someone celebrating.'

Isla nodded. 'I've just been at the most amazing birth,' she admitted, and then, to her complete surprise, she was off—telling Alessi all about Cathy and Dan's long journey and just how wonderful the birth had been. 'I'm sorry,' she said when she realised that they had been talking about it for a good ten minutes. 'I'm going on a bit.'

'I don't blame you,' Alessi said. 'I think there is no greater reward than seeing a family make it against the odds. It is those moments that we treasure and hold onto, to get us through the dark times in our jobs.'

Isla nodded, glad that he seemed to understand just how priceless this evening's birth had been.

They chatted incredibly easily, having to tear themselves away from their conversation to say goodbye to colleagues who were starting to drift off.

'I can't believe that we went to the same school!' Isla said when Alessi brought it to her attention. 'How old are you?'

'Thirty.'

'So you would have been two years above me...' Isla tried to place him but couldn't—they would, given their age difference, for the most part, have been on separate campuses. 'You might know my older sister Isabel,' Isla said. 'She would have been a couple of years ahead of you.'

'I vaguely remember her. She was head girl when I went to the senior campus. Though I didn't really get involved in the social side—I was there on scholarship so if I wanted to stay there I really had to concentrate on making the grades. Were you head girl, too?'

Isla nodded and laughed, but Alessi didn't.

Alessi was actually having a small private battle with himself as he recalled his private-school days. Alessi and his sister Allegra had been there, as he had just told Isla, on scholarship. Both had endured the taunts of the elite—the glossy, beautiful rich kids who'd felt that he and his sister hadn't belonged at their school. Alessi had for the most part ignored the gibes but when it had got too much for Allegra he would step in. They had both worked in the family café and put up with the smirks from their peers when they'd come in for a coffee on their way to school and found the twins serving. Now Allegra was the one who smirked when her old school friends came into Geo's, an exclusive Greek restaurant in Melbourne, and they realised how well the Manos family had done.

Still, just because they had been on the end of snobby bitchiness it didn't mean that Isla had been like that, Alessi told himself.

They got on really well.

Isla even texted him an image she had on her phone of a school reunion she had gone to a couple of years ago.

'I remember him!' Alessi said, and gave a dry laugh. 'And he would remember me!'

'Meaning?'

'We had a scuffle. He stole my sister's blazer and she was too worried to tell my parents that she'd lost another one.'

'Did you get it back?'

'Oh, yes.' Alessi grinned and then his smile faded as Isla pointed to a woman in the photo who he hadn't seen in a very long time.

'Do you remember Talia?' Isla asked. 'She's a doctor now, though she's moved to Singapore. She actually came all the way back just for the reunion.'

Alessi didn't really comment but, yes, he knew Talia. Her name was still brought up by his parents at times—how wrong he had been to shame her by ending things a couple of days before their engagement. How he could be married now and settled down instead of the casual dates that incensed his family so.

Not a soul, apart from Talia, knew the real reason why they had broken up.

It was strange that there on Isla's phone could be such a big part of his past and Isla now dragged him back to it.

'She's got four children,' Isla said. 'Four!'

Make that five, Alessi wanted to add, his heart black with recall. He could still vividly remember dropping by to check in on Talia—he'd been concerned that she hadn't been in lectures and that concern had tipped to panic as he'd seen her pale features and her discomfort. Alessi had thought his soon-to-be fiancé might be losing their baby and had insisted that Talia go to hospital.

He had just been about to bring the car around when she had told him there was no longer a baby. Since the morning's theatre list at a local clinic he had, without input, no longer been a father-to-be.

Of course, he chose not to say anything to Isla and swiftly moved on, asking about Isla's Debutante Ball, anything other than revisiting the painful past. She showed him another photo and though he still could not place a teenage Isla he asked who an elderly woman in the photo was.

'Our housekeeper, Evie.' Isla gave a fond smile. 'My parents couldn't make it that night but she came. Evie came to all the things that they couldn't get to. She was very sick then, and died a couple of months later. Evie was going to go into a hospice but Isabel and I ended up looking after her at home.'

Isla stared at the image on her phone. She hadn't looked at those photos for a very long time and seeing Evie's loving smile had her remembering a time that she tried not to.

'Would you like another drink?' Alessi offered as Isla put away her phone, both happy to end a difficult trip down memory lane.

'Not for me.'

'Something to eat?'

She was both hungry enough and relaxed with him enough to say yes.

Potato wedges and sour cream had never tasted so good!

In fact, they got on so well that close to midnight both realised it was just the two of them left.

'I'd better go,' Isla said.

'Are you on in the morning?'

'No.' Isla shook her head. 'I'm off for the weekend. I'm pretty much nine to five these days, though I do try to mix it up a bit and do some regular stints on nights.' They walked down the steps and out into the street. 'So you start on Monday?' she checked.

'I do,' Alessi said. 'I'm really looking forward to it. At the last hospital I worked at there was always a struggle for NICU cots and equipment. It is going to be really nice working somewhere that's so cutting-edge.' He looked at Isla—she was seriously stunning and was looking right into his eyes. The attraction between them had been instant and was completely undeniable. Alessi dated, flirted and enjoyed women with absolute ease. 'I'm looking forward to the weekend, too, though.'

'That's right, you're going away with your girlfriend…'

'No,' Alessi said. 'We broke up.'

'I'm sorry,' Isla said, which was the right response.

'I'm not,' Alessi said, which was the wrong response for Isla.

She was terribly aware how unguarded she had been tonight. Perhaps safe in the knowledge that he was seeing someone.

She looked into his black eyes and then her gaze flicked down and she watched as his lips stretched into a slow, lazy smile.

His mouth was seductive and he hadn't yet kissed her but she knew that soon he would.

As his lips first grazed hers Isla's nerves actually started to dissolve like a cube of sugar being dipped into warm coffee—it was sweet, it was pleasurable, it was actually sublime. Such a gentle, skilled kiss, so different from the forced ones with Rupert. It felt like soft butterflies were tickling her lips and Isla realised that her mouth was moving naturally with his.

Alessi's hands were on her hips, she could feel his warm hands through her denim shorts and she wanted more pressure, wanted more of something that she didn't know how to define, she simply didn't want it to end. But as the kiss naturally deepened, her eyes snapped open and she pulled back. Her first taste of tongue was shocking enough, but that she was kissing a man in the street was for Isla more terrifying.

He thought her easy, Isla was sure, panic building within her about where this might lead. She almost *was* easy with him because for the first time in her life she now knew how a kiss could lead straight to bed.

She had many weapons of self-defence in her armoury but she leapt straight for the big one and shot Alessi a look of absolute distaste.

'What the hell do you think you're doing?' she snapped, even if she had been a very willing participant. 'I was just trying to be friendly...'

Alessi quickly realised that he *had* been right to be cautious about her.

He knew the looks she was giving him well.

Very well!

She didn't actually say the words—*do you know who I am?* Though Isla's expression most certainly did. It was a snobby, derisive look, it was a get-your-hands-off-me-you-poor-Greek-boy look.

'My mistake,' Alessi shrugged. 'Goodnight, Isla.'

He promptly walked off—he wasn't going to hang around to be trampled on.

Her loss.

Alessi knew she'd enjoyed the kiss as much as he had and that her mouth, her body had invited more. He simply knew.

Isla *had* enjoyed their kiss.

As she climbed into a taxi she was scalding with embarrassment but there was another feeling, too—despite the appalling ending to tonight her lips were still warm from Alessi's and her body felt a little bit alive for the very first time, a touch awoken to what had seemed impossible before.

As she let herself into her flat, a gorgeous penthouse with a view of Melbourne that rivalled that of the Rooftop Bar, she smiled at Isabel.

'Sorry I didn't get there,' Isabel said. 'Did you have a good night?'

Isla, still flushed from his kiss, still a little shaken inside, nodded.

It had, in fact, been the best Valentine's night of her life.

Not that Alessi could ever know.

CHAPTER ONE

Isla saw the sign for the turn-off to Melbourne International Airport and carried on with her conversation as if she and Isabel were popping out for breakfast.

They were both trying to ignore the fact that Isabel was heading to live in England for a year and so, instead of talking about that, they chatted about Rupert. He was back in Melbourne for a week and the *supposed* news had broken that he'd had a fling with one of the actresses in his latest film. Not even Isabel knew that Isla's relationship with Rupert was a ruse.

'You're truly not upset?' Isabel checked, and Isla, who wore her mask well, just laughed as she turned off the freeway.

'What, I'm supposed to be upset because reports say that he got off with some actress in America a few weeks ago?' Isla shook her head. 'It doesn't bother me. I couldn't care less what they say in some magazine.'

'You're so much tougher than I am,' Isabel sighed. 'I simply can't imagine how I would feel if…' Her voice trailed off.

The conversation they had perhaps been trying to

avoid was getting closer and closer and neither wanted to face it.

Isla knew what Isabel had been about to say.

She couldn't stand to hear about Sean if he was with someone else.

Sean Anderson, an obstetrician, had been working at the Victoria since November and was the reason they were at the airport now. Sean was the reason that Isabel had accepted a professional exchange with Darcie Green and was heading for Cambridge, just to escape the re-emergence of her childhood sweetheart into her life.

The large multistorey car park at the airport had never made Isla feel sick before but it did today.

They unloaded Isabel's cases from the boot, found a trolley and then headed to the elevator. Once inside Isla pressed the button for the departure floor and forced a smile at her sister as they stood in the lift.

'If Darcie's flight gets in on time you might have time to see her,' Isla said, and Isabel nodded.

'She sounds really nice from her emails. Well, I hope she is, for your sake, given that she's going to be sharing the flat with you.'

Isla had never lived alone and so, with her older sister heading overseas and as their flat was so huge, it had seemed the perfect idea at the time. Now, though, Isla wasn't so sure. Isabel was going away to sort her heart out and Isla was going to do the same. She really wanted things to be different this year, she wanted to finally start getting on with her life, and that meant dating. That meant letting her guard down and dropping Rupert and, despite being terrified, Isla was also determined to bring on a necessary change.

Not tonight, though!

Tonight there were drinks to greet Darcie at the Rooftop Bar and Alessi would be there.

It was almost a year since that Valentine's night and since then the atmosphere between them had been strained at best. He was a playboy and made no excuse about it and Isla loathed his flirting and casual dating of her staff, though he barely glanced in her direction, let alone flirted with her. Alessi, it was clear, considered Isla to be a stuck-up cow who had somehow wormed her way into her senior position thanks to her father. They rarely worked together and that suited them both.

The early morning sun was very low and bright as Isla and Isabel crossed the tunnel that would take them from the car park to the departure lounge. A few heads turned as the sisters walked by. It wasn't just that they were both blonde and good-looking but that, thanks to their frequent appearances in the celebrity pages of newspapers and magazines, people recognised them.

Isabel and Isla were more than used to it but it felt especially invasive this morning.

Today they weren't minor celebrities but were sisters who were saying goodbye for a whole year, for a reason even *they* could not discuss—an event that had happened twelve years ago. Something that both women had fought to put behind them, though, for both, it had proved impossible.

What had happened that night had scarred them both in different ways, Isla thought as she watched Isabel check her baggage in.

She didn't really know Isabel's scars, she just knew that they were there.

They had to be.

Isla forced a smile as Isabel came back from the check-in desk.

'I'm not going to wait to meet Darcie,' Isabel said, and Isla nodded. Yes, they could stand around and talk, or perhaps go and get a coffee and extend the goodbye, but it was all just too painful. 'I think I'll just go through customs now.'

'Look out, England!' Isla attempted a little joke but then her voice cracked as they both realised that this was it. 'I'm going to miss you so much!' Isla said. She would. They not only worked and lived together but shared in the exhausting round of charity events and social engagements that took place when you were a Delamere girl.

They shared everything except a rehash of that awful night but here, on this early summer morning, for the first time it was tentatively broached. 'You understand I have to go, don't you?' Isabel asked.

Isla nodded, not trusting herself to speak.

'I don't know how to be around him,' Isabel admitted. 'Now that Sean is back, I just don't know how to deal with it. I know that he doesn't understand why I ended our relationship so abruptly. We both knew it was more than a teenage crush, he was the love of my life...' Tears were pouring down Isabel's cheeks and even though she was younger than Isabel, again, it was Isla who knew she had to be strong. She pushed aside her own hurts and fears and cuddled her big sister and told her that she was making the right choice, that she would be okay and that she could get through this.

'I know how hard it's been for you since he came to MMU,' Isla said.

'You won't say anything to Sean...'

'Oh, please,' Isla said. 'I'd never tell anyone, ever.

I promised you that a long time ago. You've got this year
to sort yourself out and I'm going to do the same.'

'You?' Isabel said in surprise. 'What could you possibly have to sort out? I've never known anyone more
together than you.'

Isla, though, knew that she wasn't together. 'I love
you,' she said, instead of answering the question.

'I love you, too.'

They had another hug and then Isla stood and watched
as her sister headed towards customs and showed her
passport and boarding pass. Just as she went past the
point of no return Isabel paused and turned briefly and
waved at a smiling Isla.

Only when Isabel had gone did Isla's smile disappear
and Isla, who never cried, felt the dam breaking then.
She was so grateful that she had an hour before Darcie
arrived because she would need every minute of it to
compose herself. As she walked back through the tunnel
towards the car Isla could hardly see where she was going
because her eyes were swimming in tears, but somehow
she made it back to the car and climbed in and sat there
and cried like she never had in her life.

Yes, she fully understood why Isabel had to get away
now that Sean had returned. The memories of that time
were so painful that they could still awake Isla in the
middle of the night. She fully understood, with Sean
reappearing, how hard it must be for Isabel to see him
every day on the maternity unit.

It was agony for Isla, too.

She sat there in her car, remembering the excitement
of being twelve years old and listening to a sixteen-
year-old Isabel telling her about her boyfriend and dating and kissing. Isla had listened intently, hanging onto

every word, but then Isabel had suddenly stopped telling her things.

A plane roared overhead and the sob that came from Isla was so deep and so primal it was as if she were back there—waking to the sound of her sister's tears and the aftermath, except this time she was able to cry about it.

Their parents had been away for a weekend. Evie, their housekeeper, had lived in a small apartment attached to the house and so, effectively, they had been alone. Isla, on waking to the sounds of her sister crying, had got out of bed and padded to the bathroom and stood outside, listening for a moment.

'Isabel?' Isla knocked on the bathroom door.

'Go away, Isla,' Isabel said, then let out very low groan and Isla realised that her sister was in pain.

'Isabel,' Isla called. 'Unlock the door and let me in.'

Silence.

But then came another low moan that had Isla gripped with fear.

'Isabel, please.' She knocked on the door again, only this time with urgency. 'If you don't let me in then I'm going to go and get Evie.'

Evie was so much more than a housekeeper. She looked after the two girls as if they were her own. She worried about them, was there for them while their parents attended their endless parties.

They both loved her.

Isla was just about to run and get Evie when the door was unlocked and Isla let herself in. She stepped inside the bathroom and couldn't believe what she saw. Isabel was drenched in sweat and there was blood on the tiles, but as she watched her sister fold over it dawned on Isla what was happening.

Isabel was giving birth.

'Please don't tell Evie,' Isabel begged. 'No one must know, Isla, you have to promise me that you will never tell anyone…'

Somehow, despite the blood, despite the terror and the moans from her sister, Isla stayed calm.

She knew what she had to do.

Isla dropped down to her knees on instinct rather than fear as Isabel lay back on the floor, lifting herself up on her elbows. 'It's okay, Isabel,' Isla said reassuringly. 'It's going to be okay.'

'There's something between my legs…' Isabel groaned. 'It's coming.'

Isla had been born a midwife, she knew that then. It was strange but even at that tender age, somehow Isla dealt with the unfolding events. She looked down at the tiny scrap that had been born to her hands and managed to stay calm as an exhausted Isabel wept.

He was dead, that much Isla knew, yet he was perfect. His little eyes were fused closed and he was so very still.

Tomorrow she would start to doubt herself. Tomorrow she would wonder if there was something more that she could have done for him. In the months and years ahead Isla would terrorise herself with those very questions and would go over and over holding her little nephew in her hands instead of doing more. But there, in that moment, in the still of the bathroom, Isla knew.

She wrapped her tiny nephew in a small hand towel. There was the placenta and the cord still attached and she continued to hold him as Isabel lay on the floor, sobbing.

'He's beautiful,' Isla said. He was. She gazed upon his features as her fingers held his tiny, tiny hands and she looked at his spindly arms and cuddled him and then, when Isabel was ready, Isla handed the tiny baby to her.

'Did you know you were pregnant?' Isla asked, but Isabel said nothing, just stared at her tiny baby and stroked his little cheek.

'Does Sean know?' Isla asked.

'No one knows,' Isabel said. 'No one is ever to know about this.' She looked at Isla, her eyes urgent. 'You have to promise me that you will never, ever tell anyone.'

Some promises were too big to make, though.

'I have to tell Evie,' Isla said.

'Isla, please, no one must know.'

'And so what are we supposed to do with him?' Isla demanded.

'I don't know.'

'You know what you *don't* want me to do, though. You know that he needs to be properly taken care of,' Isla said, and Isabel nodded tearfully.

'You won't tell anyone else,' Isabel sobbed. 'Promise me, Isla.'

'I promise.'

Isla sped through the house and to Evie. The elderly housekeeper was terribly distressed at first, but then she calmed down and dealt with things. She understood, better than most, the scandal this might cause and the terrible impact it would have on Isabel if it ever got out. She had a sister who worked in a hospital in the outer suburbs and Evie called her and asked what to do.

Isla sat, her tears still flowing as she recalled the drive out of the city to the suburbs. Isabel was holding the tiny baby and crying beside her till the lights of the hospital came into view. Evie's sister met them and Isabel was put in a wheelchair and taken to Maternity, with

Isla following behind. The midwife who had greeted them had been so lovely to Isabel, just so calm, wise and efficient.

'What happens now?' Isla asked. It was as if only then had they noticed that Isabel's young sister was there and she was shown to a small waiting room.

It had been the last time Isla had seen her nephew.

She didn't really know what had gone on.

Evie had come in at one point and said that the baby was too small to be registered. Isla hadn't known what that meant other than that no one would have to find out.

Her parents would later question Isla's decision to become a midwife. They had deemed that it wasn't good enough for a Delamere girl but Isla had stood by her calling.

She'd wanted to be as kind and as calm as the staff had been with Isabel that night.

With one modification.

Though her sister had been gently dealt with by midwives who had been used to terrified sixteen-year-old girls who did not want their parents to find out, one person had been forgotten.

Isla had sat alone and unnoticed in the waiting room.

Now she knew things should have been handled differently—the midwives, the obstetrician, at least one of them should have recognised Isla's terror and spoken at length with her about what had happened. They should have come in and taken care of the twelve-year-old girl who had just delivered her dead nephew. They should have carefully explained that the baby had been born at around eighteen weeks gestation, which had meant that there was nothing Isla could have possibly done to save him.

It would be many years before Isla got those answers and she'd had to find them out for herself.

Yes, that night had left scars.

Despite appearances, despite her immaculate clothes and long glossy hair and seemingly spectacular social life, Isla had equated sex with disaster. Not logically, of course, but throughout her teenage years she had avoided dating boys and in her final year at school Rupert had seemed the perfect solution. Still she'd kept the secret of that night to herself.

She had promised her sister after all.

CHAPTER TWO

ISLA DID WHAT she could to repair the damage to her face—her eyelids were puffy, her nose was red and her lips swollen. Isla never cried. Even at the most difficult births she was very aware that even a single tear might lead back to that memory and so she kept her emotions in check.

Always.

She put on some sunglasses and made her way to Arrivals, where she stood, her eyes moving between the three exit doors and wondering if she would even recognise Darcie when she came out.

As it turned out, it was Darcie who recognised her.

'Isla!' Her name was called from behind the rail and the second she turned Isla's face broke into a smile.

'I was watching the wrong door.' Isla greeted Darcie with a hug. 'Happy New Year,' she said.

'Happy New Year, to you, too.' Darcie smiled.

'I was starting to worry that I wouldn't recognise you when you came out,' Isla admitted.

'Well, I certainly recognised you. You're as gorgeous as you are in the magazine I was just...' Darcie's voice trailed off and she went a bit pink, perhaps guessing that the article she had read on the plane might not be Isla's favourite topic, given that it had revealed Rupert's infidelity.

Isla let that comment go and they stepped out into the morning sun. Melbourne was famous for its fickle weather but this morning the sky was silver blue and the sun had been firmly turned on to welcome Darcie.

'It shouldn't take too long to get home,' Isla said as they hit the morning rush-hour traffic. 'Did you get much sleep on the plane?'

'Not really.' Darcie shook her head. 'I shan't be much company today.'

'That's fine.' Isla smiled. 'I'm dropping you home and then I'll be going into work so you'll have the place to yourself.'

'You should have told me that you were working this morning!' Darcie said. 'I could have taken a taxi. You didn't have to come out to the airport to meet me.'

'It was no problem and I was there anyway to see Isabel off.'

'Oh, of course you were.' Darcie glanced at Isla. Despite the repair job that Isla had done with make-up and dark glasses, it was quite clear to Darcie that she had been crying. Now, though, Darcie thought she knew why. 'It must have been hard to say goodbye to your sister.'

'It was,' Isla admitted. 'I'm going to miss her a lot, though I bet she's going to have an amazing year in England.'

They chatted easily as they drove into Melbourne. Isla pointed out a few landmarks—Federation Square and the Arts Centre—and Darcie said she couldn't wait to get on a tram.

'We'll be catching one tonight,' Isla told her. 'I've organised for some colleagues to get together and have drinks tonight. It's a bit of a tradition on the maternity unit that we all try to get together before a new staff member starts, just so we can get most of the introductions out of the way and everything. If it's too much for you, given how far you've flown, everyone will understand.'

'No, it won't be too much, that sounds lovely. I'm looking forward to meeting everyone.'

'Have you left a boyfriend behind?' Isla asked, and Darcie shook her head.

'No, I'm recently single and staying that way. I'm here to focus on my career. I've heard so much about the MMU at the Victoria—I just can't wait to get started.'

'There it is.' Isla drove slowly past the hospital where Darcie would commence work the next day. It was a gorgeous old building that, contrary to outer appearances, was equipped with the best staff and equipment that modern medicine had to offer.

They soon pulled into the underground car park of the apartment block and took the lift to the penthouse.

'Wow,' Darcie said as they stepped inside. 'When you said that we'd be sharing a flat…' She was clearly a bit taken aback by the rather luxurious surroundings and looked out of the floor-to-ceiling windows to the busy city below. 'It's stunning.'

'It will soon feel like home,' Isla assured her. 'I'll give you a quick tour but then I really need to get to work.'

'There's no need for a tour,' Darcie said. 'I'll just be having a very quick shower and then bed. I'll probably still be in it when you get home.'

Isla showed Darcie to her room. It had its own en suite and Isla briefly went through how to use the remote control for the blinds and a few other things and then she quickly got changed to head into work. 'I'll try and get back about six o'clock,' Isla said. 'I've told people to get there about seven, but if I do get stuck at work I'll send a colleague to pick you up.'

'There's no need for that.' Darcie was clearly very independent, Isla realised. 'Just tell me the name of the bar and if you can't make it home in time, I'll find my own way there.'

Isla smiled, though she shook her head. 'I'm not leaving you to make your own way there on your first day in Melbourne.'

Darcie was nice, Isla decided as she drove to work. She still felt a little bit unsettled from her breakdown earlier. She had never cried like that. In fact, she did everything she could not to think about that terrible morning. The trouble was, though, since Sean had arrived, that long-ago time seemed to be catching up with both Isabel and her. As if to prove her point, the first person she saw when she walked into MMU was Sean. With no dark glasses to hide behind now, Isla's heart sank a little when he called her over.

'I was wondering if you could have a word with Christine Adams for me,' Sean said. 'I know how good you are with teenagers and, in all honesty, nothing I say about contraception seems to be getting through to her. At this rate, Christine is going to be back here in nine months' time. I inserted an IUD after delivery but, as you know, she had a small haemorrhage and it's been expelled so I can't put another one in for six weeks. She's also got a history of deep vein thrombosis so she's not able to go on the Pill. Can you just reiterate to her and her boyfriend that they need to use condoms every time? She's

told me that she doesn't want another baby for a couple
of years, and I think she's right—her body needs a rest.'

'She's very anaemic, isn't she?' Isla checked.

'She is. I was considering a transfusion when she bled
but she's going to try and get her iron up herself.'

'I'll have a chat,' Isla agreed. She was very used to
dealing with young mums and last year had started a
group called Teenage Mums-To-Be, or TMTB, as it was
known. Even though she couldn't always be there to take
the group, one of the other midwives would run it for her
if necessary and they often had an obstetrician come
along to talk to the young women, too. It was proving to
be a huge success.

Christine had attended TMTB for two babies in one
year. Robbie, who had been born a couple of days ago,
was her second baby. This morning Christine was going
home to look after a newborn *and* a ten-month-old with
her iron level in her boots. Isla knew that Sean was right,
she could be back again at the MMU very soon.

'One other thing, Isla,' Sean started as Isla went to
head off, but whatever he'd been about to say was put
on hold as he looked over Isla's shoulder. 'Good morning, Alessi, thanks for coming down—you're looking
very smart.'

Especially smart, Isla thought! Alessi's good looks and
easy smile she did not need this morning, especially as
he was looking particularly divine. He was dressed in
an extremely impressive suit, his tie was immaculately
knotted and he was, for once, freshly shaven. He might as
well be on his way to a wedding rather than dropping into
the unit to check a newborn that Sean was worried about.

'Good morning, all,' Alessi said.

'Morning, Alessi,' one of Isla's midwives called.

'Looking good,' someone else commented, and Isla bristled as she heard a wolf whistle come from the treatment room.

They were like bees to honey around him and Alessi took it all in his stride and just smiled, though it did not fall in Isla's direction. They didn't get on. Of course they were professional when they worked together. Their paths often crossed but they both tried to make sure that there was as little contact as possible. His flirting with her staff annoyed the hell out of Isla, however, and she was very tempted to have a word with him about it. She had recently found out that he was dating one of her students, Amber.

That made it sound worse than it was, Isla knew—Amber was a mature-age student and older than she herself was, but even so, Isla wasn't impressed.

What she couldn't dispute, though, was that Alessi was one of the hardest-working doctors she had ever known. As hard as he dated, he worked. He was there in the mornings when she arrived and often long after she went home.

'What do you have for me?' Alessi asked Sean, but before he could answer Isla made to go.

'I'll leave you both to it,' Isla said.

'Could you hold on a second, Isla? I still want to speak with you,' Sean said, thwarting her attempt to make a swift getaway. He turned to Alessi. 'I've got a baby I delivered in the early hours. He seemed to be fine when delivered but there's no audible cry now. All observations are normal and he seems well other than he isn't making much noise when he cries.'

'I'll take a look.' Alessi nodded.

'So why are you all dressed up?' Sean asked, given

that Alessi usually dressed in scrubs and looked as if he had just rolled out of bed.

'I'm having lunch today with the bigwigs…' Alessi rolled his eyes and then they did meet Isla's and he gave her a tight smile. 'I'm actually having lunch with Isla's father.'

She couldn't quite put her finger on it but Isla knew that he was having a little dig at her.

'Enjoy,' Isla said.

'I shan't,' Alessi tartly replied. 'Sometimes you have to just suffer through these things.'

The lunch that Alessi was speaking about was due to the fact that he was soon to be receiving an award in recognition of his contributions to the neonatal unit over the past year. There was a huge fundraising ball being held in a couple of weeks' time and Charles Delamere was attempting to push Alessi towards the charitable side of things—hence the lunch today, where it would be strongly suggested that Alessi, with his good looks and easy smile, might be a more visible presence. While Alessi knew how essential fundraising was and felt proud to have his achievements acknowledged, a part of him resented having to walk the talk. He'd far rather be getting on with the job than appearing on breakfast television to speak about the neonatal unit, as Charles had recently suggested.

Alessi chatted for a moment more with Sean but, during that brief exchange with Isla, he had noted the puffiness around her eyes and had guessed, rightly, that she had been crying. He was wrong about the reason, though. Alessi assumed Isla's tears were because of the weekend reports about her boyfriend's philandering. Even if she was upset there was still plenty of the ice-cold Isla,

Alessi thought as she stood there. Her stance was bored and dismissive and she didn't even deign to give him a glance as he headed off to examine the infant.

Isla was anything but bored, though. Seemingly together, she was shaking inside as Alessi walked off because she knew that Sean was going to ask her about Isabel.

'How was this morning?' Sean asked.

'Fine.'

'Isabel got off okay?'

'She just texted to say that she's boarding.' Isla nodded and then did her best to change the subject. 'What did you want to speak with me about?'

'Just that,' Sean answered. 'Isla, my working here didn't have any part in her decision—'

'Sean, Isabel was offered a year's secondment in England. Who wouldn't give their right arm for that?'

'It just—'

'I'm too busy to stand here, chatting,' Isla said, and walked off.

Yes, she could be aloof at times but it was surely better to be thought of as that than to stand discussing Isabel's leaving with Sean.

Isla went to the store cupboard and got some samples of condoms. She put them in a bag and then headed in to speak with Christine, who was there with Blake, her boyfriend, who was also eighteen. Little Joel, their older baby, was also there.

Isla was usually incredibly comfortable approaching such subjects with her patients. She discussed contraception many times a day both on the ward and in the postnatal clinic but when she walked behind the curtains, where Christine was nursing her baby, she also saw Alessi's shoes gleaming beneath the other side of the curtains. That he was examining the baby in the next bed to Christine made Isla feel just a little bit self-conscious.

'Hi, there, Christine.' Isla smiled. 'Hi, Blake. I hear that you're all going home this morning?'

'I can't wait to get him home,' Christine said, and gazed down at Robbie. He was latched onto Christine's breast, beautifully and happily feeding away.

'You're doing so well,' Isla commented. 'You're still feeding Joel, aren't you?'

'Just at night,' Christine replied, 'though he's jealous and wants me all the time now, too.'

Isla glanced over at Joel, who was staring at his new brother with a very put-out look on his face. Christine really was an amazing mum, but Isla could well understand Sean's concern and why he was asking her to re-iterate what he had said. Christine was incredibly pale and breastfeeding a newborn and a ten-month-old would certainly take its toll. 'I wanted to have a word with you about contraception—'

'Oh, we've already been spoken to about that,' Christine interrupted. 'The midwife said something this morning and Dr Sean has been in, so you really don't need to explain things again.'

'I do.'

'I'll leave you to it, then.' Blake went to stand but Isla shook her head.

'Oh, no.' Isla smiled as Blake reluctantly sat down. 'I want to speak with both of you. As you know, the IUD insertion didn't work. That happens sometimes, but now it's better that the doctor waits for your six-week checkup to put another in.'

'Dr Sean has explained that,' Christine sighed.

'You do know that you can't rely on breastfeeding as a form of contraception,' Isla gently reminded them, and Christine started to laugh as she looked down at Robbie.

'I know that now—given that I'm holding the proof.'

'And you understand that you can't take the Pill because of your history of blood clots,' Isla continued as Christine vaguely smiled and nodded. She really wasn't taking any of this in. 'You need to use condoms every time, or not have intercourse…'

'There's always the morning-after pill,' Christine said, and Isla shook her head. Privately she didn't like the morning-after pill, unless it was after an episode of abuse, not that she would ever push her own beliefs onto her patients. It was the fact that Christine had a history of blood clots that ruled it out for her and Isla told her so. 'You need to be careful—' Isla started, but Christine interrupted again.

'I'm not waiting six weeks and he…' she nodded her head in Blake's direction '…certainly can't wait that long.'

'I'm not asking you both to wait till then,' Isla said patiently. 'Though you don't *have* to have penetrative sex, there are other things you can do.' Christine just rolled her eyes and Isla ploughed on. 'If you are going to have sex before the IUD is put in then you are to use condoms each and every time.' She looked at Blake. 'That's why I asked to speak to you, too.'

'Oh, leave him alone.' Christine grinned.

'Christine, you're very anaemic and the last thing your body needs now is another pregnancy. I'm just asking Blake to make sure that he's careful.'

'It's not his fault, he tries to be careful,' Christine said, happy to leap to Blake's defence. 'Haven't you ever got so carried away that you just don't care, Isla?'

Isla glanced at the shoes on the other side of the curtain and just knew that Alessi could hear every word and was no doubt having a little laugh.

Rarely, her cheeks were pink as she looked back at Christine.

'Well?' Christine demanded. 'I think you know what I'm talking about, Isla.'

'But this isn't about me,' Isla answered calmly. 'I've raided the store cupboard.' She handed Blake what would hopefully be adequate supplies. 'One each time!' Isla said. 'Or I'll be seeing see you very soon. Perhaps with twins this time, wouldn't that be nice? Four under two, what fun!'

She saw Blake blink and he glanced at Christine and then back at Isla, and hopefully the message had sunk in. 'Got it?' Isla said.

'Got it,' Blake agreed.

As she left them to go through their goody bag she walked straight into Alessi, who was wearing a smile, and there was an extremely rare truce because all Isla could do was let out a little laugh.

'You didn't answer the question, Isla,' Alessi teased.

'No, I didn't.'

'A case of do as I say, not as I do?' Alessi nudged and Isla gave a non-committal smile. He'd die on the spot if he knew the truth but thankfully the small armistice was soon over and Alessi got back to talking about work, which Isla knew better how to handle. 'I'm very happy with the baby that Sean just asked me to see. There's no sign of infection—I think he has a floppy larynx, which is causing the husky cry. Still, I'm going to do a blood test and can his temperature be checked every two hours? Any deterioration at all then I'm to be called straight away.' He watched as Isla nodded and he again took in her puffy eyes and was tempted to say something.

But what could he say?

I'm sorry to hear that your boyfriend's been screwing around on you again?

Alessi wasn't sorry.

Well, perhaps he was sorry for the hurt that had been dished out to Isla but he wasn't sorry that her relationship with Rupert was over.

Close to a year on, despite not particularly *liking* her, Alessi still found himself thinking about that night.

Still, despite her cool disdain, despite having been born with a silver spoon in her mouth, as opposed to the plastic café one that he had been born to, he could not quite get her out of his head.

'What time is everybody meeting tonight?' he asked.

'About seven.'

'Good. Shall I see you there?'

'You shall.'

This was as close to a personal conversation they'd had since that night.

And that was how it would remain, he decided as he walked off.

He didn't like his attraction to her, didn't like that eleven months on, the scent of her was a familiar one whenever they were close, and he didn't like that, despite trying not to, today he had found himself with no choice but to smile into her eyes.

Stay back, Alessi, he told himself.

He liked to keep things light with women. Since Talia

he hadn't liked to get too involved. But all that aside, Alessi was determined that Isla Delamere would not be changing her mind on him twice.

CHAPTER THREE

ISLA GOT CAUGHT up in a delivery and didn't make it home until well after six, but Darcie was up and it was actually nice not to come back to an empty flat but share in a glass of wine as they got ready.

'Can I borrow your hair dryer?' Darcie asked. 'The adapter that I brought isn't working.'

'Sure,' Isla said, and went and got it. 'I'll just text Rupert and let him know that I'm running a bit late and to meet us there.'

'Oh, so you're still seeing each—' Darcie abruptly halted whatever it was she'd been about to say. 'I'm so sorry, Isla. That is absolutely none of my business. I think I must have left my manners in England!'

'It's fine.' Isla shrugged. 'My sister said pretty much the same thing this morning. Look, it really isn't awkward. I don't get upset by what's said in the magazines, they're full of rubbish and lies…'

'Of course they are. It's nice that you can trust him.' Darcie smiled but Isla could see a small flicker of pity in her eyes and knew that Darcie, like everybody else, assumed that Isla was being taken for a fool.

Isla went to have a very quick shower, though perhaps it wasn't quite as quick as the one she had intended to have.

New Year, new start, Isla decided as she soaped up.

She *was* going to break up with Rupert.

Isla already knew that she had to stop hiding behind him and certainly she didn't like it that people thought she was somehow standing by her man as Rupert seemingly made a fool of her.

Rupert had rung and explained what had happened before the news had hit. The actress had the same agent as Rupert and the supposed tell-all had been at the agent's direction. Only when the exposé had happened had Rupert found out it had been planned.

'Not good enough,' Isla had said. Still, she found it hard to be cross with him—after all, she knew that what had been said in the article was all lies.

Isla was determined to end it, though she was tempted to put off the break-up. She had asked Rupert to stick close to her tonight and she was nervous about the charity ball coming up in a couple of weeks. Alessi's award meant that he would be sitting at the same table as her father—the same table as her!

Yet things had seemed better when they'd spoken today, Isla thought, recalling the smile he had given as she'd come out from behind Christine's curtain. She closed her eyes for a moment and remembered their kiss that night and just how nice it had been to briefly be in his arms. She stood in the shower, the water cascading over her, as she returned to the blissful memory. Her hands moved over her hips as she remembered his there, and then her eyes snapped open as one hand started to move down of its own accord as she ached, honestly ached to return to the memory and bring it to a more fitting conclusion. She wanted to know what might have happened had she not said no. She wanted to explore the possibilities, her body was almost begging her to.

Isla stood, stunned by her own arousal.

She had buried her sexuality completely.

Since the night she'd delivered Isabel's baby she'd just quashed that side of herself.

Now, though, her breasts felt so heavy she was fighting herself not to touch them and the intense ache between her legs refused to recede. For the first time she wanted to explore her own body.

Shocked, Isla turned off the shower taps and stepped out. She quickly dried herself and pulled on some underwear and dressed. She wore a very pale green summer dress that did nothing to reduce the flush on her cheeks. She simply couldn't stop thinking about Alessi and that he'd be there tonight and so, too, that smile.

And the memory of that kiss.

He'd use you, Isla reminded herself as she put on lip gloss. The same way he'd worked his way through half of MMU.

Not that any of the staff seemed to regret their flings with Alessi.

Would she regret one?

Isla snapped herself out of it.

There was no way she was going to do anything about the reluctant torch she carried for Alessi. She could actually picture his incredulous smile if she told him her truth. Scrap that, incredulous laughter, she amended, and then headed out to the lounge.

'You look great.' Darcie smiled. 'I'm actually nervous about meeting everyone.'

'Well, don't be,' Isla said. 'They're a friendly bunch.'

It was a warm, sultry night and they took a tram for a couple of stops and then arrived at the bar and, as promised, everybody was incredibly friendly and pleased to meet the new obstetrician.

'This is Lucas,' Isla introduced them. 'He's a senior midwife on the MMU...'

'It's nice to meet you,' Darcie said with a smile, and Isla continued the introductions.

'And this is Sophia, a community midwife...' Thankfully, for Isla, Alessi wasn't there, and she allowed herself to relax. She went and bought some drinks and ordered a couple of bottles for the table but as she walked back she saw Alessi had just arrived. What gnawed at Isla was that he was there with Amber.

'This is Alessi.' Isla pushed out a smile. 'He's a neonatologist. Alessi, this is Darcie...' She watched as he smiled his killer smile at Darcie and then Isla continued. 'And this Amber, a *student* midwife...' Isla almost winced as she heard the tart note to her voice and she caught Alessi's eye. She wasn't jealous that he was dating her student; she wanted to tell him instead that she was cross.

'Hi, there.' Isla jumped as she heard Rupert's voice and felt his arm come around her waist. 'Sorry if I'm a bit late.'

'It's fine.' Isla had never been more pleased to see him and gave him a kiss—the practised kiss that they were both used to. What she wasn't so used to was turning back to the table and the black look Alessi was throwing in Rupert's direction.

He looked then at Isla and gave the smallest shake of his head.

All evening she found herself aware of his disapproval.

Well, she very much disapproved of who Alessi was dating, too.

Her skin prickled when he spoke with Amber. Her usually cool edge seemed to be melting and though the conversation flowed at the table, for once Isla wasn't the perfect hostess. Thankfully everybody was keen to hear about how things worked in Cambridge, where Darcie was from and where Isabel would now be working. No one, apart from Rupert and Alessi, seemed to notice her tension.

'Take it easy,' Rupert said, because Isla was again topping up her glass. Isla rarely drank more than one glass of champagne but tonight she was rather grateful for the wine, and Rupert, who could sense her volatility, was right to warn her.

Not that Alessi approved of Rupert telling her what to do—Isla saw the sharp rise of his eyebrows at Rupert's words.

Alessi didn't like it that Rupert, given what he was putting her through, had just warned Isla to slow down. He didn't like it that Rupert was here in the least. Alessi was, in fact, having an extremely uncomfortable evening, though it wasn't Isla that he felt bad for, but Amber. Alessi, even if his relationships didn't last very long, would never cheat or flirt with another woman, except his mind was fighting not to do just that.

It felt wrong to be sitting with Amber while Isla was there.

He was very aware that he was sitting next to the wrong woman.

'I'm just going to go to the loo,' Isla said, and as she got up to leave, Alessi made himself sit there, though the temptation was to follow her.

The restrooms were located right on the other side of the bar and Isla headed off. She knew she had maybe had a little bit too much to drink and was glad of the chance to just take a breath.

No one had said a word about Rupert. They were all used to Isla bringing him along but she was aware of slight pity in her colleagues' eyes and Isla loathed it.

Tonight she *was* ending it, which left her without a safety net, and as she walked out of the loos and straight into Alessi the Rupert-free tightrope got its first wobble, the first inkling of what was to come.

'Everything okay?' Alessi asked, because the look that she gave him was less than pleasant.

'Actually, no,' Isla said. 'What are you doing, dating one of my students?'

'Excuse me?'

'You heard.'

'She isn't *my* student,' Alessi pointed out. 'You're talking as if Amber's eighteen when, in fact, she's a thirty-two-year-old single mother of two. I'm hardly leading her astray—'

'I don't like the way you flirt with my midwives,' Isla interrupted, and Alessi gave her a slow smile, though his eyes told her he was less than impressed with what she was saying.

'Have there been any complaints?'

'Of course not.'

'Any hint as to inappropriateness on my part?' Alessi checked, and watched Isla's cheeks turn to fire as she shook her head. 'Then I'd tread very carefully here if I were you, Isla,' he said. 'The staff don't have an issue?' He raised an eyebrow and Isla gave a terse shake of her head. 'And I don't have an issue,' he drawled. 'So, in fact, the only person who has a problem with my dating Amber is you. I wonder why that is?'

Isla stood, her face flaming. She knew that she shouldn't have said anything, especially not tonight, but now that she had it was impossible to take it back. 'I'm just letting you know how I feel about the issue.'

'What issue?'

Isla licked her tense lips as he backed her to the wall but her lack of response didn't end the conversation.

'I flirt, Isla. I date. I enjoy women but only women who get that it's only ever going to be short-term...'

'Why?'

The question was out before she considered it but it was pertinent enough to halt Alessi in his tracks.

Why?

It was a question few, outside the family, asked him. A question he had never truthfully answered and he had no intention of doing so now.

'Because that is how I choose to live my life. I don't need your approval, or you to rubber-stamp who I date from MMU, but I can tell you now I have never once cheated on anyone. I don't have to make up lies or excuses about what's been said or where I've been...'

'I need to get back,' Isla said, not liking where this conversation was leading, but Alessi wouldn't let her off the hook.

'We've only just started talking,' he said. 'And given you're so inclined to discuss my sex life, I'm sure you won't mind if I share my feelings about yours. Have some respect for yourself...' He met her eyes and Isla took a sharp breath as he now voiced what nobody else had had the guts to. 'What are you with him for, Isla? It's all over the internet and plastered across every magazine that he's screwing around and yet you're carrying on as if nothing's happened.'

'It's none of your business.'

'Well, I'm making it mine,' Alessi said. 'Why would you let him treat you like that?' He looked over as Rupert came around the corner and stood for a moment as he witnessed the angry confrontation.

'There you are,' Rupert said, and, having been instructed by Isla to stay close, he came and put an arm around her waist, dropping a kiss on her head. 'Darcie is starting to droop. I think she might need to go home.'

'Sure,' Isla said as Alessi just stood there, staring at Rupert with a challenge in his eyes. 'If you can tell Darcie that I'll be there in a few minutes, that would be great. I just need to discuss something with Alessi.'

As Rupert walked off Alessi's angry eyes met Isla's. 'He's got a nerve,' Alessi said, 'telling you that you've had too much wine and coming to check up on you, yet he gets to carry on exactly as he chooses…'

'Our relationship is not your concern,' Isla said, her voice shaking. There was no doubt about the sudden flare of possessiveness in Alessi's voice. 'Anyway, you flirt, you…' She tripped over her words, not quite sure of the point she was trying to make. 'You're such a chauvinist.'

'It's the Greek in me.'

They stood angry and frustrated. A kiss was there but not happening. They were back to where they had been a year ago, only the stakes were much higher now. Alessi looked at her full mouth and noticed that she ran a very pink tongue over her lips as if to tempt him.

And tempt him it did.

Isla was looking at his mouth. She was back to how she'd felt in the shower, only now Alessi was less than a step away. Her body was on fire, there was sex in the air, and when walking away might be safer, because it was Alessi, he forced the issue, voiced the truth, stated what was. 'I could kiss you now.'

Isla lifted her eyes to his and saw that the lust and the want in his matched hers. 'You could,' she invited.

She wanted his kiss. The world had disappeared and she had no thought about anything other than now and a kiss that was nearing, but she blinked at his caustic response to her provocative words.

'But I won't,' Alessi said, distaste evident in his voice. 'I happen to have respect for the person I'm with. I have no intention of getting mixed up in whatever twisted game it is that you're playing.'

Isla stepped back, felt the wall behind her and wished it would swallow her up. Alessi was right. It was twisted. The wall would not give, though, and she had to stand there and take it as Alessi continued venting, eleven months of frustration contorting his lips savagely. 'And there's another reason that I shan't kiss you—I won't give you the chance to blow me off again, Isla. You'll be the one to kiss me,' he warned. 'After you've suitably apologised.'

And with that he walked off, leaving Isla standing there, trying to think of an appropriate response to that most delicious threat.

'Never,' she called to his departing back.

'We'll see,' Alessi called, without turning around.

He was furious. He flashed a look at Rupert as he left but what angered Alessi most was that to not kiss Isla had taken all the self-control he could muster. To not press her to the wall and angrily claim her mouth had taken every ounce of his resistance.

He wasn't like that.

Yes, he might have dated an awful lot of women but he was always faithful.

This was why he ended things with Amber that night.

He wanted Isla.

He wanted her in a way he never had.

He wanted to see that snobby, derisive woman begging.

Yes, for the best part of a year he'd convinced himself otherwise but the truth remained—he wanted her.

CHAPTER FOUR

DARCIE REALLY WAS DROOPING. Once home she thanked Isla and Rupert for the night out and went straight to bed. Thankfully Isla didn't have to work out what to say—Rupert said it for her.

'I'm guessing we're breaking up?'

'We are.' Isla forced a brave smile. 'You can say that I'm sick and tired of all your other women.'

'How are you going to go at the ball with your Greek friend there? I assume he's a big part of the reason for us finishing tonight.'

'He hates me,' Isla said. 'And I don't particularly like him, either.'

'Well, that sounds like a good start to me.' Rupert smiled. He knew Isla very well and there were very few people that she allowed to get under her skin. He had felt the undeniable tension all night and had seen Alessi's eyes all too often turn to look towards Isla. 'It's more than time you got out there.'

'Well, I shan't be *getting out there* with Alessi. His relationships seem to last as long as a tube of toothpaste.'

'Ah, but you have to brush your teeth, Isla.' To Rupert, it was that simple. 'Go for it. It's as clear as anything that you fancy each other. Why not just give the two of you a try? If it doesn't work out, it's no big deal.'

It was to Isla, though.

They said goodbye at the door—it was possibly the nicest break-up in the world.

'This is way overdue, Isla,' Rupert said as he gave her a cuddle. Even he didn't know about Isabel and just how deep Isla's fears ran, and saying goodbye to her rock of ten years was hard.

'I know.' She gave him a smile. 'Will you be okay?'

'I shall, but, Isla, can I ask that you don't—'

Isla knew what he was about to say and said it for him. 'I shan't tell anyone about you.'

'Promise me.' His voice was urgent. 'I'm auditioning soon for a really big role. If I do get it then I'm going to be even more in the spotlight...' She could hear his fear and she understood it. She, too, would be terrified to have her sex life, or lack of it, put under the scrutiny of anyone, let alone having it discussed the world over. 'I haven't even told my parents, Isla...'

'It's okay,' Isla soothed, remembering the promise she had made all those years ago. 'I gave you my word.'

When Isla awoke the next morning and headed into work with Darcie, the world felt very different without her safety net.

Not that anyone could know just how exposed and vulnerable she felt. She was her usual cool self while secretly hoping that the world might treat her gently.

The world, though, had other plans for Isla—around eleven, she answered a page from the antenatal clinic. It was Sophia, one of the community midwives, who, because of low staff numbers, was doing an extra shift on-site today and running the antenatal clinic.

'Thanks for answering so quickly,' Sophia said. 'I wasn't sure whether or not to page you. I'm probably—'

'Always page me,' Isla interrupted. 'It doesn't matter how small your concern is, I hope you know that.'

'I do,' Sophia said. 'It's not a patient I'm concerned about, more a situation that I'm not sure how to handle. Alessi dropped by this morning and said that when his sister arrived for her antenatal visit I was to page him so that he could come down. Allegra is actually his twin sister.'

'Okay,' Isla replied, wondering where this was leading as Sophia continued.

'She's thirty-two weeks gestation and Darcie has asked her to go onto a CTG monitor now for a checkup— all is well but Darcie just wanted to be thorough as she's taking over her care and Allegra has quite a complicated history. The trouble is, when I said that I would let Alessi know that she was here, Allegra asked me not to. She wants me to just say that I forgot to page him…'

'And no doubt you're worried about what Alessi will say when you tell him that you *forgot* to let him know?' Isla said, and then thought for a moment. 'It is a bit awkward,' she admitted as she pondered the issue while doing her level best to think this through as she would for any patient who was related to one of the staff here. She had to somehow forget that the staff member happened to be Alessi who, after last night, she was doing her level best to avoid.

Ignore that fact, she told herself.

'I'll come over to Antenatal now and speak with

Allegra,' Isla offered. 'And I'll also deal with Alessi. Thank you for letting me know, Sophia.'

Isla made her way down to the antenatal clinic and Sophia told her where Allegra was. Isla knocked on the door and went in and smiled when she saw Allegra. She was the female version of Alessi with black eyes and black hair and, while strapped to the CTG monitor, she was also doing her level best to keep a wriggling little boy of around three years old amused.

'Hi, Allegra,' Isla greeted her. 'I'm Isla, the head of midwifery.'

'Hello, Isla.' Allegra smiled. 'Is this about Alessi? I realised as soon as I said it that the midwife was feeling a bit awkward when I asked her to pretend she'd forgotten I was here. I'm so sorry about that. I should have discussed this with Alessi myself, instead of landing my problems on Sophia.'

'It's fine,' Isla said, and looked over at the little boy. 'You've got your hands full, I see.'

'Very,' Allegra agreed. 'Sophia gave him a colouring book and some pencils but he's just climbing all over me at the moment. I think Niko's starting to fathom that he's not going to have me all to himself for much longer.'

'Probably,' Isla said, and sat down in a chair near Allegra. 'They're very intuitive and they often sense that change is about to come. Hey, Niko, do you want to come and sit with me?' Isla suggested to the little black-eyed boy who had the same curls as his uncle. 'Look what I've got…'

Niko looked at Isla, who had taken out her pen torch and was flicking it on and off. It worked as a diversion tactic almost every time with three-year-olds and thankfully it worked today. Niko climbed down from his mum's lap and made his way over to Isla. She noted that he had a slightly abnormal gait as he walked over and climbed up onto her lap.

'Look,' Isla said, flicking the pen torch on and off and then giving it to Niko, who tried to do the same. Only he soon found out that it wasn't as easy as Isla had made it look and he would hopefully take several moments to work it out and give Allegra a small break while they chatted and Allegra explained her reasons for not wanting Alessi there.

'I had a very difficult labour with Niko,' Allegra said. 'We were living in Sydney at the time. He was a breech birth and I ended up having an emergency Caesarean section after a very long labour.' Allegra paused for a moment before continuing—clearly the memory of it still distressed her. 'Niko wasn't breathing when he was born and had to be resuscitated. As a consequence he was without oxygen and has now got mild cerebral palsy.'

'That must have been a very scary time for you,' Isla offered.

'It was,' Allegra agreed. 'I wasn't at all well after the birth, either. The thing is, there were a couple of mistakes made and possibly what happened could have been prevented. I chose not to pursue it. I just wanted to put it all behind me. Alessi, though, was pretty devastated as well as furious. I know he thinks if he'd been there, or at least around, then I'd have been taken to Theatre more quickly and Niko's birth injury could have been avoided. My parents said pretty much the same to him, too.'

Isla said nothing but her heart went out to them both.

'I don't want Alessi to be involved in this birth, not because I don't think he's brilliant, it's more that if something does go wrong this time around then I don't want him blaming himself for it.'

'I completely understand that you'd feel that way.' Isla nodded but because she'd had a brief look at Allegra's notes before she'd come in, she knew that there was more. 'And?'

'And?' Allegra smiled at Isla's question.

'Is there another reason that you don't want Alessi's input?'

'There is.' Allegra rolled her eyes in the very same way that her brother did. 'I want to try and have a natural birth this time. Given what happened in my previous labour, Alessi is against the idea of trial of labour and thinks I should have a planned Caesarean section.'

'So, not only do you have to convince your obstetrician, you have to convince your brother, as well?'

'Ah, not just those two,' Allegra sighed. 'I've had to convince my husband and also my mother.' She gave a tired shake of the head. 'Usually I'm the golden one and Alessi's the black sheep but in this she thinks I should listen to him, because he's a doctor.'

Isla fought her own curiosity about that statement—while she wanted to know more about Alessi, this wasn't the place, and she could see Allegra was close to tears. 'What happened with Niko has brought up a lot of stuff for my parents. Maybe I should just have a planned Caesarean. I really am sorry for trying to involve your staff in this.'

'It's our job to be involved,' Isla said, and she truly did her best to pretend this wasn't Alessi's twin pouring her heart out to her. Which meant, if this hadn't been Alessi's twin then Isla knew exactly what she would do in this case. 'It's your pregnancy and your labour. You shouldn't go through an operation just to please your family. I can explain all that to him.'

Allegra looked dubious. 'I don't know how well he'd take it.'

'I would imagine that when I explain what's going on to Alessi, he's going to feel bad for causing you so much stress...'

'I know that he shall,' Allegra agreed. 'We're very close. The thing is Alessi has always looked out for me at school and things...' She looked at Isla. 'I remember you from school.'

Isla felt a little guilty that she didn't remember Allegra clearly.

'I got picked on a lot at school,' Allegra said. 'Well, we both did.'

'Really?' Isla couldn't imagine for a moment Alessi being picked on by anyone, he was so confident and assured, but then Allegra continued speaking.

'We were scholarship kids,' she explained. 'Which meant from the day that we started we didn't belong. At every opportunity it would be rammed down our throats that we couldn't afford to go skiing or that we didn't have the right uniform. It was very cruel. Alessi looked out for me then and is just trying to do the same now. The thing is...' Allegra hesitated and Isla stepped in.

'You don't need him to any more?'

'No, I don't.' Allegra sighed. 'I'm not going to take any risks with this baby but I really do want to try and have a natural delivery.' She thought for a long moment. 'It would be great if you could speak to him for me. I really have tried and I seem to get nowhere.'

Isla nodded. 'You're not the first patient to have this sort of problem. I've dealt with this on several occasions.

No doubt I'll be the same if my sister ever gets pregnant. It's very hard to step back when you love someone, though Alessi needs to in this.'

'Thanks, Isla.'

Niko had actually fallen asleep while they'd been talking. Isla carried him over to one of the empty reclining chairs next to Allegra and laid him down, then went and looked at the CTG monitor. 'Everything looks very good,' Isla said. 'Right, I'm going to have a word with that brother of yours and don't worry. If you have any concerns, any at all, ring through to MMU and ask to be put through to me.'

'Thanks so much.'

As she walked out of the room there was Alessi, speaking with Sophia and frowning.

'I asked you to page me as soon as Allegra arrived—'

'Alessi,' Isla said, and gave a small smile to Sophia, excusing her from the conversation. 'Sophia paged me. I need to speak with you about your sister.' She saw concern flash across his features and immediately put him at ease. 'There's nothing wrong with the baby, but before you go in and see Allegra there is something that I need to discuss with you.'

Alessi's eyebrows rose and she had a feeling he was about to walk off but he gave a small nod.

'What is it that you want to discuss?'

'Perhaps not here.' Isla gestured to one of the consulting rooms and they both walked over to it.

It was awkward to be in there with him, given all that had, or rather hadn't, taken place between them, but Isla pushed all that aside and dealt with what was important—the patient. She took a seat at the desk and Alessi did the same. With the door closed she could smell his cologne and she really wished this conversation didn't have to take place on the tail end of last night, but she had no choice in the timing of things and so she pushed on.

'I've just been speaking with Allegra. We've had quite a long conversation, in fact,' she ventured. 'The thing is, while Allegra really appreciates your concern about the pregnancy—'

'I don't need you interfering in my family, Isla,' Alessi interrupted, and it was clear that he knew what the discussion would be about and wanted no part of it.

'I'd prefer not to have to but it's not about what I'd prefer and it's not about what you need—this is about Allegra.'

Alessi took a breath. 'Isla, I'm not going to discuss this with you.'

'You don't have to discuss anything with me, Alessi,' Isla answered calmly. 'I'm just asking that you take a few minutes to listen.' He went to stand but Isla halted him. 'Alessi, Allegra isn't your patient, she's *my* patient in *my* unit.'

'I'll discuss this directly with Allegra,' Alessi said, and headed for the door.

'And cause her more stress?' Isla responded, and watched as his shoulders stiffened. It really was a difficult subject to approach. She hadn't been lying when she'd said to Allegra that she'd handled this sort of situation several times and she would be blunt if she had to be. 'Allegra knows that you're just trying to look out for her and while she does appreciate it she wants you to be the baby's uncle rather than some hovering neonatologist. Everything is going well this pregnancy.'

'Everything was going well the last one,' Alessi said, though at least he sat back down.

'Do you think that Allegra doesn't already know all that?' Isla asked, and watched as Alessi closed his eyes and breathed out. 'Do you think she hasn't wrestled for a long time with her decisions before making them?'

'I'm really causing stress for her?' he asked. When she didn't say anything his black eyes met hers and he gave a wry smile as he answered his own question. 'Clearly I am. God, I never meant to, Isla. The thing is, what happened during Niko's labour was preventable. I just want to…' His voice trailed off.

'You want to ensure that nothing goes wrong with this one,' Isla finished for him, and Alessi nodded. 'I get that but if something *does* go wrong, if an emergency does arise, do you really want to be a part of it?'

'I want to be there to ensure nothing untoward happens in the first place.'

'Look, I do get that…' Isla started but Alessi didn't let her finish.

'Allegra going for a natural delivery is a crazy idea, given what happened last time.'

'It's not a crazy idea to Allegra, and it's not a crazy idea to her obstetrician—'

'Darcie's been here all of five minutes.'

Isla chose to ignore that. She knew it was hard when another doctor took over a patient's care but it wasn't for Alessi to air his concerns to his sister so she continued with what she was saying. 'And it isn't a crazy idea to me. A lot of women want to experience a natural delivery. She'd have a closely monitored trial of labour and if things didn't progress well then, perhaps more quickly, given her history, things would move towards a Caesarean. Even if Darcie is new, our recruitment policy is vigorous and she's joined an amazing team, which means that your sister *shall* be well looked after here, Alessi, you know that.'

Alessi thought for a long moment. Really, he could only admire Isla for confronting him on this difficult subject but her help didn't end there.

'If it makes it any easier for you,' she continued, 'I'm happy to oversee Allegra's care.'

Alessi's eyes jerked up and met hers.

'Whatever you think about me personally, Alessi, however you think I landed the role, the truth is I think that we both know that I do a very good job. I will, if you would like, keep an eye on Allegra during her antenatal visits and, as far as possible, I will be there for the birth.'

'You'd do that?'

'Of course.'

Alessi was surprised by her offer but, then again, was he? For nearly a year he had chosen to believe she had got the job because of who her father was. He had been wrong about that. Alessi had known it deep down and it was confirmed right now. The patients all raved about her, there was no doubt that she ran a very good midwifery unit and now she was offering to take care of Allegra when both knew how tense things were between them. Even the fact that Allegra had discussed so much with Isla told Alessi something—she didn't open up easily to anyone, yet she had with Isla. 'I would like that and I'll back off, too,' Alessi said, and then stood. 'Thank you.'

'No problem.'

He went to go but then turned around. 'I was going to come and see you later,' Alessi said. 'But now that we're here, I might as well just say it now—I would like to apologise for the things that I said last night.' Isla found she was holding her breath as he continued, 'I had no right to lecture you about your partner and the choices you make. It was out of character for me and I really would like to apologise.'

'It's fine.'

'Also, I broke up with Amber last night, so you don't have to worry that I'm dating one of your students.'

'Because of what I said?'

Alessi let out a very mirthless laugh. 'No.'

'But…'

'As I said, I don't cheat and, given that last night the only person I wanted was you, it seemed appropriate to end things.'

And with that he was gone and only when the door closed behind him did Isla let out the air trapped in her throat—her lungs were still closed tight.

Had he just said what he had?

Yes.

Did that mean…?

It did.

Oh, God.

It was like being tossed three flaming torches and having to learn to juggle with absolutely no clue how.

She walked out of the consulting room into a world that felt very different—Alessi liked her, in that way, and had made it clear that he was single. There was no Rupert to hide behind any more, not that she'd told Alessi that.

She was on the edge of something—scared to step off yet somehow compelled to.

Allegra was holding Niko and speaking with Sophia, but Isla watched her turn and smile widely at her brother as he came over, and as Isla approached she heard their conversation.

'You should have said.' Alessi gave her a cuddle.

'I tried,' Allegra gently scolded. 'Several times.'

'I'll back off and I'll make sure Mum and Dad do, too,' Alessi promised. 'I just...'

'I know,' Allegra said. 'I know you were just trying to do your best for us.' She looked at Isla as she joined them. 'Thank you so much, Isla.'

'It's no problem. I've spoken with Alessi and, if you're happy for me to do so, I can oversee things and come down and check all your antenatal visits, rather than your brother, and then, if you'd like, I'd be delighted to be there for your birth of your second child.'

'I'd really like that, Isla.'

'Good.'

She nodded goodbye and as Isla walked off Allegra smiled. 'I feel so much better. You really will speak to Mum and Dad?'

'Yep.'

'They'll give you a hard time,' Allegra pointed out.

'So, what's new?'

"Lessi!" Niko, fed up with all the adults, held out his arms to his uncle and, from a slight distance Isla watched as Alessi took his little nephew in his arms and gave him a kiss and then he must have said something funny because Niko laughed and laughed and Alessi grinned, too.

Then he turned and caught her staring at him and the smile remained as she blushed and returned it then quickly walked away, to return to the ward.

Yes, she was on the edge of something.

Something temporary, though. She knew that much about Alessi and she had almost reconciled herself to that.

Yes, this year was going to be very different. Alessi was going to be her first.

Even if he mustn't know it.

Somehow she had to hold onto her glamorous, sophisticated reputation while releasing a little of her heart.

CHAPTER FIVE

DARCIE SETTLED INTO the flat and hospital amazingly well.

With one exception.

Her first week at the Victoria passed smoothly but at the start of Darcie's second week Isla heard an angry exchange coming from the treatment room and then Darcie marched out. Frowning, Isla stepped into the treatment room to find Lucas standing there, the tension still in the air and a wry smile on his face.

'Issue?' Isla checked, trying to hide her surprise because Darcie got on with everyone, and no one, no one *ever* had an issue with Lucas—he was down-to-earth and seriously gorgeous and for him to have had upset Darcie or vice versa was a surprise indeed.

'You tell me.' Lucas shrugged.

'Lucas?' Isla frowned. He was a part of the glue that tied the MMU together. He got on with everyone, was intuitive, funny and so damn good-looking that his smile could melt anyone. It would seem it simply didn't melt Darcie.

'I don't need the new obstetrician telling me I'm late and to get my act together.'

Isla let out a breath. No, that much Lucas didn't need.

'And,' Lucas drawled, 'I also don't need you to have

a word for me, Isla. Whatever her issue with me is, I'll deal with it myself.'

'Fine,' Isla said, 'but whatever the hell your issues are with each other, keep them well away from the patients.'

'You know that I will.'

'I do,' Isla said. 'Let me know if you need anything…' She turned to go but Lucas halted her.

'Isla, I hate to say this, I know I was late in this morning but I really need to go home…' He blew out a breath and then went to explain but Lucas didn't need to explain things to Isla. She knew that his home life was complicated at best and if Lucas said that he needed to go home then he was telling the truth.

'Go, then,' Isla said. 'I'll take over your patients.'

'I've only got one,' Lucas said. 'I'm expecting her to arrive any minute, I'm just setting up for her. Donna Reece, she's pretty complex.'

'You think I can't handle complex?' Isla teased.

'No, I just feel like I'm landing an awful lot on you.'

'Return the favour someday.' Isla smiled. 'Hand over the patient to me and go home.'

As Isla wheeled through the drip Lucas had set up, there was Darcie, checking drugs for the imminent arrival of Donna Reece. She was forty years old, at twenty-four weeks gestation with twins and a direct admission from the antenatal ward as she had been found to be in premature labour.

'Where's Lucas?' Darcie frowned. 'He was supposed to—'

'I've got your orders,' Isla said. 'I'm taking over this patient.'

'Oh, so he doesn't want to work with me?'

'Lucas has gone home,' Isla said. She was about to

tell Darcie why and to tell her to back off Lucas, but then she remembered that Lucas had asked her not to step in. Anyway, there was no time for that. Donna was about to arrive.

'Did he page Alessi?'

'Yes,' Isla said, and as Donna was wheeled in, just the look on her face had Isla reaching for the phone to page for an anaesthetist to come directly to the delivery ward, too.

'Hi, Donna, I'm Isla…'

Isla kept her voice calm as she attached Donna to all the equipment. Things didn't look good at all and it was made worse that Donna's thirteen-year-old daughter was present and clearly distressed.

As Alessi arrived Isla was taking the young girl down to the waiting room and she gave him a grim smile, in way of small preparation for what he was about to face.

'Have a seat in here,' Isla said to Jessica. 'I know that you've had a horrible morning…'

'I thought that Mum was just coming here for a checkup,' Jessica said. She was holding a large backpack and Isla could see a towel sticking out of it. It was the summer holidays and clearly they had intended to head out to the beach for the day after the routine appointment that had suddenly taken a different turn. 'Mum said she didn't feel well this morning and I said she'd promised we'd go out. I should have listened…'

'Jessica, I'm going to come and talk to you later. You've done nothing wrong and your mum is going to be okay.'

'But what about the babies?' Jessica asked.

'Right now the doctors are in with your mum and we'll know a lot more soon. Is there anyone I can call for you?

Your dad's overseas?' Isla checked, because Lucas had
told her that he was.

'He is but Mum's going to ring him and tell him to
come home.'

'I'll speak to your mum and we'll see about getting
someone to come and sit with you. Right now, do your
best to take it easy and I'll go and see how Mum is doing.'

She went back into the delivery ward. Alessi was
doing an ultrasound and his face was grim and he wasn't
trying to hide it. He was clearly concerned.

'How's Jessica?' Donna asked.

'She's just worried about you and the babies,' Isla
said. 'Is there anybody that you'd like me to call who
can come and be with her?'

'Could you call my sister?' Donna asked. 'Tom, my
husband, is in Dubai. I'm going to see what Darcie has
to say and then call him and ask him to come home.'
Donna closed her eyes. 'Jessica and I had an argument
last night. I told her that I needed more help around the
house, especially with the twins coming. Then we had
another row this morning because I'd promised to take
her to the beach but I told her I was too tired, when really my back was hurting and I was starting to worry
that something was going wrong with the twins.' Donna
started to cry. 'She said in the ambulance that she thinks
this is all her fault.'

'We both know that none of this is her fault,' Isla said.
'These things happen all the time, whether there's an argument involved or not. I'll speak with your daughter at
length about this,' Isla promised, and Alessi glanced up at
the determined note in her voice. 'Right now, though,' Isla
continued, 'we need to take care of you and your babies.'

'Darcie's said that the medicine might postpone the labour.'

'That's right,' Isla nodded, and then glanced up as Alessi came over.

'Hi, Donna.' He gave a pale smile. 'As I said, I'm going to be overseeing the twins' care.'

'Hopefully not for a while,' Donna said, but Alessi glanced at Isla and her heart sank as Alessi continued to speak.

'I'm not sure. I have to tell you that I am very concerned about one of the twins on the ultrasound. Do you know what you're having?'

Donna nodded. 'Two boys.'

'That's right, and you know that they're not identical?'

Again Donna nodded.

'The twins are in two separate amniotic sacs and they each have their own placenta,' Alessi explained. 'The trouble is that one of the twins is smaller than the other, and the fluid around this twin…' he placed a hand high on Donna's stomach '…is significantly reduced. Most of the time our aim is to prolong the pregnancy for as long as possible but in some cases it is better that the baby is born.'

'Even at twenty-four weeks?' Donna asked, and there was a very long silence before Alessi answered.

'No,' he said gently. 'It is far too soon but this is where it becomes a very delicate balancing game. Darcie has given you steroids that will mean that if the twins come after forty-eight hours then their lungs will be more mature than they would otherwise be. However, I'm not sure that I want the delivery to be held off for much longer. This little one needs to born soon. The placenta isn't doing its job and that twin stands a better chance out of the womb than inside.'

'But what about the other one?'

'That is why it is such a delicate balance,' Alessi said. There were no easy answers—twin A needed as long as possible inside the womb; twin B, to have a chance of survival, desperately needed to be born. The diagnosis was indeed grim. Twenty-four weeks was, in the best of cases, extremely premature but for an already small undernourished baby it didn't look good at all. Isla listened as Alessi gently led Donna down the difficult path of realisation that the babies' chances of survival were poor and that their outlook, if they did live, might not be bright.

It really was a horrible conversation to have, and he did it kindly and with compassion, but he was also clear in that he didn't offer false hope. By the end of the consultation Donna had said that she wanted everything, *everything* possible done for both twins when they were born.

'We shall,' Alessi assured her. 'Donna, I can say that you are in the very best place for this to happen. I am going to be there for your boys and I shall do all that I can for them.' He stood and looked at Isla, asking if he could have a word outside.

'Any changes, particularly to twin B, I want to be urgently paged. I've spoken to the anaesthetist and he's going to set up an epidural so that we can do an urgent section if required.'

'How long do you think twin B has got if he isn't delivered?'

'I'm hoping to buy a few days,' Alessi said. 'Though

I doubt we can wait much longer than that, though that would be to the detriment of twin A, who looks very well.'

'It's a tough choice.'

'I don't think I'll have to make it.' Alessi sighed. 'She has marked funnelling,' he said, and Isla nodded. The cervix was dilated at the top end and that meant that Donna could deliver at any time.

'I'm going to go and speak with Jessica now,' Isla said, 'and then ring her aunt and ask her to come in.'

'Do you want me to speak with her?' Alessi offered, but Isla shook her head.

'I'm sure you'll be having a lot of contact with the family in the coming days and weeks. If you could just bear in mind that she's feeling guilty, when really, whether Donna was in labour or not when she presented in Antenatal, the outcome was always going to be that she was admitted today…'

'I'll keep it in mind,' Alessi said. 'Oh, and I just had a call from Allegra. She's very grateful to you. Things are much better.'

'That's good.'

'I spoke with my parents, as well, and they are doing their best now not to interfere.'

'How did that go?' Isla asked.

'Ha.' Alessi smiled. 'They do listen to me when it's about work.'

'Only then?' Isla asked, her curiosity permanently piqued when it came to Alessi, but he simply gave a small nod.

'Pretty much. I'd better get back.'

'Sure.'

'Isla?'

'Yes?'

Alessi changed his mind. 'It will keep.'

He left her smiling.

When Alessi had gone back to NICU and things were settling down with Donna, Isla had a very long chat with Jessica. Rather than speaking in her office, Isla took the young girl to the canteen and they had a drink as Isla did her best to reassure her that none of the situation was her fault.

'None of this happened because of your argument with your mum,' Isla said, when Jessica revealed her guilt. 'I promise you that. One of the twins is very small and we'd have picked up on that today at her appointment and she would have been admitted.'

'It's too soon for them to be born, isn't it?' Jessica asked.

'They're very premature,' Isla explained. 'But as I said, there's a problem with one of the twins and your mum was always going to have to deliver the twins early. Do you understand that you didn't cause this?'

'I think so,' Jessica said. 'I'm scared for my brothers.'

'I know that you are, but we're going to do all we can for them and for your mum. I've spoken with your aunt and she's on her way in and you're going to be staying with her tonight. Your mum's rung your dad and he's on his way back from Dubai.'

'It's serious, then.'

'It is,' Isla said. There was no point telling Jessica that everything was going to be fine. It would be a lie and even with the best possible outcome, her mum and brothers were going to be at the Victoria for a very long time. 'But your mum is in the best place. Darcie, the doctor who is looking after her, is very used to dealing with difficult pregnancies. In fact, she's just come over from England and we're thrilled to have her expertise, and Alessi, the doctor who will be in charge of your brothers' care, is one of the best in his field. He'll give them every chance.'

She let the news sink in for a moment. It was a hard conversation, but Isla knew that it might be easier on Donna if she prepared Jessica and ultimately easier on Jessica to be carefully told the truth. 'Why don't we get Mum a drink and take it up to her now?'

Jessica nodded and they headed back up to the ward. Isla was pleased to see Jessica and Donna have a cuddle and Donna reiterate to Jessica that none of this was her fault.

It was a long day and it didn't end there because just as Isla was about to head for her home she got an alert on her computer that it was her fortnightly TMTB group tonight.

'I completely forgot,' Isla groaned to Emily. 'I honestly thought it was next week.'

'Do you want me to take it?' Emily offered. 'I can go home for an hour and then come back.'

'That's lovely of you but, no, it's fine.' Isla smiled. She knew how stretched Emily was and it was incredibly generous of her to offer to stay back.

Isla did some paperwork to fill in the time and then headed over to the room they used for TMTB. She turned on the urn and put out a couple of plates of biscuits and set up. Usually there were five to ten young mums, all at various stages of pregnancy.

As Isla was setting up a young girl put her head around the door. She was clearly nervous and Isla gave her a warm smile.

'Are you looking for Teenage Mums-To-Be?' Isla asked, and the girl gave a tentative nod.

'Then you're in the right place. I'm Isla.'

'Ruby.'

'I'm just setting up but come in and help yourself to a drink. The rest of the group should start arriving any time now.'

Isla watched as the young girl came in. She was incredibly slim and, Isla guessed, around sixteen years old. She was wearing shorts and a large T-shirt and if she hadn't been here, Isla wouldn't have guessed that she was pregnant. It was good that she was here so early in her pregnancy, Isla thought, but when she looked over to where Ruby was making a drink her heart sank as she saw the young girl slipping a few biscuits into her pocket and then a few more.

She was hungry, Isla realised.

Pregnant and hungry.

'I'll be back in a moment, Ruby,' Isla said, and headed back to the ward. In her office Isla rang down to Catering and asked for sandwiches and a fruit platter and some jugs of juice to be sent up. There were some perks to being a manager because her request went through unquestioned and Isla only wished that she had thought of this long ago. Still, TMTB was a relatively new project and they were all still feeling their way.

Gradually the other girls started to arrive and at seven the group started and introductions were made. Harriet was nineteen and this was her first pregnancy. She had already been told that her baby was going to have significant issues.

'He's going to have to have an operation as soon as he's born,' Harriet said. 'I don't really understand what is happening, but Mum said that she'll come to my next appointment with me.'

'That's good,' Isla said. 'It's really helpful to have someone with you at these appointments because sometimes you can forget to ask a question or later not remember what was said.'

Then it was Alison's turn. She was about four weeks away from her delivery date and very excited. 'I didn't even want to be pregnant,' Alison admitted, 'and now I can't wait.'

Isla smiled. This was one of the reasons that she loved this group so much. It was very helpful for others to realise that the conflicting emotions they might be feeling weren't reserved for them. Here the girls got to share in each other's journeys and Isla had seen that Ruby was listening intently, though she was guarded when it was her turn to speak.

'I'm Ruby,' she said. 'I'm fourteen weeks pregnant.'

'How old are you, Ruby?' Isla asked, and suspicious eyes looked back at her before she answered the question.

'Seventeen.' She was immediately defensive. 'My mum wanted me to have an abortion but I'm not getting rid of it.'

'How are things with you and Mum at the moment?' Isla gently pushed, and Ruby shrugged.

'I haven't really seen much of her. I'm staying with friends at the moment.' Isla made a mental note to look at Ruby's file and see if there was anything more that she could do to support her during this difficult time. She would talk to her away from the group, Isla decided, but for now she moved on.

Alison had some questions about delivery and pain control and said that she didn't want to stay in bed.

'You don't have to,' Isla said. 'We usually encourage mothers to move around during labour—walking around is wonderful.'

There were always a lot of questions. Isla loved the enthusiasm of the teenage mums and more often than not both the questions and answers were interspersed with a lot of laughter.

It was that sound of laughter that alerted Alessi as he walked out of Maternity, having just checked in again on Donna.

He hadn't stopped all day and seeing a huge trolley laden with food being delivered to the room, he assumed that there was an administration meeting going on.

He was starving and, completely shameless, he followed the trolley into the room, to be greeted by a sight that he wasn't expecting!

Isla felt awkward around Alessi and possibly she had every reason to now as he put his head around the door just in time to capture her in a deep squat on the floor as she showed the girls how that position opened up the pelvis nicely!

Here, though, was not the place to be awkward and so, instead of hurriedly standing, as was her instinct, she remained in a rather embarrassing position and gave him a very bright smile as the girls turned round to see who had interrupted the group.

'Did you smell the food, Alessi?' Isla asked.

'I did.' Alessi grinned. 'Sorry to disturb you. I thought it might be a work meeting and I could steal a few sandwiches. I'll let you guys get on.'

'Shall we feed him?' Isla said to the girls, and they all agreed that they should. Well, of course they did—

Alessi was seriously gorgeous. He went over to the trolley and as he selected some sandwiches and fruit Isla introduced him.

'Alessi is one of our neonatologists. Some of you may have quite a bit to do with him once your baby is here.'

He gave a small wave but instead of taking his food and walking off he turned to the group. 'For feeding me you can ask any questions that you want.'

Isla was more than pleasantly surprised and, yes, the girls, especially Harriet, did have questions that they wanted to ask, and Isla knew she had lost her audience.

'Why don't we all get something to eat?' Isla suggested, and before she'd even finished the sentence chairs were scraping as the girls headed over for supper and to talk to the gorgeous doctor who had joined them.

She was going to provide food each time, Isla decided, watching as Ruby and another young mum really did fill up their plates. They were hungry, seriously hungry, Isla realised, kicking herself that she hadn't thought to do this before.

Well, that would change now.

'We'll have pizza next time,' Isla said, and she saw Ruby's ears prick up. Anything that brought these young mums back to the group was more than worth it. Not only did their questions get answered but through meeting regularly friendships were forged, and it also meant that Isla could keep an extra eye on these vulnerable young girls.

Alessi was really fantastic with them, answering Harriet's questions easily. 'Do you want me to come again?' Alessi asked Isla. 'I could prepare a talk if you like.'

'That would be great,' Isla said. 'We meet each fortnight.'

Alessi pulled out his phone and checked his calendar. 'I already have a meeting scheduled for the next one and the fortnight after that is my parents' wedding anniversary…' He thought for a moment. 'What time does it finish?'

'About eight thirty or nine,' Isla said.

'That's fine, then,' Alessi said, then turned to the group. 'Think up some questions for me.' He smiled at Harriet and then said goodbye to them and left. There were a few wolf whistles as he went and Isla laughed, glad to see the lift to the group that Alessi had given.

And also terribly aware of the lift in her.

After she finished up, instead of heading straight for home Isla went up to the ward.

She guessed he'd be there and she was right.

'Aren't you finished?' Isla asked.

'I'm staying tonight,' Alessi said.

'You're not on call.'

'Tell that to the twins.'

'Thanks for offering to come and speak. It will be good.'

'No problem,' Alessi said. 'They seem a nice group. Truth be told, I admire them.'

'I do, too,' Isla said, and turned to go.

'Isla?'

'Yes?'

This time he didn't tell her that whatever he had to say would keep. 'Are you ready for Saturday?' Alessi asked.

'Saturday?' Isla frowned. 'Oh, yes, the ball. I'd forgotten.'

'You attend so many things, I'm not surprised that it slipped your mind.'

It hadn't slipped her mind. It was just that she had been so focused on Donna that for a little while she had managed to push aside the fact it was the ball on Saturday.

She had seen the seating plans and would be sitting between her father and Alessi. Both were there to represent the maternity and neonatal units. She was excited, nervous and never more so than when she looked into his eyes, and Alessi touched on a necessary topic if things were going to proceed.

'I promise I'll behave this time if Rupert is there.' Even saying his name, even thinking of being there with Isla and him made Alessi's skin crawl, but he did his best not to show it as he broached the sensitive subject.

'Rupert's not going.'

'Oh,' Alessi said. 'Is he back in the States?'

'I think so.'

'Think so?'

Jump, Isla told herself, but her legs were shaking and she wanted to turn and run, not that Alessi could tell. As coolly as she would face the guests on Saturday, as easily as she delivered a speech, even if she was shaking inside, Isla somehow met his gaze as she took that dangerous leap.

'We broke up.'

'Oh.' Alessi had to concentrate on not letting out a sigh of relief. 'I'm sorry,' he said, just as Isla had said to him on the night they had met.

'I'm not,' Isla said, just as Alessi had once said to her.

She watched as his lips stretched into a smile, and either every baby on the delivery ward simultaneously stopped crying and every conversation had suddenly halted, or the world simply stopped for a moment. Whichever it was, it was irrelevant to them as silence invaded and realisation dawned on them both—Saturday night was theirs to look forward to.

CHAPTER SIX

ISLA HAD TRIED to speak with Ruby at the end of the TMTB meeting but she hadn't been able to get very far. Ruby had merely shrugged in answer to Isla's questions and given her a look that only teenagers could, a look that said, *what would you know?*

After the group there had been loads of sandwiches left over and a couple of the girls, Ruby included, had taken up Isla's suggestion to help themselves as it would only be thrown out, but when Isla had tried to speak with her Ruby had said that she had to go.

Isla didn't mind being snubbed. She was just very glad that Ruby had turned up and hoped that the promise of pizza might lure her back, if nothing else, and she dropped in on handover the following morning to tell her team the same.

'If I'm not there and one of you is taking the TMTB group, either ring down to Catering or get some pizza delivered,' Isla said.

'Can we bring in a cake?' Emily asked, and Isla smiled. Trust Emily to want to do more.

'No, Emily, you've already got more than enough on your plate without feeding hungry teenagers.' Isla shook her head. 'There's room in the TMTB budget to ring for pizza or to order from Catering. I do want to have a think about it, though. I can't stand the idea that these girls might be hungry...'

A bell buzzed and Isla gave her staff a smile. 'I'll get it. You carry on with handover.' But as she walked out of the staffroom the bell buzzed again and Isla quickly crossed the ward, her heart galloping when she saw that it was coming from Donna and that it must be urgent because she wasn't taking her finger off the bell.

Flick, one of the midwifery students, was, in fact, the one who was pressing the bell.

'Well done,' Isla said, because as soon as Isla appeared Flick moved to open a delivery pack.

'They're coming...' Donna sobbed.

'It's okay,' Isla said, pulling on gloves and giving instructions to Emily, who on hearing the urgency of the buzzer had followed Isla in. 'Fast-page Darcie and the neonatal crash team.'

'I wanted Tom to be here...' Donna sobbed.

'His flight gets in this morning, doesn't it?' Isla asked, and Donna went to answer but nature got in first.

'Something's coming...' Donna said, and Isla recognised the fear in Donna's voice, not just professionally but personally, too, and, just as she had that night with Isabel, she stayed calm.

At least now she knew what to do professionally.

'It's okay,' Isla said. 'We're ready for them.'

They were ready, almost. Staff were busy plugging in two Resuscitaires in the side room that Donna had been allocated. Isla could hear footsteps running along the corridor and was grateful for the sound for indeed a baby was coming.

'Don't push, Donna,' Isla said as she felt the baby's

little head. 'I know that you want to, but let's just try and slow this down a little.'

Isla wanted to slow things down, not just to minimise any trauma to the tiny baby's brain but also to ensure there were plenty of staff and equipment ready when this baby made its rapid entrance into the world. Isla met Donna's gaze. 'Just breathe,' Isla said, and a petrified Donna nodded, using all her power to give her baby a few more vital seconds inside her.

Alessi came in then. He was a bit out of breath from running and his hair was soaking and his scrubs were damp—clearly he had been in the shower when his pager had gone off. He stood, watching, but even with Donna doing her best not to push, the next contraction saw the baby delivered into Isla's hands.

He was tiny but vigorous and very red. He let out a small cry as Alessi quickly cut the cord, took the tiny bundle from Isla and carried him over to the resuscitation table.

'Twin A,' Isla said to Darcie, who was running in. 'Born at seven forty-eight.'

'So we're waiting on twin B,' Darcie said to Donna, who lay back on her pillow and started to cry. Isla glanced over to the Resuscitaire where Alessi was concentrating hard, and so, too, were the rest of the team.

'What's happening?' Donna asked. There was a huge crowd around the cot but it was all very calm and controlled.

'Looking beautiful!' came Alessi's strong voice. 'He is moving and fighting me, Donna, but I have put down a tube to give him some medicine to his lungs, that's why you can't hear him crying. Do you have a name?'

'Elijah.'

There was a flurry of activity and Isla looked over as the staff started to prepare to move the baby over to NICU. Then Alessi came over and spoke with Donna. 'He's doing as well as can be expected,' Alessi said. 'We are going to get Elijah over to NICU now, where they are ready for him.'

'Can I see him?'

'Briefly,' Alessi said. 'Later you will have more time with Elijah but we want him over there now.'

The incubator was wheeled over but Donna's brief time with her son was soon thwarted as she first folded over and then lay back on the bed. The second twin was coming and Alessi nodded to his team to take the baby up to NICU as Darcie took over the second delivery.

'Cord's around the neck,' Darcie said. 'Very friable...' The umbilical cord was so thin and weak that it tore as Darcie tried to loop it over the baby's head but already the tiny baby was slipping out.

When Isla saw him delivered she was holding her breath, even as she clamped the severed cord. She never made comparisons—in fact Isla did everything she could not to think of that awful night with Isabel whenever a baby was born.

She couldn't help but compare this morning, though.

He was so tiny and his arms and legs were spindly and his little eyes were fused closed. The difference was that this little one started to put up a fight. Even as Darcie lifted him and handed him straight to a neonatal nurse his arms were flailing and he let out a tiny mewing cry as the nurse took him over to Alessi.

'Let me hold him,' Donna called out. 'Alessi, I want to hold him.'

Alessi didn't say anything at that point, at least not to Donna. Instead, he spoke to the little boy.

'Hello, beautiful baby,' he said, and Isla felt tears prick at the backs of her eyes as Alessi did his best to shut out Donna's pleas to hold her baby and instead did everything he could to give this little life a chance. 'Do you have a name for your son?' Alessi asked.

'Archie,' Donna said, and then lay back on the pillow, exhausted and defeated, aching to hold her son but knowing he needed the skill of the medical team now.

Isla did her best to comfort Donna as the team worked on. There was no way to see what was happening. Alessi, the anaesthetist and two neonatal nurses were around the resuscitation cot. They could hear the baby's fast heart rate on the monitor and Alessi issuing instructions. The mood was markedly more urgent than it had been for Elijah, and Donna started to cry.

'I just want to hold him,' Donna said to Isla.

'I know you do,' Isla said. 'But right now he needs to be with the medical team—they're doing everything they can for him.'

It was an interminable wait, made all the more difficult because Donna's husband called to say that he had landed. When Donna couldn't speak Isla took over the call and Alessi glanced up at the calmness in her voice as she introduced herself to the distraught husband.

'Tom, Donna is exhausted and upset but we're taking care of her. Elijah was born first and has been taken up to the neonatal intensive care unit, and Archie...' she glanced over and met Alessi's sombre gaze '...is being worked on by the team now. We hope to get him up to the intensive care unit soon.' She took a breath. 'Have you cleared customs? Good, go over to the information desk and explain what's happening and hopefully they can see you to the front of the taxi queue.' There was another pause. 'They're very premature, Tom. Right now the team are doing their best for your sons.'

It wasn't an easy call but somehow she did her best not to scare Tom while still conveying the need for him to get there urgently because it was clear that Archie especially was struggling. That was confirmed when Alessi came over and spoke to Donna, his expression grim. 'Donna, I am very concerned for Archie. I want to move him up to NICU where we can do some more tests on him and where there is more equipment…'

'I want to hold him.'

'I know you do,' Alessi said, 'but we are not at that stage—Archie is fighting and I will do everything I can to assist him in that. For now we'll bring him over so you can have a little look at him. He's very beautiful…'

The incubator was wheeled over. Archie looked like a little washed-up frog, but Alessi was right—he was a very beautiful baby. 'Put your hand in,' Alessi said, and Donna did, stroking his little cheek and then holding his fingers. 'I'm going to take him up. I also want to see how his brother is doing. As soon as I can I'll come and speak with you or I'll send someone else if I am busy with them.'

'Thank you. If something happens…' Donna couldn't say it but Alessi did.

'If either of the twins takes a turn for the worse you will be told, Donna, and the staff here will do everything they can to get you to your babies. Right now, though, I need to get him to NICU.'

'Mummy loves you,' Donna said, and Isla felt her heart twist, and for once she was struggling to keep up her cool mask. She wanted to go over to Alessi, to tell him to just give Donna her baby, to accept the inevitable and give them this precious time.

It wasn't her place to, though. Donna had made it clear before the twins' birth that she wanted everything possible done for her sons. It was for Isla to support that decision now.

It was a long and difficult day. Isla went through the birth with Flick and all that had happened. Donna's husband arrived and he went up to NICU. Though Donna ached to go and see her twins she had a small bleed after delivery and wasn't well enough to go up till much later in the day.

Isla went with her.

First they saw Elijah, the tiny, though relatively bigger, twin. 'It seems impossible...' Donna said, and Isla just stood back and let her have the time with her son. She looked over to the next cot and Alessi was there and caught her eyes, his expression still grim.

When Isla took Donna over she knew why.

Donna completely broke down when she saw her little man hooked up to so many machines.

'He's not well enough to be held,' Alessi said. 'Just talk to him, he'll know your voice.'

Alessi, Isla noted, looked exhausted. He was also incredibly patient and kind. For close to a year she had dismissed him as some sort of killer flirt and had avoided him at all costs.

Now there was no avoiding him.

On Friday, at the end of a long shift, at the end of a very long week, she walked into her office to find Alessi sitting there with Jessica, the twins' older sister.

'Excuse me.' Alessi glanced up as she came in. 'I was

just speaking with Donna, and Jessica asked if she could have a word. I just came to the nearest room.'

'That's fine.' Isla smiled. 'I'll leave you to it.'

'No, don't go,' Alessi said. 'Jessica was just telling me that she's too nervous to see the twins but that her mother thinks that she should.'

'Do you want to see them?' Isla asked.

'I don't know,' Jessica admitted. 'I've seen their photos and there are so many machines.'

'NICU can be a scary place,' Isla said. 'Alessi is actually coming to speak to my Teenage Mums-To-Be group, in a few weeks' time, to prepare them in case their babies have to go there. It can be a bit overwhelming but once you get past the machines you'll see your brothers.'

'That is what I was just telling Jessica,' Alessi agreed. 'They are very cute. Elijah is very much the big brother. Stoic and very strong, he doesn't like to cry or make a fuss…'

'And Archie?' Jessica asked, and Isla heard the twist in the young girl's voice.

'He's way too cute,' Alessi said, and Isla smiled at the genuine warmth in his voice as he went on to tell Jessica about her youngest brother. 'His eyes have just opened and he loves the sound of voices, he really does calm down when he hears someone say his name.'

'I used to talk to him when Mum was pregnant,' Jessica said.

'Then he would know your voice.' Alessi smiled but then looked over when Isla's cool voice broke in.

'Are you scared to love them, Jessica?' she asked, and Alessi could only blink in surprise. Isla asked the tough questions and had clearly got straight to the difficult point because Jessica nodded and started crying. 'I'm guessing you already do love them,' Isla said.

'They might die, though.'

'I know,' Isla said. 'And I know that is so hard to even begin to deal with, but whatever is going to happen you can still have some time with them and let yourself be their big sister. Would you like me to come and spend some time with them with you?'

Clearly it was what Jessica did want because half an hour later, instead of collapsing on the sofa and being grateful that it was the start of Friday night and the end of a long week, Isla was up on NICU with Jessica.

There was no place she would rather be, though. Watching as Jessica's fear was replaced by smiles, seeing little Archie's eyes flicker and possibly, possibly a hint of a smile on his lips was time well spent indeed. They took photos and Jessica let her friends know all about her two brothers via social media.

'I'm off.' Alessi stood by the incubator. He had changed out of scrubs and was wearing black jeans and a gunmetal-grey top and he looked like the man who had made her heart flip over on sight all those months ago. 'I'll see you tomorrow,' he said to Isla.

'There's a big ball tomorrow night,' Isla explained to Jessica. 'Alessi's getting an award.'

'And I'll see you on Monday,' he said to little Archie. 'In the meantime, behave.' He nodded his head in the direction of the corridor and Isla excused herself from Jessica, who was holding her brother's tiny hand. 'It's good she's had some time with them.'

'I know.' Isla smiled. 'It's going to be tough on her. How do you think Archie—'

'It's minute by minute,' Alessi interrupted, the inevitable answer because there were no guarantees in NICU and especially not with a baby who was so fragile and small. 'Just take the good times, that's all you can do sometimes. Are you off now?'

Isla paused before answering; she had a feeling, more than a feeling that they were on the edge of something. That if she said yes, then she'd be joining him for dinner tonight, or for drinks, or for…

Isla looked into his black eyes and there was an absence of fear. Yes, she knew, given his reputation, it could only ever be fleeting. She knew, too, that she couldn't tell him her truth—he would surely run a mile—yet she knew she was ready.

For him.

Yet, while she wanted to say yes, some things came first. 'I think I'm going to be here for as long as Jessica wants me to be.'

'Fair enough.' Alessi smiled. 'I'll see you tomorrow, then.'

'You shall.'

'Funny, but I'm actually looking forward to it now.'

She knew what he meant and her answer told him the same. 'So am I.'

CHAPTER SEVEN

ISLA WASN'T FEELING quite so brave the next morning, though there was still a flutter of anticipation in her stomach for the coming night as she downed a grapefruit juice before heading into work for a couple of hours.

'Haven't you got a ball that you're supposed to be getting ready for?' Darcie teased as they headed out the door.

'I'm getting my hair done at two,' Isla said.

'I guess you've got this type of thing down to an art. Still, if I were going to a ball instead of working this weekend, I'd need more than a hair appointment to get me ball-ready! What are you wearing?'

'Black,' Isla said. 'Or red, I haven't decided. All I know is that I've got a mountain in my inbox that needs to be scaled. The weekends when I'm not officially there are the only times I can get anything done on the paperwork front.'

Instead of taking the tram, they walked. Darcie wasn't on until nine and Isla wasn't officially working anyway, so they took their time, enjoying the morning and stopping at Isla's favourite café. She picked up a coffee and a pastry to have at her desk and Darcie did the same.

'I love the food here,' Darcie groaned. She'd really

taken to the café culture of Melbourne and Isla was only
too happy to show her her favourite haunts. Once on the
MMU, Darcie took her breakfast to the staffroom to get
handover from Sean, and instead of saying hi to the staff
Isla headed straight for the quiet of her office. She was
just unlocking the door when she saw Alessi walking
down the corridor.

'I thought you were off this weekend?' Isla frowned.

'Not any more—I got called in at four,' Alessi said.
'I've just been speaking with Donna and her husband.'

He followed her into the office. 'Archie had a large
cerebral haemorrhage overnight. We're taking down all
the equipment and letting nature take its course. Emily
is about to take them up to NICU to have some time
with him.'

'Oh, poor Donna…'

'Poor Archie,' Alessi said. 'He's such a fighter…' And
then, to Isla's surprise, Alessi cried. Not a lot, but he'd
been tired already and being called in at four to find
hope had gone and sharing the news with Archie's loving family all caught up with him and Alessi did let out
a couple of tears.

Isla just stood there, more than a touch frozen. She
wasn't very good with her own emotions, let alone dealing with Alessi's, and her lack of response didn't go unnoticed.

'You're much kinder to your patients when they're
upset,' Alessi pointed out, and gave a wry smile as he
gathered himself back together as Isla still stood there.

She could cope when it was a patient; she could survive only by staying a step back. Alessi made her want
to take that step forward but she just didn't know how.

'I just hate it that he had everything stacked against

him. Had he been a girl he'd have been stronger,' Alessi said. 'Or had it been a single pregnancy at twenty-four weeks…even if he'd been the first to be born, he'd have had more of a chance, but everything that could go wrong went wrong for him.'

'Maybe he's getting to you because he's a twin, too…' Isla offered.

'They all get to me,' Alessi said. 'Though Archie has more than most—he really did want to live.' He looked at Isla. Was it exhaustion that made him be honest, or was it simply that it was her? 'I'm not actually a twin. I was the second born of triplets, with Allegra the last. My brother was the firstborn and died when he was five days old.'

The same age as Archie.

'Is that why you're so driven?' Isla asked.

'Oh, I'm driven now, am I?' Alessi teased. 'Last week you were warning me away from your staff.'

'It would seem you're both.'

Alessi shrugged. 'I guess. You feel you have to make up for all the opportunities that they never had.'

She remembered the black-sheep comment that Allegra had made about Alessi, and curiosity got the better of her now for she wanted to know more about him. 'Did your parents push you?'

Alessi nodded. 'You know, apparently, Geo, my brother, would never have spoken back to them. In fact, he'd be married by now and would have given them grandchildren.'

Isla smiled.

'And he wouldn't have given up piano at fifteen or…' Alessi shook his head. Things were moving closer to a painful part of his past than he would like, so he wrapped it up there. 'The list goes on. I really feel for Elijah, too. If he makes it.'

She watched as Alessi yawned. She could see he was exhausted and if it were any of her staff Isla would have told them to go home.

'Shouldn't you let Jed take over Archie's care?' Isla ventured, referring to the neonatologist on this weekend. 'You've been here all week and you've got a big night tonight. Surely you need—'

'What I *need*,' Alessi interrupted, 'are three things from you.'

'Three things?'

'Your coffee and whatever smells good in that bag...'

'What's the third?' Isla said, handing them over.

'If I don't get there tonight, can you give my speech for me?'

'Alessi, you're up for an award, I think it's taken as a given that you'll be there. My father—'

'Archie is having seizures,' Alessi interrupted. 'Violent ones, and they aren't nice for his family to see. Jessica wants to be there also and I want his death to be as gentle and as pain-free as possible. I want to be there for him. I'm sorry if it upsets your father that I might not make it but right now Archie is my priority.'

Alessi waited. He knew she was about to protest and he actually wanted her to. *That* was his tipping point. When anyone tried to come between him and his work Alessi walked away very easily. He wanted not to get in too deep; he wanted her to insist that he be there tonight.

Instead, she nodded her assent.

'Fine,' she said, though her father would think it anything but fine if Alessi didn't show up. 'What do you want me to say on your behalf?'

'Whatever is said at such things. I'm sure you'll give an excellent speech,' Alessi said.

'That sounds like an insult.'

It was, actually. He looked at her, so completely calm and unruffled, even as he had broken down, and knew she'd be the same tonight. 'Do any of them get to you?'

'Sorry?'

'I remember the night we met. You were all animated, completely enthralled about a baby that had just been delivered.' He watched her cheeks redden and rather than leave things there he chose to pursue them. 'I've seen you elated but I've never seen you upset and, though avoiding each other, we've still found ourselves working together at times.'

'When have I avoided you?'

'Come off it, Isla,' Alessi said. 'And don't avoid the question. Do any of them get to you?'

'I don't let them get to me,' Isla said, hopefully slamming the door closed on that observation, but Alessi wrenched it straight back open.

'That would take an awful lot of self-control.'

'Not really.' She tried to keep her voice even.

'Yes, really. Otherwise it would mean that you're completely burnt out and I don't believe that you are.'

'You don't know me,' Isla said.

'I know that I don't, because a year ago I could have sworn that we were getting on, that we were enjoying each other's company, that you wanted me as much as I wanted you,' he said. 'Yet it would seem I was wrong.'

Isla wanted to tear her eyes from his but somehow she made herself hold his gaze.

'I may be wrong now,' Alessi said, and Isla knew that she could turn and head to her desk and he would go, but she didn't. Instead, she stood there as he continued speaking, the air between them crackling with tension. 'The thing is, I won't put myself in that position again. You'll never give me that look again, Isla…'

She wanted to point out that she wasn't giving him *that* look now; she wanted to point out that she wasn't turning and walking off. The air seemed too thick for her lungs and Isla's eyes flicked to his mouth, to his soft, full lips, and she wanted to place hers there, or for his mouth to move to hers, but Alessi just stood his ground.

'When you're ready to apologise for that night…'

'Apologise?' Isla gave an incredulous smile.

Alessi didn't return the smile. 'Yes, apologise,' he confirmed. 'The next move is yours.'

'I'm not with you.'

'You'll kiss me, Isla.'

'And if I don't?'

'Then we both die wondering.'

She would, Isla realised.

No matter what the future held, if a part of it did not contain a night with Alessi, then she would die wondering because he was possibly the most beautiful, sensual man to cross her path and, yes, she wanted her time with him, for however long they had.

'I need to go,' Alessi said. 'Thank you for the coffee.'

'I hope today goes better than expected for you,' Isla croaked.

'It won't,' Alessi said, 'but some things have to be faced and dealt with.' He turned and opened the office door.

Her face was on fire, his words playing over and over.

Some things had to be dealt with and faced, but not this.

Alessi's invitation turned fears into pleasure.

CHAPTER EIGHT

DARCIE HAD PROVED to be a brilliant flatmate but as Isla got ready for the ball she was actually relieved to have the place to herself.

Nothing was going to happen between her and Alessi tonight, she told herself, except Isla knew where their kiss could lead.

She'd fought it once after all.

Isla got back from the hairdresser's at four, where she'd had her thick blonde hair curled and pinned up and had also had her nails done in a neutral shade as she still hadn't decided what to wear tonight.

Red, Isla thought, taking out her dress and holding it up, yet it was everything she wasn't—it was bold, confident and sexy, and Alessi could possibly sue her under the Trade Descriptions Act once he got the dress off!

Black.

Safe.

Only it felt far from safe when she put it on. It showed her cleavage, it showed the paleness of her skin and the flush in her cheeks whenever his name came to mind, which it did at regular fifteen-second intervals.

He might not even be there, Isla reminded herself. Except that thought didn't come as a relief.

She could still feel the heat between them from that morning. Her body, as she dressed for the night, acutely recalled the burn of his gaze and the delicious warning that the next move was hers. There had been no physical contact that morning yet it felt as if there had been.

Isla was shaking as she put on her make-up, shaking with want, with nerves, with the absolute shock of the availability of Alessi should she choose to make a move.

Should she choose?

Isla looked at herself in the mirror and realised she already had.

She wanted Alessi.

A car had been arranged—Charles Delamere didn't want his daughter arriving in a taxi—and Isla sat in the back, staring ahead. The sights of Melbourne were familiar; the feeling inside wasn't. There was no Isabel to chat with, no Rupert to deflect male attention.

She stepped into the venue alone.

Her eyes scanned the reception room as she drank champagne and sparkled as she was expected to.

There was no sign of him.

Relief and disappointment mingled as they were called to take their seats.

'Where's Manos?' Charles frowned at the empty seat at the table.

'I think that he may be stuck at the hospital,' Isla said. 'He's asked me to make a speech on his behalf if he can't get here.'

'You are joking?' Charles snapped. 'The whole point of this award is to raise NICU's profile. How are we going to get people signing cheques if the star of the show can't even be bothered to turn up?'

'Dad.' Isla looked at him. 'He's with a family—'

'Isla,' her father broke in. 'To be able to take care of the *families*, sometimes you have to look at the bigger picture. I told him the same when I had lunch with him the other day. Not that he wanted to hear it. He's an arrogant...' Charles's voice trailed off as Alessi approached the table but then he stood and shook Alessi's hand.

'Good to see that you *finally* made it,' Charles said. 'I thought I'd clearly outlined how important tonight was.'

'You did.' Alessi pushed out a smile but didn't elaborate or explain the reason for his lateness. He looked like heaven in a tux, but he'd clearly rushed. His hair was damp and he hadn't shaved, which somehow he got away with. There was a teeny stand-off between the two men and Isla found herself holding her breath, though why she didn't know.

Alessi took a seat beside her and the fragrance of him, the scent of him, the warmth of him was the reason Isla turned. Greeting the guest, manners, polite conversation had nothing to do with the turn of her head.

'How was today?'

'I've had better,' Alessi responded. 'I'm pretty wrecked. I don't want to talk about it here.' He wasn't in the mood for conversation. It had been a hell of a day and it had depleted him, and he didn't need Isla's coolness, neither did he need Charles's sniping.

'I'm sorry,' Isla said, and he glanced over and those two words and their gentle delivery helped.

'It was peaceful.' Alessi conceded more information. 'I'm glad that I stayed.' He couldn't think about it right now so he looked more closely at Isla, who was a very nice distraction from dark thoughts, and the night seemed a little brighter.

'You look amazing.'

'Thanks.' Isla smiled. 'So do you.'

They shared a look for a moment too long. She could have, had there been no one else present, simply reached over and kissed him. It was there, it just was, and Alessi knew it, too, and he confirmed it with words.

'You have to say sorry first.'

Isla just laughed. There was a thrill in her spine and all the nerves of today, of yesteryear just blew away. It should be just them but the entrée was being placed in front of her.

'I'm going to have to disappear,' Alessi said, 'and write my speech. I didn't get a chance today.'

'I've already written it,' Isla said, and handed him a piece of paper. 'Just lose the first part.'

'The first part?'

'"Dr Manos regrets that he's unable to be here tonight."'

'Dr Manos is suddenly very glad that he is.' Alessi smiled. It was a genuine smile and one that had seemed a long way off when he had left the hospital. Had it not been for this commitment, tonight would have been spent alone. Alessi took each death very personally and had long since found out that a night on the town or casual sex did nothing to fill up the black hole he climbed into when a little life was lost.

His grief was still there yet her smile did not dismiss it and neither did his.

Isla could hear her father asking a question, breaking the spell, dragging them back to the table, to the ball, to the world.

Dinner was long, the speeches even longer, and Alessi noted that Isla chatted easily with the guests at the table during dinner and listened attentively to the speeches.

She really was enjoying herself. Alessi shared her humour. His foot pressed into her calf on one occasion, not suggestively, more to share an unseen smile when one of the recipient's speeches went on and on and on.

Then it was Alessi's turn to take to the stage. Charles gave a rather long-winded introduction about the work he had done in the year that Alessi had been at the Victoria and how pleased they were to have such talent on board.

Isla watched as Alessi went up to the stage, the speech she had written in his hand, and he took a moment to arrange the microphone. Absolutely she could see why it was her father wanted a more visible profile for Alessi because, even before he had spoken, he held the room.

She watched him glance down at his speech and, yes, he omitted the first part where Isla had explained that, regretfully, he couldn't be there.

He thanked everyone present and then Isla froze as Alessi hesitated and she realised she had omitted to mention a small joke she had written—*I'd especially like to thank the extraordinary Isla Delamere for her amazing work on the MMU*. It would have been funny had *she* read it out. Instead, Alessi's face broke into a smile and he met her gaze.

She could feel her father's impatience at the small lull in proceedings, she could feel her own lips stretching into a smile as Alessi omitted her joke and then moved on.

"'I am very proud to receive this award,'" Alessi said, reading from Isla's notes. "'But more than that, I am incredibly grateful to work alongside skilled colleagues at such a well-equipped hospital. It helps when you can say, in all honesty, to parents that everything possible is being done or was done. It makes impossible decisions and difficult days somewhat easier to be reconciled to.'"

It was the truth, Alessi thought.

That Archie had been given every chance had been a huge source of comfort to Donna. That the facilities were top class, that there had been a private area for the family to take their necessary time with empathetic staff discreetly present had made his passing more bearable.

He wrapped up the speech and then added a line of his own, or rather he didn't completely omit Isla's.

'I would especially like to thank Isla Delamere for being here tonight and for her amazing work on the MMU.'

Ouch!

Isla was blushing as Alessi returned to his seat.

'Thank you,' Alessi said. Her words had hit home. Yes, he might loathe this side of things but he was starting to accept that it might be necessary. No, he wouldn't be appearing on morning television, as Charles had in mind for him, but he would make more effort, Alessi decided. That was the reason he stood around talking, being polite and accepting congratulations, while others headed off to dance. That was the reason he didn't make his excuses and head home.

Isla watched in mild surprise as her student Flick danced with Tristan, a cardiac surgeon. She could almost feel the sparks coming from them, or was it just that Alessi was standing close?

'Well done,' Isla said, when finally the crowd gathered around him had dispersed enough for them to have a conversation.

'Thanks,' Alessi said.

'Not too painful?' Isla checked.

'No. Your speech was perfect. I really am very grateful for such a well-run hospital. I just don't like the fact that your father seems to want me to be the poster boy for the NICU.'

'What was that?' Charles came over and Alessi didn't even flinch.

'I was just telling Isla how well run and well equipped the hospital is.'

'Because of nights such as this one,' Charles said. 'You cut it very fine getting here.'

'I already explained that, Dad,' Isla said, but Alessi didn't need Isla to speak for him and told Charles exactly how difficult it had been to get there, albeit a little late.

'I certified a patient dead at eight minutes past six,' Alessi responded coolly, and Isla frowned at the tension between the two men. 'As I said to you at lunch, please don't rely on me to be your front person. I'll do what I can on the social side of things but my job is to keep up the stats while yours is to bring in the funds.'

Isla swallowed. There were few people who spoke to Charles Delamere like that and got away with it, but it was what her father said next that truly confused her.

'You could have at least shaved before you got here.'

'Dad!' Isla was shocked that her father would be so personal but Alessi didn't seem remotely bothered.

'It's fine,' Alessi briefly addressed Isla, then turned his attention back to Charles, who was looking at Alessi with thinly disguised murder in his eyes. 'I stayed with the parents of the baby that died until seven and then I spoke at length with their daughter. Shaving really wasn't my priority.' He looked at Isla. 'Would you like to dance?'

She said yes just to get the two of them apart.

'Alessi, I'm so sorry about that!' Isla said as they hit the dance floor. She was honestly confused by the way her father was acting. 'I don't know what's wrong with him. He had no right to say anything about you not having shaved.' Privately she was glad that Alessi hadn't shaved—he looked wonderful and she actually ached to feel his jaw against her skin, but she held back from dancing with him the way she wanted to.

'Don't worry about it.' Alessi shrugged.

'Even so, I don't know what's got into him.'

'I do.' Alessi smiled. 'He knows tonight I am going to be sleeping with his daughter.'

'You assume a lot,' Isla croaked as he pulled her in closer.

'I never assume,' Alessi said. 'I just aim high.'

His fingers were stroking her arms and now his cheek was near hers as he spoke, his jaw was all scratchy against her cheek, even more delicious than Isla had predicted, and she found she could barely breathe.

'I thought you were exhausted.'

'Do I feel tired to you?' Alessi said, and Isla guessed he was referring to the hard heat that was nudging at her stomach.

'No.' A single word was all Isla could manage.

'I'm never too tired for you, Isla.'

She was beyond turned on. She wanted to move her face so their mouths could meet, she wanted the wetness of his tongue and the heat of his skin on hers.

Did she tell him how scared she was?

Did she tell him that he would be her first?

Isla would possibly die if he found out she was a virgin.

She'd had an internal when she'd had appendicitis and the doctors had thought it might be an ovarian cyst.

There was going to be no bloodshed, no 'Oh, my God,

is that your hymen?' Just utter inexperience in very experienced arms.

Yet she wanted him and she had never till now wanted a man.

She wanted to be made love to and kill this demon for ever, choke it at the neck and get on with her life.

She knew his reputation, knew his relationships were fleeting at best. This might be just a one-night stand but it would be one that would help her step into her future.

Isla pulled her head back and looked into black, smiling eyes and, no, a heavy heart was not what was needed tonight. A long confessional could not help things here.

It was lust looking back at her, not love, she reminded herself.

Yet it was the beginning of the end of the prison she had trapped herself in and, however unwittingly, Alessi could set her free.

'What are you thinking?' he asked.

'I'm not going to tell you.'

It was the truth and it was also *the* truth.

Isla's decision was made.

Alessi would never know that he was her first.

'I'm going to go soon,' he said in a low voice that made her shiver on the inside. 'I don't want to offend your father by leaving with you. I'll text you my address.'

'You don't know my number.'

'I do,' Alessi said. 'Don't you remember sending me that school reunion photo on the night we met, the night you blew me off?' She was on fire in his arms as he scolded her for her actions that night. 'You're going to apologise *properly* for that tonight.'

'Meaning?'

'Meaning I am going to go and say my goodbyes,'

Alessi said. His fingers were at the tie of her halter neck and she had an urge for him to unknot it, to be naked against him, to give in to the kiss that they both craved.

As the song ended, so, too, did their dance and Alessi gave her a brief smile of thanks before walking off.

To the world it might have looked like a duty dance, but for Isla it had been pure pleasure. She joined her father and tried to carry on a conversation with a prominent couple as her heart hammered and her mind whirred as to what to do. She saw Flick leaving with Tristan but this time Isla could only smile with the realisation that she had reprimanded Alessi just a few weeks ago for the very same thing—a doctor seeing one of her students.

She had been jealous, Isla could see it so clearly now.

Her phone buzzed and she glanced at it.

There was no message from Alessi, just his address.

'Heading off already?' Charles frowned. 'It's a bit soon.'

Isla looked at her father. She always did the right thing by her parents, by her sister, by Rupert, by her staff, her patients, by everyone but herself.

It was far from too soon.

Putting herself first was way overdue, in fact.

Isla left without another word.

CHAPTER NINE

ALESSI STEPPED INTO his apartment and swapped the crystal of his award for the crystal of a brandy glass.

He sent a text and wondered.

Would she come?

And if she did, then what would tomorrow bring?

He had spent close to a year wondering about Isla. Disliking her, yet wanting her. A whole year of trying to fathom what went on behind that cool facade.

No one had ever got into his head-space more and yet, rarely for Alessi, he did wonder about the consequences of tonight. He didn't want to be shut down by Isla again, yet a part of him knew it was inevitable. Rare were the glimpses of the true Isla and he found himself craving them. From the first unguarded night to the smile when she had walked out from speaking with Blake and Christine, or sitting on a birthing ball with her teenage mums-to-be.

It was a case of one step forward and a hundred steps back with Isla and, despite the promise of their dance, despite the passion he had felt, Alessi actually doubted now that she'd even turn up at his door.

He checked his phone and, no, she hadn't responded

and Alessi found himself scrolling back and looking at their brief communication.

There was an eighteen-year-old Isla, as blonde and as glossy as she was now and smiling for the camera, but there was still that keep-out sign in her eyes. Alessi stared at the image for a long time, zooming in to avoid seeing Talia, for she had no place here tonight. Instead, he looked into Isla's cool gaze and wondered about the secrets she kept, especially when he heard a knock at the door.

'I was wrong,' Alessi said as he opened the door to her. 'I was starting to think you wouldn't come.'

'Why would you think that?' Her voice lied—it was clear, it was confident, it was from the actress she had learnt to be.

'Because you're impossible to read.'

'Better than boring,' she said as he poured her a drink and handed it to her. She didn't like brandy but it was a necessary medicine tonight. She was on the edge of both terror and elation and she wanted her demons gone.

To him.

He really was impossibly beautiful. His tie and jacket were off. If she ignored their surroundings, if she could pretend that they weren't in his apartment, it could almost be the night they'd met for he had been wearing black pants and a white shirt then. He was just as toned, just as sensual, just as confident as he had been that night as he walked over to her, removed her now empty glass from her hand and placed it on a small table. His hands returned to her hips as they had that night, only his mouth did not take hers.

'So...' Alessi looked at her. 'Here we are again.'

He was going to keep to his word, Isla realised as his lips did nothing to meet hers.

'Up to you, Isla.'

Her lips actually ached from his ignoring them, and her body wanted to twitch from the lack of attention she craved. His hands were warm on her hips, his fingers just at the curve of her buttocks, and he moved not a muscle yet he stirred her deep on the inside. 'I thought you were the great seducer,' Isla said, willing her voice to be even, begging her heart to slow down.

'So it's my job to turn you on?' Alessi checked, staring into her eyes.

'Yes.'

'But I already have.'

Was it that simple? Isla thought. Because, yes, he already had.

'You will make the move, Isla.'

Was she here to be served her just deserts, was payback on his mind? She voiced just one of her many fears about this night. 'So you can blow me off this time?'

'God, no.' The need in his voice put paid to that fear and so did his words. 'I wanted you then and I want you now.'

Her eyes told Alessi she wanted him, too. 'So what do you have to say about that night?'

'I'm not going to apologise.'

He shrugged his shoulders but he didn't move and she thought she might die if their lips didn't meet, so she offered her haughty best.

'Sorry!'

'That's a poor excuse for an apology,' Alessi said. 'Say it with your mouth on mine.'

'Alessi...' Isla cringed. She had no idea what was

happening, no idea what his game was. She wanted to put up her hand and take a time-out, to consult the rule book, phone a friend, but there was only one other player in this game and she could hardly consult him.

I've never done this before, Alessi, she wanted to reveal. *Apart from one kiss with you, I've never really been intimate or affectionate with a man before...*

Only that wasn't true.

Thirty seconds ago she had never been this intimate or affectionate but now she was pressing her lips to his mouth as if it was the most natural thing in the world. 'Sorry,' Isla breathed, feeling his lips stretch into a smile beneath hers as she joined in the game.

And she'd just been intimate again because her hands were running over his back as she whispered to his lips again.

'I can't hear you,' Alessi said, and her lips moved to his ear, to the lovely, soft lobe, such a contrast to the scratch of his jaw, and she was saying the same word again.

'Sorry.'

Sorry for being a bitch, sorry for shutting you out, sorry for a year of deprivation when it was so easy after all.

She was unbuttoning his shirt as her mouth moved to his neck. It really was that simple. He shrugged out of his shirt and she ran her hands over the lean chest, stroking his hardening nipples, and all she had to be, Isla realised, was herself, and she knew what she wanted.

It was Isla's fingers rather than Alessi's that undid the halter neck to her dress and the feel of skin, of his firm chest against her naked one, matched the moan that escaped from him, and then she removed her mouth from his neck and stood, taking in the feast going on in his eyes as he looked at her bare breasts.

'I've run out of sorries,' Isla said.

'I haven't.' Alessi's eyes lifted to hers. 'I'm sorry for every terrible thought I have had about you and I'm even sorry for the inappropriate ones—they didn't do you justice...'

His mouth came down on hers then, so hard that Isla thought she might taste blood. Almost a year of anger and pent-up frustration was unleashed from Alessi and for Isla it was electrifying and completely consuming to be so thoroughly kissed. His fierce tongue claimed her as her breasts were crushed to his chest. One of Alessi's hands was at the back of her head, the other on her bottom, yet it was Isla who was pushing in.

She resented the bottom half of her dress for coming between them. She loathed both his trousers and his belt. She wanted them gone, she wanted them both naked, she wanted her legs wrapped around him.

Alessi pulled back and her mouth chased him for more.

'Get on the bed,' he ordered, his words harsh but necessary or they'd be doing it up the wall.

'Where is it?'

He was as disorientated as she and it took a second for him to fathom the familiar route and it was hard getting there while being down each other's throats on the way.

They stripped at the bedroom door, with the same glee and abandon as if they were taking their clothes off to jump in a river on a hot summer's day. Isla's nerves left her at the door and they dived onto his bed together, want tumbling them over and over, only tearing their mouths from each other to drink in glimpses of the other's nakedness. He loved her large pink areolas and the blonde curls between her legs, and she in turn loved the darkness of his erection that nudged for attention even as his fingers slid inside her.

Isla simply forgot her own inexperience, forgot that she didn't know what to do, or shouldn't know what to do, for all that she *could* do was try and remember to breathe as his fingers deeply stroked her and his mouth noisily worked her breasts.

He touched her where, and in a way, she had never touched herself, and her body flared at the delicious invasion. Her spine seemed to turn to lava and she rocked to his hand.

'Come,' he ordered, and yet she had never done so. 'Come,' he said urgently, 'because then I'm going to take you...'

She looked down at his fingers sliding in and out of her yet she couldn't relax to his hand, no matter how she wanted to. 'Take me now...'

They were side on and facing each other, and Alessi required no second invitation. His leg nudged hers apart so they scissored his and his fingers moved from deep within and held his thick base and teased, stroking her clitoris, toying at her entrance, till her own hand was closed over his and urged him inside.

'Condom...' He went to reach for one, but that meant rolling, that meant leaving, and her hand stayed steady over his, for she could not bear to break the spell. He nudged in just a little way and her throat closed on itself as she glimpsed how much this was going to hurt. Pain was confirmed again with the second, deeper thrust.

Alessi felt her tension and misread it. Common sense paid a very brief visit and he reached for a condom. The pause as he slid it on was enough for Isla to catch her breath. She didn't like the pale pink of the sheath, she wanted the lovely darkness of before, the softness of his wet skin and the hard feel of him inside. It was that simple, but as he squeezed into her those wants were pale compared to the pleasurable hurt of being taken.

Alessi closed his eyes in pleasure at how tight she was, her moan, her sob, the bite of Isla's teeth on his shoulder spoke not of pain to him.

Or to her.

Yes, it hurt, yes, she wanted a second to regroup, but the salt of his skin in her mouth and the immeasurable force of him thrusting within was a small price to pay for no rest. There were no thoughts to be gathered; he was driving her towards something and Isla was the most willing passenger. She could feel her first orgasm building, each deep stroke of him taking her to the edge of what was surely inevitable, but then Alessi stilled.

'Don't stop,' Isla begged, but then she looked to the reason he had. The condom was shredded, rolled around his base, and decadent wishes came true, because she had loathed him pink and sheathed. She was absolutely on the edge of coming and the sight of him dark inside her simply topped her and it was Isla who took over, who continued the dance, and how could he not join her?

Both were watching, both dizzy with pleasure as Isla came. The first jolt of her body had Isla fight it, scared to let go, but trusting in him she did and with a small scream went with the pleasure. Alessi felt the pulses, the grip of Isla's tight space dragging him in, and he simply gave in and thrust into her, loving the sense of her unleashed. He felt a pull in his stomach and the rise of his balls and somehow, *somehow* there was that brief flash of common sense and he dragged his thick length from her, and both watched as he shot silver over her.

It was delicious to look down while too scary to look up and meet the other's eye.

It had been better than good.

CHAPTER TEN

ISLA WOKE TO the roaming of his hands.

There was a moment of bliss as instinct told her to roll towards him or just lie there and relish the slow exploration, to kiss him as she wanted to, and then she remembered the sheer recklessness of last night.

It was Alessi who addressed it.

'You owe Blake and Christine an apology,' Alessi said to her ear as he kissed it. 'It *is* possible to get too carried away.'

'It's fine,' Isla said, and somehow her voice sounded together. 'I've got it covered.'

He would assume, of course, that this good-time girl would have contraception all taken care of, especially as she was a midwife.

Isla closed her eyes on sudden tears.

What the hell would he say if he knew she'd been a virgin until last night, that she wasn't even on the Pill?

Isla was starting to panic, not that she would let him see.

'I have to go.' She rolled over and gave him a smile.

'Now?'

'Now.' Isla nodded.

'Hey…' His hand was on her shoulder as she sat up. 'There's no need to rush off.'

But there was.

She had to get home.

She had to think.

And so she climbed from the bed and headed out to the lounge, where her clothes lay strewn.

'I'll drive you,' Alessi said as she pulled on her dress.

The embarrassment of getting a taxi in last night's clothes was the only reason she agreed.

Alessi made do with last night's clothes also and the lack of conversation in the car had him rolling his eyes. 'I knew that you'd do this,' he said as he pulled up at a café.

'Do what?'

Alessi gave a mirthless laugh and got out and Isla sat there, watching him order coffee through the café window. Next door the shutters were going up on a pharmacy. Once home she could go and get the morning-after pill, Isla thought, and then closed her eyes because she knew that she wouldn't. She had nothing against others taking it, it just wasn't for her.

She sat there, telling herself she was overreacting, that she couldn't be pregnant, except her assurances had the same ring to her as her teenage mums' did.

She was twenty-eight!

Damn you, Alessi, Isla thought as he walked back to the car carrying coffee. *Damn you for making me lose my head.*

Not just last night but this morning, too, for she wanted more of him. She wanted that grim mouth to smile, she wanted his kiss and to be back in his bed, she wanted more of whatever it was they'd found.

'Here.' He handed her a coffee and Isla took a sip and screwed up her face.

'I don't take sugar.'

'How the hell would I know?' Alessi said as he started the engine. 'Because you don't communicate…'

Her shoulders moved as she let out a small involuntary laugh. 'Did you plan that?'

'I did.' He glanced over and gave her a smile. 'I actually know that you don't take sugar so I asked them to put in three.

'What's your address?' he asked, and after she had given it to him he resumed the conversation. 'Do you know how I know that you don't take sugar?'

Isla said nothing, just stared ahead as he answered his own question.

'Because I don't really like how I am around you, Isla. I don't like it that even though you run so very cold, I still find myself hanging out for the occasional heat. I notice things about you that I would prefer not to. Like you don't have sugar, like the day you told someone you were going to walk in your lunch break yet you never have. How you hold back on everyone and everything…'

'I don't.'

'You do.' Alessi glanced over as he drove her home. She was back to being unreadable, back to being cool and aloof and just everything that she hadn't been last night, and he wanted her back.

'We're going out this afternoon,' he said as they pulled up at her apartment.

'I've got plans.'

'Cancel them. I'll pick you up at one.'

'I might be out.'

'Then I'll be back at two.'

'Alessi…' Isla didn't know what to make of this. 'Last night—'

'I don't want to hear you regret it,' Alessi interrupted, 'or that it was something that shouldn't have happened or that it was just a one-off. Get it into your head that I'm going to date you, Isla, and that starts today. I'm certainly not waiting until Monday to find out if you're speaking to me or avoiding me.'

Isla let out a pale smile. 'It would have been the latter.'

'Which is why we are going out today. There is one thing we need to get straight though, Isla—I don't cheat, and I expect the same from you.' Her cheeks were on fire as he continued speaking. She knew he was referring to the night when she had practically offered to get off with him while Rupert and Amber had been back in the bar. 'I don't care what you got up to when you were with Rupert but if you are seeing me, then you are seeing only me. Do you get that?'

Isla nodded but her heart was heavy.

He really didn't know her at all.

'We have a companion,' Alessi said, when Isla opened her door at one to find him there, holding Niko in his arms. 'Allegra's husband, Steve, is working and she called and asked if I would mind having Niko for the afternoon as she needs a break. She rarely asks…'

'That's fine.' Isla smiled. 'Hi, there, Niko.'

'I thought we could go to the zoo,' Alessi said, but he must have seen her startle. 'You don't like the zoo?'

'I've never been,' Isla admitted. 'Actually, that's not strictly true, I've been to a couple of dinners there and a wedding once. I've just never…'

'*Been* to the zoo,' Alessi finished for her. 'Well, I

have been many times. It's Niko's favorite place for me to take him.'

'I'd better get changed,' Isla said, because she'd put on a dress, assuming they would be going out for lunch. 'Jeans?'

'Shorts,' Alessi said. 'It will get hot walking around and, anyway, I like to see your legs.'

How could he manage to flirt while holding a three-year-old as well as offering to take her to the zoo, of all places?

It was hot and smelly and actually fun.

'Oh, my…' Isla fell in love with the orangutans, which was possibly to be expected, given her job, but the babies were so adorable.

'They are as hairy as some of my premmies,' Alessi said.

Isla glanced at him, hearing the genuine warmth in his voice.

'*Your* premmies?'

'Until they go home.' Alessi nodded.

'Wouldn't that take its toll?'

'Perhaps, but the night that my brother died it looked as if my parents might lose all three of us. There was a doctor there who stayed night after night and my parents always say that were it not for him, they could have gone home with no children.'

'That's your parents' memory, Alessi,' Isla said, ignoring the set of his jaw. It worried her, all the pressure that he put on himself. 'I'm sure there were a whole lot of others who played their part.'

'I don't need to be told to delegate.'

'Lucky you, then,' Isla said, ignoring the edge to

Alessi's voice that told her this was out of bounds. 'I'm constantly being reminded to delegate by my team. Anyway, I just hope your phone's off, because I've never been to the zoo before and I might prove a terrible disappointment for Niko if you suddenly have to dash off.'

He gave a reluctant smile, which turned to a wry one an hour or so later when Jed rang through some results that Alessi was waiting for.

'Thanks for letting me know,' Alessi said. 'Yes, just continue with the regime.' As he ended the call Alessi looked over at Isla. 'I'll never turn my phone off.'

Isla just laughed. 'Neither will I.'

They just wandered, eating ice cream and taking it in turns to push Niko in his stroller. 'He gets tired,' Alessi explained. 'He's walking so much better now but on days like today it's better to bring the stroller along.'

'How bad was he when he was born?' Isla asked.

'Bad enough that we thought he might not make it,' he said. 'Allegra was very sick, too. It was a terrible time. My parents…' He was quiet for a moment. 'I think it brought a lot back for them.'

'About your brother?'

Alessi nodded but then tried to turn the conversation a little lighter. 'God, could you imagine the pressure if anything had happened to Allegra?'

'Pressure?'

'"Do your homework, Alessi, your brother would have loved the chance. When are you going to get married…?"' He rolled his eyes. '"Your brother would have loved that chance, too!"' He gave a wry smile. 'Thankfully Allegra and Steve have taken some of that heat off by marrying and having Niko. Don't get me wrong, I love my parents but they make it clear that I'm not doing all the things a good Greek son should.'

'Well, I don't do all the things that a good Delamere girl should.'

'Such as?' Alessi asked as they headed towards the elephants and he took Niko out of the stroller and put him onto his shoulders.

'Such as being a midwife. My parents thought I should study medicine, like my sister. It caused a lot of rows. Even when I got the position of head midwife my father suggested I'd be better off heading to medical school. Finally, though, he seems to get that it's not a hobby.'

'Don't you get on with them?'

'Oh, I do,' Isla said. 'We've had our differences. My midwifery for one, and that they were pretty absent when we were growing up. I get on much better with them now that I'm an adult. I can understand better why, now—their charity work is really important.'

'Family is more so.'

'I agree,' Isla said. 'I guess it's all about balance. My parents didn't have that, it was all or nothing for them.'

They stopped at the elephants. A calf had recently been born and there was quite a crowd gathered. 'Imagine delivering that,' Isla grinned.

'You love your job, don't you?' Alessi said, feeling more than a touch guilty at his assumption that her father had paved her way—clearly she'd had to fight to get where she was.

'I do.'

'Did you always want to be a midwife?'

'Not always,' Isla said, but didn't elaborate. She just watched as the little calf peeked out from between his mother's legs.

'I love the elephants,' Alessi said into the silence. 'I like the way they always remember.'

'I hate the way they always remember,' Isla said.

'Why?'

'Because some things are best forgotten.'

'Such as?' Alessi asked.

She turned and gave a weak smile but shook her head. She simply didn't know how to tell him or how to answer his questions about when she had decided to be a midwife. At what point did you hand over your heart, your past? At what point did you reveal others' secrets?

Isla didn't know.

'He's getting tired,' Alessi said as he lowered Niko from his shoulders. 'We'll take him to see his favourite thing and then get him home.'

'What is Niko's favourite thing?' Isla asked, glad for the change in subject.

It was the meerkats!

Niko hung over the edge of the barrier, shrieking with laughter every time they stood up and froze, calling out to ''Lessi' to watch.

'Look at that one,' Alessi said to Niko. 'He's on lookout while the others dig for food.'

Niko didn't care if he was on lookout; he just laughed and laughed till in the end so, too, were Isla and Alessi.

It was fun.

Just a fun day out and Isla hadn't had too many of those. She finally felt as if she was being herself, only it was a new self, someone she had never been—someone who was honest and open, except for the lies she had promised to keep.

At six, Alessi strapped an already fast asleep Niko into his car seat. 'Hopefully he will stay that way till tomorrow,' he said. 'I'll get him home and then we can go and get some dinner.'

'Won't it look odd if I'm with you?' Isla asked.

'Odd?' Alessi checked.

'For Allegra, seeing me out with you...'

'I'm not going to hide you around the corner and pretend that I've spent the day with Niko alone. Anyway, he's three, he's going to tell her that you were there.'

'I guess.' There was a flutter in her stomach as they pulled up at Allegra's house, but thankfully Alessi didn't put her through the torture of coming up to the door when Isla said that she'd prefer to wait for him in the car.

'I'll just carry him up the stairs and put him into bed,' Alessi said. 'I won't be long.'

Famous last words.

'Is that Isla in the car?' Allegra asked as she let him in.

'It is.'

'Alessi...' Allegra started, but didn't elaborate until Niko was tucked up in bed and the bedroom door was closed behind him.

'What?' Alessi said. He'd heard the note of reprimand in his sister's voice when she'd seen who was in the car. 'It's no big deal.'

'Well, it is to me,' Allegra said. 'Can you try and not break up with *this one* before I have the baby. I don't want any bad feelings...'

'There won't be any bad feelings,' Alessi said. 'Isla would never involve you like that...' Then he halted, because he'd lied. It *was* starting to feel like a big deal. 'Anyway, I have no intention of breaking things up.'

Allegra gave a slightly disbelieving snort. 'The baby's still four weeks off, Alessi.'

'I know.'

Allegra paused at the bottom of the stairs and turned and looked at her brother, who she loved very much. 'Four weeks would be an all-time record,' Allegra said. 'Well, not an all-time…' Her voice trailed off. She didn't think the mention of Talia's name would be particularly welcome here. 'I like Isla.'

'I do, too.' Alessi admitted. 'Yes, perhaps it would be more sensible to wait till the baby is born but…' He gave a small shrug. 'I'd already waited for nearly a year.'

He had.

Alessi said goodbye to his sister and then headed back to the car. A part of him wanted to turn and retract what he'd said to his sister—push the genie back in the bottle—yet he did really like Isla.

He more than liked her, in fact.

It was a rather new feeling to have.

'Right.' Alessi climbed into the driver's seat. 'Do you want to go for dinner?'

'I do.' Isla smiled. 'I'm actually starving.'

'Name where you want to go, then,' Alessi said. 'I picked the zoo so it's your turn to choose.'

Isla thought for a moment. 'We could go to Geo's. I hear they've got a new menu.'

'Geo's?' Alessi frowned but then screwed up his nose. 'Maybe we could try somewhere else…'

'Why?' Isla pushed. 'You're Greek and I love Greek food and they do the best in Melbourne.'

'We'll never get a booking this time on a Sunday night.'

'I will,' Isla said.

'They have a dress code,' Alessi pointed out.

'Not for me…' She halted then. Geo's was one of the best Greek restaurants in Melbourne and it was booked out ages in advance, just not for the likes of Isla. She could feel the tension in the car and guessed it was thanks to her latest arrogant remark. God, she'd suggested a seriously expensive restaurant in the same way she'd asked for champagne the first night they'd met.

'Don't make me feel pretentious, Alessi.'

'I'm not.'

'Actually, you are.'

He could have driven off, Alessi realised, simply left it at that. Instead, he left the engine idling and told her the truth. 'Geo's is actually my parents' restaurant, Isla.' He watched as her eyes widened in surprise and then he surprised himself and let out the handbrake. 'Let's go there.'

'Alessi.' Isla let out a nervous laugh. 'I honestly didn't know. I don't want to make things awkward for you.'

'Why would be it awkward?' he said, while determined not to make it so.

The restaurant was packed and heads turned as Alessi led her through. Isla was acutely aware that she was wearing shorts and runners, especially when a woman, who had to be his mother, came over and gave her son a kiss.

'This is Isla,' Alessi introduced them. 'She's a friend from work and we have just taken Niko to the zoo. Isla, this is my mother, Yolanda.'

'Come upstairs,' Yolanda said. 'Introduce Isla…'

'We're going to eat downstairs,' Alessi said firmly, and guided Isla to a table near the back. And as they took a seat he explained. 'If I take you upstairs then I'd have to marry you,' he teased.

'Downstairs it is, then.'

The food was amazing—even if Yolanda did tend to hover. Isla could hear laughter from upstairs. It was clear that Alessi had a huge extended family and a couple of them stopped by, greeting Isla warmly.

'Your family are close,' Isla said.

'Very,' Alessi agreed, and then told her a little about how the restaurant had started. 'We started getting more and more orders for catering. People would bring in their own dishes and ask my mother to make her moussaka in them so that they could pass them off as their own. Once we had finished school my parents were ready to take the gamble so the café was closed and Geo's opened. Upstairs is all for family. Downstairs is the main restaurant.'

'Do you come here a lot?'

'I try to drop in once a week,' Alessi said, 'maybe once a fortnight if things are busy at work.'

'And have you ever taken anyone upstairs?' Isla smiled, more than a little nosy where Alessi was concerned.

'One person.'

The smile was wiped from her face as she heard the serious note in his voice. 'You remember Talia from school?'

Isla nodded.

'We started going out when she first went to med school.'

'How long were you going out for?' Isla asked, and his response caught her by surprise.

'Two years.'

'Oh.' She'd always thought Alessi kept his relationships short-term. 'That's a long time.'

'Especially by Greek standards,' Alessi said, and took a breath. He never went into the past with women but he was starting to hope for more of a future with Isla, and for Alessi that meant being honest. 'We were about to get engaged. Neither my parents nor hers have ever forgiven me for calling it off.'

'You were young.' Isla tried to keep things light. 'Surely that's better if you weren't sure you were ready.'

'I was ready,' Alessi said, and watched as Isla's glass paused just a little before she placed it on the table. He was close to sharing, closer than he had ever been. He liked her take on things, he actually respected her directness and the slight detachment that came from Isla. She offered a rare perspective and he wanted more of that now. 'Apart from the reunion, do you keep in touch with Talia?' Alessi asked.

'A bit,' she said. 'Just social networks and things... Why?' She smiled. 'Do you still have a thing for her?'

'God, no,' Alessi said. It was the truth.

He looked at Isla—the fact that she and Talia were loosely in touch was enough of a reason not to tell her the truth about that time.

Or an *excuse* not to.

Isla would never break a confidence, he knew that.

Alessi knew then how serious he was about Isla because in more than a decade he had never once come close to telling another woman the truth behind that time.

But not here.

Not yet.

'How serious did you and Rupert get?' Alessi asked. 'Did you ever speak of marriage?'

'No.' Isla let out a short laugh. 'Rupert and I...'

Alessi watched as she suddenly took great interest in the dessert menu, which two minutes ago Isla had declined, and he was suddenly glad he hadn't revealed all.

Yes, he knew her a bit better but despite her apparent

ease, Isla still revealed very little. 'Shall we go?' Alessi suggested, and Isla nodded.

'It seems strange not to have to wait for the bill.'

'We still have to account for our time.' Alessi smiled and rolled his eyes as his mother made her way over, insisting that they come upstairs for coffee, but Alessi declined.

'I have work at seven,' he said, determined not to let his family push things, while determined not to hide. 'So does Isla.'

He drove her back to her apartment and they chatted along the way. 'Do you miss Isabel?' Alessi asked.

'I do,' Isla said, 'though it sounds as if she's having an amazing time in Cambridge...'

'How come she went?' Alessi asked. 'It was quite sudden.'

'It just came up,' Isla said, and gave him the same answer that she had to Sean. 'Who wouldn't kill for twelve months' secondment in England?'

'It had nothing to do with Sean?'

'Sean?'

'I just picked up on something.' Alessi glanced over. 'When he first started, I was down on MMU and Isabel was blushing and avoiding him as much as you would have avoided me tomorrow had I not dragged you out today...'

'I don't know what you're talking about.'

She did, Alessi was sure, but her trust was worth his patience and so he kissed her instead.

His kiss was more intimate than last night, Isla thought. It tasted not so much of passion but of promise and possibility. His mouth was more familiar and yet more intriguing because it pushed her further along a path she had never been on with a man.

Here they could end their amazing weekend.

Right now she could climb out of the car and go up to her apartment. Both of them could gather their thoughts, ready to resume normal service on Monday.

It was Isla who pulled back. 'I don't want anyone at work to know...'

'Of course,' Alessi said, and then guessed the reason they were still in his car, rather than her asking him up. 'Oh, yes, you share with Darcie.' He hesitated, wondering if asking her back to his for a second night was too much, too soon, yet it was Isla's boldness that took him by delighted surprise.

'She's on call tonight.'

It was new, it was delicious, it was a weekend that didn't have to end just yet as Isla invited him just a little bit further into her life.

CHAPTER ELEVEN

FOR A WOMAN who had never dated, Isla got a crash course and the next two weeks were blissful. Even the hard parts, like attending Archie's funeral in the hospital chapel, were made better for being together.

'Thanks for everything you did, Isla,' Donna said as they said their farewells after the service. 'Especially with Jessica.'

'How is she doing?' Isla asked.

'She's upset, of course, but she really does know that none of this was her fault. She's so glad that they had that lovely evening together and that last day.' Donna turned to Alessi. 'Thank...' she attempted, then broke down, and Alessi gave her a cuddle.

'He was such a beautiful boy,' he said. 'I am so sorry that there wasn't more that could be done. You made the right choice, Donna. He got a whole day of being loved and cuddled by his mum and dad and big sister.'

Isla, who never cried, could feel tears at the backs of her eyes as Donna wept and nodded and then pulled away. 'I need to get back up to the unit for Elijah.'

'Go,' Alessi said. 'I will see you up there soon.'

He walked up towards Maternity with Isla. He'd felt

her standing rigid beside him during the service and had noted that not a tear had been shed by her.

'Awful, wasn't it?' Alessi said.

'Yep.'

'Does nothing move you to tears, Isla?'

She halted and turned to face him. 'Excuse me?'

'I'm just commenting...'

'What, because I don't break down and cry I'm not upset?'

'I never said that,' Alessi answered calmly. 'I was just asking if anything moves you to tears. Babies' funerals are very difficult.'

'I agree.'

'Why do you hold back?'

'What, because I don't cry...'

'You hold back in everything, Isla,' he said.

It wasn't a row, more an observation, and one Isla pondered as she set up that night for TMTB.

She was pleased to see that Ruby was back.

'Are we getting pizza tonight?' Ruby asked, and Isla nodded.

'We are. I've already ordered it so it should be here soon. How are you doing, Ruby?'

'I've got my scan tomorrow afternoon.'

'Is anyone coming with you?' Isla asked, and Ruby shook her head. 'Would you like me to come with you?'

'No, thanks.'

'Well, if you change your mind just ask them to page me.'

As everyone gathered there was one noticeable absence and Isla was delighted to tell the group the happy news. 'Alison had a little girl on Monday,' Isla said. 'The birth went really well and the baby is beautiful. I've got a photo on my phone that Alison asked me to show you.'

Her phone was passed around and Isla loved watching the smile on each of the young women's faces. It was always a nice time but it was also a little confronting for some of the group as they realised that some day soon it would be their baby being spoken about in the group. Clearly it was too much for Ruby because she quickly passed on the phone.

Isla was worried for the young girl and though Ruby hung around afterwards to take the last of the pizza, still she didn't want to speak with Isla and made her excuses and dashed off.

She needed someone she gelled with, Isla thought. Isla took no offence that that person might not be herself and the next day, when Ruby didn't page Isla to come for the ultrasound, Isla was actually trying to think who might be the best fit for Ruby when her pager went off.

'Isla, it's Darcie. I was wondering if you could come down to the antenatal clinic. I've got a patient, Ruby, and—'

'I know Ruby.' Isla smiled. 'Did she change her mind?'

'Sorry?'

'I offered to come with her for her ultrasound but she said no.'

'Well, she's asked for you now. Isla, there's an anomaly on the ultrasound. The baby has spina bifida. The poor kid has had the most terrible afternoon. Loads of tests and specialists. Heinz was speaking with her and she's got terribly upset...'

Isla groaned. As brilliant as Heinz, a paediatric neurologist, was, his people skills weren't the best. 'He broached termination and Ruby is beside herself.'

'I'll be there now. Who's the midwife?' Isla asked, wondering why she hadn't been told about this long ago. She knew Ruby's ultrasound had been scheduled for two.

'Lucas,' Darcie said, and then hesitated. 'I didn't call him in till just before that.'

'I don't know what's going on between the two of you,' Isla said swiftly, 'but sort it out. I don't care if you don't get on, I don't care if you're my flatmate. I care about my patients.'

She was furious as she walked down the corridor but took a calming breath as she stepped into the room. Lucas was sitting with a teary Ruby, who had clearly been through the wringer. She looked so young and vulnerable and she should have had an advocate with her, a friend, anyone, but instead she'd faced it all pretty much alone.

'It's okay, Ruby…' Isla said, but it was the wrong thing to say because an angry Ruby jumped to her feet.

'No, it isn't!' Ruby said. 'I've just been told that it isn't all right…'

'Ruby,' Isla said, 'I know it's so much to take in.' She just wanted to get her away from the clinic for a while, to talk to her without everyone hanging around. 'Why don't we go to the canteen?'

'I don't want to go the canteen with you, you stuckup cow,' Ruby said. 'I just want…' She didn't finish but instead ran off. Isla went after her but she knew it was pointless.

'She just needs some time,' Darcie said when Isla saw her.

'I know,' Isla said, and looked at Darcie. 'I should have been told. Just because you and Lucas aren't talking—'

'Hey!' Darcie broke in. 'Lucas did a CTG on a thirty-five-weeker at two and found no heartbeat. I'm going to deliver her tonight. He's been brilliant, he's been in with Mum and Dad all afternoon. Yes, we've had a row and we don't get on, but my not telling him about Ruby had nothing to do with that. We were swamped. I had no idea Heinz was going to talk to her, I just thought he was looking through the scans.'

'Isla—'

Isla turned as Lucas knocked on the door. 'Allegra Manos is here, she said you were to be paged when she arrived.'

'Thanks.'

'I'm sorry I didn't let you know about Ruby,' Lucas added. 'I was in with a mum—'

'Darcie explained.' Isla let out a tense breath. 'Sorry about that, Darcie.'

'Apology accepted.' Darcie smiled. 'It's just been one of those awful afternoons.'

Not that the other patients could know that, so both Isla and Darcie pushed out a smile and went in to see Allegra.

She looked fantastic and the baby seemed to be doing just fine.

'Everything,' Darcie said as she examined Allegra, 'is looking great. The baby is head down and a nice size and there's lots of fluid. How are the movements?'

'Lots of them,' Allegra said.

Darcie spoke at length with Allegra about a trial of labour and told her that they would part insert an epidural. 'It won't stop you from moving around but it means that if we do need to move to a Caesarean then everything will be set up, so we can move quickly if we have to and you can also stay awake.'

Darcie answered a few more of Allegra's questions. 'I'll be seeing you weekly from now on,' Darcie said as she stepped out.

'All looks good.' Isla smiled.

'Can you let Alessi know that for me? I know he'll be itching to find out. He's doing his best not to ring for updates.'

'I'll let him know,' Isla said, but when she paged him she got the head nurse in Neonatology, who said he was busy with an infant. 'Can I pass on a message?'

'It's fine,' Isla said. 'I'll try again later.'

Much later.

In fact, it was after eight when she made her way up to NICU and buzzed and was let in, and after washing her hands she was directed to Alessi, who was by little Elijah's cot. 'How is he?' she asked.

'Giving me far too many sleepless nights, but he's doing a bit better,' he said. He was putting an IV in Elijah's scalp and Isla stood quietly as Alessi concentrated. There was a little picture attached to his cot of him and Archie lying together on what must have been Archie's last day, and Isla tore her eyes from it as Alessi finished and peeled off his gloves. 'Thank you,' he said to the neonatal nurse who had assisted him. 'Is this a personal visit?' he asked as they walked from the cot.

'Sort of.' Isla nodded. 'I'm just here to tell you about Allegra. All went well—'

'We'll go into my office.'

Isla followed him in. 'Your office is very messy.'

'Because I'm never in it long enough to put anything away,' he said, and as a case in point his phone buzzed and he answered it. 'I'll be out in a few moments.' He then hung up the phone. 'How is Allegra?'

'Fantastic. It's all progressing well. The baby is head down and engaged and Darcie will be seeing her weekly from now on.'

'She still wants a trial of labour?'

'She does,' Isla replied. 'Darcie has gone through it all with her and Allegra will have an epidural placed just in case a Caesarean is needed.' She perched on the edge of his desk. 'What time are you finishing?' she asked, knowing that he should already be off now.

'I'm just waiting for some results to come in on Elijah.'

'I thought he was doing a bit better?'

'He is,' he said. 'I just want to check his labs.'

'Who's on call tonight?'

'Jed,' Alessi clipped.

'Can't Jed—'

'Isla, please don't,' Alessi warned, because this really was his tipping point. 'I work long hours. If it doesn't suit—'

'Oh, please.' She simply laughed in the face of his warning. 'I'm not some needy miss, worried that you're going to ruin dinner if you're late home.' She pulled him towards her and started to kiss his tired mouth. 'And I'm not trying to come between you and your prem-mies.' She locked her hands behind his neck and looked into the blackest, most beautiful eyes she had ever seen and was as honest as she had ever been. 'I don't care if you're here till five in the morning just as long as you need to be here, Alessi... I just happen to care about you. If you were one of my staff I'd have sent you home about three hours ago. In fact, I'd have told you to take tomorrow off, too.'

'I'm not one of your staff.'

'Lucky for you.'

Alessi looked at Isla. He loved how she'd bypassed his warning, how she'd admitted she cared, so he told her the truth.

'I can't send Donna and Tom home with no baby.'

'And you'll do everything to see that you don't,' Isla calmly assured him. 'But Elijah's going to be here for weeks, maybe months...' She could see the wrestle in his eyes. 'I'm not going to push it.' She gave him another quick kiss and jumped down from the desk. 'I'm heading home. Stop by if it's not too late.'

'Is Darcie on call tonight?'

'Nope.' Isla headed for the door. 'I doubt she'll drop dead with shock—half the hospital seems to have worked out that we're on.'

They *were* on.

Alessi knew that when at ten, instead of crashing in the on-call room, he was driving to Isla's. It had nothing to do with the promise of sex. He would probably be kicked out for snoring, he was so tired. It was balance, it was her, it was the calm of non-judgment and the freedom of choice along with cool reason.

'I'd just about given up,' Isla said, answering the door in her dressing gown, her hair wrapped in a towel.

'Jed might call,' he warned her. 'I might need to go in.'

'That's fine,' she said. 'Do you want something to eat?'

'I had something earlier,' he said. 'I'd kill for a shower, though.'

He'd been to the apartment a few times but never while Darcie was there. She was tapping away on her

computer while watching a movie and didn't seem remotely fazed to see him here.

'Help yourself,' Isla said, opening her bedroom door.
Alessi did.

To shampoo, to conditioner, to Isla's deodorant.

'You smell like me,' Isla said as he joined her in bed
and then kissed him. 'You taste like me, too.'

Alessi really hadn't come here with sex on his mind
and that became more apparent as their kiss deepened.
'I didn't bring anything...'

'Alessi.'

'Can we lose the condoms?' he asked. 'I don't care
what tests, I'll do them, but...'

They were just so completely into each other that this
conversation had only been a matter of time but Isla was
grateful for the very small reprieve he had just given her.

'Yes...' She knew she should tell him there was no
need for tests on her part and she would, Isla decided.
She was moving closer and closer to opening up to him,
just not now. Now she could feel his exhaustion, now it
was so easy to be bold, to just move her lips from his
mouth and kiss downwards, to hold him in her hands
and feel him grow.

For Alessi it was heaven.

Her tentative lips did not alert him to her inexperience.
Instead he just revelled in her slow explorations and the
trail of her damp hair down his body.

Isla tasted him for the first time, loved the feel of his
hand on her head and the gentle pressure that pushed
her deeper. Selfish was his pleasure and that she revelled in. She could feel his occasional restraint, when
he tried not to thrust.

Then there was the turn-on when he stopped trying and just gave in. The power, the feel, the taste, the rush of him coming had Isla come, too, at the intimate private pleasure, and then afterwards, feeling him relaxed and sated beside her, it was the closest she had ever felt to another person.

And Alessi felt it, too, for there in the dark, as pleasure receded, a deeper connection flowed in as she lay in his arms.

'I was wrong to accuse you of holding back when there are things that I haven't told you.'

Isla looked at him as he continued speaking.

'Talia was pregnant.' It was with Isla that he shared for the first time. 'When she told me I asked her to marry me and we decided to tell our parents about the pregnancy after the wedding.' He liked it that her face was still there, though her smile had gone, and he liked it that she didn't ask questions. 'We had a big dinner at the restaurant on the Saturday…'

He tried to explain better. 'In Greek families you establish a connection before the man asks the woman's father, so even though we weren't officially engaged, it was a given that it was to come. On the Wednesday Talia missed lectures. I went over to check if all was okay and it was clear she was unwell. I thought she was losing the baby. I wanted her to go to hospital but she told me there was no need…' He watched Isla's slight frown. 'She told me then that she'd had an abortion that morning.'

'Without telling you?'

'Yep. She thought I would try to talk her out of it. She said that she wanted to have children one day but that she knew she couldn't study to be a doctor and be a teenage mum…' Alessi turned from Isla and looked back at the ceiling. 'I get that, I understand that. I get that it was her body…'

'It was your baby, though?'

Alessi nodded and he waited and hoped for Isla to share.

'Go to sleep,' Isla said, and Alessi smiled into the darkness.

If it took for ever he would find out what went on in that head, and then he smiled into the darkness again. 'Jed and I have swapped. I'm working this weekend.'

'But you're already on call twice next week,' Isla pointed out sleepily.

'I know,' Alessi said, 'but it will be worth it to have next weekend off. You know what next weekend is?' he checked. 'Valentine's Day. The anniversary of when we first met.'

'And?'

'I have plans for us.'

'Such as?'

'You'll find out,' he said. Yes, he'd had plans when he'd swapped the work arrangements with Jed—an intimate meal with Isla, perhaps a night in a gorgeous hotel, but right now those plans were getting bigger and he gave a wry laugh.

'Hopefully it will end better than the last one.'

CHAPTER TWELVE

IT WAS THE promise of the weekend and the fact that her period was due that had Isla knocking on Darcie's office door on the Monday morning.

'Hi, Darcie…'

'Hey, Isla.'

'I was wondering…' Isla started, but then she changed her mind. She would make an appointment with her GP, Isla decided, and turned to go. Except her period was due any time and for it to be safe she'd need to start the Pill on her first day. She also knew that she needed to have her blood pressure checked and things… So Isla took a breath. 'Have you got a moment?'

'Sure,' Darcie said. 'I've got precisely six.' She frowned when Isla didn't smile. 'I've got all the time you need, Isla. Is everything okay?'

'Oh, it's not a biggie,' Isla said. 'It won't take long. I was just wondering if you could write me a script for the Pill…'

'Sure,' Darcie said. 'Have a seat.'

Isla did, though again she was tempted to change her mind. 'What do you usually take?' Darcie asked, pulling out a blood-pressure cuff. When Isla didn't immediately answer, Darcie said, 'Sorry, Isla, but I'm not just going to give you a repeat without checking your blood pressure.'

Isla nodded. She knew that Darcie was thorough and was starting to realise what a stupid idea this had been as Darcie quickly checked it. 'All good.' Darcie nodded. 'So, what are you on?'

'I'm not,' Isla said.

'What type of contraception do you usually use?'

'Condoms,' Isla said, and then cleared her throat.

'Okay,' Darcie answered carefully. They both knew that condoms weren't the safest of choices.

'Look, sorry, Darcie, I should have gone to my GP. I just—'

'Isla, it's fine.' Darcie interrupted. 'I'm not just going to write out a script, though, if it's something that you haven't taken before.'

Isla nodded.

'Have you any history that I should know about?'

Isla shook her head.

'Blood clots, migraines…' She went through the list of contraindications.

'Nothing.'

'Good.' Darcie smiled. 'When did you last have a smear test?'

Isla sat there, her cheeks on fire.

'Sorry, I keep forgetting I'm in Australia,' Darcie said into the silence. 'When did you last have a Pap?'

Isla had never had a Pap because she'd never been sexually active.

'It's been…' Isla gave a tight shrug. 'It's been a while.'

'I'm not going to tell you off for leaving it too long,'

Darcie said. 'Let's just get it over and done with. When is your period due?'

'Today or tomorrow.'

'Have you had any unprotected sex?'

'No.' Isla shook her head, but more to clear it. What the hell was she lying for? 'Once,' she amended. 'But he...' She let out a breath in embarrassment. God, no wonder the patients loathed all the questions. 'He withdrew.'

'Did you do it standing up?' Darcie grinned as she teased. They'd both heard it all before and knew that withdrawal was far from safe.

'I'm not pregnant,' Isla said. She knew that she wasn't—her breasts had that heavy feeling they always got when her period was near. Not that it put Darcie off.

'Fine, then you won't mind peeing in a jar to put my mind at ease. Then I'm going to do a Pap and give you a work-up and get all the boxes ticked so you can hopefully forget about things for another couple of years.'

'You don't have time.'

'I just made time.' Darcie smiled. She was a thorough doctor and refused to be rushed by anyone, especially her patients, and a little while later as she looked at the pregnancy card on the desk before her, a patient Isla suddenly was.

'Isla,' Darcie said, and Isla watched as she pushed the card over to her.

Isla stared at it for a long moment. There were possibly a thousand thoughts in her head but not a single one of them did she show on her face. She just looked up at Darcie.

'Can we leave the Pap for another time?' Isla said, her voice completely clear, her expression unreadable.

'Of course, but, Isla—'

'Can we not discuss this, please?' Isla stood. 'Just…' She turned as she got to the door. 'You won't tell anyone…'

'You don't have to ask me that, Isla,' Darcie said, and Isla nodded. 'But if you want to talk any time, you can.'

Isla muttered brief thanks and headed out to her department, and for the first time ever she left early.

She lay on her bed and just stared at the ceiling and all she felt was stupid, naïve and embarrassed at having got pregnant her *first* time.

It was all she could manage to feel as she lay there.

When the phone bleeped to indicate a text, she knew it was from Alessi but she didn't even look at it.

She simply could not bear to think of telling him or even attempt to fathom his reaction.

Far worse than his anger would be duty.

Isla lay there, recalling his words—how he'd done the right thing by Talia, how he'd offered to marry her as soon as he'd found out.

She didn't want that for either of them.

They'd been going out for a couple of weeks, which surely meant, given his track record, that they had just about run their course.

Isla tried to comfort herself, reminded herself that the reason she'd been going on the Pill in the first place was that Alessi himself had wanted to move things forward, to lose the condoms.

On the proviso that she was on the Pill, though.

Isla felt a tear slide out and she screwed her eyes shut.

She heard the door open and Darcie come home and

Isla wanted to call out to her, she wanted to sob, hell, she wanted to break down and cry.

But she didn't know how to, scared that if she let out a part of her fear then the rest would come gushing out.

Secrets she had sworn never to reveal.

CHAPTER THIRTEEN

Isla didn't have to try too hard to avoid Alessi.

That night he was too wrecked to even drive home so he sent a text to Isla to say he was crashing at the hospital. About two seconds after hitting 'send' he did just that in the on-call room on the unit.

He dived back into work at eight the next day when he was on call again. He finally saw Isla on Tuesday but it wasn't a social visit—a newborn was rapidly deteriorating and all Alessi wanted from Isla was her cool efficiency, which he got.

In fact, Isla was doing her very best to keep calm.

Wrestling with her own news, trying to fathom that she herself would, in a matter of months, be a mum, she had been checking on a newborn when she found a baby looking dusky at her mother's breast. Isla moved the infant, hoping her breathing had just been obstructed temporarily but was silently alarmed by her colour and tone.

'I'm just going to take her to the nursery,' Isla said to Karina, the mother. 'She's looking a bit pale and the light is better there...' She would have loved to speak with the mother some more but the little girl was causing Isla too much concern and she moved swiftly through the unit, glad when she saw Emily there, who instantly saw Isla's concern.

'I'll page Alessi,' Emily said as Isla suctioned the infant and started to deliver oxygen.

Yes, Isla was calm and did everything right but there was this horrible new urgency there as Karina arrived in the nursery, tears streaming down her face.

'She was fine!' Karina was saying, and Isla could hear the fear, the love, the helplessness in her voice. 'Please, help her,' she begged as Alessi dashed in and took over.

'She's going to be fine…'

Alessi's calm voice caught even Isla by surprise. 'Just a little milk that's gone down the wrong way…' He was rubbing the baby's back and gently suctioning her, and thankfully she was pinking up.

He dealt with it all very calmly, even though there was some marked concern, which he explained in more detail a little while later after some tests had been done.

'As I said…' Alessi pulled up the X-ray on his computer and went through it with the mum. 'She has inhaled some milk and we're going to be looking for infection, which is why I'm going to have her moved to NICU to keep a closer eye on her for a few days…'

It had all been dealt with well yet it left Isla more shaken than it would usually, not that she showed it.

'Thanks for that.' Isla gave him a tight smile as his team went off to NICU with their latest recruit and she headed into her office, just wanting to be alone, but Alessi followed.

'Shouldn't you be with the baby?'

'She's fine,' Alessi said. 'Are you?'

'I just got a fright,' Isla admitted. 'I'd just popped in to chat with Karina…'

'It happens. I want to take a closer look at her palate when I'm up there. I think she might have a small cleft that's been missed.'

Isla just looked at him and tried to fathom that in a few months she'd be on this roller-coaster. 'I'll try and call you tonight,' Alessi said, and gave her a light kiss on her lips. Isla wanted to grab his shoulders and cling to him; she wanted some of his ease and strength to somehow transfer to her, but instead she stood there and watched him leave.

She knew she had to tell him.

Just not yet.

She wouldn't say anything until she could tell him without breaking down, till she'd somehow got her head around the fact that she'd soon be a first-time mother herself.

It was just all too much to take in, let alone share with Alessi, when she didn't know how he'd react.

Which meant that at nine on Friday evening, after a hellish week at work, as Alessi drove home he called Isla and got her cool voice when he needed warmth.

He got distance when he needed to be closer.

'Is it too late to come over?' he asked.

'Well, it is a bit,' she said. 'I'm pretty tired.'

'Sure.' Alessi forced down his irritation. He could sleep for a whole week yet he still wanted to see her. 'Isla, I was thinking about tomorrow…' He was just so glad the weekend was finally here.

He had it planned.

He was way past the flowers and dinner stage already.

'How about I pick you up around six—'

'I actually wanted to talk about that,' Isla broke in. 'I've just realised that I can't make it.'

'You can't make it?'

'I forgot when you said you'd swapped your shift that I already had plans for this weekend...'

'Such as?'

Such as trying to get my head around the fact that I'm pregnant, Isla wanted to scream. *Such as trying to tell you that I wasn't on the Pill. That you were my first...*

She was closer to tears than she wanted to be.

'Alessi...' She swallowed. 'I just can't make it.'

'Don't do this, Isla,' he warned. 'I'm coming now and you are going to talk to me.'

'There's nothing to talk about.'

'You know, you're right,' he said, his temper bubbling to the surface. 'Because it seems to me I'm the one who does the talking. I've told you so much these past weeks, Isla, and you've told me precisely nothing.'

'That's not true.'

'Bull!' Alessi shouted. 'I know little more about you than I did the night of the ball. You tell me nothing about how you feel or what you're thinking. Oh, sorry, I do know one thing that I didn't two weeks ago—you give good head.'

No, he could never know her, neither could he read her because instead of a shocked gasp or a swift attack he got the sound of dry laughter.

'You're right, you don't know me,' Isla said, because by her own silence he didn't and she'd surely left it too late to start opening up now.

'Game over, is it, Isla?' Alessi's voice was cool. 'At least have the guts to say it.'

'Game over,' Isla said, and hung up.

As Valentine's Days went, it was a pretty terrible one.

She woke to a text from Alessi, apologising, but telling her that she'd be getting flowers as he had been unable to cancel the flower order. And then there was a snarky addition: Believe me, Isla, I damn well tried!

Isla actually smiled wryly at his text.

She answered the door to her delivery of not one but two large bouquets.

One was from Alessi, saying that he couldn't wait for tonight.

The other was from Rupert, who must have forgotten to cancel his regular order from the florist.

'You have a very interesting life,' said Darcie, smiling.

Things had been just a touch awkward between them since Isla had found out she was pregnant but Darcie was nice enough not to push her to talk. Instead, she made Isla laugh as she swiped Rupert's bunch and said that she was going to pretend they were for her.

It was the only funny part of the day.

The only funny part of the week.

Isla's heart ached in a way that it never had before. She knew she had to tell Alessi, that somehow she had to face things—he would soon find out after all—but she was worried about his reaction. Of course she expected him to be upset. In her work Isla was more than used to that. She knew, though, that after the dust settled, when the initial shock of a pregnancy wore off, rapid decisions were often made.

She had never wanted their fragile relationship to be put under such early pressure and, worse, it was her own fault. But on Wednesday night, as she set up for TMTB, Isla knew her problems were comparatively small as a very pale face came around the door, followed by a slender body that housed a growing bump.

'Come in, Ruby.' Isla smiled and she forced another one when Alessi followed her in with an empty incubator he had bought down from NICU for his talk with the girls.

He ignored her.

'I'm sorry I called you a stuck-up cow!' Ruby said.

'It's fine, Ruby. I know that I can be a stuck-up cow at times!' She gave the young girl a little hug. 'It's so good to see you here. Do you want to get something to eat?'

Ruby nodded and made her way over to the table, which was groaning under the weight of cupcakes Emily had just *happened* to have made.

Emily was always going beyond the call of duty and it dawned on Isla that she would be the perfect midwife for Ruby. Isla decided that she would have a word about Ruby with her favourite midwife tomorrow, or whenever Emily was next on.

And then, as she looked at the faces of her TMTB group, some nervous, some excited, others ready, Isla felt the first glimpse of calmness that she'd had since Darcie had pushed the pregnancy card towards her and she had found out that she'd be a mother.

She looked at Ruby and saw the fear in her eyes but also the fire. She looked at Harriet, who was facing things bravely and passing around a picture of the ultrasound.

Yes, she was twenty-eight but Isla forgave herself then because teenage, twenty, thirty or forty—when it first happened and you found out you were going to be a mum, it was an overwhelming feeling indeed.

She didn't feel so overwhelmed now.

Scared, yes, nervous, of course, but there was excitement there, too, and as she glanced over at Alessi, who was pointedly ignoring her, Isla was grateful, too, that, no matter what his reaction was, this man was the father of her child.

'It's great to see so many of you.' Isla kicked things off. They did a small catch-up, finding out where everyone was at, but when it was Ruby's turn she said little and Isla moved things on because clearly Ruby wasn't willing to share her news yet.

'Most of you met Alessi four weeks ago,' Isla introduced their guest speaker. 'He's a neonatologist here at the Victoria. A couple of you already know that your babies will be going to NICU when they're born. Some of you might not be expecting your baby to end up there and so, if it does, it will come as a huge shock. That's why Alessi is here,' Isla explained. 'If your baby is on NICU then at least you'll have a familiar face and, as well as that, he's a wonderful doctor.'

She gave him a smile but again Alessi completely blanked her and instead he addressed the group.

'Thank you for having me along tonight,' he said. 'As Isla said, I am a neonatologist. Does everyone here know what that means?' When no one answered he asked another question. 'Does everyone know what NICU stands for?'

A couple of the newer girls shook their heads and Alessi did smile now, but it was a tight one and, Isla knew, aimed at her.

It said, *Ruby was right—you are a stuck-up cow!*

'Well, a neonatologist is a doctor who takes care of newborns. In my case, I care for newborns that need, or might need, extra support. NICU stands for Neonatal Intensive Care Unit, which basically means it is a place for babies who need a lot of support. The best place for a baby to be is where it is now…' As Alessi talked, Isla could see he already had the group eating out of his hand.

He was completely lovely with them.

'I'm very good at my job,' he said, 'but even with all the technology available, I'm still not as good as you are at keeping your baby oxygenated and nourished and its temperature stable…'

He opened up the incubator and turned on a few monitors and explained how they worked and what the staff were looking for, and really he did give an excellent talk.

'The nurses there are amazing,' Alessi said. 'When a baby is especially sick there is a nurse with them at all times, sometimes two. They don't get scared by the alarms, because they are very used to them. So although the alarms will make you feel anxious, don't think that the nursing staff are ignoring anything.'

Then his phone rang and Alessi rolled his eyes.

'That's my family ringing again and asking where I am,' he said, 'and that is one alarm that I *am* going to ignore!'

Isla smiled as he turned off his phone and gave the group his full attention.

He went through many things and then asked if anyone had questions, which they all did, even Ruby.

'What happens if a baby is disabled?' Ruby asked.

Isla had sat in on a meeting just that morning about her baby. There was talk of out-of-utero surgery, if a suitable doctor could be found, though Ruby didn't know about this yet.

She was in a very fragile place and Isla was very proud of her for asking questions.

'Many of the babies I look after will have disabilities,' Alessi said. 'When you say what happens…'

'Do you care as much about them?' Ruby asked. 'Or do you think the mother should have got rid of it? What happens if the baby is up for adoption?'

There was a long stretch of silence and Isla fought not to step in yet she glanced at Alessi and knew that she didn't have to. He was taking care with his answer as he looked at the hostile and very scared girl.

'The only thing I would think in that instance,' Alessi said, 'was that by the time the mother and baby get to be in my care, a lot of very difficult decisions have already been made and a lot of obstacles faced.'

He hesitated for a moment before continuing. 'A lot of my babies will leave the unit and require a lot of extra care just to do normal things. Many, too, leave healthy. My job, my goal, is to hand the baby to its carer, who-ever that may be, in the best possible health. That is my goal every day when I go into work. You ask if I care as much. I care about every one of my patients. Some need more care than others and I see that they get it.'

She couldn't not tell him about the pregnancy. Isla had long known that but it was confirmed then.

She was keeping her baby and so the decisions that would be made for its care would involve Alessi also.

She looked at his wide, lovely smile as he even man-aged to get a small laugh from Ruby, and Isla imagined his expression when she told him they were bound for ever—that the cool and together 'I've got this covered' Isla hadn't even been on the Pill.

She deserved his reaction, she expected the row, and she'd prefer that than Alessi choosing to do the right thing, to marry her, stick together…

'Now, I'm going to have to leave.' Alessi broke into her introspection. 'I have some time for some questions but it is my parents' fortieth anniversary tonight and I am already in trouble for being late.'

He didn't rush them through the questions, though. Ruby had no more but she took a generous helping of sandwiches with her and left, while a couple of girls hung around to speak with Alessi. 'I'll return this,' Isla offered, unplugging the incubator, knowing that Alessi had other places he needed to be.

She wheeled the incubator back up to NICU and chatted with the nurses there for a while.

'How's Elijah?' Isla asked.

'Well, it's still early days,' the senior nurse said. 'He gave us all a terrible time last week but he seems to be holding his own at the moment. Donna will be coming in soon to bring in some breast milk. She generally comes in at this time if you want to hang around.'

'Not tonight,' Isla said.

Tonight she needed to get her head around her decision—somehow she would tell Alessi, but away from here, Isla thought as she walked back down to MMU.

'Oh!' As Isla pushed open the door, there was Alessi. Alone.

'I thought you had to get to your parents'…'

'They can wait,' Alessi said. 'This can't. I want to know what happened, Isla. I want to know what's going on.'

Isla took a deep breath.

'Any time now, Isla,' he said. His phone was ringing and he saw that it was Allegra, no doubt demanding to know where he was.

'I'll be there as soon as I can!' Alessi had to keep himself from shouting and Isla screwed her eyes shut as he switched to Greek.

When he ended the call she met his eyes and it was time for the truth. 'I'm pregnant, Alessi.'

His reaction was nothing like she had expected. His face had already been pale, Isla realised, but it paled a little further and then he gave her a very small smile.

'Can you hold that thought?'

'Sorry?' Isla blinked.

'Allegra is at the party and doesn't want to make a fuss but she thinks she might be in labour.'

'Oh!'

'She sounds as if she's in labour.'

'Meaning?'

'One conversation, two contractions.'

'She needs to get here.'

'Try telling her that,' Alessi said, and handed her his phone. 'While *we* get *there*.'

CHAPTER FOURTEEN

It was the strangest car ride.

Isla's news hung between them while both were grateful for the pause.

Alessi wanted some time with his thoughts rather than say something he might later regret. *Is it mine?* was, for Alessi, the obvious question.

In turn, Isla was relieved that her secret was out and that the world was still turning.

'I think I've left it too late to get to hospital...' Allegra, from the echo Isla could hear, was in the bathroom.

'That's fine.' Isla's voice was calm. 'We're a couple of minutes away. I'm going to call for backup. Are you in the bathroom?'

'Yes.'

'Where's Steve?'

'Can I hang up on you and text him?' Allegra asked. 'I don't want the whole family piling in.'

'Give me his number,' Isla said. 'I'll text him from my phone, you just keep talking to me.'

'My waters just broke.'

'Okay,' Isla said. 'What colour is the fluid?' She heard Alessi let out a tense breath as it became obvious from the conversation that things were moving along rather rapidly.

'Clear.'

'Have a feel,' Isla instructed. 'There's no cord?'

'No. Isla, I want to push.'

'Try not push,' Isla said. 'We're at the traffic lights on the corner. Alessi's swearing because they're red.'

'I don't want my brother delivering me.'

'I know you don't want your brother to deliver you,' Isla said, and she caught a glimpse of Alessi's rigid profile. 'But luckily you've got me. I'm going to ring off and I'll see you in a moment.' She turned to Alessi. 'I'm jumping out when we get to the next lights.'

Their eyes met and there was so much unsaid. 'We're talking this out tonight, Isla,' Alessi said.

'I'm sorry, Alessi.' She told him the truth as the car moved the next five hundred meters. 'I wasn't on the Pill.' She felt his eyes on her briefly. 'I know I let you think I was… I meant to take care of it the next morning, get the morning-after pill, but I didn't…' Tears were threatening and she choked them down.

'Are you considering an abortion?' Alessi asked, and Isla shook her head.

'Then never apologise for your pregnancy again.'

She arrived at Geo's and walked in as calmly as she could, grateful she had been there before and that the staff let her straight upstairs as soon as she explained that Alessi was parking.

The speeches were going on as Isla made her way through the crowd and Alessi's father was speaking.

'Tonight I celebrate forty years with the love of my life. We have been together through good times and bad…' There was a long pause before he continued. 'We were blessed with three children, Geo, Alessandro and Allegra, tonight we sit in Geo's as a family, always.'

Alessi must have ditched the car because he was right behind her as she headed to the bathroom.

'Watch the door,' Isla said, and took a deep breath and stepped inside.

She'd delivered many women on the bathroom floor but she'd only deeply loved one of them.

Make that two, Isla thought as she stepped in and saw Allegra's red face and damp curls. Steve was there beside her and he blew out a breath of relief as Isla came over. 'Talk about timing,' Steve said.

'Perfect timing.' Isla smiled, dropping to her knees, knowing what to do.

'It's coming.'

Oh, it was.

'Get behind Allegra, Steve,' Isla said. 'Help pull her legs back.'

'Where's Alessi?' Steve asked.

'Gnawing on the door with his teeth.' Isla smiled.

'He must trust you,' Allegra said.

Alessi did.

But with no equipment, no help to hand, it tested Alessi on so many levels and it was a Herculean effort to stand outside.

Last time, with Niko, Allegra had nearly died.

It wasn't like last time, Alessi told himself.

Isla was there.

Isla was pregnant.

It was then that he properly acknowledged it. He looked at his parents, who were scanning the gathered crowd, waiting for their children to start speaking. A crowd was starting to gather where Alessi was playing doorman and a paramedic was climbing the stairs, wearing a crash helmet, which was possibly a giveaway.

'Yes,' Alessi said when his mother raced over. 'Allegra is having the baby.'

'Why aren't you in there?' Yolanda demanded.

'Isla's there. She'll call if she needs me.'

Alessi closed his eyes.

She just had called.

Private, deep, she had told him she was pregnant and he was eternally grateful for the drama of tonight, for not demanding to know if the baby was his, in some Neanderthal reaction.

Whatever the answer, he was there for her, too.

Alessi knew it.

Isla didn't.

'Is everything okay?' Steve asked, his eyes anxious.

'Everything,' Isla said, 'is perfect.'

Allegra pushed and when she couldn't push, she pushed some more and then let out a scream, not that anyone would hear outside, where there was music and chattering and laughter. And as Allegra rested her body against her husband, Isla demanded more from her.

'Again.'

'No.'

'One more, come on…'

'Do what Isla says.' Steve was both supportive and firm. Behind his wife, he held up her thighs and helped Allegra bring their child into the world.

Their baby was almost here—the head was out and with the next push it would be delivered. The door opened at that moment and Isla smiled as Aiden Harrison, a rapid-response paramedic who had arrived on motorbike, stepped quietly inside.

'Put your hands down, Allegra,' Isla said.

Allegra did and together she and Isla delivered the baby.

It was a gorgeous fat baby girl with big cheeks and chunky arms and legs, who cried on entering the world and was born with her eyes open. Allegra and Steve wept when they saw her, their strong, healthy baby, and so, too, did Isla.

Not a lot, but some tears did spill out, especially as Steve cut the cord.

'I think you've stopped the party.' Isla smiled through her tears because the noise outside had faded.

'Steve…' Allegra said. 'Maybe you could let them know that everything is okay?' She glanced up from her beautiful daughter. 'And let Alessi in, poor guy.'

His face was as white as chalk but he smiled when he stepped in and saw his niece.

It was so completely different from the last time.

Then, it had needed to be all sterile equipment and everyone avoiding meeting his eyes. Then it had been his sister and nephew on different intensive care units and the joy of childbirth completely missing.

Now smiling faces greeted him and the surroundings didn't matter.

A backup ambulance had arrived and as Allegra was transferred to a stretcher it was Alessi who held the baby.

There were repercussions to his job. He generally dealt with the babies that had run into complications, with the battlers to survive, but this little girl was feisty, dark, hungry, angry… Alessi looked into very dark navy eyes that in a matter of weeks would be as black as his.

She needed no help from him, just love, and this little lady had it.

So, too, did Isla.

He loved her—of that he was completely sure.

CHAPTER FIFTEEN

A PROCESSION OF cars followed the ambulance to the hospital and once there a celebration ensued.

Isla was more than used to the excitement within a Greek family when a baby was born but it was all multiplied tonight, because this little lady had been born on her grandparents' fortieth wedding anniversary. Isla was aware, too, of the exhaustion having so many people around might cause for a new mum, but Alessi sorted it and suggested that the party continue back at his place.

'Thank you so much, Isla,' Allegra said as Isla went to go. 'It might not have been the ideal location but it really was the best birth.'

'It was wonderful.' Isla smiled. 'You made it look very easy.'

'It has been the best wedding anniversary present ever.' Yolanda was ecstatic. Niko was asleep on her shoulder and would be staying with his *yaya* tonight, but first they headed back to Alessi's, stopping for champagne on the way.

The mood was elated as corks popped and Alessi watched as Isla took a glass and pretended to take a sip so as not to draw attention to the fact she wasn't drinking.

'Are you okay?' he asked.

'Of course.' Isla smiled.

'Isla?' Alessi checked, because he could see that she was struggling.

'I'm a bit tired,' Isla admitted, which was the understatement of the year. She was exhausted. The high of the birth was fading and the enormity of her revelation was starting to make itself known. They hadn't had a chance to discuss it and from the way things were going it would be a good while yet till they could.

'Go and lie down,' Alessi suggested.

'I can't just go to bed in the middle of a party. My father would have kittens if I—'

'He's not here, though. Isla, you can do no wrong today, you just safely delivered Allegra's baby. I know they are a bit over the top but they really are so grateful and relieved.'

'I think it's lovely how happy they are,' Isla said.

He led her to the bedroom and she walked in, glad to escape from all the noise. Alessi closed the blinds and Isla undressed down to her underwear and slipped into bed. He came and sat on the edge.

'Thank you for tonight,' he said.

'I really didn't have to do much. Your niece made her entrance herself,' Isla said. 'She's such a gorgeous baby.'

'It will be you soon,' Alessi said, and watched as her eyes filled with tears. He could only guess how overwhelming this all must be for her. 'How long have you known?' he asked, and then answered his own question. 'The Monday before Valentine's Day.'

'How do you know?'

'Your texts went from ten lines to two words,' Alessi said. 'Don't worry about all that now. Just get some rest.'

'You're not cross.'

'Cross?' Alessi checked. 'Did you expect me to be cross?'

'I didn't know what to expect.'

'I only get cross when you dump me for no good reason, Isla,' he said. 'Get some sleep. We'll talk later.'

There was a lot to talk about but when Alessi finally got to bed around two, he certainly wasn't about to wake her for The Talk. He had never intended to wake her at all, but Alessi hadn't forgotten how nice it was to have her in his bed and he had missed her so much.

Asleep, Isla wriggled towards the source of warmth. Her back was to him and, deprived of his touch for ten days now, her body knew who it wanted and her bottom nudged into his groin and sank into his caress as his arm came over her.

Alessi lay there. No, it would be completely inappropriate, he told himself, because there was that damn talk to have. Except his fingers didn't care about such matters and were stroking her through the silk of her bra and then burrowing in.

'Isla…' Alessi said, which wasn't much of a conversation. His mouth was on her shoulder, tasting her skin again and then moving up to her neck. The response in her had him harden further, the craning of her neck to meet his mouth, the consent, the want had a flare of possession rise in Alessi and there was no conversation to be had.

Isla was his.

His mouth suckled her neck and Isla bit down on her bottom lip as he deliciously bruised her. His hand was sliding down her panties and she wanted to turn but she didn't. She liked the arm holding her down and Alessi's precision as he took her from behind.

Of all his responses, of all the reactions she had

anticipated, this hadn't been one of them. Alessi's hand was on her stomach, gently pressing her back into him, and Isla, who had never been taken like this, writhed in pleasure as his hand moved down and stroked her intimately.

'Alessi…' She said his name, the only thing now on her mind as he moved her towards orgasm.

And for Alessi, here in the darkness of his bedroom, yes, there were questions, but her body's response, their absolute connection meant the only truth that actually mattered was easily said. 'I love you.'

Isla stilled, but Alessi didn't. He thrust into her and didn't let her get her breath, neither did he allow the panic that suddenly built in her to settle. He just said it again, for their love was no accident.

She could feel him building to come, feel all the passion about to be unleashed, and it tipped Isla into raw honesty when she'd spent her whole life covering lies. 'I love you, too.'

Isla came before him and she loved how he held her down and didn't kiss her, or stifle her shout. He just let her be and drove her ever higher as he came deep inside her.

And still there was no need for The Talk because they had said what mattered.

Doubts belonged to the morning. There were none in his arms.

CHAPTER SIXTEEN

ALESSI WOKE BEFORE Isla and would have watched her sleeping had he not been so hungry.

Neither had had dinner, he remembered.

He wondered if she was as starving as he was.

If Isla was feeling sick in the mornings.

He just stared at her and wondered, which he'd been doing for more than a year, Alessi thought with a smile as he climbed from bed and went to the kitchen.

Coffee on, he started making breakfast and completely out of habit he checked his emails and then glanced at the news.

And then did a double take.

Yes, again she had him wondering.

'Morning, Isla…'

It was incredibly nice to be woken with coffee and breakfast and Alessi's smile, and she returned it but even as she stretched, doubts started piling in.

God, she'd told him she loved him.

Isla let out a breath.

Yes, he'd said he loved her but she was petrified of forcing his hand, thinking that Alessi might be simply making the best of a bad deal.

'This looks lovely,' she said, her hand shaking a

touch as she took the coffee from the tray, unable to meet his eyes.

'Is there something you need to tell me?' Alessi said.

'Isn't what I told you last night enough to be going on with?' Isla said. 'I know it's a shock. I know it's too soon…'

'It doesn't feel too soon,' he said. 'We're not teenagers, Isla.'

'I know, but even so…'

'It was a shock last night,' Alessi admitted, 'but it's a nice surprise now. How do you feel about it?'

'Nervous,' Isla admitted. 'I was terrified at first but now…' she looked at him '…it's starting to feel like a nice surprise, too, but I'm terrified of the pressure it might put on us.'

'Like marriage?'

Isla nodded.

'You don't want to get married?' Alessi asked. 'Isla, help me here, because the last woman I asked to marry me…' She could see him struggling. 'I don't want to put the same pressure on you. Looking back, I can see that we were far too young and not in love. You've heard the saying "Marry in haste, repent at leisure". I'm quite sure now that that would have been Talia and I.'

'I don't want it to be us.'

'It won't be,' Alessi assured her. 'Just so long as we are always honest with each other.'

'I feel like I've forced things…'

'Isla, I was going to ask you to marry me on Valentine's night. I had it all planned, right down to if you said yes, we were going to go the next day to the restaurant, upstairs this time, and tell my family…' He could see the disbelief in her eyes. He rolled his eyes and then climbed out of bed and went to a drawer, and Isla watched as he took out a small box.

'There.' He handed it to her. 'Do you believe me now?'

She looked up at him and then back to the ring.

It was white gold, with a pale sapphire. 'It matches your eyes, almost exactly,' Alessi said. 'I wanted a diamond but when I saw this...'

Again he asked a question. 'Is there something you need to tell me?'

'Such as?'

Alessi took a breath. 'Maybe there's something I need to tell you. I'm sorry if it comes as a shock. Your ex-boyfriend just came out. It's all over the news...' He saw the tears in her eyes and misread them. 'I'm sorry. Is this news to you?'

'I've always known.' Isla took a breath. 'There's never been anything sexual between us.'

'I don't understand.' Alessi frowned. 'Were you covering for him?'

'Yes,' Isla said, 'but he was covering for me, too.' It was the biggest confession of her life and far harder to admit than her pregnancy. 'I've never had a sexual relationship with anyone. Till you.'

'You're telling me that our night together was your first?' He shook his head, not so much in disbelief but that night he had felt her burn in his arms, the sex between them had been so good, so natural. 'You should have told me,' he said. 'You must have been so nervous...'

'No,' she refuted. 'I was always scared before, I wasn't that night.'

'Scared of what, Isla?'

'I don't really know,' she admitted. 'I thought I was scared of getting pregnant but I don't feel scared. Something happened when I was twelve…' She closed her eyes. 'I can't tell you.'

'I think you have to.'

'I can't tell you because it's not my secret to share, it didn't happen to me.'

'Whatever happened affected you, though,' Alessi said. 'What would you tell one of your patients?'

'To talk to someone.'

'So talk to me.'

'My sister.' Isla gulped in a breath as panic hit. 'Please, never say…'

'I would never do that.'

That much she knew.

'When I was twelve I heard her…' Isla let out a breath. 'She had a baby, I think it was about eighteen weeks…'

'You think?'

'I didn't know at the time,' Isla said. 'I delivered him. Isabel begged me not to say anything but I got our house-keeper, Evie. She took us to a hospital… It was all dealt with, our parents never found out… I promised never to tell.'

'You're not telling me about Isabel,' Alessi said. 'I don't need the details about her, I need to know what happened to you and what you went through.'

And so she told him, and Alessi watched as the su-premely confident, always cool Isla simply collapsed in tears as she released the weight of her secret.

He held her as she spoke and then, as the tears sub-sided, Isla lay there and looked up at him and found out how it felt not to be alone.

'No more secrets,' Alessi said.

'I know.'

'You could have told me...' And then he stopped. 'I guess you had to trust me.'

'I should have told you that night,' Isla said, 'because I trusted you then, Alessi, or I wouldn't have slept with you...' She looked at the smile on his face and frowned. 'What's funny?'

'Not funny,' Alessi said. 'I guess that means that the baby's mine.'

'Of course—' Isla started, and then halted. Of course he would have had doubts, he would have been doing the frantic maths. Not once had it entered her head that he might wonder if the baby was his, but of course it must have been there for him. 'You loved me, even when you didn't know that the baby was yours...'

'Isla, I love you, full stop. We'd have worked it out, whoever the father was.'

He loved her. Isla accepted it then.

'Marry me?' Alessi said.

'Try and stop me.' Isla smiled. 'Can we not tell anyone about the baby yet, though? I want to keep it to ourselves for a little while.'

'And me,' Alessi said.

'We've only being going out for a few weeks...'

'Oh, no,' Alessi said, and took her in his arms. 'I've been crazy about you since the night I first met you and I was right that night...' He gave her a slightly wicked smile of triumph. 'You *did* want me.'

'I did,' Isla said, blushing at the memory. 'God, I've wasted so much time.'

'I wouldn't change a thing about us, Isla. You know there is another saying, Isla, *"Ki'taxa vathia' mes sta ma'tia sou ke i'da to me'llon mas".*'

'What does it mean?'

'It means I looked deep into your eyes and I saw our future. That was what happened on the night we first met and that is what is happening now. You are my future, Isla.'

'And you are mine.'

They had a past, they had the future and, Isla knew as Alessi kissed her, they were for ever together now.

* * * * *

Don't miss the next story in the fabulous
MIDWIVES ON-CALL *series*
MEANT-TO-BE FAMILY
By Marion Lennox
Available in April 2015!

MEANT-TO-BE FAMILY

BY
MARION LENNOX

MILLS & BOON

Published in Great Britain 2015
by Mills & Boon, an imprint of Harlequin (UK) Limited,
Eton House, 18-24 Paradise Road, Richmond, Surrey, TW9 1SR

© 2015 Harlequin Books S.A.

Special thanks and acknowledgement are given to Marion Lennox
for her contribution to the *Midwives On-Call* series

ISBN: 978-0-263-24699-5

Printed and bound in Spain
by CPI, Barcelona

Dear Reader,

For me, there's no more powerful emotion than witnessing the miracle of birth. As a kid on a farm, birth never ceased to leave me amazed and awed, and that feeling's stayed with me all my life. So when I was asked to contribute to the *Midwives On-Call* anthology I jumped at the chance.

But my heroine has fertility issues, and as I wrote, these questions drifted through my writing—what makes a parent? What makes love? Five years ago grief drove my hero and heroine apart. How much love does it take to bring them back together?

The midwives of Melbourne Victoria Hospital are a tight-knit team, facing the complexities of birth and love—and sometimes grief and loss—as part of their working day world. Life and death, love and joy—they're what matters. In the Melbourne Maternity Unit we see those emotions every time our midwives walk through the door, so it's only fitting that my lovers can finally find the power to love again.

Families take many forms. I hope you love the crazy, mixed-up bunch of loving that my Oliver and my Emily end up with.

Enjoy!

Marion

Books by Marion Lennox

Mills & Boon® Medical Romance™

A Secret Shared...
Waves of Temptation
Gold Coast Angels: A Doctor's Redemption
Miracle on Kaimotu Island
The Surgeon's Doorstep Baby

Mills & Boon® Cherish™

Christmas Where They Belong
Nine Months to Change His Life
Christmas at the Castle
Sparks Fly with the Billionaire
A Bride for the Maverick Millionaire

**Visit the author profile page
at millsandboon.co.uk for more titles**

With thanks to my fellow authors who've
helped make this *Midwives On-Call* series fabulous.
A special thank-you to Alison Roberts, for her friendship,
her knowledge and her generosity in sharing, and to
Fiona McArthur, whose midwife skills leave me awed.

CHAPTER ONE

LATE. LATE, LATE, LATE. This was the third morning this week. Her boss would have kittens.

Not that Isla was in the mood to be angry, Em thought, as she swiped her pass at the car-park entry. The head midwife for Melbourne's Victoria Hospital had hardly stopped smiling since becoming engaged. She and her fiancé had been wafting around the hospital in a rosy glow that made Em wince.

Marriage. 'Who needs it?' she demanded out loud, as she swung her family wagon through the boom gates and headed for her parking spot on the fifth floor. She should apply for a lower spot—she always seemed to be running late—but her family wagon needed more space than the normal bays. One of the Victoria's obstetricians rode a bike. He was happy to park his Harley to one side of his bay, so this was the perfect arrangement.

Except it was on the fifth floor—and she was late again.

The car in front of her was slow going up the ramp. *Come on...* She should have been on the wards fifteen minutes ago. But Gretta had been sick. Again.

Things were moving too fast. She needed to take the

little girl back to the cardiologist, but the last time she'd taken her, he'd said...

No. Don't go there. *There* was unthinkable. She raked her fingers through her unruly curls, trying for distraction. She'd need to pin her hair up before she got to the ward. Had she remembered pins?

It didn't work. Her mind refused to be distracted, and the cardiologist's warning was still ringing in her ears.

'Emily, I'm sorry, but we're running out of time.'

Was Gretta's heart condition worsening, or was this just a tummy bug? The little girl had hugged her tight as she'd left, and it had been all she could do to leave her. If her mum hadn't been there... But Adrianna adored being a gran. 'Get into work, girl, and leave Gretta to me. Toby and I will watch *Play School* while Gretta has a nap. I'll ring you if she's not better by lunchtime. Meanwhile, go!'

She'd practically shoved her out the door.

But there *was* something wrong—and she knew what it was. The cardiologist had been blunt and she remembered his assessment word for word.

It was all very well, hearing it, she thought bleakly, but seeing it... At the weekend she'd taken both kids to their favourite place in the world, the children's playground at the Botanic Gardens. There was a water rill there that Gretta adored. She'd crawled over it as soon as she could crawl, and then she'd toddled and walked.

Six months ago she'd stood upright on the rill and laughed with delight as the water had splashed over her toes. At the weekend she hadn't even been able to crawl. Em had sat on the rill with her, trying to make her smile, but the little girl had sobbed. She knew what she was losing.

Don't! Don't think about it! Move on. Or she'd move on if she could.

'Come on.' She was inwardly yelling at the car in front. The car turned the corner ponderously then—praise be!—turned into a park on Level Four. Em sighed with relief, zoomed up the last ramp and hauled the steering wheel left, as she'd done hundreds of times in the past to turn into her parking space.

And…um…stopped.

There was a car where Harry's bike should be. A vintage sports car, burgundy, gleaming with care and polish.

Wider than a bike.

Instead of a seamless, silent transition to park, there was the appalling sound of metal on metal.

Her wagon had a bull bar on the front, designed to deflect stray bulls—or other cars during minor bingles. It meant her wagon was as tough as old boots. It'd withstand anything short of a road train.

The thing she'd hit wasn't quite as tough.

She'd ripped the side off the sports car.

Oliver Evans, gynaecologist, obstetrician and in-utero surgeon, was gathering his briefcase and his suit jacket from the passenger seat. He'd be meeting the hospital bigwigs today so he needed to be formal. He was also taking a moment to glance through the notes he had on who he had to meet, who he needed to see.

He vaguely heard the sound of a car behind him. He heard it turning from the ramp…

The next moment the passenger side of his car was practically ripped from the rest.

It was a measure of Em's fiercely practised calm that she didn't scream. She didn't burst into tears. She didn't even swear.

She simply stared straight ahead. Count to ten, she told herself. When that didn't work, she tried twenty.

She figured it out, quite quickly. Her parking spot was supposed to be wider but that was because she shared the two parking bays with Harry the obstetrician's bike and Harry had left. Of course. She'd even dropped in on his farewell party last Friday night, even though it had only been for five minutes because the kids had been waiting.

So Harry had left. This car, then, would belong to the doctor who'd taken his place.

She'd just welcomed him by trashing his car.

'I have insurance. I have insurance. I have insurance.' It was supposed to be her mantra. Saying things three times helped, only it didn't help enough. She put her head on the steering wheel and felt a wash of exhaustion so profound she felt like she was about to melt.

His car was trashed.

He climbed from the driver's seat and stared at his beloved Morgan in disbelief. The Morgan was low slung, gorgeous—and fragile. He'd parked her right in the centre of the bay to avoid the normal perils of parking lots—people opening doors and scratching his paintwork.

But the offending wagon had a bull bar attached and it hadn't just scratched his paintwork. While the wagon looked to be almost unscathed, the passenger-side panels of the Morgan had been sheared off completely.

He loved this baby. He'd bought her five years ago, a post-marriage toy to make him feel better about the world. He'd cherished her, spent a small fortune on her and then put her into very expensive storage while he'd been overseas.

His qualms about returning to Australia had been tempered by his joy on being reunited with Betsy. But now…some idiot with a huge lump of a wagon—and a bull bar…

'What the hell did you think you were doing?' He couldn't see the driver of the wagon yet, but he was venting his spleen on the wagon itself. Of all the ugly, lumbering excuses for a car…

And it was intact. Yeah, it'd have a few extra scratches but there were scratches all over it already. It was a battered, dilapidated brute and the driver'd be able to keep driving like the crash had never happened.

He wanted to kick it. Of all the stupid, careless…

Um…why hadn't the driver moved?

And suddenly medical mode kicked in, overriding rage. Maybe the driver had had a heart attack. A faint. Maybe this was a medical incident rather than sheer stupidity. He took a deep breath, switching roles in an instant. Infuriated driver became doctor. The wagon's driver's door was jammed hard against where his passenger door used to be, so he headed for its passenger side.

The wagon's engine died. Someone was alive in there, then. Good. Or sort of good.

He hauled the door open and he hadn't quite managed the transition. Rage was still paramount.

'You'd better be having a heart attack.' It was impossible to keep the fury from his voice. 'You'd better have a really good excuse as to why you ploughed this heap of scrap metal into my car! You want to get out and explain?'

No!

Things were already appalling—but things just got a whole lot worse.

This was a voice she knew. A voice from her past.

Surely not.

She *had* to be imagining it, she decided, but she wasn't opening her eyes. If it really was…

It couldn't be. She was tired, she was frantically worried about Gretta, she was late and she'd just crashed her car. No wonder she was hearing things.

'You're going to have to open your eyes and face things.' She said it to herself, under her breath. Then she repeated it in her head twice more but her three-times mantra still didn't seem to be working.

The silence outside the car was ominous. Toe-tappingly threatening.

Maybe it'd go away if she just stayed…

'Hey, are you okay?' The gravelly voice, angry at first, was now concerned.

But it was the same voice and this wasn't her imagination. This was horrendously, appallingly real.

Voices could be the same, she told herself, feeling herself veering towards hysteria. There had to be more than one voice in the world that sounded like his.

She'd stay just one moment longer with her eyes closed.

Her passenger door opened and someone slid inside. Large. Male.

Him.

His hand landed on hers on the steering wheel. 'Miss? Are you hurt? Can I help?' And as the anger in his voice gave way to caring she knew, unmistakably, who this was.

Oliver. The man she'd loved with all her heart. The man who'd walked away five years ago to give her the chance of a new life.

So many emotions were slamming through her head… anger, bewilderment, grief… She'd had five years to move on but, crazy or not, this man still felt a part of her.

She'd crashed his car. He was right here.

There was no help for it. She took a deep, deep breath. She braced herself.

She raised her head, and she turned to face her husband.

Emily.

He was seeing her but his mind wasn't taking her in. Emily!

For one wild moment he thought he must be mistaken. This was a different woman, older, a bit…worn round the edges. Weary? Faded jeans and stained windcheater. Unkempt curls.

But still Emily.

His wife? She still was, he thought stupidly. His Em.

But she wasn't his Em. He'd walked away five years ago. He'd left her to her new life, and she had nothing to do with him.

Except she was here. She was staring up at him, her eyes reflecting his disbelief. Horror?

Shock held him rigid.

She'd wrecked his car. He loved this car. He should be feeling...

No. There was no *should*, or if there was he hadn't read that particular handbook.

Should he feel grief? Should he feel guilt?

He felt neither. All he felt was numb.

She'd had a minute's warning. He'd had none.

'Em?' He looked...incredulous. He looked more shocked than she was—bewildered beyond words.

What were you supposed to say to a husband you hadn't seen or spoken to for five years? There was no handbook for this.

'H-hi?' she managed.

'You've just crashed my car,' he said, stupidly.

'You were supposed to be a bike.' Okay, maybe that was just as stupid. This conversation was going exactly nowhere. They'd established, what, that he wasn't a bike?

He was her husband—and he was right beside her. Looking completely dumbfounded.

'You have a milk stain on your shoulder.'

That would be the first thing he'd notice, she thought. Her uniform was in her bag. She never put it on at home—her chances of getting out of the house clean were about zero—so she was still wearing jeans and the baggy windcheater she'd worn at breakfast.

Gretta had had a milky drink before being ill. Em had picked her up and cuddled her before she'd left.

Strangely, the stain left her feeling exposed. She didn't want this man to see...her.

'There are child seats in your wagon.'

He still sounded incredulous. Milk stains? Family

wagon? He'd be seeing a very different woman from the one he'd seen five years ago.

But he looked…just the same. Same tall, lean, gorgeous. Same deep brown eyes that crinkled at the edges when he smiled, and Oliver smiled a lot. Same wide mouth and strong bone structure. Same dark, wavy hair, close cropped to try and get rid of the curl, only that never worked. It was so thick. She remembered running her fingers through that hair…

Um, no. Not appropriate. Regardless of formalities, this was her husband. Or ex-husband? They hadn't bothered with divorce yet but she'd moved on.

She'd just crashed his car.

'You're using Harry's car park,' she said, pointing accusingly at…um…one slightly bent sports car. It was beautiful—at least some of it still was. An open sports car. Vintage. It wasn't the sort of car that you might be able to pop down to the car parts place in your lunch hour and buy a new panel.

He'd always loved cars. She remembered the day they'd sold his last sports car.

His last? No. Who knew how many cars he'd been through since? Anyway, she remembered the day they'd sold the sleek little roadster both of them had loved, trading it in for a family wagon. Smaller than this but just as sensible. They'd gone straight from the car showroom to the nursery suppliers, and had had the baby seat fitted there and then.

She'd been six months pregnant. They'd driven home with identical smug looks on their faces.

He'd wanted a family as much as she had. Or she'd thought he did. What had happened then had proved she hadn't known him at all.

'I've been allocated this car park,' he was saying, and she had to force herself back to here, to now. 'Level Five, Bay Eleven. That's mine.'

'You're visiting?'

'I'm employed here, as of today.'

'You can't be.'

He didn't reply. He climbed out of the wagon, dug his hands deep in his pockets, glanced back at his wreck of a car and looked at her again.

'Why can't I, Em?' The wreck of the car faded to secondary importance. This was suddenly all about them.

'Because I work here.'

'It's the most specialised neonatal service in Melbourne. You know that's what I do.'

'You went to the States.' She felt numb. Stupid. Out of control. She'd been sure her ex-husband had been on the other side of world. She didn't want him to be here.

'I did specialist training in in-utero surgery in the States.' This was a dumb conversation. He was out of the car, leaning back on one of the concrete columns, watching her as she clung to the steering wheel like she was drowning. 'I've accepted a job back here. And before you say anything, no, I didn't know you were working here. I thought you were still at Hemmingway Private. I knew when I came back that there was a chance we might meet, but Melbourne's a big place. I'm not stalking you.'

'I never meant…'

'No?'

'No,' she managed. 'And I'm sorry I crashed into your car.'

Finally things were starting to return to normal. Like her heart rate. Her pulse had gone through the roof when the cars had hit. She'd been subconsciously trying to get it down, practising the deep-breathing techniques she used when she was pacing the floor with Gretta, frightened for herself, frightened for the future. The techniques came to her aid instinctively now when she was frightened. Or discombobulated.

Discombobulated was how she felt, she conceded. Stalking? That sounded as if he thought she might be frightened of him, and she'd never been frightened of Oliver.

'Can we exchange details?' she managed, trying desperately to sound normal. Like this was a chance meeting of old acquaintances, but they needed to talk about car insurance. 'Oliver, it's really nice to see you again…' Was it? Um, no, but it sounded the right thing to say. 'But I'm late as it is.'

'Which was why you crashed.'

'Okay, it was my fault,' she snapped. 'But, believe it or not, there are extenuating circumstances. That's not your business.' She clambered out of the car and dug for her licence in her shabby holdall. She pulled out two disposable diapers and a packet of baby wipes before she found her purse, and she was so flustered she dropped them. Oliver gathered them without a word, and handed them back. She flushed and handed him her licence instead.

He took it wordlessly, and studied it.

'You still call yourself Emily Evans?'

'You know we haven't divorced. That's irrelevant. You're supposed to take down my address.'

'You're living at your mother's house?'

'I am.' She grabbed her licence back. 'Finished?'

'Aren't you supposed to take mine?'

'You can sue me. I can't sue you. We both know the fault was mine. If you're working here then I'll send you my insurance details via interdepartmental memo. I don't carry them with me.'

'You seem to carry everything else.' Once more he was looking into the car, taking in the jumble of kids' paraphernalia that filled it.

'I do, don't I?' she said, as cordially as she could manage. 'Oliver, it's good to see you again. I'm sorry I wrecked your car but I'm running really, really late.'

'You never run late.' He was right: punctuality used to be her god.

'I'm not the Emily you used to know,' she managed. 'I'm a whole lot different but this isn't the time or the place to discuss it.' She looked again at his car and winced. She really had made an appalling mess. 'You want me to organise some sort of tow?'

'Your car's hardly dented. I'll handle mine.'

'I'm…sorry.' She took a deep breath. 'Oliver, I really am sorry but I really do need to go. If there's nothing I can do…'

He was peering into her wagon. 'I doubt your lock's still working,' he told her. 'Once my car's towed free…'

'Locks are the least of my worries.' She slung her bag over her shoulder, knowing she had to move. She knew Isla was short-staffed this morning and the night staff would be aching to leave. 'Look at the stains,' she told him. 'No villain in their right mind would steal my wagon and, right now, I don't have time to care. I'm sorry to leave you with this mess, Oliver, but I need to go. Welcome to Victoria Hospital. See you around.'

CHAPTER TWO

RUBY DOWELL WAS seventeen years old, twenty-two weeks pregnant and terrified. She was Oliver's first patient at the Victoria.

She was also the reason he'd started so soon. He'd been recruited to replace Harry Eichmann, an obstetrician with an interest in in-utero procedures. Oliver had started the same way, but for him in-utero surgery was more than a side interest. For the last five years he'd been based in the States but he'd travelled the world learning the latest techniques.

The phone call he'd had from Charles Delamere, Victoria's CEO, had been persuasive, to say the least. 'Harry's following a girlfriend to Europe. There's no one here with your expertise and there's more and more demand.

'It's time you came home. Oliver, right now we have a kid here with a twenty-one-week foetus, and her scans are showing spina bifida. Heinz Zigler, our paediatric neurologist, says the operation has to be done now. He can do the spinal stuff but he doesn't have the skills to stop the foetus aborting. Oliver, there are more and more of these cases, and we're offering you a full-time job. If you get here fast, we might save this kid shunts, possible brain damage, a life with limited movement below the waist. Short term, I want you to fight to give this kid a happy ending. Long term we're happy to fund your research. We'll cover the costs of whatever extra training you want, any staff you need. We want the best, Oliver, and we're prepared to pay, but we want you now.'

The offer had been great, but he'd had serious reservations about returning to Melbourne. He'd walked away from his marriage five years ago, and he'd thought he'd stay away. Em had deserved a new life, a chance to start again with someone who'd give her what she needed.

And it seemed his decision had been justified. Seeing her this morning, driving a family wagon, with milk stains on her shoulder, with every sign of being a frazzled young working mum, he'd thought…

Actually, he hadn't thought. The sight had knocked him sideways and he was still knocked sideways. But he needed to focus on something other than his marriage. After a brief introduction with Charles, he was in the examination room with Ruby Dowell. Teenage mother, pregnant with a baby with spina bifida.

'At twenty-two weeks we need to get on with this fast,' Charles had told him. 'There's such a short window for meaningful intervention.'

Ruby was lying on the examination couch in a cubicle in the antenatal clinic and, as with all his patients, he took a moment at the start to assess the whole package. Her notes said she was seventeen. She'd been attending clinics in the Victoria's Teenage Mums-To-Be programme. When the spina bifida had been detected on the scans she'd been offered termination but had declined, although the notes said she intended to give the baby up for adoption after birth. Right now she was dressed in shorts and an oversized T-shirt. Her mouse-blonde, shoulder-length hair was in need of a wash and a good cut. Apart from the bump of her pregnancy she was waif thin, and her eyes were red-rimmed and wide with fear.

She looked like a wild creature trapped in a cage, he thought. Hell, why was she alone? Her notes said she was a single mum, but she should have her mother with her, or a sister, or at least a friend.

It was unthinkable that such a kid was alone. Charles had said that Isla, his daughter and also the Victoria's head midwife, was in charge of the Teenage Mums-To-Be programme. Why hadn't she organised to be here, or at least sent a midwife in her place?

But now wasn't the time to head to the nurses' station and blast the powers that be for leaving her like this. Now was the time for reassurance.

'Hey,' he said, walking into the cubicle but deliberately leaving the screens open. He didn't need to do a physical examination yet, and he didn't want that trapped look to stay a moment longer. 'I'm the baby surgeon, Oliver Evans. I'm an obstetrician who's specially trained in operating on babies when they're still needing to stay inside their mums. And you're Ruby Dowell?'

He hauled a chair up to the bedside and summoned his best reassuring manner. 'Ruby, I'm here to get to know you, that's all. Nothing's happening right now. I'm just here to talk.'

But the terrified look stayed. She actually cringed back on the bed, fear radiating off her in waves. 'I'm… I'm scared of operations,' she stuttered. 'I don't want to be here.'

But then the screen was pulled back still further. A woman in nursing uniform, baggy tunic over loose pants, was fastening the screen so Ruby could see the nurses' station at the end of the corridor.

Emily. His wife.

His ex-wife? She'd never asked for a divorce but it had been simply a matter of signing the papers, any time these last five years.

'I'm scared of operations, too,' Em said, matter-of-factly, as if she'd been involved in the conversation from the start. 'I think everyone is. But Dr Evans here is the best baby surgeon in the known universe, I promise. I've known him for ever. If it was my baby there'd be no one else I'd want. Dr Evans is great, Ruby. He's kind, he's skilled and he'll give your baby the best chance of survival she can possibly have.'

'But I told you…I don't want her.' Ruby was sobbing now, swiping away tears with the back of her hand. 'My mum said I should have had an abortion. She would have paid. I don't know why I didn't. And now you're operating on a baby I don't even want. I just want you all to go away.'

In-utero surgery was fraught at the best of times. It was full of potential dangers for both mother and baby. To operate on a mother who didn't want her baby to survive…

He didn't know where to start—but he didn't need to, because Em simply walked forward, tugged the girl into her arms and held her.

Ruby stiffened. She held herself rigid, but Em's fingers stroked her hair.

'Hey, it's okay, Ruby. We all know how hard this is. Pregnancy's the pits. You feel so on your own, and you're especially on your own. You decided not to go ahead with an abortion, going against what your family wanted you to do. That took courage, but there's only so much courage a girl can be expected to show. That's why Isla's been helping you and it's why I'm here now. I'm *your* midwife, Ruby. I'll be with you every step of the way. All the decisions will be yours but I'm right with you. Right now, if you want Dr Evans to go away and come back later, he will. Just say the word.'

She met Oliver's gaze over Ruby's shoulder and her message was unmistakable. Back me up.

So Em was this girl's midwife? Then where the hell had she been when he'd walked in?

Coping with her crashed car, that's where, and then changing out of her mum clothes into nursing gear. Still, surely she could have made it earlier.

'We've had a drama with a prem birth I had to help with,' she said, as if he'd voiced his question out loud. She was still holding, still hugging, as Ruby's sobs went on. 'That's why I'm late, Ruby, and I'm sorry. I wanted to be here when you arrived. But I'm here now, and if you decide to proceed with this operation then you're my number one priority. Do you need some tissues? Dr Evans, hand me some tissues.'

'You helped with an earlier birth?' he asked, before he could help himself, and she had the temerity to glare at him.

'Yep. I had to step in and help the moment I hit the wards. Plus I crashed my car this morning. I crashed my wagon, Ruby, and guess whose gorgeous car I drove into? None other than Dr Evans. It's his first day on the job and I hit him. It's a wonder he hasn't tossed me out of the room already.'

And Ruby's sobs hiccupped to a halt. She pulled back and looked at Em, then turned and stared at Oliver.

'She hit your car?'

'Yes,' he said. He wouldn't normally impart personal information to a patient but he guessed what Em was doing, and he could only agree. What Ruby needed was space to settle. He could help with that—even though he had to get personal to give it to her.

'I have a sixty-four Morgan Plus-4 sports car,' he said, mournfully, like the end of the world was nigh, which was about how he'd felt when he'd seen the damage— before he'd realised the driver of the other car had been Em. 'It's two-tone burgundy with black interior, a gorgeous two-seater. It's fitted with super sports upgrades, including twin Weber carbs, a Derrington header and a bonnet scoop. It also has chrome wire wheels, a badge bar with twin Lucas fog lamps and a tonneau cover. Oh, and it's retrofitted with overdrive transmission. Now it's also fitted with one smashed side—courtesy of your midwife.'

'Yikes,' Em said, but she didn't sound in the least subdued. 'Twin Weber carbs and a Derrington header, hey? Did I damage all that?'

'And if you knew how long it took to get those fog lamps…'

'Whoops. Sorry. But you scratched my car, too.' But Em was talking at Ruby rather than at him and she still sounded cheerful. Chirpy even.

'Scratched…' he muttered, and she grinned.

'That's okay. I forgive you. And they're cars. They're just things. That's what insurance is for. Whereas babies aren't things at all,' Em continued, leading seamlessly back to the reason they were all there. 'Ruby, your little girl is a person, not a thing, and she's far, far more precious. You made the decision to go ahead with this pregnancy. You made the decision early not to choose abortion and you chose it again when the scan showed spina bifida. But you've been telling me you think you might have her adopted when she's born...'

'I can't...deal with it.'

'You don't have to deal with it,' Em said soundly. 'There are lots of parents out there who'll give their eye teeth to have a baby like yours to love. That's right, isn't it, Dr Evans?'

'I... Yes.' But her words were like a punch in the gut. That last night... He'd tried to make her see one last time. *Em, I can't. I know adoption's the only way, but I can't do it. I can't guarantee to love a child who's not our own.*

'It will be our own.'

'Em, no.'

It had been their last conversation. He'd turned and walked away from the only woman he'd ever loved and it had nearly killed him. But she'd deserved the family she'd wanted so much. He'd had to give her that chance, and from the evidence he'd seen today, she'd taken it.

But now wasn't about him. It was all about Ruby. The kid's terror had been put aside. He had to take advantage of it.

Which meant putting thoughts of Em aside. Putting aside the knowledge that his wife, his ex-wife, presumably—did you need to formally sign papers to accept a marriage was over?—was in the same room.

'Ruby, you created this little girl,' he said, as Em continued to hold her. 'You can have her adopted at birth, but until then you need to look after her. And the staff here have already explained to you—to look after her means an operation now.'

'But why?' Ruby demanded, suddenly belligerent. 'I

don't understand. The kid's got spina bifida—Dr Zigler showed me on the scans. What difference does it make whether you operate now or operate when it's born?'

There was fear behind the question. Oliver recognised it. He'd done many in-utero procedures by now, and sometimes one of the hardest things was having the mum understand that the tiny child inside her was an independent being already. Something totally separate from her. This was a child who could be shifted in her uterus, who even at twenty-two weeks could cope with complex surgery and then be resettled, because, no matter how amazing the technology, the womb was still the safest place for her to be.

'Ruby, you know your baby has spina bifida,' he said now, gently. Em still had her arm around the girl. He was talking to them both, as he'd normally talk to a woman and her partner, or a woman and her mum or support person. Em had slid naturally into that role. A good midwife sometimes had to, he thought, and Em had always been brilliant at her job. Efficient, kind, skilled and empathic. He'd worked with her once and he'd loved it.

It was totally disconcerting to be working with her again, but he needed to focus on Ruby.

'You know we've picked up the spina bifida on the ultrasound,' Oliver said matter-of-factly, trying to take the emotion out of the situation. 'You've seen it?'

'It just looked blurry. I couldn't figure it out.'

So she didn't understand. 'Heinz Zigler's a great paediatric neurologist,' Charles had told him. 'He's technically brilliant, but communication's not his strong suit. He'll do the spinal surgery but everything else—including explanations to the mum—we're leaving to you.'

So now he needed to explain from the ground up.

'The scans do look blurry,' he admitted. 'I have trouble reading them myself. Fine detail like the nerve exposure around vertebrae needs incredibly specialised knowledge to see, but the radiologists here are superb. They've double-checked each other's work, and Dr Zigler agrees. Everyone's sure. But would you like me to explain what I think is happening? I don't talk in fine detail, Ruby. I just see the overview. That's actually what I do, total patient care, looking after you as well as your baby. I'm an obstetrician and a surgeon who specialises in looking after mums and bubs if bub needs an operation before it's time for her to be born.'

Silence. Ruby cast him a scared look and subsided. He waited, while Ruby pulled herself together a bit more, while Em handed her a wad of tissues, while both women readied themselves to front what was coming.

'Heinz says he told you the fine detail,' he said at last, when he thought Ruby was as ready as she was going to be. 'But here's the broad outline. The bones of your baby's spine—the vertebrae—haven't formed properly to protect your baby's spinal cord. The spinal cord holds the nerves that control your baby's movements. Because those nerves run right through the body, if the cord gets damaged then long term, your baby might not be able to walk. She might not have control of her bladder and bowel. If she has a severe problem she can also end up with a build-up of fluid in her brain. Then she'll need a shunt, all her life, to drain the excess fluid and relieve pressure.'

Ruby was crying again now, but not sobbing. Em's arm was around her, holding her close, but Ruby's attention was held. Her distress was taking second place to her need to know, and she seemed to be taking it in.

'So,' she whispered. 'So?'

'So the good thing is,' he said, still gently, 'that many problems of spina bifida aren't directly caused by the spina bifida itself. Doctors cleverer than me, like Heinz—did you know he's top in his field in research?— have worked out that the exposure of the spinal cord to the normal fluid in your womb, the amniotic fluid, is what progressively destroys the exposed nerves during pregnancy. If we can operate now, really early, and cover the exposed cord, then we prevent much of the damage. Your baby's much more likely to be able to live a normal, happy life.'

'But not with me,' Ruby whispered.

That was another issue altogether. Adoption. This was a single mum, a teenager, facing a life apart from the baby she was carrying.

'You haven't decided definitely on adoption,' Em murmured, and the girl shook her head.

'I can't think…'

'And you don't need to think.' Em's hold on her tightened. 'There's too much happening now for you to think past what you need to face right now. But, Ruby, regardless of what you decide to do when your baby's born, regardless of whether you decide you can care for her yourself or if you want to give her to parents who need a baby to love, she'll still be your daughter. You have the choice now to make a huge difference in your daughter's life.'

'You're…sure she has to have this operation?' Ruby whispered. 'I mean…really sure?'

'We're sure,' Oliver told her, suddenly immensely grateful for Em's presence. Without Em he doubted whether he'd have been able to get past the fear. 'But the operation's not without risks.' He had to say that. There was no way he could let this kid agree to surgery without warning her. 'Ruby, there are risks to you and risks to your baby. I believe those risks are small but they're still there.'

'But…I will make a difference.'

'Heinz tells me that because the spinal cord exposure is relatively high and very obvious on the ultrasound, then if we leave the operation undone, your daughter will probably spend her life in a wheelchair,' he said bluntly. 'And with the amount of exposure…there will be fluid build-up in the brain. She'll need a shunt and there may even be brain damage.'

'That's why Dr Evans has arrived here so fast,' Em went on smoothly. 'We haven't had a specialist in-utero surgeon on staff, but when we saw your ultrasound Dr Zigler knew we had to get the best obstetrician here as fast as we could. That's who Dr Evans is. The best. So now it's up to you, Ruby, love. Will you let us operate on your baby?'

'Heinz and I can close the gap over the cord,' Oliver told her. 'There's probably already a little damage done, but it's so early that damage should be minimal. What we'll do is put you to sleep, cut the smallest incision in your tummy as possible—you'll be left with a scar but I'm very neat.' He grinned at the girl, knowing a bit of pseudo modesty often worked, and he got a shaky smile in return. 'Then we'll gently turn your baby over where she's lying—with luck we won't have to take her out. Once her back is exposed Heinz will check everything, tweak things to where they should be, then we'll close the gap over her spinal cord. We'll settle her back down again and tuck her in, stitch you up and leave you both to get on with your pregnancy. You'll need to stay in hospital for about a week, maybe a bit longer, until we're sure we haven't pressured bub into coming early, but then everything should proceed as normal.'

'And she won't have to be in a wheelchair?'

'Ruby, we can't make any promises.' He caught her hand and held it. Em was still hugging her, and Oliver thought, not for the first time, Em was a wonderful midwife. She knew when to intervene and she knew when to shut up. She also exuded a quiet calm that was a tranquilliser all by itself.

He'd met her ten years ago. He'd been a barely qualified doctor, she'd been a student nurse, but already the confidence she'd engendered in the patients he'd worked with had been impressive. He'd seen her with some terrified teenage mums.

There was no nurse he'd rather have by his side and by the time they'd dated twice he'd known there was no woman he'd rather have with him for ever. Their attraction had been instant, their marriage inevitable.

It was only babies…or lack of babies…that had driven them apart.

The night their son had been stillborn had been the worst night of his life. He'd watched Em's face contort with an anguish so deep it had seemed endless, and there had been nothing he could do to stop it. He'd been unable to help her. He'd been unable to reach her.

But it was hardly the time to be thinking of that now. It was hardly the time to be thinking of it ever. After five years, they'd moved on.

'I can't make any promises,' he repeated, hauling himself back to the here and now, to the needs of the teenage kid in front of him. 'The procedure Heinz and I are trained to perform usually has an excellent outcome but there are exceptions. I won't hide that from you, Ruby. There are risks. There's a chance of infection, for you as well as your baby. We'll take every care in the world…'

'But no guarantees.'

'No guarantees,' he agreed. 'So it's up to you. This is your daughter, Ruby. It's up to you to make the choice.'

'I'm too young to have a daughter.' It was a wail and Em's arm tightened around her.

'That's where I come in,' she said solidly, a blanket of comfort and reassurance. 'You want advice, I'm full of advice. You want a hug, that's what I'm here for, too.'

'You can't be here with me all the time.'

'I can't,' Em agreed. 'I have my own son and daughter to look after. But I'm here every day during the week, and if I'm needed, I can come in at other times. My mum lives with me so I can usually drop everything and come. I don't do that for all my mums, but I'll try for you.'

'Why?' Ruby demanded, suspicious.

'Because you're special,' she said soundly. 'Isn't that right, Dr Evans? You're one special woman, and you're about to have one special daughter.'

But Oliver was hardly listening. Somehow he managed to make a grunt of acquiescence but his mind felt like it was exploding.

I have my own son and daughter to look after.

Somehow…a part of his brain had hoped—assumed?—that she'd stayed…as Em. The Em he'd left five years ago.

She hadn't. She'd moved on. She was a different woman.

I have my own son and daughter to look after…

'What do you think, Ruby?' Em was saying gently.

'Do you want to go ahead with the operation? Do you want time to think about it?'

'I don't have a choice,' Ruby whispered. 'My baby… It's the best thing…'

It was. Oliver watched Ruby's hand drop to cover the faint bulge of her tummy, the instinctive gesture of protection that was as old as time itself.

And the gesture brought back the wedge that had been driven so deep within his marriage that it had finished it. Em had wanted to adopt, and he'd known he couldn't love like parents were supposed to love. He was right, he thought bleakly. He'd always been right. What was between Ruby and her baby was what her baby needed. Ruby was this baby's mum. Adoption was great if there was no choice, but how could an adoptive parent ever love a child as much as this?

He knew he couldn't and that knowledge had torn his marriage apart.

But Em was watching him now, with those eyes he'd once thought he could drown in. He'd loved her so much, and yet he'd walked away.

And she'd walked, as well.

I have my own son and daughter to look after.

It was nothing to do with him. He'd made his choice five years ago, and Em had obviously made choices, too.

He needed to know what those choices had been.

But now wasn't the time or the place to ask. All he could do was turn his attention back to Ruby, reassure her as much as possible and then set about working out times and details of the forthcoming surgery.

As they finished, a woman who introduced herself as one of the hospital social workers arrived. It seemed Ruby needed help with housing—as well as everything else, she'd been kicked out of her parents' house. She was staying in a boarding house near the hospital but she wouldn't be able to stay there when the baby was born.

There'd be more talk of adoption. More talk of options.

Ruby's surgery was scheduled for the day after tomorrow, but for now he was redundant. He was free to head to the next mum Charles had asked him to see.

He left, but his head was spinning.

Em was still sitting on the bed, still hugging Ruby. *I have my own son and daughter to look after.*

Whatever she'd done, it had been her choice. He'd walked away so she'd have that choice.

Why did it hurt so much that she'd taken it?

CHAPTER THREE

EM GOT ON with her day, too.

One of the wonderful things about being a midwife was that it took all her care, all her attention. She had little head-space for anything else. What was the saying? Find a job you love and you'll never have to work again? She'd felt that the first time she'd helped deliver a baby and she'd never looked back.

She sometimes…okay, she often…felt guilty about working when her mum was home with the kids, but the decision to foster had been a shared one. Her mum loved Gretta and Toby as much as she did. They had the big old house, but they needed Em's salary to keep them going.

Sometimes when Em got home her mother was more tired than she was, but whenever she protested she was cut off at the pass.

'So which baby are we giving back? Don't be ridiculous, Em. We can do this.'

They could, and knowing the kids were at home, waiting…it felt great, Em thought as she hauled off her uniform at the end of her shift and tugged on her civvies. Right, supermarket, pharmacy—Gretta's medications were running low—then home. She'd rung her mum at lunchtime and Adrianna had been reassuring.

'She's looking much better.' But, still, there was no way she was risking running out of Gretta's drugs.

'Big day?' Sophia Toulson, one of the more recent arrivals to the Victoria's midwifery staff, was hauling her uniform off, too, but instead of pulling on sensible clothes like Em's—yikes, where had that milk stain come from?—she was putting on clothes that said she was heading out clubbing or to a bar—to a life Em had left behind years ago.

Not that she missed it—much. Though there were times...

'It has been a big day,' she agreed, thinking of the night to come. Em had had three sleepless nights in a row. Gretta needed to be checked all the time. What she'd give for a solid eight-hour sleep...

'But have you met the new obstetrician? You must have—he's been fast-tracked here to operate on your Ruby. Em, he's gorgeous. No wedding ring, either. Not that that tells you anything with surgeons—they hardly ever wear them. It's not fair. Just because rings can hold infection it gives them carte blanche to disguise their marital state. But he's come from the States and fast, so that hints at single status. Em, you'll be working with him. How about giving it a shot?'

Yeah, right. Propositioning Oliver? If Sophia only knew... But somehow she managed to grimace as if this conversation were completely normal, an anonymous, gorgeous obstetrician arriving in the midst of midwives whose first love was their job, and whose second love was dissecting the love lives of those around them.

She turned to face the full-length mirror at the end of the change room. What she saw there made her grimace. Faded jeans, with a rip at the knee. Trainers with odd shoelaces. A windcheater with a milk stain running down the shoulder—why hadn't she noticed that before she'd left the house?

Her hair needed a cut. Oliver had loved her hair. She'd had it longer then and the dull brown had been shiny. It had bounced—she'd spent time with decent shampoo and conditioner, and she'd used a curling wand to give it body.

Now she bought her shampoo and conditioner in bulk at the discount store and her curling wand was rusting under the sink.

Oliver had never seen her like this—until today.

Sophia was suggesting she make a play for him?

'Can you see Oliver Evans with someone like me?' she asked incredulously. 'Sophia, get real.'

'You could try,' Sophia said, coming up behind her friend and staring over her shoulder at the reflection. 'Em, you're really pretty. With a bit of effort...'

'All my effort goes into the kids.'

'You're burying yourself.'

'I'm giving them a chance.' She glanced at her watch and grimaced again. 'Ouch. I need to go. Have a great time tonight.'

'I wish I could say the same for you. Home with your mum and two kids...' She bit her lip and Em knew why. Sophia had the same problem she did—she'd barely worked with her for a month before she'd winkled out of her the reason for the gravity behind what somehow seemed a forced gaiety.

Did all women who couldn't have children feel like this? Maybe they did, but Em's solution horrified Sophia.

'I love it,' she said soundly, even defiantly, because she did. Of course she did. 'And you have fun at... Where are you going?'

'The Rooftop Bar. Madeleine just happened to mention to your Dr Evans that we might be there.' She grinned and started searching her bag for her lipstick. 'If you're not interested…'

'He's all yours,' Em said tightly. 'Best of luck. The supermarket's waiting for me. Whoo-hoo, a fabulous night for both of us.'

'Right,' Sophia said dryly. 'Em, I wish…'

'Well, don't wish,' Em said, more sharply than she'd intended. 'Don't even think about it. This is the life I chose for myself, and I'm happy. Dr Oliver Evans might be at the bar and I guess that's the life he's chosen, too. We're all where we want to be, and we can't ask for more than that.'

Oliver's day wasn't supposed to be frantic. Weren't new staff supposed to have an orientation day, a shift where they spent the time acquainting themselves with ward and theatre staff, meeting everyone in the canteen, arranging stuff in their office? Not so much. Harry, it seemed, had left in a hurry. His lady had been enticing; he'd left without giving proper notice and the work had backed up.

Apart from that, Harry hadn't had specialist in-utero surgical training. It seemed that word of Oliver's arrival had flown around Melbourne before he arrived. He had three consultations lined up for the afternoon and more for the next day.

Ruby's case was probably the most complex. No, it *was* the most complex, he thought, mostly because the scans showing the extent of the problem had made him wince.

Plus she was alone. His next mum, Lucy, arrived with

a support cast, husband, parents, an entourage of six. Her baby had a congenital heart malfunction. The little boy in utero was a twenty-four-weeker. He needed an aortic valvuloplasty—opening the aortic foetal heart valves to allow blood flow. It was one of the most common reasons for in-utero surgery, the one that Oliver was most comfortable with—as long as he had the backup of decent cardiac surgeons.

Oliver had already met Tristan Hamilton, the Victoria's neonatal cardiothoracic surgeon—in fact, they'd gone to university together. Tristan had backed up Charles's calls, pressuring him to come, and he had been one of the inducements. Tristan was incredibly skilled, and if he could work side by side with him, for this mum, things were likely to be fine.

But what seemed wrong was that Lucy and her little boy had huge family backup—and Ruby had no one.

But Ruby had Em.

That had to be compensation. Em would be terrific.

If indeed she was with her. She'd been running late that morning. She'd looked harassed, like she had one too many balls in the air.

She'd come flying into Ruby's room half an hour after she'd hit his car, burbling about an early delivery. Really? Or had she spent the half hour on the phone to her insurance people?

It was none of his business.

Still, it was a niggle…

Isla Delamere was the Victoria's head midwife—plus she was the daughter of the CEO. Apparently she'd also just become engaged to the hospital's neonatal intensive care specialist. Isla was not a person to mess with, he'd decided. He'd been introduced to her by Charles, and as he was about to leave he saw her again.

'You have how many in-utero procedures lined up for me?' he said, half joking. 'You guys believe in throwing me in at the deep end.'

'You just do the surgery,' she said, smiling. 'My mid-wives will keep everything running smoothly. I have the best team…'

'My midwife this morning was running late.' He shouldn't have said it. He knew it the moment he'd opened his mouth. The last thing he wanted was to get Em into trouble and this woman had power at her finger-tips, but Isla didn't seem bothered.

'I'm sorry about that. We had three births within fifteen minutes of each other just as Em came on duty. I know her care of Ruby's a priority, but one of the births was prem, the mum was out of her tree, and there's no one better at calming a frantic mum than Em. I only used her for the final fifteen minutes but it made a difference. You did cope by yourself until then?'

She raised her beautifully formed eyebrows quizzically… head midwife wondering if surgeon could cope without a little assistance…

Right. He'd got his answer but now Isla thought he was a wimp. Great start.

'Some of the staff are going to the Rooftop Bar after work,' Isla told him. 'Have you been invited? You're welcome to join us.'

'Thanks but I have a problem to sort.'

'Your car?' She was still smiling and, he thought, that was just the sort of thing that hospital staff the world over enjoyed. Specialist's car being trashed, especially since most staff here could never afford to run a car like Betsy.

He loved that car and now she was a mess. But…

'Em's promised to sort it,' Isla told him. 'She's not the sort of woman to let her insurance lapse.'

'It's not the insurance…'

'And she's really sorry. She was stricken when she first came in this morning. She's been so busy all day I suspect she hadn't had time to apologise but—'

'Will she be at the bar now?'

'Em? Heavens, no. She has two kids waiting for her at home.'

'Two?'

'Gretta's four and Toby's two. They're special kids but, wow, they're demanding.'

'I guess…' And then he asked because he couldn't help himself. Had a miracle happened? *Gretta's four…* She must have moved like the wind. 'Her partner…' He knew there couldn't have been a marriage because there'd never been a divorce but…there must be someone. 'Is he a medic? Does she have help?'

But Isla's eyebrows hit her hairline. Her face closed, midwife protecting her own. 'I guess that's for you to ask Em if it's important for you to know,' she said shortly, clearing her desk, making signals she was out of there. Off to the Rooftop Bar to join her colleagues? 'She doesn't talk about her private life. Is there anything else you need?'

More information, he thought, and he'd bet Isla knew everything he wanted to know. But he couldn't push without opening a can of worms. Evans was a common name. Em had clearly not told anyone there was a connection.

Better to leave it that way, maybe.

'Thanks, no.'

'Goodnight, then. And good luck with the car. You might let Em know when you have it sorted. She's beating herself up over it. She's a great midwife and I don't like my midwives stressed. I'd appreciate it if you could fix it.'

'I'll try,' he said, but it was too late. Isla had gone.

He headed down to the car park. He hadn't been back to assess the damage during the day—he hadn't had time.

The park next to his was empty. Em was gone.

Her wagon had still been drivable. Her doors had been bent, but the wheels were still okay, whereas his... One of the wheels was far from okay and he wasn't driving anywhere. He stooped and examined it and thought of the hassle it had been to find the right parts for his little beauty. Where was he going to find another wheel rim? And the panels were a mess.

Strangely, it didn't upset him as much as he'd thought it might. He checked the damage elsewhere and knew he'd have to get her towed—actually, carried, as there was no way she could be towed like this. And then he'd go searching for the parts he needed.

He kind of liked searching the internet for car parts. It was something to do at three in the morning when he couldn't sleep.

Which was often.

He rounded the front of the car and there he saw a note in his windshield. Em?

Oliver, I really am sorry about this. I've put my hand up, it was all my fault, and I've told my insurance company to pay without arguing. I photocopied my driver's licence and my insurance company details—they're attached. One of the girls

on the ward knows of a great repair place that spe-
cialises in vintage cars—the details are here, too.
See you when you next see Ruby.
Em

It was all about the car. There was nothing personal
at all.

Well, what did he expect? A *mea culpa* with extras?
This was more than generous, admitting total culpabil-
ity. Her insurance company would hate her. As well as
that, she'd probably have to pay the first few hundred
dollars, plus she'd lose her no-claim bonus.

He could afford it. Could she?

He re-read the note. What was he hoping for? Personal details?

Her driver's licence told him all he was going to get.
Emily Louise Evans. She was still using his name, then.
So…single mother? How? Had she gone ahead and adopted by herself? He checked again, making sure he was
right—she was living at her mother's address.

He liked Adrianna. Or he had liked her. He hadn't
seen his mother-in-law for years.

He could drop in…

Why?

'Because she shouldn't accept full responsibility,' he
said out loud. 'If she's supporting kids…'

She'd said she'd already phoned her insurance company and confessed, but maybe he could reverse it.
Maybe he could take some of the load.

The independent Em of five years ago would tell him
to shove it.

Yeah? He thought back to the Em of five years ago,

shattered, gutted, looking towards the future with a bleakness that broke his heart.

'If you won't do it with me then I'll do it alone. If you think I can go back to the life we led... I'm over night-clubs, Oliver. I'm over living just for me.'

'Isn't there an us in there?'

'I thought there was, but I thought we wanted a family. I hadn't realised it came with conditions.'

'Em, I can't.'

'So you're leaving?'

'You're not giving me any choice.'

'I guess I'm not. I'm sorry, Oliver.'

Five years...

Okay, their marriage was long over but somehow she still seemed...partly his responsibility. And the cost of this repair would make her insurance company's eyes water.

It behoved him...

'Just to see,' he told himself. He'd thought he'd drop in to visit Adrianna when he'd come to Melbourne anyway, to see how she was.

And talk to Adrianna about Em?

Yeah, but he was over it. He'd had a couple of relationships in the last five years, even if they had been fleeting. He'd moved on.

'So let's be practical,' he told himself, and hit his phone and organised a tow truck, and a hire car, and half an hour later he was on the freeway, heading to the suburb where his ex-mother-in-law lived. With his wife and her two children, and her new life without him.

'You hit who?'

'Oliver.' Em was feeding Toby, which was a messy joy. Toby was two years old and loved his dinner. Adrianna had made his favourite animal noodles in a tomato sauce. Toby was torn between inspecting every animal on his spoon and hoovering in the next three spoonfuls as if there was no tomorrow.

Adrianna was sitting by the big old fire stove, cuddling Gretta. The little girl's breathing was very laboured.

Soon...

No. It hurt like hot knives to have to think about it. Much better to concentrate on distractions, and Oliver was surely a distraction.

'He's working at the Victoria?'

'Yep. Starting today.'

'Oh, Em... Can you stay there?'

'I can't walk away. We need the money. Besides, it's the best midwifery job in Melbourne. I love working with Isla and her team.'

'So tell him to leave. You were there first.'

'I don't think you can tell a man like Oliver Evans to leave. Besides, the hospital needs him. I read his CV on the internet during lunch break. His credentials are even more awesome than when I knew him. He's operating on Ruby's baby and there's no one better to do it.'

And that had Adrianna distracted. 'How is Ruby?'

Em wasn't supposed to bring work home. She wasn't supposed to talk about patients outside work, but Adrianna spent her days minding the kids so Em could work. Adrianna had to feel like she was a part of it, and in a way she was. If it wasn't for her mum, she'd never be able to do this.

This. Chaos. Animal noodles. Mess on the kitchen floor. Fuzzy, a dopey half-poodle, half something no one could guess at, was currently lurking under Toby's highchair on the off-chance the odd giraffe or elephant would drop from on high.

'Hey, it's all done.' There was a triumphant bang from the laundry and Mike appeared in the doorway, waving his spanner. 'That's that mother fixed. I'd defy any drop to leak anywhere now. Anything else I can do for you ladies?'

'Oh, Mike, that's fabulous. But I wish you'd let us pay—'

'You've got free plumbing for life,' Mike said fiercely. Mike was their big, burly, almost scary-looking next-door neighbour. His ginger hair was cropped to almost nothing. He wore his jeans a bit too low, he routinely ripped the sleeves out of his T-shirts because sleeves annoyed him, and in his spare time he built his body. If you met Mike on a dark night you might turn the other way. Fast.

Em had met Mike on a dark night. He'd crashed into their kitchen, banging the back door so hard it had broken.

'Em, the wife… My Katy… The baby… There's blood, oh, my God, there's blood… You're a midwife. Please…'

Katy had had a fast, fierce delivery of their third child, and she'd haemorrhaged. Mike had got home to find her in the laundry, her baby safely delivered, but she'd been bleeding out.

She'd stopped breathing twice before the ambulance had arrived. Em had got her back.

Mike and Katy were now the parents of three boys who promised to grow up looking just like their dad, and Mike was Em's slave for ever. He'd taken Em and her household under his wing, and a powerful wing it was. There were usually motorbikes parked outside Mike and Katy's place—multiple bikes—but no matter what the pressure of his family, his job or his biker mates, Mike dropped in every night—just to check.

Now, as Toby finished the last mouthful of his noodles, Mike hefted him out of his highchair and whirled him round and hugged him in a manner that made Em worry the noodles might come back up again. But Toby crowed in glee.

'Can I take him next door for a few minutes?' he asked. 'We've got a new swing, a double-seater. My boys'll be outside and Henry and Tobes'll look a treat on it. Give you a bit of peace with Gretta, like.'

He glanced at Gretta but he didn't say any more. What was happening was obvious. Gretta was more and more dependent on oxygen, but more and more it wasn't enough.

If Mike took Toby, Em could sit by the fire and cuddle Gretta while Adrianna put her feet up and watched the telly. Toby was already lighting up with excitement.

'That'd be great, Mike, thank you,' Em told him. 'I'll pop over and pick him up in an hour.'

'Bring Gretta with you,' Mike said. 'Give her a go on the swing. If she's up for it.'

But she wasn't up for it. They all knew it, and that knowledge hung over the house, a shadow edging closer.

Today Oliver's presence had pushed that shadow back a little, made Em's thoughts fly sideways, but, Oliver or not, the shadows were there to stay.

CHAPTER FOUR

THE LAST TIME Oliver had visited his ex-mother-in-law, her house had looked immaculate. Adrianna was devoted to her garden. At this time of year her roses had always looked glorious, her herbaceous borders had been clipped to perfect symmetry and her lawns had always been lush and green, courtesy of the tanks she'd installed specifically so she could be proud of her garden the year round.

Not now.

The grass on the lawn was a bit long and there were bare patches, spots where things had been left for a while. Where once an elegant table setting had stood under the shade of a Manchurian pear, there was now a sandpit and a paddling pool.

A beach ball lay on the front path. He had to push it aside to reach the front door.

It took him less than a minute to reach the door but by the time he had, the last conversation he'd had with Em had played itself out more than a dozen times in his head.

'Em, I can't adopt. I'm sorry, but I can't guarantee I can love kids who aren't my own.'

'They would be your own,' she'd said. She'd been emotional, distraught, but underneath she'd been sure. *'I want kids, Oliver. I want a family. There are children*

*out there who need us. If we can't have our own...to not
take them is selfish.'*

'To take them when we can't love them is selfish.'

'I can love them. I will.'

'But I can't.' He'd said it gently but inexorably, a truth
he'd learned by fire.

'You're saying I need to do it alone?'

'Em, think about it,' he'd said fiercely. *'We love each
other. We've gone through so much...'*

'I want a family.'

*'Then I can't give it to you. If this is the route you're
determined to take, then you'll need to find someone
who can.'*

He'd walked away, sure that when she'd settled she'd
agree with him. After all, their love was absolute. But
she'd never contacted him. She hadn't answered his calls.

Adrianna had spoken to him. 'Oliver, she's gutted.
She knows your position. Please, leave her be to work
things out for herself.'

It had gutted him, too, that she'd walked away from
their marriage without a backward glance. And here was
evidence that she'd moved on. She'd found herself the
life she wanted—without him.

He reached the door, lifted his hand to the bell but as
he did the door swung inwards.

The guy opening the door was about the same age
as Oliver. Oliver was tall, but this guy was taller and
he was big in every sense of the word. He was wearing jeans, a ripped T-shirt and big working boots. His
hands were clean but there was grease on his forearms.
And on his tatts.

He was holding a child, a little boy of about two. The
child was African, Oliver guessed, Somalian maybe, as

dark as night, with huge eyes. One side of his face was badly scarred. He was cradled in the guy's arms, but he was looking outwards, brightly interested in this new arrival into his world.

Another kid came flying through the gate behind Oliver, hurtling up the path towards them. Another little boy. Four? Ginger-haired. He looked like the guy in front of him.

'Daddy, Daddy, it's my turn on the swing,' he yelled. 'Come and make them give me a turn.'

The guy scooped him up, as well, then stood, a kid tucked under each arm. He looked Oliver up and down, like a pit bull, bristling, assessing whether to attack.

'Life insurance?' he drawled. 'Funeral-home plans? Not interested, mate.'

'I'm here to see Emily.'

'She's not interested, either.'

He was still wearing his suit. Maybe he should have changed. Maybe a tatt or two was necessary to get into this new version of his mother-in-law's home.

'I'm a friend of Em's from the hospital.' Who was this guy? 'Can you tell her I'm here, please?'

'She's stuffed. She doesn't need visitors.' He was blocking the doorway, a great, belligerent bull of a man.

'Can you ask her?'

'She only has an hour at most with Gretta before the kid goes to sleep. You want to intrude on that?'

Who was Gretta? Who was this guy?

'Mike?' Thankfully it was Em, calling from inside the house. 'Who is it?'

'Guy who says he's a friend of yours.' Mike didn't take his eyes off Oliver. His meaning was clear—he didn't trust him an inch. 'Says he's from the hospital. Looks like an undertaker.'

'Mike?'

'Yeah?'

'It'll be Oliver,' she called, and Mike might be right about the 'stuffed' adjective, Oliver conceded. Her voice sounded past weariness.

'Oliver?'

'He's the guy I was married to.' *Was?*

'Your ex is an undertaker? Sheesh, Em...'

'He's not an undertaker. He's a surgeon.'

'That's one step before the undertaker.'

'Mike?'

'Yeah?'

'Let him in.'

Why didn't Em come to the door? But Mike gave him a last long stare and stepped aside.

'Right,' he called back to Em. 'But we're on the swings. One yell and I'll be here in seconds. Watch it, mate,' he growled at Oliver, as he pushed past him and headed down the veranda with his load of kids. 'You upset Em and you upset me—and you wouldn't want to do that. You upset Em and you'll be very, very sorry.'

He knew this house. He'd been here often with Em. He'd stayed here for weeks on end when, just after they were married, Em's dad had been diagnosed with inoperable lung cancer.

It had taken the combined skill of all of them—his medical input, Em's nursing skill and Adrianna's unfailing devotion—to keep Kev comfortable until the end, but at the funeral, as well as sadness there had also been a feeling that it had been the best death Kev could have asked for. Surrounded by his family, no pain, knowing he was loved...

'This is how I want us to go out when we have to,' Em had whispered to him at the graveside. 'Thank you for being here.'

Yeah, well, that was years ago and he hadn't been with her for a long time now. She was a different woman.

He walked into the kitchen and stopped dead.

Different woman? What an understatement.

She was sitting by Adrianna's old kitchen range, settled in a faded rocker. Her hair was once more loose, her curls cascading to her shoulders. She had on that baggy windcheater and jeans and her feet were bare.

She was cuddling a child. A three- or four-year-old?

A sick child. There was an oxygen concentrator humming on the floor beside them. The child's face was buried in Em's shoulder, but Oliver could see the thin tube connected to the nasal cannula.

A child this small, needing oxygen... His heart lurched. This was no ordinary domestic scene. A child this sick...

The expression on Em's face...

Already he was focusing forward. Already he was feeling gutted for Em. She gave her heart...

Once upon a time she'd given it to him, and he'd hurt her. That she be hurt again...

This surely couldn't be her child.

And who was Mike?

He'd paused in the doorway and for some reason it took courage to step forward. He had no place in this tableau. He'd walked away five years ago so this woman could have the life she wanted, and he had no right to walk back into her life now.

But he wasn't walking into her life. He was here to talk to her about paying for the crash.

Right. His head could tell him that all it liked, but his gut was telling him something else entirely. Em… He'd loved her with all his heart.

He looked at her now, tired, vulnerable, holding a child who must be desperately ill, and all he wanted was to pick her up and carry her away from hurt.

From loving a child who wasn't hers?

Maybe she was hers. Maybe the in-vitro procedures had finally produced a successful outcome. But if this was her child…

His gut was still churning, and when she turned and gave him a tiny half-smile, a tired acknowledgement that he was there, a sort of welcome, the lurch became almost sickening.

'Ollie.'

No one had called him Ollie for five years. No one dared. He'd hated the diminutive—Brett, his sort of brother, had mocked him with it. *'Get out of our lives, Pond Scum Ollie. You're a cuckoo. You don't belong here.'*

Only Em had whispered it to him in the night, in his arms, when their loving had wrapped them in their own cocoon of bliss. Only Em's tongue had made it a blessing.

'Hey,' he said softly, crossing to where she sat, and, because he couldn't help himself, he touched her hair. Just lightly. He had no right, but he had to…touch.

It was probably a mistake. It hauled him into the intimate tableau. Em looked up at him and smiled, and it was no longer a half-smile. It was a smile of welcome. Acceptance.

A welcome home? It was no such thing. But it was a

welcome to *her* home, to the home she'd created. Without him.

'Gretta, we have a visitor,' she murmured, and she turned slightly so the child in her arms could see if she wanted.

And she did. The little girl stirred and opened her eyes and Oliver's gut lurched all over again.

Isla had said Em had a two- and a four-year-old. This little one was older than two, but if she was four she was tiny. She was dressed in a fuzzy pink dressing gown that almost enveloped her.

She was a poppet of a child, with a mop of dark, straight hair, and with huge eyes, almost black.

Her lips were tinged blue. The oxygen wasn't enough, then.

She had Down's syndrome.

Oh, Em… What have you got yourself into?

But he couldn't say it. He hauled a kitchen chair up beside them both, and took Gretta's little hand in his.

'I'm pleased to meet you, Gretta.' He smiled at the little girl, giving her all his attention. 'I'm Oliver. I'm a friend of your…' And he couldn't go on.

'He's Mummy's friend,' Em finished for him, and there was that lurch again. 'He's the man in the picture next to Grandma and Grandpa.'

'Ollie,' the little girl whispered, and there was no outsider implication in that word. She was simply accepting him as part of whatever this household was.

There was a sudden woof from under the table, a scramble, another woof and a dog's head appeared on his knee. It was a great, boofy, curly brown head, attached to a body that was disproportionly small. It woofed again but its tail wagged like a flag in a gale.

'This is Fuzzy,' Em said, still smiling at him. His presence here didn't seem to be disconcerting her. It was as if he was simply an old friend, dropping by. To be welcomed and then given a farewell? 'Mike gave us Fuzzy to act as a watchdog. He sort of does, but he's always a bit late on the scene.'

'Oliver!' And here was the last part of the tableau. Adrianna was standing in the door through to the lounge and her eyes weren't welcoming at all. 'What are you doing here?'

Here was the welcome he'd expected. Coldness and accusation…

'Mum…' Em said warningly, but Adrianna was never one who could be put off with a mere warning.

'You hit Em's car.'

'Mum, I told you. I hit his.'

'Then he shouldn't have been parked where you could hit him. What are you doing here?'

'Offering to pay for the damage.'

Her eyes narrowed. 'Really?'

'Really.'

'Mum, it was my fault,' Em protested, but Adrianna shook her head.

'It's your no-claim bonus that's at risk. Oliver's a specialist obstetric surgeon, and I'm betting he has no mortgage and no kids. He can afford it.'

'Mum, it's my debt.'

'You take on the world,' her mother muttered. 'Oliver owes you, big time. My advice is to take his money and run. Or rather take his money and say goodbye. Oliver, you broke my daughter's heart. I won't have you upsetting her all over again. Raking up old wounds…'

'He's not,' Em said, still gently, and Oliver was aware

that her biggest priority was not Em or the emotions his presence must be causing, but rather on not upsetting the little girl in her arms. 'Mum, he's welcome. He's a friend and a colleague and he's here to do the honourable thing. Even if I won't let him. I can afford to pay, Oliver.'

'I won't let you,' he told her.

'I'll make you a cup of tea, then,' Adrianna said, slightly mollified. She humphed across to the kettle, made tea—and, yep, she remembered how he liked it. She plonked two mugs on the table, one for Em, one for him. Then she hoisted Fuzzy into one arm, took her own mug in the other hand and headed back to the sitting room. 'Semi-final of *Boss of My Kitchen*,' she said briefly over her shoulder. 'Shall the croquembouche disintegrate into a puddle? The tension's a killer. Nice to see you, Oliver—sort of—but don't you dare upset Em. Goodbye.'

And she disappeared, using a foot to shove the door closed behind her.

Her message couldn't be clearer. *My daughter wants me to be polite so I will be, but not one inch more than I must.*

He was left with Em, and the little girl in her arms. Sitting in Adrianna's kitchen.

It was a great kitchen.

He'd always loved this house, he thought, inconsequentially. Kevin and Adrianna had built it forty years ago, hoping for a huge family. They'd had four boys, and then the tail-ender, Emily. Adrianna's parents had moved in, as well, into a bungalow out the back. Em had said her childhood had been filled with her brothers and their mates, visiting relations, cousins, friends, anyone Adrianna's famous hospitality could drag in.

Oliver and Em had built a house closer to the hospital they both worked in. They'd built four bedrooms, as well, furnishing them with hope.

Hope hadn't happened. The IVF procedures had worn them down and Josh's death had been the final nail in the coffin of their marriage. He'd walked out and left it to her.

'You're not living in our house?' He'd signed it over to her before going overseas, asking their lawyer to let her know.

'It's better here,' she said simply. 'My brothers are all overseas or interstate now, but I have Mum, and Mike and Katy nearby. The kids are happy here. I've leased our house out. When I emailed you, you said I could do what I like. I use half the rent to help with expenses here. The other half is in an interest-bearing deposit for you. I told you that in the email. You didn't answer.'

He hadn't. He'd blocked it out. The idea of strangers living in the gorgeous house he and Em had had built with such hopes...

'I couldn't live there,' Em said, conversationally. 'It doesn't have heart. Not like here. Not like home.'

Yeah, well, that was another kick in the guts, but he was over it by now. Or almost over it. He concentrated on his tea for a bit, while Em juggled Gretta and cannula and her mug of tea. He could offer to help but he knew he'd be knocked back.

She no longer needed him. This was her life now.

Gretta was watching him, her great brown eyes carefully assessing. Judging? Who knew? The IQs of kids with Down's syndrome covered an amazingly broad spectrum.

He touched the cannula lightly. 'Hey, Gretta,' he said softly. 'Why do you need this?'

'For breeving,' she lisped, but it was as if even saying the words was too much for her. She sank back against Em and her eyes half closed.

'Gretta has an atrioventricular septal defect,' Em said matter-of-factly, as if it was a perfectly normal thing for a kid to have. No problem at all.

But those three words told Oliver all he needed to know about the little girl's condition.

An atrioventricular septal defect... Common term—hole in the heart.

A large percentage of babies with Down's syndrome were born with congenital heart defects. The most common problem was atrioventricular septal defects, or holes in the heart. That this little one was at home with oxygen, with a cannula helping her breathe, told Oliver there was more than one hole. It must be inoperable.

And he had to ask.

'Em, is she yours?'

The words echoed around the kitchen, and as soon as they came out he knew it was the wrong thing to ask. The arms holding Gretta tightened, and so did the look on Em's face.

'Of course she's mine,' she whispered, but the friendliness was gone. 'Gretta's my daughter. Oliver, I think you should leave.'

'I meant—'

'You meant is she adopted?' Her face was still bleak. 'No, she's not adopted. I'm Gretta's foster-mum, but her birth mother has given all responsibility to me. That means I can love her as much as I want, and that's what I do. I love her and love her and love her. Gretta's my daughter, Oliver, in every sense of the word.'

'You have another...son?'

'You'll have met Toby on the way out with Mike, and he's my foster-child, too. He has spinal kyphoscoliosis. He's the bravest kid. I'm so proud of my kids. Mum's so proud of her grandkids.'

He got it. Or sort of. These were fostered kids. That's what Em had wanted him to share.

But that's what he'd been, he thought bleakly. Someone else's reject. Much as he approved of the idea in theory, in practice he knew it didn't work.

But what Em did was no longer his business, he reminded himself. This was what she'd decided to do with her life. He had no business asking...

How could he not?

'Who's Mike?' he asked, and he hadn't known he was going to ask until he did.

'My lover?' Her lips twitched a little at the expression on his face. 'Can you see it? Nope, Mike's our next-door neighbour, our friend, our man about the house. He and Katy have three kids, we have two, and they mix and mingle at will. You like going to Katy's, don't you, Gretta?'

There was a faint nod from Gretta, and a smile.

And the medical part of Oliver was caught. If Gretta was responding now, as ill as she was, her IQ must be at the higher end of the Down's spectrum.

He watched Em hold her tight, and he thought, She's given her heart...

And he never could have. He'd never doubted Em's ability to adopt; it was only his reluctance...his fear...

'Is there anything I can do to help?' he found himself saying. 'Now that I'm here?'

'But you don't want to be here.' Em shifted a little, making herself more comfortable. 'You've moved on. At least, I hope you have. I'd have thought you'd have asked for a divorce, found a new partner and had kids by now. You wanted kids. What's stopping you?'

And there was a facer. He had wanted children, they both had, but after a stillbirth and so many attempts at IVF it had worn them—and their marriage—into the ground. Em had told him to leave.

No. She hadn't. She'd simply said she wanted to adopt a child, and that was a deal-breaker.

'I haven't found the right person,' he said, trying to make it sound flippant, but there was no way he could make anything about what had happened to them flippant. The last year or so of their marriage had been unswervingly grey. He looked at Em now and he thought some of the grey remained.

A lot of the grey?

He glanced around the kitchen, once sparkling and ordered, if a bit cluttered with Adrianna's bits and pieces from the past. But now it was all about the present. It was filled with the detritus of a day with kids—or a life with kids.

But this was what Em wanted. And he hadn't?

No, he thought fiercely. It had been what he'd wanted more than anything, and that's why he'd walked away.

So why hadn't he found it?

There was the sound of feet pounding up the veranda, a perfunctory thump on the door and two little boys of about six and four burst in. They were followed by Mike, carrying the toddlers. The six-year-old was carrying a bunch of tattered kangaroo paws, flowers Oliver had seen in the next-door front garden. Tough as nails, Australian perennials, they hardly made good cut flowers but these were tied with a gaudy red bow and presented with pride.

'These are for Gran Adrianna,' the urchin said. And when she obviously wasn't in the kitchen, he headed through the living-room door and yelled for her. 'Gran? Gran Adrianna, we've got you a present. Mum says happy birthday. She was coming over to say it but she's got a cold and she says she wants to give you flowers for your birthday and not a cold.'

And Em turned white.

CHAPTER FIVE

EVERYONE ELSE WAS looking at the kid with the flowers, and then at Adrianna, who reappeared and stooped to give the kids a hug. Only Oliver saw the absolute mortification that crossed Em's face.

She'd forgotten, he thought. Of course she had. Even if she'd remembered this morning, after crashing her car, doing a huge day on the wards, then coming home to such a sick kid, forgetting was almost inevitable.

Think. Think! he told himself. He used to live in this town. Cake. St Kilda. Ackland Street. Cake heaven. It wasn't so far, and the shops there stayed open late.

'Are you guys staying for the cake?' he asked, glancing at his watch, his voice not rising, speaking like this was a pre-ordained plan. 'It'll be here in about twenty minutes. Em asked me to order it but it's running a bit late. Adrianna, is it okay if I stay for the celebration? Em thought it might be okay, but if you'd rather I didn't... Mike, can you and the kids show me the swing while we wait? I'm good at pushing.'

'Em asked you to order a cake?' Adrianna demanded, puzzled, and Oliver spread his hands.

'I crashed into her car this morning. She's been run off her legs all day and I asked if there was anything I could do. Therefore, in twenty minutes there'll be cake. Swing? Kids?'

'Oliver…' Em started, but Oliver put up his hand as if to stop her in mid-sentence. Which was exactly what he intended.

'She always wants to pay,' he told his ex-mother-in-law, grinning. 'She's stubborn as an ox, your Em, but you'd know that, Adrianna. We seem to have been arguing about money all day. I told you, Em, I'm doing the cake, you're on the balloons. Sorry I've mistimed it, though. I'll pay ten percent of the balloons to compensate. Any questions?'

'N-no,' Em said weakly, and his grin widened.

'How about that? No problems at all. Prepare for cake, Adrianna, and prepare for Birthday.'

And suddenly he was being towed outside by kids who realised bedtime was being set back and birthday cake was in the offing. Leaving an open-mouthed Em and Adrianna in the kitchen.

Two minutes later, Mike was onside. They were pushing kids on swings and Oliver was on the phone. And it worked. His backup plan had been a fast trip to the supermarket for an off-the-shelf cake and blow-them-up-yourself balloons but, yes, the shop he remembered had decorated ice cream cakes. They were usually pre-ordered but if he was prepared to pay more… How fast could they pipe Adrianna's name on top? Candles included? Could they order a taxi to deliver it and charge his card? Did they do balloons? Next door did? Was it still open? How much to bung some of those in the taxi as well? He'd pay twice the price for their trouble.

'You're a fast mover,' Mike said, assessing him with a long, slow look as they pushed the double swing together.

And then he said, not quite casually, 'Should I worry? If Em gets hurt I might just be tempted to do a damage.'

So Em had a protector. Good. Unless that protector was threatening to pick him up by the collar and hurl him off the property. He sighed and raked his hair and tried to figure how to respond.

'Mate, I'm not a fast mover,' he said at last. 'For five years I haven't moved at all. I'm not sure even what's happening here, but I'm sure as hell not moving fast.'

'Oh, Em, you remembered.' The moment the boys were out of the house Adrianna stooped and enveloped Em— and Gretta—in a bear hug. 'I've been thinking all day that no one's remembered and... Oh, sweetheart, I'm sorry.'

'You're sorry!' Em struggled to her feet, still cradling Gretta. She should confess, she thought, but as she looked at her mum's face she thought, no. Confession might make her feel better, but right now Adrianna was happy because her daughter had remembered. Oliver had given her that gift and she'd accept, because to do anything else would be cruel. Her mum did so much...

Oliver had rescued her. It'd be dumb to spoil his efforts with more than Adrianna had to know.

But she wasn't going to be dishonest. Not entirely. 'Mum, I remembered when I woke up this morning,' she said. 'But when Gretta was sick I forgot to say it. It was such a rush all day and there's been nothing I could do. But when I met Oliver—'

'You knew he was coming?'

'He ordered the cake. And you know he's always loved you.' And that at least was the truth.

'Oh, Em...'

'And I've bought you a half-day spa voucher.' Yeah, she was lying about that but she could order and get it printed tonight. 'And if we can, I'll do it with you.' That's what Adrianna would like most in the world, she knew, but how would she manage that? But she looked at her mum's tired face and thought she had to do it. It might have to wait until Gretta was better, but she would do it.

If Gretta got better.

'Oh, but, Em…Gretta…'

'It can't be all about Gretta,' Em said gently, and that, too, was true. No matter how much attention Gretta needed, there were others who needed her, as well. It'd be a wrench to spend one of her precious free days…

But, no. This was her mum.

Oliver had saved the situation for now. The least she could do was take it forward.

The cake was amazing, an over-the-top confection that made the kids gasp with wonder. The taxi driver brought it in with a flourish then directed the kids to bring in the balloons. Whatever Oliver had paid, Em thought numbly, it must have been well and truly over the top, as the balloons were already filled, multi-coloured balls of floating air, bursting from the cab as soon as the doors were open, secured only by ribbons tied to the cab doors.

The kids brought them in, bunch upon bunch, and the kitchen was an instant party.

Katy arrived from next door, summoned by her kids. She wouldn't come right in—her flushed face verified her self-diagnosis of a streaming head cold and she declared there was no way she was risking Gretta catching anything—but she stood in the doorway and sang 'Happy Birthday' with the rest of them and watched while Adrianna blew out the candles and sliced the creamy caramel and chocolate and strawberry confection into slices that were almost cake-sized each.

'I can't believe it,' Adrianna said mistily, between mouthfuls of cake. 'Thank you all so much.'

And Em looked across at Oliver, who was sitting with Toby on his knee, one spoonful for Oliver, one spoonful for Toby, and she caught his gaze and tried to smile. But it didn't come off.

This was how it could have been, she thought. This was what she'd dreamed of.

But she'd pushed too hard, too fast. Josh's death had gutted her. She remembered sobbing, 'I can't do IVF any more, I'm too tired. There are babies out there who need us. We'll adopt. You're adopted, Oliver, you know it can work.'

But: 'It doesn't work,' he'd said, not angrily, just flatly, dully, stating immutable facts. 'It's second best and you know it.'

His reaction had shocked her. She'd been in no mood to compromise, and suddenly everything had escalated. The tension of five years of trying for a family had suddenly exploded. Leaving them with nothing.

What had he been doing for five years? Building his career, by the look of his CV. Turning into a wonderful doctor.

A caring doctor… His patience with two-year-old Toby, not the easiest kid to feed, was wonderful. The way he responded to the kids around the table, the mess, the laughter…

The way he smiled up at Adrianna and told her he was so sorry he'd missed her last five birthdays, she'd have to have five slices of cake to make up for it…

He was wonderful.

She wanted to weep.

She wanted to set Gretta down, walk around the table and hug him. Hold him.

Claim him again as her husband?

Right, like that was about to happen. The past was the past. They'd made their decisions and they'd moved on.

'Em's given me an afternoon at the day spa,' Adrianna said happily, cutting across her thoughts. Or almost. Her thoughts were pretty intense right now, pretty much centred on the gorgeous guy with the toddler, right across the table from her. She was watching his hands. She'd loved those hands—surgeon's hands. She remembered what those hands had been able to do.

She remembered…

'That's gorgeous,' Katy was saying from the doorway. 'But, Em, you still haven't had that colour and cut Mike and I gave you for Christmas. Right, Adrianna, this time it's going to work. As soon as I get over my snuffles I'm taking all five kids and you two are having your Christmas and birthday treats combined. This weekend?'

Once again, right. As if. Em gave her a smile, and then went to hug Adrianna, but she thought Katy would still be recovering by this weekend and her boys would probably catch her cold after her and Gretta was still so weak…

Adrianna should—and would—have her day spa but there'd be no day spas or colour and cuts for Em until… until…

The *until* was unthinkable. She hugged Gretta and her mind closed.

'What about this Saturday and using me?' Oliver asked, and she blinked. Had she misheard?

'You?'

'Anyone can see you've got the cold from hell,' he told Katy. 'Even if you're not still contagious you'll be wiped out, and you have three of your own to look after. Whereas I've just moved to Melbourne and my job hasn't geared up yet. There's nothing to stop me coming by and taking care of a couple of kids for a few hours.' He spooned chocolate ice-cream cake into Toby's waiting mouth and grinned at the little boy. 'Piece of cake, really. We'll have fun.' And then he smiled across at Gretta, focusing entirely on the little girl. 'How about it, Gretta? Will you let me take care of you and Toby?'

Gretta gazed back at him, clearly not understanding what was happening, but Oliver was smiling and she responded to the smile. She tried a tentative one of her own.

She was one brave kid, Oliver thought. But she looked so vulnerable... Her colour... Oxygen wasn't getting through.

'That'd be fantastic,' Adrianna breathed. 'Em worries about Gretta's breathing, but with you being a doctor...'

'Is he a doctor?' Katy demanded.

'He's Em's ex,' Mike growled, throwing a suspicious, hard stare at Oliver.

'But I'm still reliable,' Oliver said—hopefully—and Katy laughed.

'Hey, I hooked with some weirdos in my time,' she told the still-glowering Mike. 'But a couple of them turned into your mates. Just because they didn't come up to my high standards doesn't mean they're total failures as human beings. What do you say, Em? Trust your kids for a few hours with your ex? And him a doctor and all. It sounds an offer too good to refuse to me.'

And they were all looking at her. From what had

started as a quiet night she was suddenly surrounded by
birthday, kids, mess, chaos, and here was Oliver, threatening to walk into her life again.

No. Not threatening. Offering.

She'd been feeling like she was being bulldozed.
Now… She looked at Oliver and he returned her gaze,
calmly, placidly, like he was no threat at all. Whatever
he'd been doing for the last five years it was nothing to
do with her, but she knew one thing. He was a good man.
She might not know him any more, but she could trust
him, and if a specialist obstetrician and surgeon couldn't
look after her Gretta, who could?

Her mind was racing. Gretta and Toby were both ac-
customed to strangers minding them—too many stays
in hospital had seen to that. Oliver was currently feeding Toby like a pro.

She *could* take Adrianna for an afternoon out. She
glanced again at her mum and saw the telltale flicker of
hope in her eyes. She was so good… Without Adrianna,
Em couldn't have these kids.

The fact that she'd once hoped to have them with
Oliver…

No. Don't go there. She hauled herself back from the
brink, from the emotions of five years ago, and she managed a smile at Oliver.

'Thank you, then,' she said simply. 'Thank you for offering. Mum and I would love it. Two p.m. on Saturday?
We'll be back by five.'

'I'll be here at one.'

Four hours… Did she trust him that long?

Of course she did, she told herself. She did trust him.
It was only… She needed to trust herself, as well. She

needed to figure out the new way of the world, where Oliver Evans was no longer a lover or a husband.

It seemed Oliver Evans was offering to be a friend.

An hour later she was walking him out to his car. Amazingly, he'd helped put the kids to bed. 'If I'm to care for them on Saturday, they should see me as familiar.' The children had responded to his inherent gentleness, his teasing, his smile, and Em was struggling not to respond, as well.

But she was responding. Of course she was. How could she not? She'd fallen in love with this man a decade ago and the traces of that love remained. Life had battered them, pushed them apart, but it was impossible to think of him other than a friend.

Just a friend? He had to be. She'd made the decision five years ago—Oliver or children. She'd wanted children so much that she'd made her choice but it had been like chopping a part of herself out. Even now... The decision had been made in the aftermath of a stillbirth, when her emotions had been all over the place. If she was asked to make such a decision again...

She'd make it, she thought, thinking of the children in the house behind her. Gretta and Toby. Where would they be without her?

Someone else might have helped them, she thought, but now they were hers, and she loved them so fiercely it hurt.

If she'd stayed with Oliver she would have had... nothing.

'Tell me about the kids,' he said, politely almost, leaning back on the driver's door of his car. His rental car.

It had been a lovely car she'd destroyed. That's what

Oliver must have decided, she thought. He'd have a gorgeous car instead of kids—and now she'd smashed it.

'I'm sorry about your car,' she managed.

He made an exasperated gesture—leave it, not important. But it was important. She'd seen his face when he'd looked at the damage.

'Tell me about the kids,' he said again. 'You're fostering?'

'Mum and I decided…when you left…'

'To have kids?'

'You know I can't,' she said, evenly now, getting herself back together. 'For the year after you left I wasn't… very happy. I had my work as a midwife. I love my work, but you know that was never enough. And then one of my mums had Gretta.'

'One of your mums.'

'I know… Not very professional, is it, to get so personally involved? But Gretta was Miriam's third child. Miriam's a single mum who hadn't bothered to have any prenatal checks so missed the scans. From the moment the doctors told her Gretta had Down's she hadn't wanted anything to do with her. Normally, Social Services can find adoptive parents for a newborn, even if it has Down's, but Miriam simply checked herself out of hospital and disappeared. We think she's in Western Australia with a new partner.'

'So you've taken her baby…'

'I didn't take her baby,' she said, thinking suddenly of the way he'd reacted to her suggestion of adoption all those years ago. It had been like adoption was a dirty word.

'I wasn't accusing…'

'No,' she said and stared down at her feet. She needed

new shoes, she thought inconsequentially. She wore lace-up trainers—they were the most practical for the running she had to do—and a hole was starting to appear at her left big toe. Not this pay, she thought. Maybe next? Or maybe she could stick a plaster over the toe and pretend it was a new fashion. One of the kids' plasters with frogs on.

'What do you know about Miriam?' Oliver asked, and she hauled her attention back to him. Actually, it had never really strayed. But distractions were good. Distractions were necessary.

'We…we don't hear from Miriam,' she told him. 'But it's not for want of trying. Her two older children are in foster care together on a farm up near Kyneton—they're great kids and Harold and Eve are a wonderful foster-mum and dad—but Gretta couldn't go with them. Her heart problems have meant constant hospitalisation. We knew from the start that her life would be short. We knew it'd be a fight to keep her alive, so there was a choice. She could stay in hospital, institutionalised until she died, or I could take her home. She stayed in hospital for two months and then I couldn't bear it. Mum and I reorganised our lives and brought her home.'

'But she will die.' He said it gently, as if he was making sure she knew, and she flushed.

'You think we don't know that? But look at her tonight. She loved it. She loves…us.'

'I guess…'

'And don't you dare bring out your "Well, if she's adopted you can't possibly love her like your own" argument to say when she dies it won't hurt,' she snapped, suddenly unable to prevent the well of bitterness left from an appalling scene five years ago. 'We couldn't possibly love her more.'

'I never said that you couldn't love an adopted child.'

'Yes, you did.'

'I just said it's different and I hold by that. It's not the same love as from birth parents and you know it.'

'As Miriam's love? No, it's not and isn't Gretta lucky that it's not?'

'Em...'

'What?' She had her hands on her hips now, glaring. He'd shocked her so much, all those years ago. She'd been totally gutted when Josh had been stillborn, devastated beyond belief. She'd curled into a tight ball of misery, she'd hardly been able to function, but when finally daylight had begun to filter through the blackness, she'd clung to what had seemed her only hope.

'Oliver, let's stop with the in-vitro stuff. It's tearing me apart—it's tearing us apart. Let's try instead for adoption.'

But his reaction had stunned her.

'Em, no.' He'd said it gently but the words had been implacable. *'I can't guarantee to love a child who's not my own. I won't do that to a child.'*

It had been a divide neither of them could cross. She had been so desperate for a child that she couldn't accept his refusal to consider adoption—and Oliver had walked away rather than concede.

'I love Gretta and so does Adrianna,' she said now, forcing herself to stay calm. Forcing herself to put the hurt of years ago on the back burner. 'So, moving on...'

'Toby?'

And mentioning her son's name was a sure way to defuse anger. Even saying his name made her smile.

'Adrianna found Toby,' she told him. 'Or rather Adrianna helped Toby find us.'

'Would you like to tell me about him?'

She'd prefer not to, actually. She was finding it disturbing on all sorts of levels to stand outside in the dusk with this man who'd once been her husband. But he had offered to take the children on Saturday, and she did need help. These last few months, with Gretta's health deteriorating, had been taking their toll on Adrianna. This Saturday would be gold for both of them, she knew, and Oliver had offered.

Therefore she had to be courteous. She had to share.

She had to stand outside with him a moment longer, even though a part of her wanted to turn around and run.

Why?

It was how he made her feel. It was the way her body was responding. He'd been her husband. She'd thought she knew this man at the deepest, most primeval level—yet here he was, standing in the dusk asking polite questions about children he knew nothing about.

Her children.

'Toby has multiple problems.' Somehow she'd pulled herself together...sort of. 'He's African, as you can probably guess. He has scoliosis of the spine; his spine was so bent he looked deformed even when he was born, and his family abandoned him. One of the poorest families in the village took him in. His pseudo-mum did the best she could for him but he hadn't been fed properly and he was already suffering from noma—a facial bacterial infection. She walked for three days to the nearest hospital to get him help—can you imagine that? But then, of course, she had to go back to her own family. But she'd fought for him first. One of the international aid agencies took on his case and brought him over here for facial reconstruction. So far he's been through six operations. He's doing great but…'

'But you can't keep him.'

She stilled. 'Why not? The hospital social worker in charge of his case knew Adrianna and I were already fostering Gretta, and she took a chance, asking us if we'd be willing to take him on. Adrianna did all the paperwork. Mum drove this, but we both want it. Theoretically he's supposed to go home when he's been treated. We're still in touch with his African foster-mum but she's so poor and she's very happy that he stays here. So in practice we're fighting tooth and nail to keep him.'

'Em, for heaven's sake…' He sounded appalled. 'You can't look after the world's waifs and strays. There are too many.'

'I can look after the ones I love,' she threw back at him, and tilted her chin. Defiant. She knew this argument—and here it came.

'You can't love him.'

'Why not?'

'He's not your kid.'

'Then whose kid is he? The woman who bore him? The woman who walked for three days to save him but can't afford to feed him? Or Mum and me, who'll do our damnedest to keep him healthy and safe?'

'Em…' He raked his hair, a gesture she knew all too well. 'To take two kids like Gretta and Toby… A kid who'll die and a kid you might lose. They'll break your heart.'

'You just said I can't love them. You can't have it both ways, Oliver.'

'Is this what you wanted me to do? Adopt the kids the world's abandoned?'

'I don't think I expected anything of you,' she managed, and was inordinately proud of how calm she sounded. 'At the end of our marriage all I could see was what I needed. I know that sounds selfish, and maybe it is, but it's what I desperately wanted. Despite loving you I couldn't stop that wanting. You always knew I wanted a family. I'm a midwife, and I'm a midwife because watching babies come into the world is what I love most. I'd dreamed we could have our own family...'

'And when that didn't happen you walked away.'

'As I remember it, you walked.'

'Because it's not fair for me to adopt. These kids need their own parents.'

'They don't have them. Are you saying second best is worse than nothing?'

'They'll know...that they're second best.'

'Oliver, just because that happened to you...'

And she watched his face close, just like that.

He didn't talk about it, she thought. He'd never talked about it but she'd guessed.

She thought, fleetingly, of her in-laws, of Oliver's adoptive parents. But she had to think fleetingly because thinking any more made her so angry she could spit.

She only knew the bare bones but it was enough. She could infer the rest. They'd had trouble conceiving so they'd adopted Oliver. Then, five years later, they'd conceived naturally and their own son had been born.

Oliver never talked about it—never would talk about it—but she'd seen the family in action. Brett was five years younger than Oliver, a spoiled brat when Em had first met him and now an obnoxious, conceited young man who thought the world owed him a living.

But his parents thought the sun shone from him, and it seemed to Em that they'd spent their lives comparing their two sons, finding fault with Oliver and setting Brett on a pedestal.

Even at their wedding…

'He's done very well for himself,' Em had overheard his adoptive mother tell an aunt. *'Considering where he comes from. We've done what we could, but still… I know he's managed to get himself qualified as a doctor but… His mother was a whore, you know, and we can never forget that. Thank God we have Brett.'*

It had been as much as Em could do not to front the woman and slap her. It wouldn't have been a good look on her wedding day—bride smacks mother-in-law—but she'd come awfully close. But Oliver had never talked of it.

It was only when the adoption thing had come up when Josh had died that the ghosts had come from nowhere. And she couldn't fight them, for Oliver wouldn't speak of them.

'Oliver, we're doing our best,' she told him now, gentling, reminding herself that it was his ghosts talking, not him. She knew it was his ghosts, but she'd never been allowed close enough to fight them. 'Mum and I are loving these kids to bits. We're doing all we possibly can…'

'It won't be enough.'

'Maybe it won't.' She was suddenly bone weary again. Understanding could only go so far. 'But we're trying the best that we can. We'll give these kids our hearts, and if that's not enough to let them thrive then we'll be incredibly sad but we won't be regretful. We have love to give and we're giving it. We're trying, whereas you… You lacked courage to even think about it. "No adoptions," you said, end of story. I know your background. I know how hard it was for you to be raised with Brett but your parents were dumb and cruel. The whole world doesn't have to be like that.'

'And if you ever had a child of your own?'

'You're saying I shouldn't go near Gretta or Toby because I might, conceivably, still have a child biologically?'

'I didn't mean that.' He raked his hair again, in that gesture she'd known and loved. She had a sudden urge to rake it herself, settle it, touch his face, take away the pain.

Because there was pain. She could see it. This man was torn.

But she couldn't help him if he wouldn't talk about it. To be helped you had to admit you needed help. He'd simply closed off, shut her out, and there was nothing she could do about it.

She'd moved on, but he was still hurting. She couldn't help him.

'Go home,' she said, gently again. 'I'm sorry, Oliver, I have no right to bring up the past, but neither do you have a right to question what I'm doing. Our marriage is over and we need to remember it. We need to finalise our divorce. Meanwhile, thank you for tonight, for Adrianna's birthday. I'm deeply appreciative, but if you want to pull out of Saturday's childminding, I understand.'

'I'll be here.'

'You don't need to…'

'I will be here.'

'Fine, then,' she said, and took a step back in the face

of his sudden blaze of anger. 'That's good. That's great. I'll see you then.'

'I'll see you at the hospital tomorrow,' he said. 'With Ruby.'

And her heart sank. Of course. She was going to see this man, often. She needed to work with him.

She needed to ignore the pain she still saw in his eyes. She needed to tell herself, over and over, that it had nothing to do with her.

The problem was, that wasn't Em's skill. Ignoring pain.

But he didn't want her interference. He never had.

He didn't want her.

Moving on…

'Goodnight, then,' she managed, and she couldn't help herself. She touched his face with her hand and then stood on tiptoe and lightly kissed him—a feather touch, the faintest brush of lips against lips. 'Goodnight, Oliver. I'm sorry for your demons but your demons aren't mine. I give my heart for always, non-negotiable, adoption, fostering, marriage… Ollie, I can no more change myself than fly. I'm just sorry you can't share.'

And she couldn't say another word. She was suddenly so close to tears that she pushed away and would have stumbled.

Oliver's hand came out to catch her. She steadied and then brushed him off. She did it more roughly than she'd intended but she was out of her depth.

'Thank you,' she whispered, and turned away. 'Goodnight.' And she turned and fled into the house.

Oliver was left standing in the shadows, watching the lights inside the house, knowing he should leave, knowing he had to.

'I give my heart for always.'

What sort of statement was that?

She'd been talking about the kids, he told himself, but still...

She'd included marriage in the statement, and it was a statement to give a man pause.

CHAPTER SIX

EM HARDLY SAW Oliver the next day. The maternity ward was busy, and when she wasn't wanted in the birthing suites, she mostly stayed with Ruby.

The kid was so alone. Today was full of fill-in-the-blanks medical forms and last-minute checks, ready for surgery the next day. The ultrasounds, the visit and check by the anaesthetist, the constant checking and rechecking that the baby hadn't moved, that the scans that had shown the problem a week ago were correct, that they had little choice but to operate... Everything was necessary but by the end of the day Ruby was ready to get up and run.

She needed her mum, a sister, a mate, anyone, Em thought. That she was so alone was frightening. Isla dropped in for a while. Ruby was part of Isla's teen mums programme and Ruby relaxed with her, but she was Ruby's only visitor.

'Isn't there anyone I can call?' Em asked as the day wore on and Ruby grew more and more tense.

'No one'll come near me,' Ruby said tersely. 'Mum said if I didn't have an abortion she'd wash her hands of me. She said if I stayed near her I'd expect her to keep the kid and she wasn't having a thing to do with it. And she told my sisters they could stay away, too.'

'And your baby's father?'

'I told you before, the minute I told him about it, he was off. Couldn't see him for dust.'

'Oh, Ruby, there must be someone.'

'I'll be okay,' Ruby said with bravado that was patently false. 'I'll get this kid adopted and then I'll get a job in a shop or something. I just wish it was over now.'

'We all wish that.'

And it was Oliver again. He moved around the wards like a great prowling cat, Em thought crossly. He should wear a bell.

'What?' he demanded, as she turned towards him, and she thought she really had to learn to stop showing her feelings on her face.

'Knock!'

'Sorry. If I'm intruding I'll go away.'

'You might as well come in and poke me, too,' Ruby sighed. 'Everyone else has. I'm still here. Bub's still here. Why is everyone acting like we're about to go up in smoke before tomorrow? Why do I need to stay in bed?'

'Because we need your baby to stay exactly where she is,' Oliver told her, coming further into the room. He had a bag under his arm and Ruby eyed it with suspicion. 'Right now she's in the perfect position to operate on her spine, and, no, Ruby, there's not a single thing in this bag that will prod, poke or pry. But I would like to feel your baby for myself.'

Ruby sighed with a theatrical flourish and tugged up her nightie.

'Go ahead. Half the world already has.'

'Has she moved?'

'Nah.' She gave a sheepish grin. 'I feel her myself.

I'm not stupid, you know.' And she popped her hand on her tummy and cradled it.

There was that gesture again. Protective. *'Mine.'*

Oliver sat down on the bed and felt the rounded bump himself, and Em looked at the way he was examining the baby and thought this was a skill. Ruby had been poked and prodded until she was tired of it. Oliver was doing the same thing but very gently, as if he was cradling Ruby's unborn child.

'She's perfect,' he said at last, tugging Ruby's nightie back down. 'Like her mother.'

'She's not perfect. That's why I'm here.'

'She's pretty much perfect. Would you like to see a slide show of what we're about to do?' He grinned at Ruby's scared expression. 'There's not many gory bits and I can fast-forward through them.'

'I'll shut my eyes,' Ruby said, but he'd caught her, Em thought. She wasn't dissociated from this baby. Once again she saw Ruby's hand move surreptitiously to her tummy.

He flicked open his laptop. Fascinated, Em perched on the far side of the bed and watched, too.

'This is one we prepared earlier,' Oliver said, in the tone TV cooks used as they pulled a perfect bake from the oven. 'This is Rufus. He's six months old now, a lovely, healthy baby, but at the start of this he was still inside his mum, a twenty-two-weeker. This is the procedure your little one will have.'

The screen opened to an operating theatre, the patient's face hidden, the film obviously taken for teaching purposes as identities weren't shown. But the sound was on, and Em could hear Oliver's voice, calmly directive, and she knew that it was Oliver who was in charge.

She was fascinated—and so was Ruby. Squeamishness was forgotten. They watched in awe as the scalpel carefully, carefully negotiated the layers between the outside world and the baby within. It would be an intricate balance, Em knew, trying to give the baby minimal exposure to the outside world, keeping infection out, disturbing the baby as little as possible yet giving the surgeons space to work.

There were many doctors present—she could hear their voices. This was cutting-edge surgery.

'I can see its back,' Ruby breathed. 'Oh…is that the same as my baby?'

'They're all different,' Oliver said. 'Your daughter is tilted at a better angle.'

'Oh…' Ruby's eyes weren't leaving the screen.

They could definitely see the baby now, and they could see how the baby was slightly tilted to the side. Carefully, carefully Oliver manoeuvred him within the uterus, making no sudden movements, making sure the move was no more dramatic than if the baby himself had wriggled.

And now they could see the spine exposed. The telltale bulge…

'Is that the problem? The same as mine?' Ruby whispered, and Oliver nodded.

'Rufus's problem was slightly lower, but it's very similar.'

Silence again. They were totally focused, all of them. Oliver must have seen this many times before, Em thought—and he'd been there in person—but he was still watching it as if it was a miracle.

It was a miracle.

'This is where I step back and let the neurosurgeon

take over,' Oliver said. 'My job is to take care of the whole package, you and your baby, but Dr Zigler will be doing this bit. He's the best, Ruby. You're in the best of hands.'

They watched on. The surgery was painstaking. It was like microsurgery, Em thought, where fingers were reattached, where surgeons fought hard to save nerves. And in a way it was. They were carefully working around and then through the bulge. There'd be so many things to work around. The spinal cord was so fragile, so tiny. The task was to repair the damage already done, as far as possible, and then close, protecting the cord and peripheral nerves from the amniotic fluid until the baby was born.

'Is…is it hurting?' Ruby breathed, as the first incision was made into the tiny back.

'Is *he* hurting? No. Rufus is anaesthetised, as well as his mum. Did you see the anaesthetist working as soon as we had exposure? The jury's out on whether unborn babies can feel pain. There are those who say they're in a state similar to an induced coma, but they certainly react to a painful touch. It makes the procedure a little more risky—balancing anaesthetic with what he's receiving via his mum's blood supply—but the last thing we want is to stress him. Luckily the Victoria has some of the best anaesthetists in the world. Vera Harty will be doing your anaesthetic and your daughter's. I'd trust her with a baby of my own.'

Ruby was satisfied. She went back to watching the screen.

Em watched, too, but Oliver's last statement kept reverberating.

I'd trust her with a baby of my own.

The sadness was flooding back. Oliver had been

unable to have a baby of his own—because of her. She had fertility problems, not Oliver.

He'd left her years ago. He could have found someone by now.

Maybe he had. Maybe he just wasn't saying.

But he hadn't. She knew him well, this man.

There'd been an undercurrent of longing in the statement.

They'd both wanted children. She'd released him so he could have them. Why hadn't he moved on?

Watch the screen, she told herself. Some things were none of her business. Oliver was none of her business— except he was the obstetrician treating her patient.

She went back to being professional—sort of. She went back to watching Rufus, as Oliver and Ruby were doing.

The procedure was delicate and it took time but it seemed Oliver was in no hurry to finish watching, and neither was Ruby. Em couldn't be, either. Her job was to keep Ruby calm for tomorrow's operation, and that's what was happening now. The more familiar the girl was about what lay ahead, the more relaxed she'd be.

And not for the first time, Em blessed this place, this job. The Victoria considered its midwives some of the most important members of its staff. The mothers' needs came first and if a mum needed her midwife then Isla would somehow juggle the rest of her staff to cover.

Unless there was major drama Em wouldn't be interrupted now, she thought, and she wasn't. They made an intimate trio, midwife and doctor, with Ruby sandwiched between. Protected? That's what it felt like to Em, and she suspected that's how Ruby felt. Had Oliver set this up with just this goal? She glanced at him and knew her suspicion was right.

The first time she'd met him she'd been awed by his medical skills. Right now, watching him operate on screen, feeling Ruby's trust growing by the second, that awe was escalating into the stratosphere.

He might not make it as a husband, but he surely made it as a surgeon.

Back on screen, the neurosurgeon was suturing, using careful, painstakingly applied, tiny stitches, while Oliver was carefully monitoring the levels of amniotic fluid. This baby would be born already scarred, Em thought. He'd have a scar running down his lower back—but with luck that was all he'd have. Please…

'It worked a treat,' Oliver said, sounding as pleased as if the operation had happened yesterday, and on screen the neurosurgeon stood back and Oliver took over. The final stitches went in, closing the mum's uterus, making the incision across the mum's tummy as neat as the baby's. 'Rufus was born by Caesarean section at thirty-three weeks,' Oliver told them. 'He spent four weeks in hospital as a prem baby but would you like to see him now?'

'I… Yes.' Ruby sounded as if she could scarcely breathe.

'We have his parents' permission to show him to other parents facing the same procedure,' Oliver told her. 'Here goes.'

He fiddled with the computer and suddenly they were transported to a suburban backyard, to a rug thrown on a lawn, to a baby, about six months old, lying on his back in the sun, kicking his legs, admiring his toes.

There was a dog at the edge of the frame, a dopey-looking cocker spaniel. As they watched, the dog edged forward and licked the baby's toes. Rufus crowed with laughter and his toes went wild.

'He doesn't…he doesn't look like there's anything wrong with him,' Ruby breathed.

'He still has some issues he needs help with.' Oliver was matter-of-fact now, surgeon telling it like it was. 'He'll need physiotherapy to help him walk, and he might need professional help to learn how to control his bladder and bowels, but the early signs are that he'll be able to lead a perfectly normal life.'

'He looks…perfect already.' Ruby was riveted and so was Em. She was watching Ruby's face. She was watching Ruby's hand, cradling her bump. 'My little one…my little girl…she could be perfect, too?'

'I think she already is.' Oliver was smiling down at her. 'She has a great mum who's taking the best care of her. And you have the best midwife…'

Em flashed him a look of surprise. There was no need to make this personal.

But for Ruby, this was nothing but personal. 'Em says she'll stay with me,' Ruby told him. 'At the operation and again when my baby's born. There's a chance that she can't—she says no one's ever totally sure because babies are unpredictable—but she's promised to try. I hope she can, but if she's not then she's introduced me to Sophia, or Isla will take over. But you'll look after…' Her hand cradled the bump again as she looked anxiously at Oliver. 'You'll look after us both?'

'I will.' And it was a vow.

'Tell me again why I need a Caesarean later—when my baby's born properly?'

He nodded, closed his laptop and sat back in a visitor's

chair, to all appearances prepared to chat for as long as Ruby wanted. He was busy, Em knew. As well as the promises he'd made her to childmind on Saturday, she knew he already had a full caseload of patients. But right now Ruby was being given the impression that he had all the time in the world, and that time was Ruby's.

He was…gorgeous. She knew it, she'd always known it, but suddenly the thought almost blindsided her.

And it was more than him being gorgeous, she thought, feeling dazed. She was remembering why she'd loved this man.

And she was thinking—idiotically—that she loved him still.

Concentrate on medicine, on your patient, on anything other than Oliver, she told herself fiercely. Concentrating on Oliver was just too scary.

What had Ruby asked? Why she needed a Caesarean?

'You see the incision we just cut in Rufus's mum's uterus?' Oliver was saying, flicking back to the screen, where they could see the now closed incision in the abdomen. 'I've stitched it with care, as I'll stitch you with care, but when your bub comes out, she'll push. You have no idea how hard a baby can push. She wants to get out to meet you, and nothing's going to stop her. So maybe she'll push against that scar, and if she pushes hard enough on very new scar tissue she might cause you to bleed. I have two people I care about, Ruby. I care about your daughter but my absolute priority is to keep you safe. That means a Caesarean birth, because, much as I want to meet your baby, we'll need to deliver her before she even thinks about pushing.'

'But if you wanted to keep me really safe you wouldn't operate in the first place,' Ruby muttered, a trace of the old resentment resurfacing. But it didn't mess with Oliver's composure.

'That's right,' he agreed, his tone not changing. 'I believe we *will* keep you safe but there are risks. They're minor but they're real. That's why it's your choice. You can still pull out. Right up to the time we give you the anaesthetic, you can pull out, and no one will think the worse of you. That's your right.'

The room fell silent. It was such a hard decision to make, Em thought, and once again she thought, Where was this kid's mum?

But, surprisingly, when Ruby spoke again it seemed that worry about the operation was being supplanted by something deeper.

'If I had her...' Ruby said, and then amended her statement. '*When* I have her...after she's born, she'll have a scar, too.'

'She will,' Oliver told her, as watchful as Em, waiting to know where Ruby was going with this.

'And she'll have it for ever?'

'Yes.'

'She might hate it—as a teenager,' Ruby whispered. 'I know I would.'

'I'll do my best to make it as inconspicuous as possible—and cosmetic touch-ups when she's older might help even more. It shouldn't be obvious.'

'But teenagers freak out about stuff like that. I know I would,' Ruby whispered. 'And she won't have a mum to tell her it's okay.'

'If she's adopted, she'll have a mum,' Em ventured. 'Ruby, we've gone through what happens. Adoption is your choice all the way. You'll get to meet the adoptive parents. You'll know she goes to parents who'll love her.'

'But…I'll love her more. She's *my* baby.'

And suddenly Ruby was crying, great fat tears slipping down her face, and Em shifted so she could take her into her arms. And as she did so, Oliver's laptop slid off the bed and landed with a crash on the floor.

Uh-oh. But Em didn't move. For now she couldn't afford to think of computers. For now holding this girl was the most important thing in the world.

But still… A car and then a laptop…

She was starting to be an expensive ex-wife, she thought ruefully, and she almost smiled—but, of course, she didn't. She simply held Ruby until the sobs receded, until Ruby tugged away and grabbed a handful of tissues. That was a bit late. Em's shoulder was soaked, but who cared? How many times had Em ever finished a shift clean? She could count them on one hand. She always got her hands dirty, one way or another.

And it seemed, so did Oliver, for he was still there. Most consultants would have fled at the first sign of tears, Em thought. As a breed, surgeons weren't known for their empathy.

He'd risen, but he was standing by the door, watching, and there was definitely sympathy. Definitely caring.

He was holding the two halves of his laptop. The screen had completely split from the keyboard. And the screen itself…smashed.

'Whoops,' she said, as Ruby blew her nose.

He glanced down at the ruined machine. 'As you say, whoops.'

And as Ruby realised what he was holding, the teenager choked on something that was almost a laugh. 'Em's smashed your computer,' she said, awed. 'Do you mind?'

'I can't afford to mind.'

'Why not?' She was caught, pulled out of her misery by a smashed computer.

'Priorities,' he said. 'You. Baby. Computer. In that order.'

'What about Em?' she asked, a touch of cheekiness emerging. 'Is she a priority?'

'Don't you dare answer,' Em told him. 'Not until you've checked that your computer is covered by insurance. Ruby, if you're rethinking your plans to adopt…'

'I think…I might be.'

'Then let's not make any decisions yet,' she said, hurriedly. Surely now wasn't the time to make such an emotional decision? 'Let's get this operation over with first.'

Ruby took a deep breath and looked from Oliver to Emily and back again. 'Maybe I do need a bit of time,' she conceded. 'Maybe a sleep…time to think.'

'Of course you do.' She pulled up her covers and tucked her in. 'Ruby, nothing's urgent. No decisions need to be made now. Just sleep.'

'Thank you. And, Dr Evans…'

'Mmm?' Oliver was about to leave but turned back.

'I hope your computer's all right.'

'It will be,' he said. But it wouldn't. Em could see the smashed screen from where she stood. 'But even if it's not, it's not your problem,' he said, gently now, almost as a blessing. 'From here on, Ruby, we don't want you to worry about a thing. You've put yourself in our hands and we'll keep you safe. Em and I are a great team. You and your baby are safe with us.'

His lovely, gentle bedside manner lasted until they were ten feet from Ruby's door. Em closed the door behind her, looked ahead—and Oliver was staring straight at her. Vibrating with anger.

'You're planning on talking her out of keeping her baby?'

The turnabout from empathy to anger was shocking. The gentleness had completely gone from his voice. What she saw now was fury.

She faced him directly, puzzled. 'What are you saying? I didn't. I'm not.'

'You are. She'd decided on adoption but now she's changing her mind. But you stopped her.'

'I didn't stop her. I'd never do that.' She thought back to the scene she'd just left, trying to replay her words. 'I just said she had time…'

'You told her not to make a decision now. Why not? Right now she's thinking of keeping her baby. You don't think it's important to encourage her?'

'I don't think it's my right to direct her one way or another.' She felt herself getting angry in response. 'All I saw in there was a frightened, tired kid who's facing major surgery tomorrow. Who needs to stay calm and focused. Who doesn't need to be making life-changing decisions right now. She's already decided enough.'

'But maybe when you're emotional, that's the time to make the decision. When she knows she loves her baby.'

'She'll always love her baby.' Em was struggling to stay calm in the face of his anger—in the face of his accusation? 'Ruby is a seventeen-year-old, terrified kid with no family support at all. If she decides to keep this baby, it'll change her life for ever. As it will if she gives it up for adoption. What I did in there—and, yes, I interceded—was give her space. If she wants to keep her baby, she'll need every ounce of strength and then some.'

'She'll get support.'

'And she can never be a kid again. But, then, after this, maybe being a kid is no longer an option. But I agree, that's none of my business. Oliver, is this discussion going anywhere? I've been away from the birthing suites for over an hour and I don't know what's going on. I may well be needed.'

'You won't influence her?'

'Why would I influence her?'

'Because you believe in adoption.'

'And you don't? Because of what happened to you when you were a kid?' Anger was washing over her now. Yes, she should get back to the birthing suites but what was it he was accusing her of? 'Get over it, Oliver. Move on. Not every adoptive mother is like yours, and not every birth mother is capable of loving. There's a whole lot of grey in between the black and white, and it's about time you saw it.'

'So you won't encourage her to adopt?'

'What are you expecting me to do?' She was confused now, as well as angry. She put her hands on her hips and glared. 'Are you thinking I might pop in there, offer to adopt it myself and get myself another baby? Is that what you're thinking?'

'I would never—'

'You'd better not. A midwife influencing a mother's decision is totally unethical. How much more so is a midwife offering to adopt? I'll do neither. I have my kids, Oliver, and I love them to bits. I have no wish for more.'

'But Gretta's going to die.'

Why had he said it? It had just come out, and he could have bitten his tongue from his head. Em's face bleached white and she leaned back against the wall for support.

Dear heaven… What sort of emotional drop kick was he? Suggesting one kid was going to die so she was lining up for another? Where had the thought come from?

It was confusion, he thought. Maybe it was even anger that she'd got on with her life without him.

Or maybe it was sheer power of testosterone washing through him—because the woman who should be his wife was looking at him as if he was a piece of dirt.

Where to start with apologies? He'd better haul himself back under control, and fast. 'Hell, Em, I'm sorry. I didn't mean that the way it came out, truly.' He reached out and touched her stricken face, and the way he felt… sick didn't begin to describe it. 'Can you forget I said it? Of all the insensitive oafs… I know Gretta's health has nothing to do with…anything. I'm so sorry. Can you wipe it? I know you love Gretta…'

'Are you talking about Emily's little girl?'

They both turned to face the newcomer, and it was a relief to turn away from each other. The tension between them was so tight it was threatening to break, to fly back and hit both of them.

Oliver recognised the young man heading towards them. Oliver had been introduced to Noah Jackson earlier in the week. He was a surgical registrar, almost at the end of his training. 'Technically brilliant,' Tristan, the paediatric cardiologist, had told him. 'But his people skills leave a whole lot to be desired.'

And now he proceeded to display just that.

'Hi, Em,' he called, walking up to them with breezy insouciance. 'Are you discussing Gretta's progress? How's she going?'

'She's…okay,' Em said, and by the way she said it Oliver knew there was baggage behind the question.

'You ought to meet Gretta,' Noah told Oliver, seemingly oblivious to the way Em's face had shuttered. 'She's worth a look. She has Down's, with atrioventricular septal defects, massive heart problems, so much deformity that even Tristan felt he couldn't treat her. Yet she's survived. I've collated her case notes from birth as part of my final-year research work. I'd love to write her up for the med journals. It'd give me a great publication. Em's care has been nothing short of heroic.'

'I've met her,' Oliver said shortly, glancing again at Em. Gretta—a research project? He could see Em's distress. 'Now's not...' he started.

But the young almost-surgeon wouldn't be stopped. 'Gretta wasn't expected to live for more than a year,' he said, with enthusiasm that wouldn't be interrupted. 'It'll make a brilliant article—the extent of the damage, the moral dilemma facing her birth mother, her decision to walk away—Em's decision to intervene and now the medical resources and the effort to keep her alive this far. Em, please agree to publication. You still haven't signed. But Tristan says she's pretty close to the end. If I could examine her one last time...'

And Oliver saw the wash of anger and revulsion on Em's face—and finally he moved.

He put his body between the registrar and Em. Noah was tall but right now Oliver felt a good foot taller. Anger did that. Of all the insensitive...

'You come near Em again with your requests for information about her daughter—her *daughter*, Noah, not her patient—and I'll ram every page of your case notes down your throat. Don't you realise that Em loves Gretta? Don't you realize she's breaking in two, and you're treating her daughter like a bug under a microscope?'

'Hey, Em's a medical colleague,' Noah said, still not getting it. 'She knows the score—she knew it when she took Gretta home. She can be professional.'

'Is that what you're being—professional?'

'If we can learn anything from this, then, yes…'

Enough. Em looked close to fainting.

The lift was open behind them. Oliver grabbed Noah by the collar of his white jacket, twisted him round and practically kicked him into the lift.

'What…?' Noah seemed speechless. 'What did I say?'

'You might be nearing the end of your surgical training,' Oliver snapped. 'But you sure aren't at the end of your training to be a decent doctor. You need to learn some people skills, fast. I assume you did a term in family medicine during your general training, but whether you did or not, you're about to do another. And another after that if you still don't get it. I want you hands-on, treating people at the coal face, before you're ever in charge of patients in a surgical setting.'

'You don't have that authority.' The young doctor even had the temerity to sound smug.

'You can believe that,' Oliver growled. 'You're welcome—for all the good it'll do you. Now get out of here while I see if I can fix the mess you've made.'

'I haven't made a mess.'

'Oh, yes, you have,' Oliver snapped, hitting the 'Close' button on the lift with as much force as he'd like to use on Noah. 'And you've messed with someone who spends her life trying to fix messes. Get out of my sight.'

The lift closed. Oliver turned back to Em. She hadn't moved. She was still slumped on the wall, her face devoid of colour. A couple of tears were tracking down her face.

'It's okay,' she managed. 'Oliver, it's okay. He's just saying it like it is.'

'He has no right to say anything at all,' Oliver snapped, and he couldn't help himself. She was so bereft. She was so gutted.

She was...his wife?

She wasn't. Their long separation to all intents and purposes constituted a divorce, but right now that was irrelevant.

His Em was in trouble. *His Em.*

He walked forward and took her into his arms.

She shouldn't let him hold her. She had no right to be in his arms.

She had no right to want to be in his arms.

Besides, his words had upset her as much as Noah's had. His implication that she could replace Gretta...

But she knew this man. She'd figured it out—the hurt he'd gone through as a kid, the rejection, the knowledge that he'd been replaced by his adoptive parents' 'real' son.

Noah was just plain insensitive. He was arrogant and intelligent but he was lacking emotional depth. Oliver's comments came from a deep, long-ago hurt that had never been resolved.

And even if it hadn't, she thought helplessly, even if he was as insensitive as Noah, even if she shouldn't have anything to do with him, for now she wanted to be here.

To be held. By her husband.

For he still felt like her husband. They'd been married for five years. They'd lain in each other's arms for five years.

For five years she'd thought she had the perfect marriage.

But she hadn't. Of course she hadn't. There had been ghosts she'd been unable to expunge, and those ghosts were with him still. He couldn't see…

Stop thinking, she told herself fiercely, almost desperately. Stop thinking and just be. Just let his arms hold me. Just feel his heart beat against mine. Just pretend…

'Em, I'm sorry,' he whispered into her hair.

'For?'

'For what I said. Even before Noah, you were hurt. I can't begin to think how I could have said such a thing.'

'It doesn't matter.' But it did. It was the crux of what had driven them apart. For Oliver, adoption was simply a transaction. Hearts couldn't be held…

As theirs hadn't. Their marriage was over.

But still she held. Still she took comfort, where she had no right to take comfort. They'd been separated for five years!

So why did he still feel like…home? Why did everything about him feel as if here was her place in the world?

'Hey!' A hospital corridor was hardly the place to hold one's ex-husband—to hold anyone. It was busy and bustling and their sliver of intimacy couldn't last.

It was Isla, hurrying along the corridor, smiling—as Isla mostly smiled right now. The sapphire on her finger seemed to have changed Em's boss's personality. 'You know I'm all for romance,' she said as she approached. 'But the corridor's not the place.' She glanced down at the sapphire on her finger and her smile widened. 'Alessi and I find the tea room's useful. No one's in there right now…'

'Oh, Isla…' Em broke away, flushing. 'Sorry. It's not… Dr Evans was just…just…'

But Isla had reached them now and was seeing Em's

distress for herself. 'Nothing's wrong with Ruby, is there?' she asked sharply.

'No.' Oliver didn't break his composure. 'But you have a problem with Dr Noah Jackson. He seems to think Em's Gretta is a research experiment.'

'Noah's been upsetting my midwife?' Isla's concern switched to anger, just like that. 'Let me at him.'

'I don't think there's any need,' Em managed. 'Oliver practically threw him into the lift.'

'Well, good for you,' Isla said, smiling again. 'I do like an obstetrician who knows when to act, and one who knows the value of a good cuddle is worth his weight in gold.' She glanced again at her ring. 'I should know. But, Em, love, if you've finished being cuddled, I would like you back in the birthing suite.'

'Of course,' Em said, and fled.

There was a moment's silence. Then...

'Don't you mess with my midwives,' Isla said, and Oliver looked at her and thought she saw a whole lot more than she let on.

'I won't.'

She eyed him some more. 'You two have baggage? Your name's the same.'

'We don't have...baggage.'

'I don't believe it.' She was still thoughtful. 'But I'll let it lie. All I'll say is to repeat—don't mess with my midwives.'

Thursday night was blessedly uneventful. Gretta seemed to have settled. Em should have had a good night's sleep.

She didn't but the fact that she stared into the dark and thought of Oliver was no fault of...anyone.

Oliver was no business of hers.

But he'd held her and he felt all her business.

Oliver…

Why had he come here to work? Of all the unlucky coincidences…

But it wasn't a simple coincidence, she conceded. The Victoria had one of Australia's busiest birthing units. It was also right near her mother's home so it had made sense that she get a job here after the loss of Josh.

And after the loss of Oliver.

Don't go there, she told herself. Think of practicalities.

It made sense that Oliver was back here, she told herself. Charles Delamere head-hunted the best, and he'd have known Oliver had links to Melbourne.

So she should leave?

Leave the Victoria? Because Oliver had…cuddled her?

It's not going to happen again, she told herself fiercely. And I won't leave because of him. There's no need to leave.

He could be a friend. Like Isla. Like Sophia.

Yeah, right, she told herself, punching her pillow in frustration. Oliver Evans, just a friend?

Not in a million years.

But she had no choice. She could do this. Bring on tomorrow, she told herself.

Bring on a way she could treat Oliver as a medical colleague and nothing else.

CHAPTER SEVEN

FRIDAY. EM'S DAY was cleared so she could focus on Ruby. Isla was aware of the situation. 'If she really has no one, then you'd better be with her all the way.'

So she stayed with Ruby in the hour before she was taken to Theatre. She spent their time discussing—of all things—Ruby's passion for sewing. Ruby had shyly shown her her handiwork the day before, so Em had brought in one of Toby's sweaters. Ruby was showing her how to darn a hole in the elbow.

'Darning's a dying art,' she'd told Em, so Em had found the sweater and brought a darning mushroom— Adrianna had one her grandmother had used!—and needle and thread and asked for help.

Ruby took exquisite care with the intricate patch. When she was finished Em could scarcely see where the hole had been, and darning and the concentration involved worked a charm. When the orderlies came to take Ruby to Theatre, Ruby was shocked that the time had already arrived.

She squeezed Em's hand. 'Th-thank you. Will I see you later?'

'I'm coming with you,' Em declared, packing up the darning equipment. 'Isla's told me if I'm to help deliver your baby at term then I should introduce myself to her now. So I'm to stay in the background, not faint, and admire Dr Evans's handiwork.'

'You'd never faint.'

'Don't you believe it,' Em told her, and proceeded to give her some fairly gross examples. She kept right up with the narrative while Ruby was pushed through to Theatre, while pre-meds were given, while they waited for the theatre to be readied. Finally, as Ruby was wheeled into Theatre, they were both giggling.

Oliver was waiting, gowned and ready. So, it seemed, was a cast of thousands. This was surgery at its most cutting edge. They were operating on two patients, not one, but one of those patients was a foetus that was not yet viable outside her mother. The logistics were mind-bending and it would take the combined skills of the Victoria's finest to see it succeed.

Shock to the foetus could cause abortion. Therefore the anaesthetic had to be just right—they had not only the Victoria's top anaesthetist, but also the anaesthetic registrar. Heinz Zigler was gowned and ready. Tristan Hamilton, paediatric cardiologist, was there to check on the baby's heart every step of the way. There were so many possible complications.

The surgery itself was demanding but everything else had to be perfect, as well. If amniotic fluid was lost it had to be replaced. If the baby bled, that blood had to be replaced, swiftly but so smoothly the loss couldn't be noticed. Everything had to be done with an eye to keeping the trauma to the baby at the absolute minimum.

'Hey, Ruby.' Oliver welcomed the girl warmly as she was wheeled in, and if he was tense he certainly wasn't showing it. 'What's funny?'

'Em's been telling me—' Ruby was almost asleep from the pre-meds but she was still smiling '—about muddles. About her work.'

'Did she tell you about the time she helped deliver twins and the team messed up their bracelets?' Oliver was smiling with his patient, but he found a chance to glance—and smile—at Em. 'So Mathew Riley was wrapped in a pink rug and Amanda Riley was wrapped in a blue rug. It could have scarred them for life.'

Em thought back all those years. She'd just qualified, and it had been one of the first prem births where she'd been midwife in charge. Twins, a complex delivery, and the number of people in the birthing room had made her flustered. Afterwards Oliver had come to the prem nursery to check on his handiwork. The nurse in charge—a dragon of a woman who shot first and asked questions later—had been in the background, as Oliver had unwrapped the blue bundle.

Em had been by his side. She'd gasped and lost colour but Oliver hadn't said a word; hadn't given away by the slightest intake of breath that he'd become aware she'd made a blunder that could have put her job at risk. But the mistake was obvious—the incubators had been brought straight from the birthing suite and were side by side. There was no question who each baby was. Without saying a word, somehow Oliver helped her swap blankets and wristbands and the charge nurse was unaware to this day.

That one action had left her…smitten.

But it hadn't just been his action, she conceded. It had also been the way he'd smiled at her, and then as she'd tried to thank him afterwards, it had been the way he'd laughed it off and told her about dumb things he'd done as a student…and then asked her to have dinner with him…

'I reckon I might like to be a nurse,' Ruby said sleepily. 'You reckon I might?'

'I reckon you're awesome,' Oliver told her. 'I reckon you can do anything you want.'

And then Ruby's eyes flickered closed. The chief anaesthetist gave Oliver a nod—and the operation was under way.

Lightness was put aside.

Oliver had outlined the risks to Ruby—and there were risks. Exposing this tiny baby to the outside world when she was nowhere near ready for birth was so dangerous. Em had no idea how many times it had been done in the past, how successful it had been, but all she knew as she watched was that if it was her baby there was no one she'd rather have behind the scalpel than Oliver.

He was working side by side with Heinz. They were talking through the procedure together, glancing up every so often at the scans on the screens above their heads, checking positions. They wanted no more of the baby exposed than absolutely necessary.

Another screen showed what they were doing. To Em in the background she could see little of the procedural site but this was being recorded—to be used as Rufus's operation had been—to reassure another frantic mum?

Please let it have the same result, she pleaded. She was acting as gofer, moving equipment back and forth within reach of the theatre nurse as needed, but she still had plenty of time to watch the screen.

And then the final incision was made. Gently, gently, the baby was rotated within the uterus—and she could see the bulge that was the unsealed spine.

There was a momentary pause as everyone saw it. A collective intake of breath.

'The poor little tacker,' Tristan breathed. 'To be born like that…she'd have had no chance of living a normal life.'

'Then let's see if we can fix it,' Oliver said in a voice Em had never heard before. And she knew that every nerve was on edge, every last ounce of his skill and Heinz's were at play here.

Please…

The complexity, the minuscule size, the need for accuracy, it was astounding.

Oliver was sweating. Not only was the intensity of his work mind-blowing, but the theatre itself had to be set at a high enough temperature to stop foetal shock.

'Em.' Chris, the chief theatre nurse, called back to her. 'Take over the swabs.'

All hands were needed. Em saw where she, too, was needed. She moved seamlessly into position and acted to stop Oliver's sweat obscuring his vision.

He wasn't aware of her. He wasn't aware of anything.

They were using cameras to blow up the images of the area he and Heinz were working on. Every person there was totally focused on the job or on the screens. Two people at once—two hearts, two lives…

She forgot to breathe. She forgot everything but keeping Oliver's vision clear so he could do what had to be a miracle.

And finally they were closing. Oliver was stitching—maybe his hands were steadier than Heinz's because he was working under instruction. He was inserting what seemed almost microstitches, carefully, carefully manoeuvring the spinal wound closed. Covering the spinal cord and the peripheral nerves. Stopping future damage.

The spine was closed. They were replacing the amniotic fluid. Oliver was closing the uterus, conferring with Heinz, seemingly relaxing a little.

The outer wound was being closed.

The thing was done.

Emily felt like sagging.

She wouldn't. She wiped Oliver's forehead for the final time and at last he had space to turn and give her a smile. To give the whole team a smile. But his smile ended with Em.

'We've done it,' he said with quiet triumph. 'As long as we can keep her on board for another few weeks, we've saved your baby.'

'Your baby'...

Where had that come from?

And then she thought back to the teasing he'd given her when they'd first met, when they'd been working together, she as a brand-new nurse, he as a paediatric surgeon still in training.

'Em, the way you expose your heart... You seem to greet every baby you help deliver as if it's your own,' he'd told her. *'By the end of your career, you'll be like Old Mother Hubbard—or the Pied Piper of Hamelin. Kids everywhere.'*

And wouldn't she just love that! She thought fleetingly of the two she was allowed to love. Gretta and Toby.

She did love them, fiercely, wonderfully, but she looked down at Ruby now and she knew that she had love to spare. Heart on her sleeve or not, she loved this teenage mum, and she loved the little life that was now securely tucked back inside her.

The heart swelled to fit all comers…

She thought back to Oliver's appalling adoptive mother and she thought he'd never known that.

He still didn't know it and they'd gone their separate ways because of it.

She stood back from the table. Her work there was done. She'd wait for Ruby in the recovery ward.

The team had another patient waiting for surgery. Oliver was moving on.

Em already had moved on. She just had to keep moving.

'Well done.' Out at the sinks the mood was one of quiet but deep satisfaction. There'd be no high fives, not yet—everyone knew the next few days would be critical—but the procedure had gone so smoothly surely they'd avoided embryo shock.

Tristan hitched himself up on the sinks and regarded his friend with satisfaction. He and Oliver had done their general surgical training together. They'd split as Oliver had headed into specialist surgical obstetrics and Tristan into paediatric cardiology, but their friendship was deep and longstanding.

Tristan alone knew the association between Em and Oliver. They'd had one heated discussion about it already…

'The hospital grapevine will find out. Why keep it secret?'

'It's not a secret. It's just a long time ago. Moving on…'

But now…

'Are you telling me you and Em have really moved on?' Tristan demanded as he watched his friend ditch his theatre garb. 'Because, sure, Em's your patient's midwife and she was in Theatre as an observer in that capacity, but the contact you and she had… You might not have been aware how often you flicked her a glance but every time you were about to start something risky, it was like you were looking to her for strength.'

'What the…?' Where had this come from? As if he needed Em for strength? He'd been operating without Em for years.

He'd never depended on her.

'You might say it's in the past,' Tristan went on, inexorably. 'But she's still using your name, and as of today, as an onlooker, it seems to me that the marriage isn't completely over.'

'Will you keep your voice down?' There were nurses and orderlies everywhere.

'You think you can keep this to yourself?'

'It's not obvious.'

'It's obvious,' Tristan said, grinning. 'Midwife Evans and Surgeon Evans. Sparks. The grapevine will go nuts.'

'You're not helping.'

'I'm just observing.' Tristan pushed down from the bench. He and Oliver both had patients waiting. Always there were patients waiting.

'All I'm saying is that I'm interested,' Tristan said, heading for the door. 'Me and the rest of staff of the Victoria. And some of us are even more interested than others.'

Trained theatre staff were rostered to watch over patients in Recovery, but Isla had cleared the way for Em to stay with Ruby. With no family support, the need to keep Ruby calm was paramount. So Em sat by her bedside and watched. Ruby was drifting lightly towards consciousness, seeming to ease from sedation to natural sleep.

Which might have something to do with the way Em was holding her hand and talking to her.

'It's great, Ruby. You were awesome. Your baby was awesome. It's done, all fixed. Your baby will have the best of chances because of your decision.'

She doubted Ruby could hear her but she said it anyway, over and over, until she was interrupted.

'Hey.' She looked up and Sophia was watching her. Sophia was a partnering midwife, a friend, a woman who had the same fertility issues she did. If there was anyone in this huge staff she was close to, it was Sophia. 'Isla sent me down to see how the op went,' she said, pulling up a chair to sit beside Em. 'All's quiet on the Western Front. We had three nice, normal babies in quick succession this morning and not a sniff of a contraction this arvo. Isla says you can stay here as needed; take as long as you want.'

'We're happy, aren't we, Ruby?' Em said gently, squeezing Ruby's hand, but there was no response. Ruby's natural sleep had grown deeper. 'The operation went brilliantly.' And then, because she couldn't help herself, she added a rider. 'Oliver was brilliant.'

'Yeah, I'd like to talk to you about that,' Sophia said, diffidently now, assessing Ruby as she spoke and realising, as Em had, that there was little chance of Ruby taking in anything she said. 'Rumours are flying. Someone heard Tristan and Oliver talking at the sinks. Evans and Evans. No one's put them together until now. It's a common name. But…Evans isn't your maiden name, is it? Evans is your married name. And according to the rumours, that marriage would be between you and Oliver.'

Whoa. Em flinched. But then…it had to come out sooner or later, she thought. She might as well grit her teeth and confess.

'It was a long time ago,' she murmured. 'We split five years ago but changing my name didn't seem worth the complications. I was Emily Green before. I kind of like Emily Evans better.' She didn't want to say that going to a lawyer, asking for a divorce, had seemed…impossibly final.

'As you kind of like Oliver Evans?' Sophia wiggled down further in her chair, her eyes alight with interest. 'The theatre staff say there were all sorts of sparks between you during the op.'

'Ruby's in my care. Oliver was…keeping me reassured.' But she'd said it too fast, too defensively, and Sophia's eyebrows were hiking.

Drat hospitals and their grapevines, she thought. Actually, they were more than grapevines—they were like Jack's beanstalk. Let one tiny bean out of the can and it exploded to the heavens.

What had Oliver and Tristan been talking about to start this?

And…how was she to stop Sophia's eyebrows hitting the roof?

'You going to tell Aunty Sophia?' she demanded, settling down further in a manner that suggested she was going nowhere until Em did.

'You knew I was married.'

'Yeah, but not to Oliver. Oliver! Em, he's a hunk. And he's already getting a reputation for being one of those rarest of species—a surgeon who can talk to his patients. Honest, Em, he smiled at one of my mums on the ward this morning and my heart flipped. Why on earth…?'

'A smile doesn't make a marriage.' But it did, Em thought miserably. She'd loved that smile. What they'd had…

'So will you tell Aunty Sophia why you split?'

'Kids,' she said brusquely. She'd told Sophia she was infertile but only when Sophia had told her of her own problems. She hadn't elaborated.

'He left you because you couldn't have babies?'

'We…well, I already told you we went through IVF. Cycle upon cycle. What I didn't tell you was that finally I got pregnant. Josh was delivered stillborn at twenty-eight weeks.'

'Oh, Em…' Sophia stared at her in horror. 'You've kept that to yourself, all this time?'

'I don't…talk about it. It hurts.'

'Yeah, well, I can see that,' Sophia said, hopping up to give her friend a resounding hug. 'They say IVF can destroy a marriage—it's so hard. It split you up?'

'The IVF didn't.' Em was remembering the weeks after she'd lost Josh, how close she and Oliver had been, a couple gutted but totally united in their grief. If it hadn't been for Oliver then, she might have gone crazy.

Which had made what had come next even more devastating.

'So what…?'

'I couldn't…do IVF any more,' Em whispered.

Silence.

Ruby seemed soundly asleep. She was still holding the girl's hand. She could feel the strength of Ruby's heartbeat, and the monitors around her told her Ruby's baby was doing fine, as well. The world went on, she thought bleakly, remembering coming out of hospital after losing Josh, seeing all those mums, all those babies…

'Earth to Em,' Sophia said gently at last, and Em hauled herself together and gave her a bleak little smile.

'I wanted a family,' she whispered. 'I think…I was a bit manic after the loss but I was suddenly desperate. Maybe it was an obsession, I don't know, but I told Oliver I wanted to adopt, whatever the cost. And in the end, the cost was him.'

'He didn't want to adopt?'

'He's adopted himself. It wasn't happy, and he wouldn't concede there was another side. He wouldn't risk adoption because he didn't think he could love an adopted kid. And I wasn't prepared to give, either. We were two implacable forces, and there was nowhere to go but to turn away from each other. So there you have it, Sophia. No baby, no marriage. Can I ask you not to talk about it?'

'You don't have to ask,' Sophia said roundly. 'Of course I won't. But this hospital…the walls have ears and what it doesn't know it makes up. Now everyone knows you were married…'

'It'll be a one-day wonder,' Em told her, and then Ruby stirred faintly and her eyes flickered open.

'Well, hi,' Em said, her attention totally now on Ruby. 'Welcome to the other side, Ruby, love. The operation was a complete success. Now all we need to do is let you sleep and let your baby sleep until we're sure you're settled into nice, normal pregnancy again.'

CHAPTER EIGHT

SATURDAY.

Oliver did a morning ward round, walked into Ruby's room—and found Em there.

According to his calculations—and he'd made a few—Em should be off duty. Why was she sitting by Ruby's bedside?

She was darning…a sock?

Both women looked up as he walked in and both women smiled.

'Hey,' Ruby said. 'Is it true? Were you two married?'

'How…?' Em gasped.

'I just heard,' Ruby said blithely. 'It's true, isn't it?'

Em bundled up her needlework and rose—fast. 'Yes,' she managed. 'But it was a long time ago. Sorry, Oliver, I'll be out of your way.'

'Why are you here?' Damn, that had sounded accusatory and he hadn't meant to be.

'I'm off duty but Ruby's teaching me how to darn.'

'That's…important?'

'It is, as a matter of fact,' she said, tossing him a look that might well be described as a glower. And also a warning to keep things light. 'The whole world seems to toss socks away as soon as they get holes. Ruby and I are doing our bit to prevent landfill.'

'Good for you.' He still sounded stiff but he couldn't help it. 'Are you going home now?'

'Yes.'

'So why did you two split?' Ruby was under orders for complete bed rest but she was recovering fast, the bed rest was more for her baby's sake than for hers, and she was obviously aching for diversion.

'Incompatibility,' Em said, trying for lightness, stooping to give Ruby a swift kiss. 'He used to pinch all the bedcovers. He's a huncher—you know the type? He hunches all the covers round him and then rolls in his sleep. I even tried pinning the covers to my side of the bed but I was left with ripped covers and a doomed marriage. I'll pop in tomorrow, Ruby, but meanwhile is there anything you need?'

'More socks?' Ruby said shyly, and Em grinned.

'Ask Dr Evans. I'll bet he has a drawer full. I need to go, Ruby, love. Byee.'

And she was gone.

It had been an informal visit. She'd been wearing jeans and a colourful shirt and her hair was down. She had so much to do at home—he knew she did.

Why was she here on a day off?

Because she cared?

She couldn't stop caring. That had been one of the things he'd loved about her.

He still loved?

'You're still dotty about her,' Ruby said, and he realised he'd been staring at the corridor where she'd disappeared.

'Um…no. Just thinking I've never walked in on a darning lesson before. How's bub?'

'Still kicking.'

'Not too hard?'

'N-no.' And once again he copped that zing of fear.

This was why Em had 'popped in', he thought. This kid was far too alone.

That was Em. She carried her heart on her sleeve.

If it was up to Em they would have adopted, he thought, and, despite the things he'd said to her after Josh had died, he was beginning to accept she was capable of it. *It?* Of loving a child who wasn't her own. The way she'd held Gretta… The way she'd laughed at Toby… Okay, Em was as different from his adoptive mother as it was possible to be, and it had been cruel of him to suggest otherwise.

It had taken him a huge leap of faith to accept that he'd loved Em. Even though he'd supported her through IVF, even though he'd been overjoyed when she'd finally conceived, when Josh had died…

Had a small part of him been relieved? Had a part of him thought he could never extend his heart to all comers?

He would have loved Josh. He did. The morning when they'd sat looking down at the promise that had been their little son had been one of the worst of his life. But the pain that had gone with it…the pain of watching Em's face…

And then for Em to say let's adopt, let's put ourselves up for this kind of pain again for a child he didn't know…

'Let's check your tummy,' he told Ruby, but she was still watching him.

'You are still sweet on her.'

'She's an amazing woman. But as she said, I'm a huncher.'

'Is it because you couldn't have children?'

How...? 'No!'

'It's just, one of the nurses told me Em's got two foster-kids she looks after with her mum. If you and she were married, why didn't you have your own?'

'Ruby, I think you have quite enough to think about with your own baby, without worrying about other people's,' he said, mock sternly.

'You're saying butt out?'

'And let me examine you. Yes.'

'Yes, Doctor,' she said, mock meekly, but she managed the beginnings of a cheeky grin. 'But you can't tell me to butt out completely. It seemed no one in this hospital knew you guys have been married. So now everyone in this hospital is really, really interested. Me, too.'

After that he was really ambivalent about the babysitting he'd promised. Actually, he'd been pretty ambivalent in the first place. Work was zooming to speed with an intensity that was staggering. He could easily ring and say he was needed at the hospital and it wouldn't have been a lie.

But he'd promised, so he put his head down and worked and by a quarter to one he was pulling up outside the place Em called home.

Em was in the front yard, holding Toby on a push-along tricycle. When she saw him she swung Toby up into her arms and waved.

Toby hesitated a moment—and then waved, too.

The sight took him aback. He paused before getting out of the car. He knew Em was waiting for him, but he needed a pause to catch his breath.

This was the dream. They'd gone into their marriage expecting this—love, togetherness, family.

He'd walked away so that Em could still have it. The fact that she'd chosen to do it alone…

But she wasn't alone. She had her mum. She had Mike next door and his brood. She had great friends at the hospital.

The only one missing from the picture was him, and the decision to walk away had been his.

If he'd stayed, though, they wouldn't have had any of this. They'd be a professional couple, absorbed in their work and their social life.

How selfish was that? The certainties of five years ago were starting to seem just a little bit wobbly.

'Hey, are you stuck to the seat?' Em was carrying Toby towards him, laughing at him. She looked younger today, he thought. Maybe it was the idea that she was about to have some free time. An afternoon with her mum.

She was about to have some time off from kids who weren't her own.

But they were her own. Toby had his arms wrapped around her, snuggling into her shoulder.

He had bare feet. Em was tickling his toes as she walked, making him giggle.

She loved these kids.

He'd thought… Okay, he'd thought he was being selfless, walking away five years ago. He'd been giving up his marriage so Em could have what she wanted. Now… Why was he now feeling the opposite? Completely, utterly selfish?

Get a grip, he told himself. He was here to work.

'Your babysitter's here, ma'am,' he said, finally climbing from the car. 'All present and correct.'

She was looking ruefully at the car. 'Still the hire car? Can't you get parts?'

'They're hard to come by.' He'd spent hours on the internet tracking down the parts he needed.

'Oh, Ollie…'

No one called him Ollie.

Em did.

She put her hand on his arm and he thought, She's comforting me because of a wrecked car. And she's coping with kids with wrecked lives…

How to make a rat feel an even bigger rat.

But her sympathy was real. Everything about her was real, he thought. Em… He'd loved this woman.

He loved this woman?

'Hey, will you go with Uncle Ollie?' Em was saying, moving on, prising Toby away from his neck-hugging. 'I bet he knows how to tickle toes, too.'

'I can tickle toes.' He was a paediatric surgeon. He could keep a kid entertained.

But Toby caught him unawares. He twisted in Em's arms and launched himself across, so fast Oliver almost didn't catch him. Em grabbed, Oliver grabbed and suddenly they were in a sandwich hug, with Toby sandwiched in the middle.

Toby gave a muffled chortle, like things had gone exactly to plan. Which, maybe in Toby's world, they had.

But he had so much wrong with him. His tiny spine was bent; he'd have operation after operation in front of him, years in a brace…

He'd have Em.

He should pull away, but Em wasn't pulling away. For this moment she was holding, hugging, as if she needed it. As if his hug was giving her something…

Something that, as his wife, had once been her right?
'Em…'

But the sound of his voice broke the moment. She tugged away, flipped an errant curl behind her ear, tried to smile.

'Sorry. I should expect him to do that—he does it all the time with Mike. He has an absolute conviction that the grown-ups in his life are to be trusted never, ever to drop him, and so far it's paid off. One day, though, Toby, lad, you'll find out what the real world's like.'

'But you'll shield him as long as you can.'

'With every ounce of power I possess,' she said simply. 'But, meanwhile, Mum's ready to go. She's so excited she didn't sleep last night. Gretta's fed. Everything's ready, all I need to do is put on clean jeans and comb my hair.'

'Why don't you put on a dress?' he asked, feeling… weird. Out of kilter. This was none of his business, but he was starting to realise just how important this afternoon was to Em and her mum. And how rare. 'Make it a special occasion.'

'Goodness, Oliver, I don't think I've worn a dress for five years,' she flung at him over her shoulder as she headed into the house. 'Why would the likes of me need a dress?'

And he thought of the social life they'd once had. Did she miss it? he wondered, but he tickled Toby's toes, the little boy giggled and he knew that she didn't.

They left fifteen minutes later, like a pair of jail escapees, except that they were escapees making sure all home bases were covered. Their 'jail' was precious.

'Mike might come over later to collect Toby,' Em told him. 'Toby loves Mike, so if he does that's fine by us.

That'll mean you only have Gretta so you should cope easily. You have both our cellphone numbers? You know where everything is? And Gretta needs Kanga…if she gets upset, Kanga can fix her. But don't let her get tired. If she has trouble breathing you can raise her oxygen…'

'Em, trust me, I'm a doctor,' he said, almost pushing them out the door.

'And you have how much experience with kids?'

'I'm an obstetrician and a surgeon.'

'My point exactly. Here they're outside their mum, not inside, and you don't have an anaesthetist to put them to sleep. There's a stack of movies ready to play. You can use the sandpit, too. Gretta loves it, but you need to keep her equipment sand-free…'

'Em, go,' he said, exasperated. 'Adrianna, take Em's arm and pull. Em, trust me. You can, you know.'

'I do know that,' Em told him, and suddenly she darted back across the kitchen and gave him a swift kiss on the cheek. It was a thank-you kiss, a perfunctory kiss, and why it had the power to burn… 'I always have,' she said simply. 'You're a very nice man, Oliver Evans. I would have trusted you to be a great dad, even if you couldn't trust yourself. That's water under the bridge now, but I still trust you, even if it's only for an afternoon.'

And she blinked a couple of times—surely they weren't tears?—then ducked back and kissed Gretta once again—and she was gone.

And Oliver was left with two kids.

And silence.

The kids were watching him. Toby was in his arms, leaning back to gaze into his eyes. Cautiously assessing? Gretta was sitting in an oversized pushchair, surrounded by cushions.

To trust or not to trust?

Toby's eyes were suddenly tear-filled. A couple of fat tears tracked down his face.

Gretta just stared at him, her face expressionless. Waiting to see what happened next?

Both were silent.

These were damaged kids, he thought. Rejects. They'd be used to a life where they were left. They'd come from parents who couldn't or wouldn't care for them and they had significant medical problems. They'd be used to a life where hospital stays were the norm. They weren't kids who opened their mouths and screamed whenever they were left.

Could you be stoic at two and at four? That's how they seemed. Stoic.

It was a bit…gut-wrenching.

Kanga—it must be Kanga: a chewed, bedraggled, once blue stuffed thing with long back paws and a huge tail—was lying on the table. He picked it—him?—up and handed him to Toby. Gretta watched with huge eyes. This wasn't what was supposed to happen, her eyes said. This was *her* Kanga.

He lifted Gretta out of her chair with his spare arm and carried both kids out into the yard, under the spreading oak at the bottom of the garden where the lawn was a bit too long, lushly green.

He set both kids down on the grass. Fuzzy the dog flopped down beside them. He, too, seemed wary.

Toby was still holding Kanga. Warily.

He tugged Gretta's shoes off so both kids had bare feet. Em had made the tickling thing work. Maybe it'd work for him.

He took Kanga from Toby, wriggled him slowly towards Gretta's toes—and ticked Gretta's toes with Kanga's tail.

Then, as both kids looked astonished, he bounced Kanga across to Toby and tickled his.

Toby looked more astonished. He reached out to grab Kanga, but Oliver was too fast. The tickling tail went back to Gretta's toes—and then, as Toby reached further, Kanga bounced sideways and tickled Fuzzy on the nose.

Fuzzy opened his mouth to grab but Kanga boinged back to Gretta, this time going from one foot to the other.

And then, as Gretta finally reacted, Kanga boinged up and touched her nose—and then bounced back to Toby.

Toby stared down in amazement at his toes being tickled and his eyes creased, the corners of his mouth twitched—and he chuckled.

It was a lovely sound but it wasn't enough. Kanga bounced back to Gretta, kissed her nose again, then bounced right on top of Fuzzy's head.

Fuzzy leaped to his feet and barked.

Kanga went back to Toby's toes.

And finally, finally, and it was like a minor miracle all by itself, Gretta's serious little face relaxed. She smiled and reached out her hand.

'Kanga,' she said, and Kanga flew to her hand. She grabbed him and held, gazing dotingly at her beloved blue thing.

'Kanga,' she said again, and she opened her fingers—and held Kanga back out to Oliver.

Her meaning was clear. He's mine but it's okay to play. In fact, she wanted to play.

But that one word had left her breathless. What the…? He'd seen the levels of oxygen she was receiving and she was still breathless? But she was still game.

She was trusting.

He wanted to hug her.

She was four years old. He'd met her twice. He was feeling…feeling…

'Hey!' It was Mike, and thank heaven for Mike. He was getting emotional and how was a man to keep tickling when he was thinking of what was in store for this little girl? He looked across at the gate and smiled at Mike with gratitude.

'Hey, yourself.'

'We're going to the beach,' Mike called. 'You want to come?'

'I'm sitting the kids,' he said, and Mike looked at him like he was a moron.

'Yeah. Kid-sitting. Beach. It's possible to combine them—and your two love the beach. Katy and Drew are staying home—Katy's still under the weather but her mum's here and Drew has a mate over. But we have four kid seats in the wagon—we always seem to have a spare kid—and why not?'

Why not? Because he'd like to stay lying under the tree, tickling toes?

It wouldn't last. His child entertainment range was limited, to say the least, and both kids were looking eager.

But, Gretta… Sand… Maybe he could sort it.

'What if we put one of the car seats into your car,' Mike said, eyeing the rental car parked at the kerb. 'Rental cars always have bolts to hold 'em. That way you can follow me and if Gretta gets tired you can bring her straight home. And we have beach shelters for shade. We have so much beach gear I feel like a pack mule going up and down the access track. Katy's mum's packed afternoon tea. Coming?'

'Yeah,' he said, because there was nothing else he could say. But there was part of him that was thinking as he packed up and prepared to take his charges beachwards, I wouldn't have minded caring for them myself. I wouldn't have minded proving that I could be a...

A father? By minding them for a couple of hours? Would that make him a hero? Could it even disprove what he'd always felt—that you couldn't love a kid who wasn't your own? Of course it couldn't.

It was just that, as the kids had chuckled, he'd felt, for one sliver of a crazy moment, that he could have been completely wrong. That maybe his judgement five years ago had been clouded, distorted by his own miserable childhood.

And an afternoon alone with these kids would prove what? Nothing. He'd made a choice five years ago. It had been the only honest option, and nothing had changed.

Except the way Gretta was smiling at the thought of the beach seemed to be changing things, like it or not. And the knowledge that Em would think giving Gretta an afternoon at the beach was great.

Would it make Em smile?

'You coming, mate, or are you planning on writing a thesis on the pros and cons?' Mike demanded, and he caught himself and took Kanga from Toby and handed him to Gretta.

'We're coming,' he told him. He looked at the muscled hulk of a tattooed biker standing at the gate and Oliver Evans, specialist obstetric surgeon, admitted his failings. 'But you might need to help me plan what to take. I'm a great obstetrician but as a father I'm the pits.'

* * *

'You reckon he'll be okay? You reckon he'll manage?'

'If you're worried, ring Mike.'

Em and her mum were lying on adjoining massage tables. They had five minutes' 'down' time before the massage was to begin. The soft, cushioned tables were gently warmed, the lights were dim, the sound of the sea washed through the high windows and a faint but lovely perfume was floating from the candles in the high-set sconces.

They should almost be asleep already but Em couldn't stop fretting.

'Ring Mike and ask him to check,' Adrianna said again. 'We all want you to enjoy this. I want to enjoy this. Check.'

So she rang. She lay on her gorgeous table and listened to Mike's growl.

'You're not supposed to be worrying. Get back to doing nothing.'

'You've got Toby?'

'Me and Oliver—that's one hell of a name, isn't it?—we're gunna have to think of something shorter—have Toby—and my kids and Gretta. We're at the beach. Want to see? I'm sending a video. Watch it and then shut up, Em. Quit it with your worrying. Me and your Ollie have things in hand.'

He disconnected. She stared at the phone, feeling disconcerted. Strange. That her kids were somewhere else without her... With Oliver. Ollie...

No one called him Ollie except her, but now Mike was doing the same. It was like two parts of her life were merging.

The old and the new?

It was her imagination. Oliver…Ollie?…would do this afternoon of childminding and move on.

A ping announced the arrival of a message. She clicked and sure enough there was a video, filmed on Mike's phone and sent straight through.

There was Toby with Mike's two littlies. They were building a sandcastle—sort of. It was a huge mound of sand, covered with seaweed and shells. Fuzzy was digging a hole on the far side and Mike's bitser dog was barking in excitement.

As Em watched, Toby picked up a bucket of water and spilt it over the castle—and chuckled. Mike laughed off camera.

'If you think I don't have anything better to do than fill buckets for you, young Toby—you're right…'

And then the camera panned away, down to the shoreline—and Em drew in her breath.

For there was Oliver—and Gretta.

They were sitting on the wet sand, where the low, gentle waves were washing in, washing out.

Oliver had rigged a beach chair beside them, wedging it secure with something that looked like sandbags. Wet towels filled with sand?

Gretta's oxygen cylinder was high on the seat, safe from the shallow inrushes of water, but Ollie and Gretta were sitting on the wet sand.

He had Gretta on his knee. They were facing the incoming waves, waiting for one to reach them.

'Here it comes,' Oliver called, watching as a wave broke far out. 'Here it comes, Gretta, ready or not. One, two, three…'

And he swung Gretta back against his chest, hugging

her as the water surrounded them, washing Gretta's legs, swishing around his body.

He was wearing board shorts. He was naked from the waist up.

She'd forgotten his body...

No, she hadn't. Her heart couldn't clench like this if she'd forgotten.

'More,' Gretta whispered, wriggling her toes in the water, twisting so she could see the wave recede. Her eyes were sparkling with delight. She was so close to the other side, this little one, and yet for now she was just a kid having fun.

A kid secure with her... Her what?

Her friend. With Oliver, who couldn't give his heart.

Silently Em handed her phone to her mum and waited until Adrianna had seen the video.

Adrianna sniffed. 'Oh, Em...'

'Yeah.'

'Do you think...?'

'No.'

'It's such a shame.'

'It's the way it is,' Em said bleakly. 'But...but for now, he's making Gretta happy.'

'He's lovely,' Adrianna said stoutly.

'Don't I know it?' Em whispered. 'Don't I wish I didn't?'

'Em...'

The door opened. Their massage ladies entered, silently, expecting their clients to be well on the way on their journey to complete indulgence.

'Are you ready?' the woman due to massage Em asked. 'Can you clear your mind of everything past, of everything future and just let yourself be. For now there should be nothing outside this room.'

But there was, Em thought as skilful hands started their skin-tingling work. There was a vision of her ex-husband holding her little girl. Making Gretta happy.

Massages were wonderful, she decided as her body responded to the skill of the woman working on her.

They might be wonderful but thinking about Oliver was…better?

He sat in the waves and watched—and felt—Gretta enjoy herself. She was a wraith of a child, a fragile imp, dependent on the oxygen that sustained her, totally dependent on the adults who cared for her.

She trusted him. She faced the incoming waves with joy because she was absolutely sure Oliver would lift her just in time, protect the breathing tube, hug her against his body, protect her from all harm.

But harm was coming to this little one, and there was nothing anyone could do about it. He'd mentioned Gretta to Tristan and Tristan had spelt out the prognosis. With so much deformity of the heart, it was a matter of time…

Not very much time.

That he had this time with her today was precious. He didn't know her, she wasn't his kid, but, regardless, it was gold.

If he could somehow take the pain away…

He couldn't. He couldn't protect Gretta.

He couldn't protect Em.

Hell, but he wanted to. And not just for Em, he conceded. For this little one. This little girl who laughed and twisted and buried her face in his shoulder and then turned to face the world again.

Em loved her. *Loved her.*

An adopted child.

He'd thought… Yeah, okay, he knew. If Em was able to have her own child it'd all change. Gretta would take second place.

But did he know? Five years ago he'd been sure. He'd been totally judgmental and his marriage was over because of it.

Now the sands were shifting. He was shifting.

'More,' Gretta ordered, and he realised two small waves had washed over her feet and he hadn't done the lift and squeal routine. Bad.

'Em wouldn't forget,' he told Gretta as he lifted and she squealed. 'Em loves you.'

But Gretta's face was buried in his shoulder, and that question was surfacing—again. Over and over.

Had he made the mistake of his life?

Could he…?

Focus on Gretta, he told himself. Anything else was far too hard.

Anything else was far too soon.

Or five years too late?

CHAPTER NINE

BY THE TIME Em and Adrianna arrived home, Oliver had the kids squeaky clean. He'd bathed them, dressed them in their PJs, tidied the place as best he could and was feeling extraordinarily smug about his child-minding prowess.

The kids were tired but happy. All Em and Adrianna had to do was feed them and tuck them into bed. He could leave. Job done.

They walked in looking glowing. They both had beautifully styled, shiny hair. They both looked as squeaky clean as the kids—scrubbed? They'd obviously shopped a little.

Em was wearing a new scarf in bright pink and muted greens. It made her look…how Em used to look, he thought. Like a woman who had time to think about her appearance. Free?

And impressed.

'Wow.' Both women were gazing around the kitchen in astonishment. The kids were in their chairs at the table. Oliver had just started making toast to keep them going until dinner. 'Wow,' Adrianna breathed again. 'There's not even a mess.'

'Mike took them all to the beach,' Em reminded her, but she was smiling at Oliver, her eyes thanking him.

'Hey, I had to clean the bathroom,' Oliver said, mock wounded. 'I've had to do some work.'

'Of course you have.' Adrianna flopped onto the nearest chair. 'Hey, if we make some eggs we could turn that toast into soldiers, and the kids' dinner is done. Kids, how about if I eat egg and toast soldiers too, and then I'll flop into bed, as well. I'm pooped.' But then she turned thoughtful. 'But, Em, you aren't ready for bed yet. You look fabulous, the night's still young, the kids are good and Oliver's still here. Why don't you two go out to dinner?'

Em stared at her like she'd lost her mind. 'Dinner…'

'You know, that thing you eat at a restaurant. Or maybe it could be fish and chips overlooking the bay. It's a gorgeous night. Oliver, do you have anything else on?'

'No, but—'

'Then go on, the two of you. You know you want to.'

'Mum, we don't want to.'

'Really?' Adrianna demanded. 'Honestly? Look at me, Em, and say you really don't want to go out to dinner with Oliver. Oliver, you do the same.'

Silence.

'There you go, then,' she said, satisfied. 'Off you go. Shoo.'

What else could they do but follow instructions? The night was warm and still, a combination unusual for Melbourne, where four seasons were often famously represented in one day. But this night the gods were smiling. Even the fish-and-chip kiosk didn't have too long a queue. Oliver ordered, then he and Em walked a block back from the beach to buy a bottle of wine, and returned just as their order was ready.

They used to do this often, Em thought. Once upon a time...

'I still have our picnic rug,' Oliver said ruefully, as they collected their feast. 'But it's in the back of the Morgan.'

'I'm sorry.'

'Don't be. Just be glad your wagon only got scratches—you're the one who's dependent on it. Moving on... Hey, how about this?' A family was just leaving an outside table and it was pretty much in the best position on the beachfront. Oliver swooped on it before a bunch of teenagers reached it, spread his parcels over it and signalled her to come. Fast.

'You're worse than the seagulls,' she retorted, smiling at his smug expression. 'Talk about swoop for the kill...'

'Table-swooping's one of my splinter skills,' he told her. 'Surely you remember.'

'I try...not to.'

'Does that help? Trying not to?'

Silence. She couldn't think of an answer. They unwrapped their fish and chips and ate a few. They watched a couple of windsurfers trying to guide their kites across the bay with not enough breeze, but the question still hung.

How soon could you forget a marriage? Never? It was never for her.

'I... How was America?' she asked at last, because she had to say something, the silence was becoming oppressive.

'Great. I learned so much.'

'You went away an obstetrician and came back...'

'I'm still first and foremost an obstetrician.'

'But you have the skills to save Ruby's baby—and countless others. You must feel it's worth it.'

'Em...'

'And you wouldn't have done that if we'd stayed together.' She was determined to get this onto some sort of normal basis, where they could talk about their marriage as if it was just a blip in their past. It was nothing that could affect their future. 'But I'm surprised you haven't met anyone else.' She hesitated but then ploughed on. She needed to say this. Somehow.

'You ached to be a dad,' she whispered, because somehow saying it aloud seemed wrong. 'I thought... There's nothing wrong with you. It's me who has the fertility problems. I thought you'd have met someone else by now and organised our divorce. Isn't that why we split? I sort of...I sort of wanted to think of you married with a couple of kids.'

'Did you really want that?' His curt response startled her into splashing her wine. She didn't want it anyway, she decided. She put down her glass with care and met his look head-on.

Say it like it is.

'That's what you wanted. That's why I agreed to separate.'

'I thought ending the marriage was all about you needing a partner so you could adopt.'

'It's true I wanted kids,' she managed, and her voice would hardly work for her. It was hard even to whisper. 'But I never wanted another husband than you.'

'You didn't want me.'

'Your terms were too hard, Oliver. Maybe now... maybe given some space it might be different. But we'd lost Josh and I was so raw, so needy. All I wanted was a child to hold… I think maybe I was a little crazy. I demanded too much of you. I hadn't realised quite how badly you'd been wounded.'

'I hadn't been wounded.'

'I've met your adoptive parents, remember? I've met your appalling brother.'

'I'm well over that.'

'Do you ever get over being not wanted? You were adopted, seemingly adored, and then suddenly supplanted by your parents' "real" son. I can't imagine how much that must have hurt.'

'It's past history.'

'It's not,' she said simply. 'Because it affects who you are. It always will. Maybe…' She hesitated but this had been drifting in and out of her mind for five years now. Was it better left unsaid? Maybe it was, but she'd say it anyway. 'Maybe it will affect any child you have, adopted or not. Maybe that's why you haven't moved on. Would you have loved Josh, Oliver, or would you have resented him because he'd have had the love you never had?'

'That's nuts.'

'Yeah? So why not organise a divorce? Why not remarry?'

'Because of you,' he said, before he could stop himself. 'Because I still love you.'

She stilled. The whole night seemed to still.

There were people on the foreshore, people on the beach. The queue to the fish-and-chip shop was right behind them. Kids were flying by on their skateboards. Mums and dads were pushing strollers.

Because I still love you…

He reached out and touched her hand lightly, his lovely

surgeon's fingers tracing her work-worn skin. She spent too much time washing, she thought absently. She should use more moisturiser. She should…

Stop blathering. This was too important.

Five years ago they'd walked away from each other. Had it all been some ghastly mistake? Could they just… start again?

'Em…' He rose and came round to her side of the table. His voice was urgent now. Pressing home a point? He sat down beside her, took both her hands in his and twisted her to face him. 'Do you feel it, too?'

Did she feel it? How could she not? She'd married this man. She'd loved him with all her heart. She'd borne him a son.

He was holding her, and his hold was strong and compelling. His gaze was on her, and on her alone.

A couple of seagulls, sensing distraction, landed on the far side of the table and edged towards the fish-and-chip parcel. They could take what they liked, she thought. This moment was too important.

Oliver… Her husband…

'Em,' he said again, and his hold turned to a tug. He tugged her as he'd tugged her a thousand times before, as she'd tugged him, as their mutual need meant an almost instinctive coming together of two bodies.

Her face lifted to his—once again instinctively, because this was her husband. She was a part of him, and part of her had never let go. Never thought of letting go.

And his mouth was on hers and he was kissing her and the jolty, nervy, pressurised, outside world faded to absolutely nothing.

There was only Oliver. There was only this moment. There was only this kiss.

She melted into him—of course she did. Her body had spent five years loving this man and it responded now as if it had once again found its true north. Warmth flooded through her—no, make that heat. Desire, strength and surety.

This man was her home.

This man was her heart.

Except he wasn't. The reasons they'd split were still there, practical, definite, and even though she was surrendering herself to the kiss—how could she not?—there was still a part of her brain that refused to shut down. Even though her body was all his, even though she was returning his kiss with a passion that matched his, even though her hands were holding him as if she still had the right to hold, that tiny part was saying this was make-believe.

This was a memory of times past.

This would hurt even more when it was over. Tug away now.

But she couldn't. He was holding her as if she was truly loved. He was kissing her regardless of the surroundings, regardless of the wolf whistles coming from the teenagers at the next table, regardless of…what was true.

It didn't matter. She needed this kiss. She needed this man.

And then the noise surrounding them suddenly grew. The whistles stopped and became hoots of laughter. There were a couple of warning cries and finally, finally, they broke apart to see…

Their fish…

While they had been otherwise…engaged, seagulls

had sneaked forward, grabbing chips from the edge of their unwrapped parcel. Now a couple of braver ones had gone further.

They'd somehow seized the edge of one of their pieces of fish, and dragged it free of the packaging. They'd hauled it out…and up.

There were now five gulls…no, make that six…each holding an edge of the fish fillet. The fish was hovering in the air six feet above them while the gulls fought for ownership. They'd got it, but now they all wanted to go in different directions.

The rest of the flock had risen, too, squawking around them, waiting for the inevitable catastrophe and broken pieces.

Almost every person around them had stopped to look, and laugh, at the flying fish and at the two lovers who'd been so preoccupied that they hadn't even defended their meal.

A couple more gulls moved in for the kill and the fish almost spontaneously exploded. Bits of fish went everywhere.

Oliver grabbed the remaining parcel, scooping it up before the scraps of flying fish hit, and shooed the gulls away. They were now down to half their chips and only one piece of fish, but he'd saved the day. The crowd hooted their delight, and Oliver grinned, but Em wasn't thinking about fish and chips, no matter how funny the drama.

How had that happened? It was like they'd been teenagers again, young lovers, so caught up in each other that the world hadn't existed.

But the world did exist.

'I believe I've saved most of our feast,' Oliver said ruefully, and she smiled, but her smile was forced. The world was steady again, her real world. For just a moment she'd let herself be drawn into history, into fantasy. Time to move on...

'We need to concentrate on what's happening now,' she said.

'We do.' He was watching her, his lovely brown eyes questioning. He always could read her, Em thought, suddenly resentful. He could see things about her she didn't know herself.

But he'd kept himself to himself. She'd been married to him for five years and she hadn't known the depth of feeling he'd had about his childhood until the question of adoption had come up. She'd met his adoptive parents, she'd known they were awful, but Oliver had treated them—and his childhood—with light dismissal.

'They raised me, they gave me a decent start, I got to be a doctor and I'm grateful.'

But he wasn't. In those awful few weeks after losing Josh, when she'd finally raised adoption as an option, his anger and his grief had shocked them both. It had resonated with such depth and fury it had torn them apart.

So, no, she didn't know this man. Not then. Not now.

And kissing him wasn't going to make it one whit better.

He'd said he still loved her. Ten years ago he'd said that, too, and yet he'd walked away, telling her to move on. Telling her to find someone else who could fit in with her dreams.

'Em, I'd like to—'

'Have your fish before it gets cold or gets snaffled by another bird?' She spoke too fast, rushing in before he could say anything serious, anything that matched the look on his face that said his emotions were all over the place. That said the kiss had done something for him that matched the emotions she was feeling. That said their marriage wasn't over?

But it was over, she told herself fiercely. She'd gone through the pain of separation once and there was no way she was going down that path again. Love? The word itself was cheap, she thought. Their love had been tested, and found wanting. 'That's what I need to do,' she added, still too fast, and took a chip and ate it, even though hunger was the last thing on her mind right now. 'I need to eat fast and get back to the kids. Oliver, that kiss was an aberration. We need to forget it and move on.'

'Really?'

'Really. Have a chip before we lose the lot.'

The kids were asleep when she got home, and so was Adrianna. The house was in darkness. Oliver swung out of the driver's seat as if he meant to accompany her to the door, but she practically ran.

'I need my bed, Oliver. Goodnight.'

He was still watching her as she closed the front door. She'd been rude, she admitted as she headed for the children's bedroom. He'd given her a day out, a day off. If he'd been a stranger she would have spent time thanking him.

She should still thank him.

Except…he'd kissed her. He'd said he loved her.

She stood in the kids' bedroom, between the two cots, watching them sleeping in the dim light cast by a Humpty Dumpty figure that glowed a soft pink to blue and then back again.

She had to work with him, she reminded herself. She needed to get things back to a formal footing, fast.

Resolute, she grabbed her phone and texted.

Thank you for today. It was really generous. The kiss was a mistake but I dare say the gulls are grateful. And Mum and I are grateful, too.

That's what was needed, she thought. Make it light. Put the gratitude back to the plural—herself and her mother—and the seagulls? She was thanking someone she'd once known for a generous gesture.

Only...was it more than that? Surely.

He'd kissed her. Her fingers crept involuntarily to her mouth. She could still feel him, she thought. She could still taste him.

After five years, her body hadn't forgotten him.

Her body still wanted him.

He'd said he still loved her.

Had she been crazy to walk away from him all those years ago? Her body said yes, but here in this silent house, listening to the breathing of two children who'd become her own, knowing clearly and bleakly where they'd be if she hadn't taken them in, she could have no regrets. Her mind didn't.

It was only her heart and her body that said something else entirely.

What he wanted to do was stand outside and watch the house for a while. Why? Because it felt like his family was in there.

That was a dumb thought. He'd laid down his ultimatum five years ago and he'd moved on. He'd had five professionally satisfying years getting the skills he needed to be one of the world's top in-utero surgeons. Babies lived now because of him. He'd never have had that chance if he'd stayed here—if he'd become part of Em's menagerie.

He couldn't stay standing outside the house, like a stalker, like someone creepy. What he'd like was to take his little Morgan for a long drive along the coast. The car was like his balm, his escape.

Em had smashed his car. She'd also smashed…something else.

She'd destroyed the equilibrium he'd built around himself over the last few years. She'd destroyed the fallacy that said he was a loner; that said he didn't need anyone.

He wanted her. Fiercely, he wanted her. He'd kissed her tonight and it would have been worth all the fish.

It had felt right.

It had felt like he'd been coming home.

His phone pinged and he flipped it open. Em's polite thank-you note greeted him, and he snapped it shut.

She was making light of the kiss. Maybe that was wise.

Dammit, he couldn't keep standing here. Any moment now she'd look out the window and see him. Ex-husband loitering…

He headed back to the hire car. He had an apartment at the hospital but he wasn't ready for sleep yet. Instead, he headed back to the beach. He parked, got rid of his shoes and walked along the sand.

The night was still and warm. This evening the beach had been filled with families, kids whooping it up, soaking up the last of Melbourne's summer, but now the beach seemed to be the domain of couples. Couples walking hand in hand in the shallows. Couples lying on rugs on the sand, holding each other.

Young loves?

He walked on and passed a couple who looked to be in their seventies, maybe even older. They were walking slowly. The guy had a limp, a gammy hip? The woman was holding his hand as if she was supporting him.

But the hold wasn't one of pure physical support, he thought. Their body language said they'd been holding each other for fifty years.

He wanted it still. So badly…

Could he take on the kids? Could he take that risk?

Was it a risk? He'd held Gretta today and what he'd felt…

She had Down's syndrome with complications. Tristan said her life expectancy could be measured in months. It was stupid—impossible even—to give your heart to such a kid.

He could still hear his adoptive mother…

'It's not like he's really ours. If we hadn't had Brett then we wouldn't have known what love really is. And now…we're stuck with him. It's like we have a cuckoo in the nest…'

If he ever felt like that…

It was too hard. He didn't know how to feel.

But Em had made the decision for him. She'd moved on, saying he was free to find someone and have kids of his own. Kids who he could truly love.

Hell. He raked his hair and stared out at the moonlit water.

Melbourne's bay was protected. The waves were small, even when the weather was wild, but on a night like this they were practically non-existent. The windsurfers had completely run out of wind. The moonlight was a silver shimmer over the sea and the night seemingly an endless reflection of the starlit sky.

He wanted Em with him.

He wanted her to be…free?

It wasn't going to happen. She had encumbrances. No, he thought, she has people she loves. Kids. Her mother.

Not him.

It's for the best, he thought, shoving his hands deep into his pockets and practically glaring at the moon. I should never have come to the Victoria. I wouldn't have if I'd known Em would be here.

So leave?

Maybe he would, he thought. He'd agreed with Charles Delamere on a three-month trial.

Twelve weeks to go?

CHAPTER TEN

On Monday Oliver hit the wards early. He'd been in the day before, not because he'd been on duty but because he'd wanted to check on Ruby. But Ruby was doing all the right things and so was her baby, so he didn't check her first. He worked on the things he needed for his embryonic research lab, then decided to check the midwives' roster and choose a time to visit Ruby when he knew Em wouldn't be around.

So he headed—surreptitiously, he thought—to the nurses' station in the birthing centre—just as Isla Delamere came flying down the corridor, looking, for Isla, very harassed indeed.

When she saw Oliver she practically sagged in relief.

'Dr Evans. Oliver. I know your specialty's in-utero stuff and I know Charles has said you can spend the rest of your time on your research but you're an obstetrician first and foremost, yes?'

'Yes.' Of course he was.

'I have four births happening and we're stretched. Two are problems. Emily's coping with one, I have the other. Mine's a bit of a spoilt socialite—she was booked at a private hospital but had hysterics at the first labour pain so her husband's brought her here because we're closer.

I can deal with that. But Em's looking after a surrogate mum. She's carrying her sister's child—her sister's egg, her sister's husband's sperm, all very organised—but the emotion in there seems off the planet. Maggie's a multi-gravida, four kids of her own, no trouble with any, but now she's slowed right down and her sister's practically hysterical. But we can't kick her out. Oliver, Em needs support. Our registrar's off sick, Darcie's at a conference, Sean's coping with a Caesar so that leaves you. Can you help?'

'Of course.'

'Excellent. Here are the case notes. Suite Four.'

'You're okay with yours?'

'My one wants pethidine, morphine, spinal blocks, amputation at the waist, an immediate airlift to Hawaii and her body back,' Isla said grimly. 'And she's only two centimetres dilated. Heaven help us when it's time to push. But I've coped with worse than this in my time. What Em's coping with seems harder. She needs you, Dr Evans. Go.'

The last time he'd seen her he'd kissed her. Now...

Em seemed to be preparing to do a vaginal examination. She was scrubbed, dressed in theatre gear, looking every inch a midwife. Every inch a professional. And the look she gave him as he slipped into the room had nothing to do with the kiss, nothing to do with what was between them. It was pure, professional relief.

'Here's Dr Evans,' she said briskly to the room in general. 'He's one of our best obstetricians. You're in good hands now, Maggie.'

'She doesn't need to be in good hands.' A woman who looked almost the mirror image of the woman in the bed—

except that she was smartly dressed, not a hair out of place, looking like she was about to step into a board-room—was edging round the end of the bed to see what Em was doing. She ignored Oliver. 'Maggie, you just need to push. Thirty-six hours... You can do this. It's taking too long. Just push.'

Em cast him a beseeching look—and he got it in one. The whole set-up.

A guy who was presumably Maggie's husband was sitting beside her, holding her hand. He looked almost as stressed as his labouring wife.

The other woman had a guy with her, as well, presum-ably her husband, too? He was dressed in casual chinos and a cashmere sweater. Expensive. Smooth.

Both he and his wife seemed focused on where the action should be taking place. Where their child would be born. Even though the woman had been talking to Maggie, she'd been looking at the wrong end of the bed.

Surrogate parenthood... Oliver had been present for a couple of those before, and he'd found the emotion in-volved was unbelievable. Surrogacy for payment was il-legal in this country. It had to be a gift, and what a gift! To carry a child for your sister...

But Maggie wasn't looking as if she was thinking of gifts. She was looking beyond exhaustion.

Thirty-six hours...

'Can't you push?' Maggie's sister said again, fretfully. 'Come on, Maggie, with all of yours it was over in less than twelve hours. The book says it should be faster for later pregnancies. You can do it. You have to try.'

'Maggie needs to go at her own pace,' Em said, in a tone that told him she'd said it before, possibly a lot more than once. 'This baby will come when she's ready.'

'But all she needs to do is push…'

He'd seen enough. He'd heard enough. Oliver looked at Maggie's face, and that of her husband. He looked at Em and saw sheer frustration and he moved.

'Tell me your names,' he said, firmly, cutting off the woman who looked about to issue another order. 'Maggie, I already know yours. Who are the rest of you?'

'I'm Rob,' said the man holding Maggie's hand, sounding weary to the bone. 'I'm Maggie's husband. And this is Leonie, Maggie's sister, and her husband, Connor. This is Leonie and Connor's baby.'

'Maybe we need to get something straight,' Oliver said, gently but still firmly. He was focusing on Maggie, talking to the room in general but holding the exhausted woman's gaze with his. 'This baby may well be Leonie and Connor's when it's born, but right now it has to be Maggie's. Maggie needs to own this baby if she's going to give birth successfully. And I'm looking at Maggie's exhaustion level and I'm thinking we need to clear the room. She needs some space.'

'But it's our baby.' Leonie looked horrified. 'Maggie's agreed—'

'To bear a baby for you,' he finished for her. Em was watching him, warily now, waiting to see where he was going. 'But right now Maggie's body's saying it's hers and her body needs that belief if she's to have a strong labour. I'm sorry, Leonie and Connor, but unless you want your sister to have a Caesarean, I need you to leave.'

'We can't leave,' Leonie gasped. 'We need to see her born.'

'You may well—if it's okay with Maggie.' They were in one of the teaching suites, geared to help train students. It had a mirror to one side. 'Maggie, that's an observation window, with one-way glass. Is it okay if your sister and her husband move into there?'

'No.' Leonie frowned at Oliver but the look on both Maggie and Rob's faces was one of relief.

'I just…need…to go at my own pace,' Maggie whispered.

'But I want to be the first one to hold our baby,' Leonie snapped, and Oliver bit his tongue to stop himself snapping back. This situation was fraught. He could understand that sisterly love was being put on the back burner in the face of the enormity of their baby's birth, but his responsibility was for Maggie and her baby's health. Anything else had to come second.

'What Maggie is doing for you is one of the most generous gifts one woman can ever give another,' he said, forcing himself to stay gentle. 'She's bearing your baby, but for now every single hormone, every ounce of energy she has, needs to believe it's her baby. You need to get things into perspective. Maggie will bear this baby in her own time. Her body will dictate that, and there's nothing you or Connor can say or do to alter it. If Maggie wants to, she'll hold her when she's born. That's her right. Then and only then, when she's ready and not before, she'll make the decision to let her baby go. Emily, do you agree?'

'I agree,' she said.

Em had been silent, watching not him but Maggie. She was a wonderful midwife, Oliver thought. There was no midwife he'd rather have on his team, and by the look on her face what he was suggesting was exactly what she wanted. The problem, though, was that the biological parents exuded authority. He wouldn't mind betting Leonie was older than Maggie and that both she and her husband held positions of corporate power. Here they looked like they'd been using their authority to push Maggie, and they wouldn't have listened to Em.

Isla had sent him in for a reason. If this had been a normal delivery then Em could have coped alone, but with the level of Maggie's exhaustion it was getting less likely to be a normal delivery.

Sometimes there were advantages to having the word *Doctor* in front of his name. Sometimes there were advantages to being a surgeon, to having given lectures to some of the most competent doctors in the world, to have the gravitas of professional clout behind him.

Sometimes it behoved a doctor to invoke his power, too.

'Maggie, would you like to have a break from too many people?' he asked now.

And Maggie looked up at him, her eyes brimming with gratitude. 'I… Yes. I mean, I always said that Leonie could be here but—'

'But your body needs peace,' Oliver said. He walked to the door and pulled it wide. 'Leonie, Connor, please take seats in the observation room. If it's okay with Maggie you can stay watching. However, the mirror is actually an electric screen. Emily's about to do a pelvic examination so we'll shut the screen for that so you can't see, but we'll turn it back on again as soon as Maggie says it's okay. Is that what you want, Maggie?'

'Y-yes.'

'But she promised…' Leonie gasped.

'Your sister promised you a baby,' Oliver told her, still gently but with steel in every word. 'To my mind, that gift needs something in return. If Maggie needs privacy in this last stage of her labour, then surely you can grant it to her.'

And Leonie's face crumpled. 'It's just… It's just… Maggie, I'm sorry…'

She'd just forgotten, Oliver thought, watching as Leonie swiped away tears. This was a decent woman who was totally focused on the fact that she was about to become a mother. She'd simply forgotten her sister. Like every other mother in the world, all she wanted was her baby.

She'd have to wait.

He held the door open. Leonie cast a wild, beseeching look at Maggie but Em moved fast, cutting off Maggie's view of her sister's distress. Maggie didn't need anyone else's emotion. She couldn't handle it—all her body needed to focus on was this baby.

'We'll call you in when Maggie's ready to receive you,' Oliver said cheerfully, as if this was something that happened every day. 'There's a coffee machine down the hall. Go make yourself comfortable while Maggie lets us help her bring your baby into the world.'

And he stood at the door, calm but undeniably authoritative. This was his world, his body language said, and he knew it. Not theirs.

They had no choice.

They left.

Em felt so grateful she could have thrown herself on his chest and wept.

The last couple of hours had been a nightmare, with every suggestion she made being overridden or simply talked over by Leonie, who knew everything. But Maggie had made a promise and Maggie hadn't been standing up to her. Em had had to respect that promise, but now Oliver had taken control and turned the situation around.

Now there were only four of them in the birthing suite. Oliver flicked the two switches at the window.

'I've turned off sight and sound for the moment,' he told Maggie. 'If you want, we'll turn on sight when you're ready, but I suggest we don't turn on sound. That way you can say whatever you want, yell whatever you want, and only we will hear you.'

'She wants to be here...' Maggie whispered, holding her husband's hand like she was drowning.

'She does, but right now this is all about you and your baby.' He put the emphasis on the *your*. 'Emily, you were about to do an examination. Maggie, would you like me to leave while she does?'

Em blinked. An obstetrician, offering to leave while the midwife did the pelvic exam? Talk about trust...

'But you're a doctor,' Maggie whispered.

'Yes,'

'Then stay. I sort of... I mean... I need...'

'You need Oliver's clout with your sister,' Em finished for her. 'You need a guy who can boss people round with the best of them. You've got the right doctor for that here. Oliver knows what he wants and he knows how to get it. Right now Oliver wants a safe delivery for your baby and there's no one more likely than Oliver to help you achieve it.'

He stayed. Maggie's labour had eased right off. She lay back exhausted and Em offered to give her a gentle massage.

He watched as Em's hands did magical things to Maggie's body, easing pain, easing stress.

Once upon a time she'd massaged him. He'd loved...
He loved...

Peace descended on the little room. At Maggie's request Oliver flicked the window switch again so Leonie and Connor could watch, but she agreed with Oliver about the sound.

As far as Leonie and Connor were concerned, there was no audio link. Any noise Maggie made, anything they said, stayed in the room.

Maggie's relief was almost palpable, and as Em's gentle fingers worked their magic, as Maggie relaxed, the contractions started again. Good and strong. Stage two was on them almost before they knew it.

'She's coming,' Maggie gasped. 'Oh, I want to see.'

And Oliver supported her on one side and Rob supported her on the other, while Em gently encouraged.

'She's almost here. One more push... One more push, Maggie, and you'll have a daughter.'

And finally, finally, a tiny scrap of humanity slithered into the world. And Em did as she did with every delivery. She slid the baby up onto Maggie's tummy, so Maggie could touch, could feel, could savour the knowledge that she'd safely delivered a daughter.

The look on Maggie's face...

Oliver watched her hand touch her tiny baby, he watched her face crumple—and he made a fast decision. He deliberately glanced at the end of the bed and carefully frowned—as if he was seeing something that could be a problem—and then he flicked the window to black again.

He put his head out the door as he did.

'It's great,' he told Leonie and Connor, whose noses were hard against the glass, who turned as he opened the door as if to rush in, but his body blocked them. 'You can see we have a lovely, healthy baby girl, but there's been a small bleed. We need to do a bit of patching before you come in.'

'Can we take her? Can we hold her?'

'Maggie needs to hold her. The sensation of holding her, maybe letting her suckle, will help the delivery of the placenta; it'll keep things normal. Maggie's needs come first right now. I assume you agree?'

'I… Yes,' Leonie whispered. 'But we agreed she wouldn't feed her. I just so want to hold her.'

'I suspect you'll have all the time in the world to hold her,' Oliver told her. 'But the feeding is part of the birthing process and it's important. I'm sorry but, promises or not, right now my focus is on Maggie.'

Em's focus was also on Maggie. She watched while Maggie savoured the sight of her little daughter, while she watched, awed, as the little girl found her breast and suckled fiercely.

Her husband sat beside her, silent, his hand on her arm. He, too, was watching the baby.

Without words Em and Oliver had changed places—Oliver was coping with the delivery of the placenta, checking everything was intact, doing the medical stuff. This was a normal delivery—there was no need for him to be here—but still there was pressure from outside the room and he knew that once he left Leonie and Connor would be in here.

'You know,' he said mildly, to the room in general, 'there's never been a law that says a surrogate mother has to give away her baby. No matter how this baby was conceived, Maggie, you're still legally her birth mother. If you want to pull back now...'

But Maggie was smiling. She was cradling her little one with love and with awe, and tears were slipping down her face, but the smile stayed there.

'This little one's Leonie's,' she whispered. 'You've seen Leonie at her worst—she's been frantic about her baby and it was no wonder she was over the top at the end. But I can't tell you how grateful I am that you've given us space to say goodbye. To send her on with love.'

How could she do this? Oliver wondered, stunned. She'd gently changed sides now so the baby was sucking from the other breast. The bonding seemed complete; perfect.

'It's not like we're losing her,' Rob ventured, touching the little one's cheek. 'She'll be our niece and our goddaughter.'

'And probably a bit more than that,' Maggie said, still smiling. 'Our kids will have a cousin. My sister will have a baby. To be able to do this... She's not ours, you can see. She has Connor's hair. None of ours ever looked like this. But, oh, it's been good to have this time.' She looked up at them and smiled, her eyes misty with tears. 'Em, would you like to ask them to come in now?'

'You're sure?' Em asked, with all the gentleness in the world. 'Maggie, this is your decision. As Oliver says, it's not too late to change your mind.'

'My mind never changed,' Maggie said, serene now, seemingly at peace. 'While I was having her she felt all mine and that was how I wanted to feel. Thank you for realising that. But now...now it's time for my sister to meet her baby.'

* * *

'How could she do that?'

With medical necessities out of the way, Oliver and Em were able to back out of the room. Leonie was holding her daughter now, her face crumpled, tears tracking unchecked. Connor, too, seemed awed.

Rob was still holding Maggie but the two of them were watching Leonie and Connor with quiet satisfaction.

'Love,' Em said softly, as they headed to the sinks. 'I don't know how surrogacy can work without it.'

'Do you seriously think Leonie can make a good mother?'

'I do. I've seen her lots of times during Maggie's pregnancy—she's been with her all the way. Yeah, she's a corporate bigwig, but her life has been prescribed because she and Connor couldn't have children. Maggie seems the ultimate earth mother—and she is—but she and Leonie love each other to bits. I suspect the over-the-top reaction we saw from Leonie in there—and which you saved us from—was simply too much emotion. It felt like her baby was being born. She wanted what was best for her baby and everything else got ignored. Mums are like that,' she said simply. 'And thank God for it.'

'You really think she can look after the baby as well as Maggie could?'

'I have no idea. I do know, though, that this baby will be loved to bits, and that's all that counts.'

'She can love it as much as Maggie?'

'That's right, you don't think it's possible.' She lowered her voice to almost a whisper. 'It's a bleak belief, Ollie, caused by your own grief. Have you ever thought about counselling?'

'Counselling?' In the quiet corridor it was almost a

shout. He stood back and looked at her as if she was out
of her mind.

'Counselling,' she said, serenely. 'It's available here.
We have the best people...'

'I don't need counselling.'

'I think you do. You have so much unresolved anger
from your childhood.'

'I'm over it.'

'It destroyed our marriage,' she said simply. 'And you
haven't moved on. I expected you to have a wife and a
couple of your own kids by now. You were scared of
adoption—are you worried about your reaction to any
child?'

'This is nuts.'

'Yeah, it is,' she said amiably, tossing her stained robes
into the waiting bins. 'And it's none of my business. It's
just... I've got on with my life, Oliver. You kissed me
on Saturday and I found myself wondering how many
women you'd kissed since our split. And part of me
thinks...not many? Why not?'

Silence.

She was watching him like a pert sparrow, he thought,
as the rest of his brain headed off on tangents he didn't
understand. She was interested. Clinically interested.
She was a fine nurse, a midwife, a woman used to dealing with babies and new parents all the time. Maybe she
had insights...

Maybe she didn't have any insights. Maybe she was
just Em, his ex-wife.

Maybe that kiss had been a huge mistake.

Step away, he told himself. He didn't need her or anyone else's analysis. But...

'Em, I would like to see Gretta and Toby again.'

Where had that come from? His mouth? He hadn't meant to say it, surely he hadn't.

But…but…

On Saturday he'd sat on the beach and he'd held Gretta, a little girl who had very little life left to her. He should have felt…what? Professional detachment? No, never that, for once an obstetrician felt removed from the joy of children he might as well hand in his ticket and become an accountant. Grief, then, for a life so short?

Not that, either.

He'd felt peace. He acknowledged it now. He'd sat in the waves and he'd felt Gretta's joy as the water had washed her feet. And he'd also felt Em's love.

Em made Gretta smile. He was under no illusions— with Gretta's myriad medical problems and her rejection by her birth mother, she'd faced spending her short life in institutions.

And watching Em now, as she looked at him in astonishment, he thought, what a gift she's given her children.

It was his cowardice that had made that possible. He'd walked away from Em, so Em had turned to fostering.

If he'd stayed with her maybe they could have adopted a newborn, a child with no medical baggage, a child Em could love with all her heart. Only he'd thought it wasn't possible, to love a child who wasn't his own. He'd walked away because such a love wasn't possible, and yet here was Em, loving with all her heart when Gretta's life would be so short…

Had he been mistaken? Suddenly, fiercely, he wanted that to be true. For he wanted to be part of this—part of Em's loving?

Part of her hotchpotch family.

'Oliver, there's no need—'

'I'd love to spend more time with Gretta.' He was wise enough to know that pushing things further at this stage would drive her away. The way he felt about Em…it was so complicated. So fraught. He'd hurt her so much… Make it about her children, he thought, and even that thought hurt.

Her children.

'What time do you finish tonight?' he asked.

'Six.'

'I'm still reasonably quiet and I started early.' He glanced at his watch. 'I should be finished by five. What say I head over there and give Adrianna a break for an hour?'

'Mum'd love that.' She hesitated. 'You could…stay for tea?'

'I won't do that.' And it was too much. He couldn't stop his finger coming up and tracing the fine lines of her cheek. She looked exhausted. She looked like she wasn't eating enough. He wanted to pick her up, take her somewhere great, Hawaii maybe, put her in a resort, make her eat, make her sleep…

Take her to his bed…

Right. In his dreams. She was looking at him now, confused, and there was no way he was pushing that confusion.

'I have a meeting back here at the hospital at seven,' he lied. 'So I'll be leaving as you get home.'

'You're sure you want to?'

'I want to. And if I can…for what time Gretta has left, if you'll allow me, it would be my privilege to share.'

'I don't—'

'This is nothing to do with you and me,' he said, urgently now. 'It's simply that I have time on my hands—and I've fallen for your daughter.'

CHAPTER ELEVEN

SHE SHOULD HAVE said no. The thought of Oliver being with the kids when she wasn't there was disconcerting, to say the least. She rang Adrianna and warned her and Adrianna's pleasure disconcerted her even more.

'I always said he was a lovely man. I was so sorry when you two split. It was just that awful time—it would have split up any couple.'

'We're incompatible, Mum,' she said, and she heard Adrianna smile down the phone.

'You had differences. Maybe those differences aren't as great as they once seemed.'

'Mum…'

'I'm just saying. But, okay, sweetheart, I won't interfere. I'll say nothing.'

Which didn't mean she was thinking nothing, Em decided as she headed to her next case. Luckily, it was a lovely, normal delivery, a little girl born to an Italian couple. Their fourth baby—and their fourth daughter—was greeted like the miracle all babies were.

She left them professing huge gratitude, and Em thought: How come the cases where all I do is catch are the ones where I get the most thanks? But it cheered her immeasurably and by the time she went to see Ruby, her complications with Oliver seemed almost trifling.

Ruby was about to bring those complications front and centre. The teenager was lying propped up on pillows, surrounded by glossy magazines. She had the television on, but she looked bored. And fretful. She lightened up when Em came in, and before Em could even ask her how she was, she put in a question of her own.

'Emily, I've been thinking. You and Dr Evans split because you couldn't have a baby. That's what I guessed, but it's true, I know it is.'

Whoa! Hospital grapevine? Surely not. Sophia was the only one she'd told. Surely Sophia wouldn't break a confidence and even if she had, surely no member of staff would tell a patient things that were personal.

'How—'

'I'm sure I heard it.' Ruby's eyes were alight with interest, a detective tracking vital clues. 'When I was asleep. After Theatre. You and that other nurse were talking.'

Sophia. Em did a frantic rethink of what they'd talked about. Uh-oh.

'So I've been thinking. I've got a baby I don't want,' Ruby said, and suddenly the detective Ruby had given way to a scared kid. 'Maybe you could have mine.'

There was an offer. It took her breath away.

She plonked down on the bed and gazed at Ruby in stupefaction. 'Ruby,' she said at last. 'How can you think such a thing?'

'I can't keep it,' she said fretfully. 'Dr Evans says I have to stay in bed so I don't go into labour and it's driving me nuts, but it's giving me time to think. Ever since I got pregnant…first Jason said he didn't want anything to do with it, or me. Then Mum said she'd kick me out if I kept it. And I was pig stubborn—it just seemed so wrong. I thought I was in love with Jason, and when I realised I was pregnant I was happy. I wasn't even scared. I even thought I might make a good mum. It was only after that…the complications came in.'

'Most of those complications are over,' Em said gently. 'Your daughter has every chance of being born healthy.'

'Yeah, but I've been couch-surfing since Mum found out,' she said fretfully. 'I had to leave school because I had nowhere to stay, and how can I couch-surf with a kid—no one's going to want me.'

'Then this isn't about adoption,' Em told her, forcing herself to sound upbeat and cheerful. 'This is all about plans for the future. We have a couple of excellent social workers. I'll get one of them to pop in and talk to you. She can help you sort things out.'

'But there are so many things…and if the baby's prem, which Dr Evans says is even probable, how can I cope with a baby? If she had a good home…if you and Dr Evans could look after her…'

'Ruby, leave this.' The girl's eyes had filled with tears and Em moved to hug her. 'Things will work out. You won't have to give away your baby, I promise.'

'But you need her. It could save your marriage.'

'My marriage was over a long time ago,' she said, still hugging. 'It doesn't need your daughter to try and mend it. Ruby, I want you to stop worrying about me and my love life. I want you to only think about yourself.'

Oliver arrived at Em's house right on five. Adrianna greeted him with unalloyed pleasure—and promptly declared her intention of taking a nap.

'When Em rang, that's what I decided I'd do,' she told him. 'The tea hour's the hell hour. If I can have a nap first it'll take the pressure off both of us when Em comes home.' She smiled and suddenly he found himself being hugged. 'It's great to have you back, Oliver,' she told him. 'And it's great that you arrived just when we need you most.'

He was left with the kids.

He carried them out into the soft autumn evening, stupidly grateful that Mike from next door was nowhere to be seen. Both kids seemed a bit subdued, pleased to see him, relaxed but tired.

The end of a long day? He touched Toby's forehead and worried that he might have a slight fever.

Katy next door had a cold. Had she or her kids spread it?

Maybe he was imagining things. He was like a worried parent, he thought, mocking himself.

He wasn't a parent. Not even close.

He had these kids for an hour.

He set them on the grass under the tree. Fuzzy the dog came out and loped herself over Gretta's legs. Gretta's oxygen cylinder sat beside her, a harsh reminder of reality, but for now there was no threat. A balmy evening. Warm, soft grass.

'Look up through the trees and tell me what you see,' he said, and both kids looked up obediently.

'Tree,' Gretta said.

'Tree,' Toby agreed, and he found himself smiling. Gretta and her parrot.

Together they were family, he thought. They were a fragile family at best, but for today, well, for today this was okay.

'I'm seeing a bear,' he said, and both kids looked at him in alarm.

'Up there,' he reassured them. 'See that big cloud? It has a nose on the side. See its mouth? It's smiling.'

Neither kid seemed capable of seeing what he was seeing but they looked at each other and seemed to decide mutually to humour him.

'Bear,' Gretta said.

'Bear,' Toby agreed.

'He must live up there in the clouds,' Oliver decreed. 'I think he might be the bear from "Goldilocks". Do you guys know that story?'

Toby was two, a tiny African toddler suffering the effects of early malnutrition as well as the scoliosis and scarring on his face from infection. Gretta was a damaged kid with Down's. 'Goldilocks' was way out of their sphere.

'Well,' Oliver said serenely, settling himself down. The kids edged nearer, sensing a story. 'Once upon a time there were three bears and they lived up in the clouds. Baby Bear had a lovely soft little cloud because he was the smallest. Mumma Bear had a middly sort of cloud, a bit squishy but with a nice high back because sometimes her back hurt, what with carrying Baby Bear all the time.'

'Back,' said Toby.

'Back,' Gretta agreed, obviously deeply satisfied with the way this story was progressing.

'But Papa Bear had the biggest cloud of all. It was a ginormous cloud. It had great big footprints all over it because Papa Bear wore great big boots and, no matter what Mumma Bear said, he never took them off before he climbed onto his cloud. Mumma Bear should have said no porridge for Papa Bear but Mumma Bear is really kind…'

'My Emmy,' Gretta murmured, and he wondered how much this kid knew. How much did she understand?

My Emmy…

It had been a soft murmur, a statement that Gretta had her own Mumma Bear and all was right with that arrangement.

'Porridge,' Toby said, and Oliver had to force his thoughts away from Em, away from the little girl who was pressed into his side, and onto a story where porridge was made in the clouds.

And life was fantasy.

And the real world could be kept at bay.

Em arrived home soon after six, walked in and Adrianna was in the kitchen, starting dinner. She was singing.

Oliver's hire car was parked out the front.

'Where's Oliver?' she asked cautiously, and then gazed around. 'Where are the kids?' Had he taken them out? It was late. They'd be tired. Maybe they'd gone next door. But Katy had passed her cold on to her youngest. She didn't want them there, not with Gretta's breathing so fragile.

'Hey, don't look so worried.' Her mum was beaming and signalling out the window. 'Look.'

She looked.

The two kids were lying under the spreading oak in the backyard. Oliver was sandwiched between them. He had an arm round each of them and they were snuggled against him.

Fuzzy was draped over his stomach.

'You can hardly see him,' Adrianna said with satisfaction. 'It's an Oliver sandwich. He's been telling them stories. I went for a nap but I left my window open. He's an excellent storyteller. He makes them giggle.'

'They can't understand.'

'They can understand enough to know when to giggle. Cloud Bears. Porridge stealing. High drama. Lots of pouncing, with Fuzzy being the pouncee.'

'You're kidding.'

'He's adorable,' Adrianna said. 'He always was. He always is.'

'Mum...'

'I know.' Her mother held up her hands as if in surrender. 'It's none of my business and I understand the grief that drove you apart.'

'It wasn't the grief. It was...'

'Irreconcilable differences,' Adrianna said sagely. She looked out the window again. 'But from this angle they don't look so irreconcilable to me. You want to go tell him dinner is ready?'

'I... No.'

'Don't be a coward.'

'Mum, don't.' She swiped a stray curl from her tired eyes and thought she should have had more cut off. She needed to be practical. She wanted...

She didn't want.

'I don't want to fall in love with him again,' she whispered. 'Mum...'

And her mother turned and hugged her.

'It's okay, baby,' she told her as she held her close. 'There's no fear of that, because you've never stopped loving him anyway.'

* * *

She came out to tell the kids dinner was ready. She was looking tired and worried. She stood back a bit and called, as if she was afraid of coming further.

Fuzzy raced across to her, barking. The kids looked round and saw her and Toby started beetling across the lawn to her. The scoliosis meant he couldn't walk yet, but he could crawl, and crawl he did, a power crawl, his stiff legs making him look like a weird little bug. He was a bug who squealed with joy as Em swung him up in her arms.

Gretta couldn't crawl. She lay and smiled, waiting for Em to come and fetch her, and Oliver thought that, combined, these kids weighed heaps and Em was slight and...

And it was the life she'd chosen. The life she'd wanted as an alternative to staying married to him.

He rose, lifted Gretta and her oxygen cylinder and carried her across to Em. Gretta reached out her arms to be hugged. Oliver tried for a kid swap in midair and suddenly they were all squeezed together. Kids in the middle. Him on one side, Em on the other, Fuzzy bouncing around in the middle of all their feet.

It was a sandwich squeeze, he thought, a group hug, but he was holding Em. They were the wagons circling the kids. Keeping them safe?

Nothing could keep Gretta safe.

And then Toby coughed and Em tugged away with quick concern. 'Oh, no,' she whispered as she took in Toby's flushed face. 'Katy's bug...'

'I've had them lying on either side of me, and that's the first cough. In the fresh air it should be okay. Should we try and isolate them?'

'It'll be too late, if indeed it's Katy's cold. And besides…' Her voice fell away.

'Besides?'

'We made a decision, Mum and I. The first couple of years of Gretta's life were practically all spent in hospital. She was growing so institutionalised she was starting to not respond at all. Tristan's been her doctor from the beginning. After the last bout of surgery—it was a huge gamble but it didn't pay off—he told us to take her home and love her. And that's what we're doing. We'll be a family until the end.'

Her voice broke a little as she finished but her eyes were still resolute. 'She's Toby's sister,' she said. 'We know there are risks, but the fact that she's family overrides everything.'

'So you'll let her catch—'

'I'll do as much as I can to not let her catch whatever this is,' she said. 'Toby can sleep with Mum and I'll sleep with Gretta so they're not sharing a room. We'll wash and we'll disinfect. But that's all we'll do.'

'That alone will take a power of work.'

'So what's the alternative?' she demanded, lifting her chin. 'Gretta's my daughter, Oliver. The decision is mine.'

Toby's cold was minor, a sniffle and a cough, no big deal. He was quieter than usual, but that was okay because it meant he was supremely happy to lie under the oak tree every evening and listen to Oliver's stories.

Because Oliver kept coming every evening.

'Why?' Em demanded on the third evening. 'Oliver, you don't need to. You owe me nothing.'

'This is little to do with you,' he said, and was surprised into acknowledging that he spoke the truth. For at first these kids had seemed like Em's kids, the kids he'd refused her, a part of Em. And at first he'd agreed to take care of them because of Em. It had been a way to get to know her again—and there was a hefty dose of guilt thrown in for good measure.

But now... He lay under the oak and the bears became tortoises or heffalumps or antigowobblers—that one took a bit of explaining—and he found he was taking as much pleasure as he was giving. And as much quiet satisfaction.

The last five years had been hectic, frantic, building up a career to the point where he knew he was one of the best in-utero surgeons in the world. It hadn't been easy. He'd had little time for anything else, and in truth he hadn't wanted time.

If he'd had free time he'd have thought about Em.

But now, with his career back in Australia yet to build up, he did have that time. And he wasn't thinking about Em—or not all the time, he conceded. He was thinking of two kids.

Of what story he could tell them tonight to make them laugh.

Of how to lessen the burden on Em's shoulders while acknowledging her right to love these two.

How had he ever thought she couldn't love an adopted child?

And as time went on, he thought...How could he have thought that of himself? These kids were somehow wrapping themselves around his heart like two tiny worms. They were two brave, damaged kids who, without Em's big heart, would be institutionalised and isolated.

These were kids who could well break her heart.

Gretta's prognosis was grim. Once Toby's medical condition improved, the paperwork to keep him in the country would be mind-blowing.

It didn't seem to matter. Em just…loved. Her courage took his breath away.

Her love made him rethink his life.

What sort of dumb, cruel mistake have I made? he demanded of himself after his first week of childminding. What have I thrown away?

For he had thrown it. Em was always happy to see him, always grateful for the help he gave, always bubbly with the kids when he was around. But as soon as possible she withdrew. What would she say if he asked her to reconsider their relationship? He had no right to ask, he thought. And besides… How could he cope with the pain she was opening herself up to? To adopt these kids…

Except he didn't seem to have a choice. He might not be able to adopt them but, lying under the tree evening after evening, he knew he was beginning to love them.

As he'd always loved their mother?

Every night Em got home from work and he was there. Unbidden, Adrianna pushed mealtime back a little. So instead of coming home to chaos, sometimes Em had time to lie under the tree with them.

It became a routine—they greeted her with quiet pleasure, shifted a little to make room for her on the lushest part of the lawn, Fuzzy stretching so he managed to drape over everyone.

Oliver never tried to talk to her. There was no 'How was your day, dear?' He simply kept on with his stories, but he included her in them.

He found an Emily-shaped cloud and demanded the kids acknowledge it had the same shaped nose, and the same smile. And then he made up a story about Emily and the beanstalk.

It was better than any massage, Em conceded, lying back, looking up through the trees, listening to Oliver making her kids happy.

For he did make them happy. They adored this story time. Gretta probably understood little, but she knew this was story time. Lying on the grass, she was totally relaxed. Her breathing wasn't under pressure, she wriggled closer to Oliver and Em felt her heart twist with the pleasure she was so obviously feeling.

And Toby… The scarring on his face had left the side of his mouth twisted. He had trouble forming words, but with Oliver's gentle stories he was trying more and more.

'And here comes the giant…' Oliver intoned, and Toby's scarred little face contorted with delight.

'S-stomp…stomp…stomp…' he managed.

And Em thought, How smart is my little son? And she watched Oliver give the toddler a high five and then they all said, 'Stomp, stomp, stomp,' and they all convulsed into giggles.

And Em thought…Em thought…

Maybe she'd better not think, she decided. Maybe it was dangerous to think.

What had her mum said? She'd never stopped loving him?

She had, she told herself fiercely. She'd thrown all her love into her children. She had none left over for Oliver.

But she lay and listened to giants stomping, she lay and listened to her children chuckling, and she knew that she was lying.

* * *

And she couldn't get away from him. The next morning she walked into Ruby's room and Oliver was there. Of course he was.

It seemed the man had slipped back into her world and was there to stay. He was an obstetrician, and a good one, so of course he was on the wards. He'd offered to help with Gretta and Toby, so of course he was at her house every night when she got home. He was the doctor in charge of making sure Ruby's baby stayed exactly where she was, so of course he was in Ruby's room.

It was just… Why did he take her breath away? Every time she saw him she lost her breath all over again.

She couldn't still love him, she told herself, more and more fiercely as time went on. Her marriage was five years past. She'd moved on. Oliver was now a colleague and a friend, so she should be able to treat him as such.

There was no reason for her heart to beat hard against her ribs every time she saw him.

There was no reason for her fingers to move automatically to her lips, remembering a kiss by the bay…

'Hey,' she managed now as she saw Ruby and Oliver together. She was hauling her professional cheer around her like a cloak. 'I hope Dr Evans is telling you how fantastic you've been,' she told Ruby. 'Because she has been fantastic, Dr Evans. She's been so still, she's healing beautifully and she's giving her baby every chance and more. I can't believe your courage, Ruby, love. I can't believe your strength.'

'She'll be okay,' Ruby said in quiet satisfaction, and her hand curved around her belly.

'We're going to let you go home,' Oliver told her. He'd been examining her, and now he was tucking her bedclothes around her again. 'As long as you keep behaving. Do you have somewhere to go?'

And Em blinked again. This was a surgeon—*a surgeon*—tucking in bedclothes and worrying about where his patient would go after hospital.

'Wendy, the social worker, has organised me a place at a hostel near here,' she told them. 'Mum won't let me home but Wendy's organised welfare payments. She's given me the name of a place that'll give me free furniture and stuff for the baby. It's all good.'

'You'll be alone.' Oliver was frowning. 'I'm not sure—'

'Wendy says the lady who runs the hostel has had other pregnant girls there. If I'm in trouble she'll bring me to the hospital. It sounds okay.' She hesitated. 'But there is something I wanted to talk to you about.'

She was speaking to Oliver. Em backed away a little. 'You want me to come back later?'

'No,' Ruby said, firmly now, looking from one to the other. 'I wanted you both here. I've been thinking and thinking and I've decided. I want you to adopt my baby.'

For Em, who'd heard this proposition before, it wasn't a complete shock. For Oliver, though... He looked like he'd been slapped in the face by a wet fish. How many times in his professional career had he been offered a baby? Em wondered. Possibly never.

Probably never.

'What are you talking about?' he asked at last. 'Ruby, I'm sorry, but your baby has nothing to do with us.'

'But she could have everything to do with you.' Ruby pushed herself up on her pillows and looked at them with eagerness. More, with determination. 'I've been thinking and thinking, and the more I think about it the more I know I can't care for her. Not like she should be cared for. I didn't even finish school. All my friends are doing uni entrance exams this year and I can't even get my Year Twelve. I don't have anyone to care for my baby. I don't have any money. I'll be stuck on welfare and I can't see me getting off it for years and years. I can't give my baby…what she needs.'

'She needs you,' Em said gently. 'She needs her mum.'

'Yes, but she needs more. What if she wants to be a doctor—how could someone like me ever afford that sort of education? And there'll be operations for the spina bifida—Dr Zigler's already told me there'll be more operations. She'll need special things and now I don't even have enough to buy her nappies. And the choice is adoption but how will I know someone will love her as much as I do? But I know you will. I heard…when I was asleep… It was like it was a dream but I know it's true. You two need a baby to love. You split up because you couldn't have one. What if you have my baby? I could… I dunno…visit her… You'd let me do that, wouldn't you? Mum probably still won't let me go home but I could go back to school. I'd find a way. And I could make something of myself, have enough to buy her presents, maybe even be someone she can be proud of.'

'Ruby…' Doctors didn't sit on patients' beds. That was Medical Training 101, instilled in each and every trainee nurse and doctor. Oliver sat on Ruby's bed and he took her shoulders in his hands. 'Ruby, you don't want to give away your baby.'

Em could hardly hear him. Look up, she told herself fiercely. If you look up you can't cry.

What sort of stupid edict was that? Tears were slipping down her face regardless.

'I want my baby to be loved.' Ruby was crying, too, and her tears were fierce. 'And you two could love her. I know you could. And you love each other. Anyone can see that. And I know Em's got two already, but Sophia says you're round there every night, helping, and Em's mum helps, too, and she has a great big house…'

'Where did you hear all this?' Em managed.

'I asked,' she said simply. 'There are so many nurses in this hospital and they all know you, Em. They all say you're a fantastic mum. And you should be married again. And it'd be awesome for my baby. I'd let you adopt her properly. She'd be yours.' She took another breath, and it seemed to hurt. She pulled back from Oliver and held her tummy again, then looked from Oliver to Em and back again.

'I'd even let you choose her name,' she managed. 'She'd be your daughter. I know you'd love her. You could be Mum and Dad to her. You could be married again. You could be a family.'

There was a long silence in the room. So many elephants… So much baggage.

Oliver was still sitting on the bed. He didn't move, but he put a hand out to Em. She took a step forward and sat beside him. Midwife and doctor on patient's bed… No matter. Rules were made to be broken.

Some rules. Not others. Other rules were made to protect patients. Ethics were inviolate. No matter what happened between Em and himself, the ethics here were clear-cut and absolute.

But somehow he needed to hold Em's hand while

he said it. Somehow it seemed important to say it as a couple.

'Ruby, we can't,' he said gently, and Em swiped a handful of tissues from the bedside table and handed them to Ruby, and then swiped a handful for herself.

The way Oliver was feeling he wouldn't mind a handful for himself, too.

Get a grip, he told himself fiercely, and imperceptibly his grip on Em's hand tightened.

Say it together. Think it together.

'Ruby, what you've just offered us,' he said gently but firmly—he had to be firm even if he was feeling like jelly inside—'it's the greatest compliment anyone has ever given me, and I'm sure that goes for Em, too. You'd trust us with your baby. It takes our breath away. It's the most awesome gift a woman could ever give.'

He thought back to the birth he'd attended less than a week ago, a sister, a surrogate mother. A gift.

And he thought suddenly of his own birth mother. He'd never tried to find her. He'd always felt anger that she'd handed him over to parents who didn't know what it was to love. But he looked at Ruby now and he knew that there was no black and white. Ruby was trying her best to hand her daughter to people she knew would love her, but they couldn't accept.

Would it be Ruby's fault if the adoptive parents turned out…not to love?

His world was twisting. So many assumptions were being turned on their heads.

He saw Em glance at him and he was pathetically grateful that she spoke. He was almost past it.

'Ruby, we're your treating midwife and obstetrician,' she said, gently, as well, but just as firmly. 'That puts us in a position of power. It's like a teacher dating a student—there's no way the student can divorce herself from the authority of the teacher. That authority might well be what attracted the student to the teacher in the first place.'

'I don't know what you mean.'

'I mean we're caring for you,' Em went on. 'And you're seeing that we're caring. It's influencing you, whether you know it or not. Ruby, we couldn't adopt your baby, even if we wanted to. It's just not right.'

'But you need a baby. You said…it'll heal your marriage.'

'I'm not sure what you heard,' Em told her. 'But no baby heals a marriage. We don't need a baby. Your offer is awesome, gorgeous, loving, but, Ruby, whatever decision you make, you need to take us out of it. We're your midwife and your obstetrician. We look after you while your baby's born and then you go back to the real world.'

'But I don't want to go back to the real world,' Ruby wailed. 'I'm scared. And I don't want to give my baby to someone I don't know.'

'Do you want to give your baby to anyone?' Oliver asked, recovering a little now. Em had put this back on a professional basis. Surely he could follow.

'No!' And it was a wail from the heart, a deep, gut-wrenching howl of loss.

And Em moved, gathering the girl into her arms, letting her sob and sob and sob.

He should leave, Oliver thought. He wasn't needed. He was this girl's obstetrician, nothing else.

But the offer had been made to him and to Em. Ruby had treated them as a couple.

Ruby had offered them her baby to bind them together, and even though the offer couldn't be accepted, he felt…bound.

So he sat while Ruby sobbed and Em held her—and somehow, some way, he felt more deeply in love with his wife than he'd ever felt.

His wife. Em…

They'd been apart for almost five years.

She still felt…like part of him.

Em was pulling back a bit now, mopping Ruby's eyes, smiling down at her, pushing her to respond.

'Hey,' she said softly. 'Hey… You want to hear an alternative plan?'

An alternative? What was this? Surely alternatives should be left to the social workers?

If Em was offering to foster on her own he'd have to step in. Ethics again, but they had to be considered, no matter how big Em's heart was.

But she wasn't offering to foster. She had something bigger…

'My mum and I have been talking about you,' she told Ruby, tilting her chin so she could mop some more. 'I know that's not the thing to do, to talk about a patient at home, but I did anyway. My mum lives with me, she helps care for my two kids and she's awesome. She also has a huge house.'

What…what?

'Not that we're offering to share,' Em said, diffidently now, as if she was treading on shifting sand. 'But we have a wee bungalow at the bottom of the garden. It's a studio, a bed/sitting room with its own bathroom. It has a little veranda that looks out over the garden. It's self-contained and it's neat.'

Ruby's tears had stopped. She looked at Em, caught, fascinated.

As was Oliver. He knew that bungalow. He and Em had stayed in it in the past when they'd visited Adrianna for some family celebration and hadn't wanted to drive home.

Josh had been conceived in that bungalow.

'Anyway, Mum and I have been talking,' Em repeated. 'And we're throwing you an option. It's just one option, mind, Ruby, so you can take it or leave it and we won't be the least offended. But if you wanted to take it…you could have it for a peppercorn rent, something you could well afford on your welfare payments. You'd have to put up with our kids whooping round the backyard and I can't promise they'd give you privacy. But in return we could help you.

'The school down the road is one of the few in the state that has child care attached—mostly for staff but they take students' children at need. They have two young mums doing Year Twelve now, so if you wanted to, you could go back. Mum and I could help out, too. It would be hard, Ruby, because your daughter would be your responsibility. But you decided against all pressure not to have an abortion. You've faced everything that's been thrown at you with courage and with determination. Mum and I think you can make it, Ruby, so we'd like to help. It's an option. Think about it.'

What the…?

But they couldn't take it further.

Heinz Zigler arrived then, with an entourage of medical students, ostensibly to talk through the success of the operation with Ruby but in reality to do a spot of teaching to his trainees.

They left Ruby surrounded by young doctors, smiling again, actually lapping up the attention. Turning again into a seventeen-year-old?

They emerged into the corridor and Oliver took Em's arm.

'What the hell…'

The words had been running through his head, over and over, and finally he found space to say them out loud.

'Problem?' Em turned and faced him.

'You'd take them on?'

'Mum and I talked about it. It won't be "taking them on". Ruby's lovely. She'll be a great little mum, but she's a kid herself. She made the bravest decision when she chose not to terminate. It's becoming increasingly obvious that she loves this baby to bits and this way…we could maybe help her be a kid again. Occasionally. Go back to school. Have a bit of fun but have her baby, as well.'

'She offered it to you.' He hesitated. 'To us. I know that's not possible.' He was struggling with what he was feeling; what he was thinking. 'But if it was possible… would you want that?'

'To take Ruby's baby? No!'

'I was watching your face. It's not possible to accept her offer but if it was it'd be your own baby. A baby you could love without complications. Is this offer to Ruby a second-best option?'

'Is that what you think?' She was leaning back against the wall, her hands behind her back, watching him. And what he saw suddenly in her gaze…*was it sympathy?*

'You still don't get it, do you?' she said, gently now.

This was a busy hospital corridor. Isla and Sophia were at the nurses' station. They were glancing at Em and Oliver, and Oliver thought how much of what had just gone on would spin around the hospital. How much of what he said now?

He should leave. He should walk away now, but Em was tilting her chin, in the way he knew so well, her lecture mode, her 'Let's tell Oliver what we really think of him'. Uh-oh.

'You scale it, don't you?' Her voice was still soft but there was a note that spoke of years of experience, years of pain. 'You scale love.'

'I don't know what you mean.'

'You think you couldn't love a baby because it's not yours. That's your scale—all or nothing. Your scale reads ten or zero. But me…you've got it figured that my scale has a few more numbers. You're thinking maybe ten for my own baby, but I can't have that. So then—and this is how I think your mind is working—you've conceded that I can love a little bit, so I've taken in Gretta and Toby.

'But according to your logic I can't love them at ten. Maybe it's a six for Toby because he'll live, but he's damaged and I might not be able to keep him anyway so maybe we'd better make it a five. And Gretta? Well, she's going to die so make that a four or a three, or maybe she'll die really soon so I'd better back off and even make it a two or a one.

'But Ruby's baby…now, if she could give her to me then she'd be a gorgeous newborn and I'd have her from the start and she'll only be a little bit imperfect so maybe she'd score an eight. Only of course, I can't adopt her at all, so you're thinking now why am I bothering to care when according to you she's right off the bottom of the caring scale? Baby I can't even foster—zero? So why are we offering her the bungalow? Is that what you don't understand?'

He stared at her, dumbfounded. 'This is nonsense. That's not what I meant.'

'But it's what you think.' She was angry now, and she'd forgotten or maybe she just didn't care that they were in a hospital corridor and half the world could hear. 'Yes, your adoptive parents were awful but it's them that should be tossed off the scale, Oliver, not every child who comes after that. I work on no scale. I love my kids to bits, really love them, and there's no way I could love them more even if I'd given birth to them. And I'll love Ruby's baby, and Mum and I will love Ruby, too, because she's a kid herself.

'And it won't kill us to do it—it'll make us live. The heart expands to fit all comers—it does, Oliver. You can love and you can love and you can love, and you know what? All that loving means is that you can love some more.'

'Em—'

'Let me finish.' She put up her hands as if to ward off his protests. 'I almost have. All I want to say is that you've put yourself in some harsh, protective cage and you're staying there because of this stupid, stupid scale. You can't have what you deem worthy of ten, so you'll stick to zero. And I'm sorry.'

She took a deep breath, closed her eyes, regrouped. When she opened them again she looked resolute. Only someone who knew her well—as well as he did—could see the pain.

'I loved you, Oliver,' she said, gently again. 'You were my ten, no, more than ten, you were my life. But that love doesn't mean there can't be others. There are tens all over the place if you open yourself to them. If you got out of your cage you'd see, but you won't and that has to be okay with me.' She pushed herself off the wall and turned to go. She had work to do and so did he.

'That's all I wanted to say,' she managed, and she headed off down the corridor, fast, throwing her last words back over her shoulder as she went.

'That's all,' she said again as she went. 'We agreed five years ago and nothing's changed. You keep inside your nice safe cage, and I'll just keep on loving without you.'

CHAPTER TWELVE

SHE SPENT THE rest of the day feeling shaken. Feeling ill. She should never have spoken like she had, especially in such a public place. She was aware of silences, of odd looks, and she knew the grapevine was going nuts behind her back.

Let it, she thought, but as the day wore on she started feeling bad for the guy she'd yelled at.

Oliver kept himself to himself. He was a loner. His one foray out of his loner state had been to marry her. Now he'd withdrawn again.

But now she'd put private information into the public domain. He might quit, she thought. He could move on. He hadn't expected her to be here when he'd taken the job. Would the emotional baggage be enough to make him leave?

She'd lose him again.

She'd told him it didn't matter. She'd told him she had plenty of love to make up for it.

She'd lied.

That was problem with tens, she thought as the long day continued. If you had a heap of tens it shouldn't matter if one dropped off.

It did matter. It mattered especially when the one she was losing was the man who still felt a part of her.

Her mother was right.

She still loved Oliver Evans.

He was kept busy for the rest of the day, but her words stayed with him. Of course they did. Tens and zeroes. It shouldn't make sense.

Only it did.

Luckily, he had no complex procedures or consultations during the day—or maybe unluckily, because his mind was free to mull over what Em had said. Every expectant mum he saw during the day's consultations… he'd look at them and think ten.

He wasn't so sure about a couple of the fathers, he decided. He saw ambivalence. He also saw nerves. Six, he thought, or seven. But in the afternoon he helped with a delivery. In the early stages the father looked terrified to be there, totally out of his comfort zone, swearing as he went in… 'This wasn't my idea, babe. I dunno why you want me here…'

But 'Babe' clung and clung and the father hung in there with her and when finally a tiny, crumpled little boy slipped seamlessly into the world the man's face changed.

What had looked like a three on Em's scale became a fourteen, just like that.

Because the baby really was his? Maybe, yes, Oliver thought, watching them, but now…with Emily's words ringing in his ears he conceded, not necessarily.

Afterwards he scrubbed and made his way back to the nursery. There was a premmie he'd helped deliver. He wanted to check…

He didn't make it.

A baby was lying under the lights used to treat jaundice. Two women were there, seated on either side. Maggie and Leonie. Surrogate mum and biological mum.

They didn't see him, and he paused at the door and let himself watch.

Leonie's hand was on her baby's cheek, stroking it with a tenderness that took his breath away. Where was the tough, commanding woman of the birth scene? Gone.

Maggie had been expressing milk, the staff had told him. Leonie had paid to stay in with the baby, as his mum.

She looked a bit dishevelled. Sleep-deprived? He'd seen this look on the faces of so many new mums, a combination of awe, love and exhaustion.

Maggie, though, looked different. She'd gone home to her family, he knew, just popping back in to bring her expressed milk, and to see her sister—and her daughter?

Not her daughter. Her sister's daughter.

Because while Leonie was watching her baby, with every ounce of concentration focused on this scrap of an infant, Maggie was watching her. She was watching her sister, and the look on her face...

Here it was again, Oliver thought. Love off the Richter Scale.

Love.

Zero or ten? Em was right, it came in all shapes and sizes, in little bits, in humungous chunks, unasked for, involuntarily given, just there.

And he thought again of his adoptive parents, of the tiny amount of affection they'd grudgingly given. He thought of Em and her Gretta and her Toby. He thought of Adrianna, quietly behind the scenes, loving and loving and loving.

He stood at the door and it was like a series of hammer blows, powering down at his brain. Stupid, stupid, stupid... He'd been judging the world by two people who were incapable of love outside their own rigid parameters.

He'd walked away from Em because he'd feared he'd be like them.

His thoughts were flying everywhere. Em was there, front and foremost, but suddenly he found himself thinking of the woman who'd given him up for adoption all those years ago. He'd never wanted to find her—he'd blamed her.

There were no black and whites. Maybe he could... Maybe Em could help...

'Can I help you?' It was Isla, bustling in, wheeling a humidicrib. 'If you have nothing to do I could use some help. I'm a man short and Patrick James needs a feed. Can you handle an orogastric tube?'

Patrick James was the baby he'd come to see. He'd been delivered by emergency Caesarean the day before when his mother had shown signs of pre-eclampsia. Dianne wasn't out of the woods yet, her young and scared husband was spending most of his time with her, and their baby son was left to the care of the nursery staff.

He was a thirty-four-weeker. He'd do okay.

It wasn't an obstetrician's job to feed a newborn. He had things to do.

None of them were urgent.

So somehow he found himself accepting. He settled by the humidicrib, he monitored the orogastric tube, he noted with satisfaction all the signs that said Patrick James would be feeding by himself any day now. For a thirty-four-weeker, he was amazing.

All babies were amazing.

Involuntarily, he found himself stroking the tiny, fuzz-covered cheek. Smiling. Thinking that given half a chance, he could love…

Love. Once upon a time he'd thought he'd had it with Emily. He'd walked away.

If he walked back now, that love would need to embrace so much more.

Black and white. Zero or ten. Em was right, there were no boundaries.

He watched Patrick James feed. He watched Leonie love her baby and he watched Maggie love her sister.

He thought about love, and its infinite variations, and every moment he did, he fell deeper and deeper in love with his wife.

She arrived home that night and Oliver's car was parked out the front. His proper car. His gorgeous Morgan. Gleaming, immaculate, all fixed. It made her smile to see it. And it made her feel even more like smiling that she'd yelled at Oliver this morning and here he was again. Gretta and Toby would miss his visits if they ended.

When they ended?

The thought made her smile fade. She walked into the kitchen. The smell of baking filled the house—fresh bread! Oliver's nightly visits were spurring Adrianna on to culinary quests. Her mum was loving him coming.

She was loving him coming.

'Mumma,' Toby crowed in satisfaction, and she scooped him out of his highchair and hugged him. Then, finally, she let herself look at Oliver.

He was sitting by the stove, holding Gretta in his arms. Gretta wasn't smiling at her. She looked intent, a bit distressed.

Her breathing…

The world stood still for a moment. Still hugging Toby, she walked forward to see.

'It's probably nothing,' Adrianna faltered. 'It's probably—'

'It's probably Katy's cold,' Oliver finished for her. 'It's not urgent but I was waiting… Now you're here, maybe we should pop her back to the Victoria so Tristan can check.'

Congestive heart failure. Of course. She'd been expecting it—Tristan had warned her it would happen.

'You won't have her for very long,' he'd told Em, gently but firmly. 'Love her while you can.'

One cold… She should never…

'You can't protect her from everything,' Oliver murmured during that long night when Gretta's breathing grew more and more labored. 'You've given her a home, you've given her love. You know that. It was your decision and it was the right one. If she'd stayed in a protective isolette then maybe she'd survive longer, but not lived.'

'Oh, but—'

'I know,' he said gently, as Gretta's breathing faltered, faltered again and then resumed, even weaker. 'You love, and love doesn't let go.' And then he said…

'Em, I'm so sorry I let you go,' he said softly into the ominous stillness of the night. 'I was dumb beyond belief. Em, if you'll have me back…'

'Ollie…'

'No, now's not the time to say it,' he said grimly. 'But I love you, Em, and for what it's worth, I love Gretta, too. Thank you for letting me be here now. Thank you for letting me love.'

* * *

She was past exhaustion. She held and she held, but her body was betraying her.

Gretta was in her arms, seemingly asleep, but imperceptibly slipping closer to that invisible, appalling edge.

'You need to sleep yourself,' Oliver said at last. 'Em, curl up on the bed with her. I promise I'll watch her and love her, and I'll wake you the moment she wakes, the moment she's conscious.'

They both knew such a moment might not happen. The end was so near…

But, then, define *near*. Who could predict how long these last precious hours would take? Death had its own way of deciding where and when, and sometimes, Oliver thought, death was decided because of absence rather than presence.

Even at the time of death, loved ones were to be protected. How many times had a child slipped away as a parent had turned from a bed—as if solitude gave permission for release? Who knew? Who understood? All he knew was that Em was past deciding.

'I'll take your chair,' he told her, laying his hand on her shoulder, holding. 'Snuggle onto the bed.'

'How can I sleep?'

'How can you not?' He kissed her softly on her hair and held her, letting his body touch hers, willing his strength into her. This woman… She gave and she gave and she gave…

How could he possibly have thought her love could be conditional? How could he possibly have thought adoption for Em could be anything but the real thing?

And how could he ever have walked away from this

woman, his Em, who was capable of so much love and who'd loved him?

Who still loved him, and who'd shown him that he, too, was capable of such love.

'I'll wake you if there's any change. I promise.'

'You do…love her?'

'Ten,' he said, and he smiled at her and then looked down at the little girl they were watching over. 'Maybe even more.'

She nodded, settled Gretta on the bed, then rose and stumbled a little. He rose, too, and caught her. He could feel her warmth, her strength, the beating of her heart against his. The love he felt for this woman was threatening to overwhelm him, and yet for this moment another love was stronger.

Together they looked down at this tiny child, slipping away, each breath one breath closer…

Em choked back an involuntary sob, just the one, and then she had herself under control again. There would be no deathbed wailing, not with this woman. But, oh, it didn't mean she didn't care.

'Slip in beside her,' he said, and numbly she allowed him to tug off her windcheater, help her off with her jeans.

She slid down beside Gretta in her knickers and bra, then carefully, with all the tenderness in the world, she held Gretta, so the little girl's body was spooned against hers.

Gretta stirred, ever so slightly, her small frame seeming to relax into that of her mother's.

Her mother. Em.

Somewhere out there was a birth mother, the woman who'd given Gretta up because it had all been too hard.

Down's syndrome and an inoperable heart condition that would kill her had seemed insurmountable. But Em hadn't seen any of that when she'd decided to foster her, Oliver thought. She'd only seen Gretta.

She'd only loved Gretta.

'Sleep,' he ordered as he pulled up the covers, and she gave him a wondering look in the shadows of the pale nightlight.

'You'll watch?'

'I swear.'

She smiled, a faint, tremulous smile, and closed her eyes.

She was asleep in moments.

The quiet of the night was almost absolute. The only sound was the faint in-drawing of breath through the oxygen tube. Gretta's tiny body was almost insignificant on the pillows. Em's arms were holding her, mother and child ensconced in their private world of love.

Mother and child… That's what these two were, Oliver thought as he kept his long night-time vigil. Mother and child.

In the next room, Adrianna had Toby in bed with her. Whether Toby needed comfort—who knew what the little boy sensed?—or Adrianna herself needed comfort and was taking it as parents and grandparents had taken and given comfort since the beginning of time—who knew?

Adrianna's love for Toby was almost as strong as Em's.

Grandmother, mother, child.

He wanted to be in that equation, and sitting there in the stillness of the night, he knew he wanted it more than anything else in the world. What a gift he'd had. What a gift he'd thrown away.

But Em had let him into her life again. She'd allowed him to love…

Gretta shifted, a tiny movement that he might not have noticed if all his senses weren't tuned to her breathing, to her chest rising and falling. There was a fraction of a grimace across her face? Pain? He touched her face, and she moved again, just slightly, responding to his touch as he'd seen newborns do.

On impulse he slid his hands under her body and gathered her to him. Em stirred, as well, but momentarily. Her need for sleep was absolute.

'I'm cuddling her for a bit,' he whispered to Em. 'Do you mind?'

She gave a half-asleep nod, the vestige of a smile and slept again.

He gathered Gretta against his chest and held.

Just held.

The night enfolded them. This was a time of peace. A time of blessing?

Gretta was snuggled in his arms, against his heart, and she fitted there. Em slept on beside them.

His family.

Gretta's breathing was growing more shallow. There was no longer any trace of movement. No pain. Her face was peaceful, her body totally relaxed against his.

He loved her.

He'd known this little girl for only weeks, and her courage, her strength, her own little self had wrapped her around his heart with chains of iron. She was slipping away and his chest felt as if it was being crushed.

Her breathing faltered. Dear God…

'Em?'

She was instantly awake, pushing her tumbled curls

from her hair, swinging her legs over the side of the bed, her fingers touching her daughter's face almost instantly. .

She just touched.

The breathing grew shallower still.

'Would you like to hold her?' How hard was it to say that? How hard, to hand her over to the woman who loved her?

But he loved her, too.

'I'm here,' Em whispered. 'Keep holding her. She loves you, Oliver. You've lit up our lives in these last weeks.'

'Do you want to call Adrianna?'

'She says she couldn't bear it. If it's okay with you... just us.'

Her fingers stayed on her daughter's face as Gretta's breathing faltered and faltered again. Gretta's frail body was insubstantial, almost transient, but Oliver thought there was nothing insubstantial about the power around them.

A man and a woman and their child.

'I wish I'd been here,' he said fiercely, though he still whispered. 'I wish I'd had the whole four years of her.'

'You're here now,' Em whispered as her daughter's breathing faltered yet again. 'That's all that matters.'

And then the breathing stopped.

They didn't move. It was like a tableau set in stone.

'Stop all the clocks...' Who had said that? Auden, Oliver thought, remembering the power of the poem, and somehow, some way it helped. That others had been here. That others had felt this grief.

Grief for parents, for lovers, for children. Grief for those who were loved.

Gretta had been loved, absolutely. That his own parents had doled out their love according to some weird formula of their own making—this much love for an adopted child; this much love for a child of their own making—it was nothing to do with now, or what he and Em decided to do in the future.

Their loving was so strong it would hold this little girl in their hearts for ever.

It would let them go on.

And Em was moving on. She was removing Gretta's oxygen cannula. She was adjusting Gretta's pink, beribboned pyjamas. She was wiping Gretta's face.

And finally she was gathering her daughter's body into her own arms, holding her, hugging her, loving her. And then, finally, finally the tears came.

'Go call Mum,' she managed, as Oliver stood, helpless in his grief as well as hers. 'She needs to be here now. And Toby... You need to bring him in, Oliver. For now, for this moment, we need to be together. Our family.'

They buried Gretta with a private service three days later. It was a tiny service. Only those who loved Gretta most were there to share.

Gretta's birth mother, contacted with difficulty, chose not to come. 'I don't want to get upset. You take care of her.'

'We will,' Em promised, and they did, the best they could. They stood by the tiny graveside, Oliver at one side of Em, Adrianna at the other, and they said goodbye to a part of themselves.

Such a little time, Oliver thought. How could you love someone so deeply after such a little time?

But he did. Years couldn't have made this love deeper.

He gathered Em into his arms afterwards and there were no words needed for the promises that were being made.

She knew and he knew. Here was where they belonged.

Katy had looked after Toby during the service—there were some things a two-year-old could never remember and couldn't hope to understand—but afterwards she brought him to them. 'Let's go to the Children's Garden,' Mike had suggested. 'The Botanic Gardens is a great place to play. That's where I think we all need to be.'

And it wasn't just Katy and Mike and the kids who arrived at the Gardens. Their hospital friends met them there, appearing unbidden, as if they sensed that now was the time they were needed. Isla and Alessi, Sophia, Charles, Tristan, even the obnoxious Noah—so many people who loved Em and knew the depths of Em's grief.

Heaven knew who was looking after midwifery and neonates at the Victoria, for at two o'clock on this beautiful autumn afternoon it seemed half the staff were here.

And suddenly, as if by magic, pink balloons were everywhere. They wafted upwards through the treetops and spread out. It seemed that each balloon contained a tiny packet of seeds—kangaroo paws, Gretta's favourite—with instructions for planting. Who knew who'd organised it, and who knew how many kangaroo paws would spring up over Melbourne because of Gretta? It didn't matter. All that mattered was that the love was spreading outwards, onwards. Gretta's life would go on.

There were blessings here, Oliver thought as he gazed around at the friends he'd made in such a short time, the friends that had been Em's supports while he'd been away, the friends who'd stand by them for ever.

For ever sounded okay to him.

Their friends drifted away, one by one, hugging and leaving, knowing that while friends were needed, alone was okay, as well. Sophia and Isla took Adrianna by an arm apiece. 'Rooftop Bar?' they queried, and Adrianna cast an apologetic glance at her daughter.

'If it's okay…I'd kill for a brandy.'

'If anyone deserves a brandy or three, it's you. I… We'll meet you there,' Em said, holding back, watching Oliver hugging Toby.

'Do you want me to take Toby?' her mum asked.

'I need Toby right now,' Oliver said, and Em blinked. Of all the admissions…

But no more was said. She stood silent until Sophia and Isla and Adrianna disappeared through the trees and they were alone. With her son. With…*their* son?

Then Oliver tugged her down so they were in their favourite place in the world, lying under a massive tree, staring up through the branches.

Toby, who'd submitted manfully to being hugged all afternoon, took off like a clockwork beetle, crawling round and round the tree, gathering leaves, giggling to himself. Death held no lasting impression for a two-year-old and Em was grateful for it.

'I think that's Gretta's nose,' Oliver said, pointing upwards at a cloud. 'I think she's up there, deciding whose porridge is hers.'

And to her amazement Em heard herself chuckle. She rolled over so her head lay on his chest, and his lovely fingers raked her hair.

'I love you, Em,' he said, softly into the stillness. 'I love you more than life itself. Will you let me be part of your family?'

She didn't speak. She couldn't.

She could feel his heart beneath her. His fingers were drifting through her hair, over and over. Toby crawled around them once and then again before she found her voice. Before she trusted herself to speak.

'You've always been my family, Oliver,' she said, slowly, hardly trusting herself to speak. 'Five years ago I was too shocked, too bereft, too gutted to see your needs. So many times since, I've rerun that time in my head, trying to see it as you saw it. I put a gun to your head, Ollie. Black or white. Adoption or nothing. It wasn't fair.'

'Even if your way was right? Even if your way *is* right?'

She could feel his heart but she could no longer feel hers. There'd been so many emotions this day… Her world was spinning…

No, she thought. Her world had settled on its right axis. It had found its true north.

'I'm so glad I came back in time to meet Gretta,' Oliver said softly, still stroking her hair. 'I'm so glad I was able to be a tiny part of her life. If I hadn't… She's a part of you, now, Em, and, believe it or not, she's a part of me. A part of us. Like Toby is. Like Adrianna. Like everyone is who released a pink balloon today. You're right, there is no scale. Loving is just loving. But most of all, Em, I love you. Will you take me on again, you and all your fantastic menagerie? Toby and Adrianna and Fuzzy and Mike and Katy and the kids, and Ruby and her baby when she's born? Will you let me love them with you? Will you let me love you?'

Enough. Tears had been sliding down her cheeks all day and it was time to stop. She swiped them away and tugged herself up so she was looking into his face. She gazed into his eyes and what she saw made her heart twist with love. She saw grief. She saw love.

She saw hope.

And hope was all they needed, she thought. Heaven knew how their family would end up. Heaven knew what crazy complications life would send them.

All she knew for now was that somehow, some way, this man had been miraculously restored to her.

Her husband. Her life.

'I can't stop you loving me,' she managed, swiping yet more tears away. 'And why would I want to? Oh, Oliver, I'd never want to. I love you with all my heart and that it's returned...well, Gretta's up there making miracles for us; I know she is.'

There was a crow of laughter from right beside them. They turned and Toby had a handful of leaves. He threw them at both their faces and then giggled with delight.

Oliver tugged Em to lie hard by his side, and then picked Toby up and swung him up so he was chortling down at them.

'You're a scamp,' he told him. 'We love you.'

And Toby beamed down at both of them. God was in his heaven, all was right in Toby's world.

He had his Em and now he had his Oliver. His Gretta would stay with him in the love they shared, in the love they carried forward.

Toby was with his family.

And two weeks later they went back to the gardens, for a ceremony they both decreed was important. For the things they had to say needed to be said before witnesses. Their friends who'd been with them in the tough times now deserved to see their joy, and they were all here. Even Ruby was here this time, carefully cosseted by Isla and Sophia but increasingly sure of herself, increasingly confident of what lay ahead.

Oliver had asked Charles Delamere to conduct this unconventional ceremony—Charles, the man who'd recruited him—Charles, the reason Oliver had finally come home.

Charles, the head of the Victoria Hospital. The man who seemed aloof, a powerful business tycoon but who'd released balloons for Gretta two weeks before. Who'd promised all his support, whatever they needed. Who'd also promised to move heaven and earth to cut bureaucratic red tape, so Toby could stay with them for ever.

But the successful bureaucratic wrangling was for later. This day was not official, it was just for love.

They chose a beautiful part of the garden, wild, free, a part they both loved. They stood under a tangled arch, surrounded by greenery. They held hands and faced Charles together, knowing this was right.

'Welcome,' Charles said, smiling, because what he was to do now was all about joy. 'Today Em and Oliver have asked me if I'll help them do something they need to do, and they wish to do it before all those who love them. Ten years ago, Emily and Oliver made their wedding vows. Circumstances, grief, life, drove them apart but when the time was right fate brought them together again. They've decided to renew their vows, and they've also decided that here, the gardens that are—and have been—loved by the whole family, are the place they'd like to do it. So if I could ask for your attention…'

He had it in spades. There was laughter and applause as their friends watched them stand before Charles, like two young lovers with their lives ahead of them.

'Emily,' Charles said seriously. 'What would you like to say?'

They'd rehearsed this, but privately and separately.

Oliver stood before Emily and he didn't know what she'd say but he didn't care. He loved her so much.

But then the words came, and they were perfect.

'Just that I love him,' Em said, mistily, lovingly. 'That I married Oliver ten years ago with all my heart and he has my heart still. What drove us apart five years ago was a grief that's still raw, but it's a part of us. It'll always be a part of us, but I don't want to face life's griefs and life's joys without him.'

She turned and faced Oliver full on. 'Oliver, I love you,' she told him, her voice clear and true. 'I love you, I love you, I love you, and I always will. For better and for worse. In sickness and in health. In joy and in sorrow, but mostly in joy. I take you, Oliver Evans, back to be my husband, and I promise to love you now and for evermore.'

He'd thought he had it together. He hadn't, quite. When he tried to speak it came out as a croak and he had to stop and try again.

But when he did, he got it right.

'I love you, too, Em,' he told her, taking her hands in his, holding her gaze, caressing her with his eyes. 'Those missing years are gone. We can't get them back, but for now this is all about the future. We have Toby, our little son, and with the help of our friends we'll fight heaven and earth to keep him. As well as that, we have the memory of a baby we once lost, our Josh, and we have so many wonderful memories of our beloved Gretta. And we have all our friends, and especially we have Adrianna, to love us and support us.'

He turned and glanced at Adrianna, who was smiling and smiling, and he smiled back, with all the love in his heart. And then he turned back to his wife.

'But for now...' he said softly but surely. 'For now I'm

holding your hands and I'm loving you. I love you, Emily Louise, as surely as night follows day. I love you deeply, strongly, surely, and I swear I'll never let you down again. From this day forth I'll be your husband. You hold my heart in the palm of your hand. For richer, for poorer, in sickness and in health, we're a family. But maybe…not a complete family. I'm hoping there'll be more children. More friends, more dogs, more chaos. I'm hoping we can move forward with love and with hope. Emily Louise, will you marry me again?'

'Of course I will,' Em breathed, as Toby wriggled down from Adrianna's arms and beetled his way between legs to join them. Oliver scooped him up and held and they stood, mother, father and son, a family portrait as every camera in Melbourne seemed to be trained on them.

'Of course I will,' Em whispered again, and the cameras seemed to disappear, as their surroundings seemed to disappear. There was only this moment. There was only each other.

'Of course I will,' Em whispered for the third time, as they held each other and they knew these vows were true and would hold for all time. 'I'm marrying you again right now, my Oliver. I'm marrying you for ever.'

* * * * *

Don't miss the next story in the fabulous
MIDWIVES ON-CALL *series*
ALWAYS THE MIDWIFE
by Alison Roberts
Available in May 2015!

MILLS & BOON®

The Sharon Kendrick Collection!

1 BOOK FREE!

Passion and seduction....

If you love a Greek tycoon, an Italian billionaire or a Spanish hero, then this collection is perfect for you. Get your hands on the six 3-in-1 romances from the outstanding Sharon Kendrick. Plus, with one book free, this offer is too good to miss!

Order yours today at
www.millsandboon.co.uk/Kendrickcollection

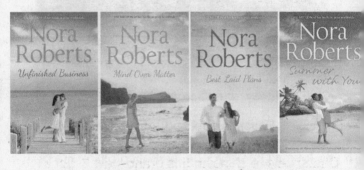

MILLS & BOON®

The Chatsfield Collection!

Style, spectacle, scandal...!

With the eight Chatsfield siblings happily married and settling down, it's time for a new generation of Chatsfields to shine, in this brand-new 8-book collection! The prospect of a merger with the Harrington family's boutique hotels will shape the future forever. But who will come out on top?

Find out at
www.millsandboon.co.uk/TheChatsfield2

MILLS & BOON®

MEDICAL ROMANCE™

THE ULTIMATE IN ROMANTIC MEDICAL DRAMA

A sneak peek at next month's titles...

In stores from 6th February 2015:

- **A Date with Her Valentine Doc** – Melanie Milburne
  and **It Happened in Paris...** – Robin Gianna

- **The Sheikh Doctor's Bride** – Meredith Webber
  and **Temptation in Paradise** – Joanna Neil

- **A Baby to Heal Their Hearts** – Kate Hardy
- **The Surgeon's Baby Secret** – Amber McKenzie
